ORIGINAL DEATH

Library of Congress Cataloging-in-Publication Data

Pattison, Eliot.
 Original death : a mystery of colonial America / Eliot Pattison.
    pages cm
 ISBN 978-1-58243-731-6
 1. Scots—North America—History—18th century—Fiction. 2. Indians of North America—Crimes against—Fiction. 3. Murder—Investigation—Fiction. 4. United States—History—Colonial period, ca. 1600-1775—Fiction. 5. Historical fiction. 6. Mystery fiction. I. Title.

 PS3566.A82497O75 2013
 813ʼ.54—dc23

2013006093

ISBN 978-1-58243-731-6

Cover and Interior design by Domini Dragoone

Counterpoint Press
1919 Fifth Street
Berkeley, CA 94710
www.counterpointpress.com

Original Death

ELIOT PATTISON

A
MYSTERY
OF
COLONIAL
AMERICA

COUNTERPOINT PRESS

ACKNOWLEDGMENTS

For information, and inspiration, special thanks to Connor Pattison,
Dr. Harry Light, Bear Berner, and Sergeant John Ordway.

LATE SUMMER 1760

Chapter One

The dead Highlanders lined the road for as far as Duncan McCallum could see, swaying from the English gibbets as crows pecked their flesh. He recognized the lifeless, sunken faces as he stumbled along in the chill grey dawn, seeing his grandfather, his uncles, then the bayoneted bodies of his mother and sisters heaped on the ground below a gallows lit by a solitary shaft of sunlight. From it his father raised a skeletal arm to point an accusing finger at him, then shouted angry words Duncan could not understand.

The cold water hit him like a violent slap. He sat up, gasping, looking into the worried, weathered countenance of his friend Conawago. The old Nipmuc Indian extended a hand to help Duncan to his feet. "You were crying out again. Your clan?"

Duncan, his heart still thundering, managed a short, sober nod. For years he had suffered nightmares of the English slaughter of his clan, but after arriving in the New World they had subsided until he had been nearly free of them. Suddenly, as soon as Duncan and Conawago had set out on their northern quest two weeks earlier, his dead family, some killed in battle, others executed as Jacobite rebels, the remainder brutally murdered by English plunderers, had come back, the nightmares growing more and more frequent. Conawago, revered among the tribes as a reader of dreams, had declared that his family on the other side was telling him it had unfinished business with him. As they moved ever closer to the bloody battlefields of the North, however, Duncan could not shake the nagging sense that they were summoning him to join them. Dreams were always messages from the other side, the people of the forest believed, and those messages had to be obeyed.

He watched as the old Nipmuc stepped to a wide, flat rock lapped by the shimmering lake and looked up to the sky, a hand on the amulet around his neck. Not for the first time he was invoking his totem to protect Duncan, the pitiful European who had not yet learned how to take a protector deity of his own. When he finished, he turned with a weary grin and gestured the young Scot toward the lake.

"These waters have been touched by the spirits today," Conawago declared. "We go no farther until you wash your darkness away."

Duncan quickly stripped off his waistcoat and shirt, shoes and stockings, then took two long strides and dove into the shimmering waters of the lake called Champlain.

The spirits were indeed in the lake that day. The water seemed unnaturally clear as he swam through it, invigorating in a way he had not known since swimming the Hebrides waters of his boyhood. As he surfaced for a breath and looked back at Conawago sunning on the rocks, he felt his foreboding fade. He resolved to speak no more of his nightmares. He would do nothing that might disturb the joy on the old man's face. Never in all the time he had known the Nipmuc had Duncan seen him so contented.

"Only eight or nine more miles," Conawago declared as Duncan pulled himself out onto the rock. "Fifty years of searching, and I am but two hours away." With boyish energy he tossed Duncan an apple and went back to the tattered letter in his hand, even though by now, after weeks of repeated reading, Duncan was certain Conawago had committed the extraordinary words to memory. He himself could have recited them.

Brother of my clan, the letter began. The four simple words had changed Conawago's life forever.

> *Once a year before the harvest moon I send this letter to a different location in the hope of reconnecting the chain of our blood. Some say you are still in Europe with kings and queens. Some say you stayed with the Jesuits and became a monk in Canada. Some say you lie in the sea in the hull of an English ship blasted by the French. Last year a woman told me she saw you making firkins in Boston. Now another says you may be teaching children in Edentown, in the Catskills. The one I seek is the last of us Nipmucs, the Conawago taken by Jesuits from the banks of the Hudson in the year 16 and 90, the one Europeans call Socrates Moon. If you are that one, I am Towantha, the son of your dead brother, though most know me as Hickory John. With me is my grandson Ojiwa, named Ishmael by those of the second world, whose parents died when he was an infant. He is twelve years of age this month. The seed of our tribe is not dead. We two yet breathe and can be found in Bethel Church, near the southern shore of Lake Champlain, on the army's new road to Ticonderoga.*

In the parchment envelope had been a short strand of white wampum beads, a tribal warranty to the truth of the words.

Conawago had collapsed onto a chair when he had first read the letter, uttering syllables of surprised joy as tears ran down his cheeks. For two hours the Nipmuc had not left the chair in the kitchen of the Ramsey great house in Edentown, reciting the letter again and again as Duncan sat grinning, with Sarah Ramsey, proprietress of the town and holder of Duncan's bond of indenture, at his side.

Not for the first time Duncan recalled the bittersweet smile on Sarah's face when he had looked up after the first reading. Her hand had gone to his and squeezed it. She had instantly known that Duncan would have to leave again, had known that Duncan would accompany Conawago to the settlement near Lake Champlain to at last complete his decades-long quest to reconnect with his family. Conawago's hope of ever doing so had died to a tiny flickering ember, and seeing it rekindled in the gentle old man's eyes had been the closest Duncan had ever been to witnessing a miracle. The years had fallen away from the wrinkled old face.

Conawago looked up and returned Duncan's gaze. "I have seen many men swim in my time," he declared, cocking his head in curiosity. "They have always stayed on the surface. But you always seek the full embrace of the water spirits."

Duncan grinned. "My grandfather," he explained. "His idea of swimming was diving for oysters and clams." He grinned at the memory of the sturdy old Highland Scot, of whom Conawago so often reminded him.

"My grandfather," Conawago replied in a whimsical tone, "taught me the magic of their feathers."

Duncan paused, then realized Conawago was now gazing over his shoulder. He turned just in time to see a huge white-headed eagle land in its nest on a tiny island a hundred yards offshore.

"It would be a gift of great power for my nephew," Conawago suggested.

Duncan hesitated, not understanding until he realized his friend stared at the bird. Conawago raised a hand to stop him as he took a long step toward the water. "There are words to be spoken," his friend said, and he quickly recited a prayer in the tongue of the Mohawk, the Iroquois tribe whose land they journeyed through. Duncan repeated it back to him and then with a running leap dove back into the cool water of the lake. He cleared the shore with a few powerful strokes then drew in a deep breath and slipped beneath the surface.

It was a world all his own, with a wonder and freedom he knew nowhere else. He glided through the diamond-bright water, pulling with cupped hands, working his feet like the seals he swam with among the islands of his youth. Schools of small fish scattered before him. Huge trout, each a living kaleidoscope, paused to watch his passage. From the shadows at the edge of his vision, one of the lake's hulking sturgeon watched like a wise old sentinel.

Only his eyes and nose breached the surface as he reached the island. The great eagle cocked his head at him but did not move. Duncan eased forward, well aware that before he had met Conawago, his presence would have frightened the bird. Something new, wild yet calming, had quickened inside him during his months in the wilderness with the old Nipmuc.

He slowly rose, pulling his lanky six-foot frame onto the stone shingle of the island, the water running off the dark blond tail of hair at his nape. "I am Duncan, chieftain of clan McCallum," he announced to the majestic creature, and then he spoke the words Conawago had given him. "I come to honor you and your kind, as a poor human who cannot soar with the gods." He spoke the words in English and Mohawk, then added a prayer of his own. "I come to ask you to bless the blood bond between two great men," he said, thinking of the glorious reunion that would come later that day. When he lowered his head, he spied what he sought, a long tail feather, brilliantly white, lying on the ground below the huge nest. He looked up and returned the intense stare of the bird. The eagle had the air of an expectant teacher.

"I fear for the bloodlines of both our clans," he confessed to the bird. "If you find us worthy, I ask that you watch over them, the Nipmuc and the McCallum." His own clan, like that of Conawago, had grown nearly extinct at the hands of the English.

Duncan stepped to the long feather, and when the bird did not react, he slowly bent to lift it, raising it up toward the sun before dipping it toward the water and then to the great bird. "*Tapadh leat*," he said. I thank you, first in Gaelic and then in the tongue of the Mohawks. The eagle watched with interest as Duncan carefully stuffed the feather into the tight leg of his britches, then the huge creature abruptly swooped down, nearly touching Duncan's cheek with the tip of its massive wing before gliding over the water.

He watched the graceful flight and was about to turn away when the eagle circled and swooped again, dragging its feet in the water a stone's throw from the island before pulling sharply upward. At first Duncan thought it had taken a fish, but then he saw its talons were empty. The bird cut a long arc in the sky, wheeling as if to see if Duncan watched, then glided down to precisely the same place where the water still rippled and touched it again before rising and returning to its nest. It turned to Duncan with the same expectant gaze.

The university-trained Scot within him knew better than to think the bird was communicating with him. But he had spent too long with Conawago to ignore such a sign. The tribes believed birds to be messengers of the gods, and he and Conawago were on a tribal quest. When he turned back to the water, he saw something floating a few feet away. He lifted the little swath of bear fur, thinking it was likely something that had adorned an Iroquois warrior, but then he saw the winding of thread that bound it to a little brass pin. It was a cockade, worn on the bonnet of Highland troops, and someone had fastened a small dried thistle into the fur.

He lowered himself into the lake and with quiet breaststrokes moved to the point where the eagle had touched, then dove.

No fish were to be seen. The patch of water was like a clearing in the forest where all the creatures had been frightened away. He pulled himself deeper, ten feet, twelve feet, and suddenly the death was upon him. He jerked backward, choking, and shot to the surface, coughing and spitting up water.

Duncan looked back at the eagle, who still watched, then gripped his fear, caught his breath, and dove again.

The man lay on the bottom as if resting, looking up at the thin blue sky. He was not much older than Duncan, with red hair tightly braided at the back. The military sash over his shoulder held a dirk but not the usual broadsword. His waist belt did not hold the regulation cartridge box, only a sporran, the front pouch worn over Highland kilts. The red and brown tartan he wore was pressed tight to his legs by the rope that bound him to the spokes of a heavy wheel. Another rope around his neck clamped his head against the iron rim of the wheel. Duncan could not bring himself to touch the body, but he gripped the wheel to study it with the more deliberate gaze of the doctor he had trained to be. The man's face was badly bruised. His right calf had been savaged, probably by a musket ball shot at close range. There were no other wounds, no apparent deathblow. He had drowned.

The Highland soldier had been dead only a few hours at most. He had been disabled with the shot, then beaten and tied to the wheel before being dumped into the lake while still alive. Seeing a clan emblem on the dirk, Duncan grabbed it before drifting up to the surface.

When Duncan emerged from the water, Conawago was carving a small piece of wood, which he quickly hid. The Nipmuc hesitated, a strange foreboding in his eyes, then he brightened and nodded his gratitude as Duncan extended the feather. He accepted the treasure, holding it in both hands toward the eagle, still watching from its nest, then whispered in the words of his people.

There had been an unspoken vow between them not to speak of the war on their journey. This journey was more important than the battles between distant kings. They had become like pilgrims who spoke no unpure thought, lest they disturb their sacred quest. Duncan dared not break the magic by speaking of his own foreboding or of his grisly discovery in the lake. The man was a casualty of the blood-soaked war between the French and British, and they were removed from that war, worked their hardest to have nothing to do with it. But as they moved back up the trail that hugged the shoreline, the image of the dead Scot haunted him. The death had a slow, organized aspect to it, not the quick work of the raiders who hit supply convoys and outposts then fled, undermining the British while their main forces were in the North, preparing for the looming battle at Montreal. But, Duncan reminded himself, the French relied heavily on irregular troops, trappers and natives of the Huron and Abenaki tribes, some of who clung to the old ways of honoring a victory by the slow death of captives.

As they paused, Duncan checked the flint of his long rifle and freshened the powder in the pan. Conawago watched him but said nothing. He too would not break the magic.

The old Nipmuc increased the pace, consuming the lakeside trail with the steady loping gait the people of the forest used to traverse long distances. Conawago was more than three times Duncan's age but never lagged, never was the first to call for a rest. Although he had traveled to both England and France, spoke several languages, and could articulate as well as any scholar Duncan had ever known, this was his home, here was where he was most comfortable, here was where he honored what the natives called his true skin. He was an aged sinewy stag who moved with graceful instinct through the forest.

That instinct had saved Duncan's life more than once, and he knew to respect it without hesitation. As Conawago abruptly halted and stepped behind the cover of a tree, Duncan dropped beside a boulder, raising his rifle as he followed the old Indian's gaze through the birches that lined the shore.

The boat they saw was broad in beam and shallow in draft, powered by four long oars on either side. It was surprisingly close to shore, no more than fifty yards away, in a channel between the shore and a long narrow island. Between the rowing benches, crates and barrels were stacked, covered by canvas.

"Army supplies," Conawago declared with relief, and stepped away from the tree. The boat was clearly one of the squat supply bateaux that plied the water passage of the long lakes, bound for the forts at Ticonderoga or Crown Point, perhaps even the depot at the far northern end of Champlain that supported the regiments in Quebec.

The old Indian stepped toward the water onto a narrow pebbly beach and waved good-naturedly toward the men on the boat. A man at the bow instantly snapped up a musket and aimed at him.

"No!" Duncan cried, and sprang forward in a long desperate leap, pushing his friend away as the musket fired. Conawago's body jerked as it fell to the ground. Without conscious thought Duncan raised his own rifle, still in his hands, and aimed at a second man who was raising another musket at them. He shot an instant before the musket fired. The man spun about, his shot gone wild, dropping his gun to clutch at his upper arm.

Duncan pulled Conawago into a thick clump of cedars that obscured them from the water. To his relief the old Nipmuc began to stir. "I am a fool," he groused as he clutched at his shoulder. "Of course they would think we were raiders. They saw those canoes."

Duncan only half heard his words. He pulled away Conawago's fingers, soaked in blood. He ripped apart the linen where it had been torn by the ball, muttering a Gaelic curse as he saw the ugly gout of flesh. The ball had scraped along the top of the shoulder, breaking the skin along its passage before digging into the flesh at his back.

"It's still in there," Duncan declared in an apologetic tone, "lodged between the skin and the shoulder blade."

Conawago grimaced, then reached into his belt and handed Duncan his skinning knife before taking a stick in his mouth and leaning over to tightly grip a thick root with both his hands. Duncan had nearly completed the full course of medical studies in Edinburgh before being arrested and transported to America for harboring a Highland rebel, yet he often sensed Conawago had a better understanding of the ways of healing. He tore the shirt another few inches and bent over his friend's shoulder with the blade.

He sliced the skin quickly but had to press against the wound to force the ball out. He gritted his teeth as Conawago moaned, cursing the luck of the shot. He would have gladly taken the wound himself to keep the old Nipmuc out of harm's way.

As was often the case, Conawago seemed to read his mind. He spat the stick out when Duncan showed him the ball. "If you hadn't pushed me, my friend, it would have been in my chest."

"But why?" Duncan asked as he wiped the bullet on his britches and dropped it into the pocket of his waistcoat.

"The Canadians grow desperate. Disrupting supplies means disrupting the British attacks in Canada."

"Canoes. You mentioned canoes."

"Where the shore curves around ahead of us. In the shadows of a big sugar tree hanging over the water."

From his pack Duncan pulled out the small copper pot they used for cooking. "I need to wash the wound," he said, gesturing toward the lake." Before stepping away he reloaded his gun and placed it within reach of Conawago.

The supply boat was disappearing behind the curve of the shore Conawago had described, beyond the huge maple. Not for the first time he marveled at his companion's eyesight. If he had not known what to look for, he would never have seen the four bark canoes. They had been pulled into low shrubs so that only their ends were visible.

When he returned, Conawago had his sewing kit in his lap, tying a piece of thread onto a needle. "We can still make it before dusk," he said to Duncan.

"Nonsense. We're making camp here. You're in no shape."

"It was not my leg that was shot. Of course we are going on." He handed Duncan the needle and thread. "You can return the favor."

Duncan's hand unconsciously went to the long scar along his hairline, where a raider had tried to scalp him the year before. Conawago had saved his life for the first time that day, then sewn up his wound. Duncan returned his friend's expectant gaze and grimaced, but found himself unable to argue. "This is going to hurt," he warned.

A quarter hour later they were under the shadow of the massive maple, studying the canoes with new worry. They had not been pulled from the water for safekeeping. They had been disabled with several holes in their bottoms, then hidden.

"Why take an ax to a perfectly good canoe?" Duncan asked.

"Because you don't intend for it to be used again. That is not the real question. If you smash a canoe you no longer care about it, no longer need to travel on the water. But why does someone smash a canoe and then hide it?" Without waiting for a reply Conawago wrapped the deerhide strap of his pack around his uninjured shoulder, hitched the arm with the injured shoulder into his belt, and set off down the path. Duncan cast a worried gaze down the lake, where a young Scot had been killed that day, then followed.

Conawago's wound kept him from running, but he set a fast walking pace for the last miles to Bethel Church. Duncan saw the effort it took for the old Nipmuc to push back his pain, but he succeeded in doing so, murmuring once more the joyful songs of the woodland peoples reserved for reunions between long-separated family members. Half a century before, Conawago had returned to his clan's home after years of studying and travel with the Jesuits only to find his people gone, the little valley where they had lived decimated by farmers. He had never seen his people again, and all the emotion he had pushed down after losing his mother and siblings and failing to find any trace of them for so long was rising to the surface. There was weariness in his voice now, sometimes a hint of melancholy, but most of all there was joy.

When at last the little settlement came into view below the long ridge they descended, Conawago paused. "I almost forgot," he declared, and Duncan watched in confusion as he settled onto a fallen log and extracted the eagle feather Duncan had retrieved. Then he saw the little jars and pouches Conawago produced from his pack, and he understood. The feather, meant as a gift to Conawago's long lost nephew, had to be blessed and adorned with the marks of their tribe. The old Nipmuc looked up for a moment with the smile of an excited boy. "Within this hour I will have embraced members of my tribe!" he exclaimed, then bent to his solemn task.

As Conawago offered the feather up to the four points of the compass and began a chant, Duncan turned toward the buildings in the distance. They questioned those they had met in their rapid passage from the Catskills, learning that Bethel Church was a community of Christian Iroquois constructed on the army's supply road between Albany and Ticonderoga, two miles from the lakeshore. The settlement had been built around a small church established by one of the Anglican missionaries who had started competing with the Jesuits and Moravians for the souls of the woodland tribes. The inhabitants of the mission had taken up farming and wagon building as a means of livelihood, and to Conawago's obvious pride a teamster near Albany had proclaimed Hickory John to be the best maker of wheels in the Champlain Valley. It was a hard life for the natives who embraced their new faith so fervently. They were often treated as outcasts by their own people and never fully trusted by the Europeans, though often they were the most devout Christians Duncan had ever met.

As Conawago drew a pattern with ocher on the feather, Duncan settled onto a boulder and studied the little collection of log structures half a mile below them. So late in the afternoon he would have expected to see more activity. As Duncan tried to recall what day of the week it was, his gaze settled on a square structure in the center of the settlement, marked by a timber cross fastened above its roof. The inhabitants were no doubt in church.

His friend was changing his shirt when Duncan turned around, wincing as he struggled to pull the bloodstained one over his shoulder. Duncan sprang to his side to help, then held the little mirror they shared, suffering Conawago's warning glances, as if the old Indian dared him to comment on his unusual show of vanity in wiping the grime from his face and straightening his long greying hair.

At last Conawago wrapped the precious eagle feather in a piece of doeskin, hitched the hand of his injured arm into his belt, and with an eager grin led Duncan down the narrow path. His journey of five decades had come to an end.

"A handsome creature," Conawago declared of a draft horse grazing in the pasture where the trail met the road. "A noble village, Duncan," he added, gesturing toward the sturdy houses they approached. He was going out of his way to show pride in the settlement, where more Nipmucs lived than anywhere else on the planet. It was indeed a tidy, well-kept community, the hands of craftsmen evident in the construction of its dozen buildings. Firewood was stacked neatly by each house. A well with a long sweep for dipping buckets stood near the little church. Smoke threaded lazily out the chimney of what looked like a smithy.

"An animal to treasure," the Nipmuc said of a large brown cow that called out as they passed. He said nothing about the expectant way the cow stood beside the large barn. Its swollen udders meant it was overdue for milking.

Their heads snapped up at movement at the far end of the village. Two dogs were tussling, each pulling an end of a small red scrap. Duncan's contentment began to wane. He glanced uneasily into the trees. A flock of crows watched the buildings.

"We can wait outside the church," Conawago suggested. "No need to disturb them."

But when they reached the building its door hung open, a solitary shoe on its side at the threshold. When Conawago hung back, Duncan stepped past him to enter the little structure. The chamber was empty. He approached the simple altar and turned to face the rough-hewn benches. On one, two prayer books lay open. On another, knitting needles had been dropped on top of what appeared to be a child's sock. Four wide-rimmed black hats occupied the row of pegs along the back wall.

With new foreboding he stepped out the door and discovered that Conawago had disappeared. Tightening his grip on his rifle he ran out into the road. He jogged to the far end of the little community, seeing nothing but the two dogs, now fleeing into a patch of pumpkins, and then he turned and quickly paced back down the road. The doors of the houses he passed were open. The cow called out her discomfort. The crows stared at him.

At first Duncan thought the sound he heard was a rustle of wind, but he saw no leaves moving. He began running, glancing into the empty barn, then stopped to survey the buildings again. The sound, now an anguished moan, grew louder—a human moan. He quickened his pace and followed it toward the building with the smoking chimney. Two wide bay doors on the side hung open. He reached the entrance and froze.

Conawago had collapsed onto the floor, the bloody head of a man in his lap, the mourning chant of his people coming from his throat in sobs. Before him was a line of bodies that extended into the shadows. The gentle folk of Bethel Church had all been killed.

Chapter Two

Conawago took no notice as Duncan inched toward the nightmare. His legs were leaden. His gun fell from his hand. He gasped suddenly and realized he had not been breathing.

He forced himself to the closest body, a girl no older than fifteen, whose long black braids draped over her calico dress. She lay straight on her back as if she had just lain down for a rest. He bent to lift her wrist, but he knew from her dull unseeing eyes he would find no pulse. He moved on to the next body, and the next, futilely touching wrists and necks. Two middle-aged men in tattered homespun clothes. Three tall women approaching middle age, each wearing a pewter cross around her neck. A strapping man who appeared to be in his thirties. None had a visible wound, and all had died with strangely serene, almost reverent expressions. He knelt at the last body in the line, that of a teenaged youth, and saw the dark pool on the packed earth under his head. The back of his skull had been crushed. He looked about the smithy. A heavy wooden spoke lay on the earthen floor, stained red at one end. The smith's hammer that lay on the anvil still held a sheen of blood.

Duncan closed the youth's eyes then stood. Eight dead, plus the man in Conawago's lap. They were all of the woodland tribes, and all but the man Conawago embraced were dressed in European-style clothes. He bent over each again, seeing now that every head had the same pool of blood under it. The blood was not yet dry, meaning the killings had taken place less than two or three hours earlier. With a chill he realized they had not died at the same time but in sequence. They had waited in line, with no trace of fear or alarm on their faces as, one by one, their skulls had been crushed from behind.

Only the man with Conawago was different. He was clearly older than the others and wore deerskin leggings gartered with strips of rabbit fur. The sleeveless waistcoat that he wore over his worn linen shirt had small bits of fur sewed into it. His long black hair was tied at the back. A bright bloom of blood leaked over his heart. His dead, defiant eyes were fixed on a carved wooden medallion on the earthen floor beside him. Down his left cheek was a vertical line of four small, intricately worked tattoos. A fish, a deer, a bear, and a snake, in a distinctive style Duncan had never seen except on Conawago, who bore identical images, in the same sequence, on his neck and shoulders. Conawago had found Hickory John.

Duncan's heart seemed to rip out of his chest as he watched Conawago rock with his dead nephew in his lap. For the first time in half a century he embraced someone of his own flesh and blood, and the flesh was now growing cold. There were no words to say. The grief sliced deep into the Nipmuc's soul. This was a wound that would never heal.

He scooped up the medallion on the floor and backed away. Duncan was still numb as he retreated out of the building and stood gazing vacantly at the little settlement. Finally he was stirred out of his paralysis by the caws of the gathering crows. A long sobbing shout left his throat and, suddenly enraged, he hurled stones until the birds flew away. Slowly his eyes focused again, studying the village with cold deliberation. Lifting his gun from where he had dropped it, he began exploring the other structures.

The sparsely furnished houses were empty, with no evidence of the day's horror. A loaf of bread stood on a table in the first, waiting to be sliced. A bowl of peeled apples sat beside a piecrust in the kitchen of another. Little corn cakes made in the Iroquois fashion lay charred on a flat stone by a hearth, the ashes in the big fireplace cool to the touch.

He paced along the road, studying the tracks now. It was the supply road to the British forts, the only road west of the lake, carved out of the wilderness shoreline after hostilities with the French had broken out. The ruts of wagons pulled by horse and ox teams were crusted into the road, some of the tracks less than a day old. Faintly visible were the prints of the studded footwear favored by heavy infantry, several days old.

Set back from the road was a building he had taken to be a small barn. But he saw now the worn path that led to it and the stone chimney that rose up from the far side of its shake roof. Well-tended beds of blooming asters and daisies flanked its narrow entry. The door was ajar. He pushed it open with his foot and saw four benches with narrow rough-hewn tables in front of each, facing a larger table at the back. Small slates lay on the smaller tables. It was a schoolhouse.

He counted eight student slates on the tables. Two held Bible verses transcribed in neat hands, two showed numbers and simple stick figures, two more had crudely formed letters, another a careful drawing of a coach. Two of the dead had probably been of school age, certainly no more than two, and both were older than Hickory John's grandson. On the wall were eight drawings, each with a different name. Six children of Bethel Church, including Ishmael, were unaccounted for.

The cow lowed again, in obvious distress. As he left the schoolhouse he glimpsed the two dogs, once more tugging over the red object he had seen from a distance. They did not notice his approach until he was nearly upon them, then they looked up with startled expressions and fled, drop-ping their prize.

The bloody piece of fur was so mutilated that he held it in his hand for a long moment before he recognized it. It was a badger-hair sporran, the pouch in which Highlanders kept their valuables. But this one was ripped into shreds and half covered with blood. The large numeral 42 was stamped onto its black leather cover. He touched the dirk he had taken from the dead man in the lake. The 42nd Regiment of Foot, the Black Watch, wore black and green tartan. The soldier in the lake had worn a different plaid.

He kept a tight grip on the sporran as he searched the other buildings, finding all of them empty. The cow bleated again, and he turned toward the barn. It was a large structure, built to accommodate at least two wagons in its long center aisle. The floor of the first stall was covered in straw bedding, with a milking stool in the corner. The walls of the next stall were lined with careful rows of woodworking tools hanging on pegs, with the body of a small wagon under construction resting on trestles. The third chamber was dark, its window shuttered. He opened the shutter and gazed outside a moment at the mare pacing skittishly along the side of the pasture. As he turned away he tripped on something, falling to a knee, then gasped. The face of a dead man stared back at him.

The soldier had fought, taking several bruises and slices on the back of his hands and cheek before receiving the wound in his chest that had killed him. His right hand still held his broadsword. He had been in his thirties and, judging from the scars across his jaw and hands, was the veteran of more than one battle. The tartan of his kilt was black and green, that of the Black Watch, renowned as the toughest, most seasoned troops in America. The sight of another dead Scot seemed to sap Duncan's strength. The deaths suddenly bore down on him with a crushing weight. Despite all their efforts, he and Conawago had stumbled into the war. He had to pull Conawago away, had to flee into the mountains. But instead he found himself kneeling in front of the dead Highlander. Something inside Duncan seemed to find familiar features in the dead man. He did not know the man, but he knew the long craggy features, the aquiline nose and unkempt blond hair with a red ribbon twisted into its braid. The man was the image of so many who had visited his family's croft and danced at their gatherings. His gaze paused on the man's dirk, whose hilt bore the embossed image of a bull between two flags, and his heart grew yet colder. The man was a MacLeod, the largest clan of the islands and coasts where Duncan had been raised.

He was so weary of death, so weary of it always taking the ones the world needed the most. His eyes misted and his hands rose in a strange pantomime, reaching out to touch the man's wounds as if he might yet save the Scot. He did not know how long he knelt, desolate and numbed, probing the wounds without conscious thought. Suddenly a whistle broke the stillness of the dead town.

"*Allons!*" someone shouted from the road. The French command triggered a cold fury inside him. He grabbed his rifle and was rising when he heard the hammer being pulled back on a gun and spun about.

"*Mon Dieu!* T'is a fine gory mess ye made of the place." The man who spoke was in the shadows, but the barrel of his pistol was not.

"If this is how you wage your war," Duncan snapped, "then the sooner Montreal falls the better." He began shifting his weight back and forth, readying to throw his gun and leap, praying he could make the man shoot wild.

"If we was French, lad," the man said, "we wouldn't be having this entertaining conversation. Ye'd be dead already. We shout a little Frenchie just to flush out bastards like ye."

Duncan tensed for his jump then froze. The blade at his neck seemed to come from nowhere, pressing against his skin. He instinctively pulled away, only to be jerked back by someone gripping his shirt. As he turned a gasp escaped his throat.

The first time Duncan had encountered a native warrior adorned for battle, he had felt like a child cringing before some mythic monster come to life. Even now as the Indian came into view, a shiver of fear ran down his spine. The man was taller than Duncan's six feet, his flinty countenance decorated with a horizontal band of black paint that ran over his eyes and back to his ears, with parallel red stripes below it on each cheek. The front of his scalp was shaven, the remaining hair tied in braids into which bits of fur had been woven. The bare skin of his scalp had been adorned with red paint, with streams running down the side of his head to resemble dripping blood. His naked chest was covered only by a tattered sleeveless waistcoat. The warrior fixed him with a cold, hungry stare. As the man reached for his rifle, Duncan thought he recognized the wolf tattooed on his shoulder.

"I am a friend of the Mohawk," he said as he yielded his gun.

"No," the man with the pistol declared as he stepped into the light. "Ye killed a friend of the Mohawk. Which makes ye an enemy of the Mohawk, an enemy of blessed King George, and especially an enemy of my friend Sagatchie," he said with a nod to the warrior. The Englishman had a square, brutish face, scarred from battle. He was dressed in a green wool jerkin with leather leggings over his britches.

"Perhaps one of us committed murder," Duncan shot back. "But it was not me."

The Indian lowered his blade to lift a piece of rope from a peg on the wall, then roughly pulled Duncan's hands behind him, tying them tightly together. The man in green bent over the dead soldier and cursed. As he straightened, his fist slashed out, slamming across Duncan's jaw so hard it knocked him back to his knees.

His assailant whistled and another figure emerged from the aisle of the barn to confer with him. As his head cleared, Duncan saw that the sinewy newcomer was dressed in the same green jerkin as his companion.

"If you are truly rangers you have a chance of catching these killers," Duncan interrupted. "My name is McCallum. I just arrived in search of someone who lived here. This happened only two or three hours ago. The raiders probably fled up the slope into the mountains."

The man with the scarred face turned with a sour expression. "I am not inclined to take advice from a murderer." The cow bleated again, and the man kicked a pail to the second man. "Get someone to milk the damned beast, Corporal," he spat, "then search every house and find me a witness."

"Sergeant Hawley," the soldier acknowledged with a knuckle to his temple and disappeared.

"Don't waste your time," Duncan said. "Everyone's dead. The children must have—"

"Sagatchie," the sergeant muttered impatiently.

Duncan only saw a quick motion out of the corner of his eye before something hard slammed into his skull. He collapsed unconscious to the floor.

HE AWOKE CHOKING on dirt. A cruel laugh rose nearby, and more dirt landed on his face. Despite the throbbing pain at the back of his skull, Duncan shook the dirt off his head and struggled to rise. He was being buried. His legs and half his torso were under a foot of fresh earth. He tried to push himself up only to find his hands still tied. He spat a Gaelic curse, then leaned back on the ground and with great effort heaved his hips upward, pushing away enough soil to free his legs. Duncan rolled and began to stand, only to be pulled backward by a sudden strangling pressure on his neck. He was bound to a tree by one of the neck straps used by the tribes to restrain their captives.

He turned toward the jeers, louder now, discovering three men leaning on shovels, staring at him in amusement. "Every hour you wait," he growled, "makes it more likely these killers will not find justice."

The nearest man, the wiry corporal from the barn, swung his spade as if to spray more dirt at Duncan, then laughed at Duncan's reaction and lowered it. "We don't waste time, lad. We be giving these poor souls the Christian burial they deserve. And the king's justice has already found the one who did this butcher's work. Your hands were covered with their blood when we found you."

"I did nothing more than try to help a fellow Scot," Duncan snapped. His voice trailed away as he surveyed his surroundings. They were behind the little church. Along the building's rear was a row of bodies wrapped in blankets, makeshift shrouds no doubt taken from the beds of the houses. Crude plank crosses leaned on the wall above all but the last two bodies. *Joshua Halftree* read the first, then *Rebecca Halftree, Martha Strong, Ezekial Strong, Barnabas Wolf,* and *Lizzie Oaks.*

"You knew them, Corporal?" he asked the ranger.

The soldier gestured toward the south. "There's a farm down the road. Sergeant Hawley sent for them. This was their church. They could at least put names to most of the dead."

"Most?" Duncan asked.

"There be a nameless corporal of the 42nd of Foot," the ranger declared. "The one you gloated over in the barn. His body was sent back with the dispatch rider for Fort Edward."

Duncan found he had no stomach for argument. Four open graves lay before him. "Let me help with the digging," he said in a weary voice.

The corporal studied him, then approached Duncan. He gestured to the guns leaning near the first cross. "We have ranger loads in those barrels. Know what that means?"

"Swan shot on top of a full ball."

"Tends to take a man down permanently," the ranger declared as he loosened the strap on Duncan's neck. "If ye try to run we'll all fire. Ye'll be in pieces before ye reach thirty paces."

A cool determination settled in Duncan. "If I turn my back on these dead," he vowed, "you are welcome to put a bullet in me." Though he had not known any of the inhabitants of Bethel Church, he felt an unexpected affinity for them. They had given a home to Conawago's kin. In their way they too were more last ones of their kind, and too many last ones were falling.

They dug in silence, Duncan pausing every few minutes to look around, hoping for a sign of Conawago but not daring to ask about him for fear it could risk his friend's arrest.

They had finished another grave when a stranger wearing clothes of brown homespun cloth appeared, carrying another rough cross. *Abraham Oaks*, it read. They were all the names of Christian Indians, names assigned upon christening.

"There were children," Duncan said.

The corporal gestured toward two shrouds lying together. "Brought from the smithy with the rest."

"There were more. Young ones taken from the schoolhouse," Duncan said.

The ranger shrugged and kept digging.

As they finished another grave, a sturdy blond woman in her thirties wearing a bloodstained apron appeared with the last cross, for Rachel Wolf.

Duncan looked at it in surprise. "But there was another in the smithy," he called out to the woman.

She shook her head but said nothing, just pointed to the cross above the church. The man in brown homespun appeared beside her. "My wife means that although the wheelmaker discussed the one God with great interest, he had not been touched by holy water."

Hickory John would not be buried in the churchyard.

"But surely—" Duncan's protest faded as the tall Mohawk from the barn walked around the corner of the building, leading a horse. Draped over the back of the animal was another shrouded body.

"Sergeant Hawley says Sagatchie knows a place," the farmer declared. As he spoke, the sour man who had arrested Duncan appeared behind the horse.

A place. The Mohawk meant a ground sacred for the Haudenosaunee, the Iroquois, where the dead were laid on platforms with offerings to take on the long journey to the spirit world. The tribal ranger stared at Duncan without expression. His war paint was gone in preparation for his solemn duty.

"He'll need help," Duncan suggested to the sergeant. "He will have to build a platform as high as his head and lift the body onto it. Not a job for one man alone."

Hawley frowned. "My men are plenty experienced in handling the dead. One of my corporals will go," Hawley spat, then he turned to the wiry man with the spade, who muttered under his breath.

"Something to say, corporal?" Hawley growled.

"Only how it seems a lot of trouble for a dead savage. Any fool can throw a body into a boneyard." The rough men of the frontier became rangers for many reasons. Some did so for the money, which was greater than that paid to garrison soldiers. Others signed on to keep their homes safe from raiders. Some did so just to kill Indians.

"There're words that must be spoken," Duncan pressed. "Hickory John was one of the last of a great tribe. He must be honored." The Mohawk ranger cocked his head toward Duncan, surprise now in his deep black eyes. "The spirits must be made aware of his coming," Duncan added, addressing the Mohawk now.

The man with the spade gave another jeer. "I know the Psalms, boy," the corporal growled. "The Lord maketh me lie down in green pastures."

Duncan shook his head. "Do you know the names of the spirits that must be called to admit Towantha to the next world? Can you speak the condolence of the tribes? Will you find a snake to carry the news of his journey to the other side?"

When Duncan turned to the sergeant, Hawley's gaze was locked on Sagatchie, who stared contemptuously at the corporal. The tribal rangers were critical to the success of the irregular units, and they had to be respected. The sergeant stepped to the Mohawk's side and quietly conferred. Sagatchie hesitantly handed him the treacherous war ax slung over his back. The sergeant turned to Duncan, lifting the curved club that ended with a hard ball on one side and an iron spike on the other. "Do you have any notion how many this ax has killed, McCallum? Near a dozen I know of, and no doubt there's more. Sagatchie can split your brainpan at fifty feet if he has to." Duncan offered a quick bow of his head toward the Mohawk. "Corporal!" The sullen ranger looked up at Hawley. "You'll go too." The corporal cursed.

"If the prisoner offends the spirits, Sagatchie, you can teach him proper respect," Hawley added. "Just bring him back mostly alive."

Duncan eyed the Mohawk uneasily. Sagatchie's face seemed chiseled in stone, its expression somber, but in his eyes Duncan recognized the anger that smoldered in such warriors, never totally dying away. He looked over the Indian's shoulder, increasingly concerned that he had not seen Conawago. Surely his friend would want to be present for the death rites of his kin.

Sagatchie stepped forward and extended the lead rope of the horse toward Duncan. Hawley refastened the strap around Duncan's neck then untied it from the tree, handing the end to the Mohawk. Duncan cast one more worried glance toward the settlement before yielding to Sagatchie's tug on the prisoner strap and following him up the trail into the forest.

They climbed up steep switchbacks for over an hour, Sagatchie chanting in his own tongue the entire time, until they reached a small valley dominated by hemlocks, interspersed with maples. When they reached a flat where all the foliage was blood red, Sagatchie tossed down the end of the prisoner strap. The surly corporal lowered himself against a massive sugar tree and cut a piece of tobacco.

"Careful, Corporal," Duncan said in a casual tone. "Some in the tribes say the spirits of such trees can reach out and pull in humans who show no respect for the place."

"What kind of fool talk is that?" the corporal spat.

"My friend Conawago and I found a skeleton once. The tree was growing over the bones. I said the man must have died many years before. Conawago insisted it had happened only days earlier, because the man had not shown the proper reverence. Of course such a powerful tree would have to have the mark of the spirits on it."

The corporal seemed about to curse again, but as he turned he saw Sagatchie untying the horse's burden, then nervously studied the landscape beyond the tree. A casual glance may have dismissed the regularly spaced, thin timbers in the shadows as a grove of saplings, but now the corporal saw them for what they were, the posts of more than two score platforms, each topped with a decomposing body.

The soldier shot up and looked uneasily at the massive trunk he had been leaning against. "Jesus weeps!" he gasped and quickly backed away from the tree. Above his head were carved symbols, worked in the wood by many different hands over many years. A human skull had been carved into it, and also a bear's paw with long curving claws, a leaping deer, and at least a dozen snakes, creatures understood by the woodland tribes to be particularly important messengers to the gods.

"A sentinel tree," Duncan explained. "It protects the other side."

The corporal frowned but warily looked around the back of the tree as if taking Duncan's words literally.

"Some of the ghosts may still linger," Duncan suggested, "trying to find their way across."

He picked up the ranger's musket, which the corporal had abandoned in his hasty retreat. "Perhaps you'd best keep watch from the creek," he suggested to the ranger, and extended the weapon to him. "But I would like the loan of your belt ax, Corporal."

The corporal grabbed the gun with a sour look, then cocked it, aiming it in Duncan's direction before tossing his ax to Duncan's feet and marching to a log by the nearby stream. Duncan gathered his neck strap into a coil, pulled the loop over his head and tucked it into his belt, then paused for a silent prayer with his palm on the venerable tree before moving toward some sturdy saplings.

As Duncan worked at cutting poles, Sagatchie consulted the sky, the wind, the surrounding trees, and finally a hawk circling high above before selecting a sunlit patch above a short waterfall. The Mohawk made a round of each of the scaffolds, murmuring quiet words, as Duncan worked the posts into the earth.

There should be other rites, Duncan knew, daylong rites spoken by wise old sachems and tribal matrons, with loved ones joining in, but for Hickory John there was no sachem but Conawago, no matrons, no clan members to gather and recall the heroic deeds of his long life. Like Conawago he was of a disappearing breed, not just because he was Nipmuc but because he was a woodland Indian. Perhaps his greatest achievement of all was that he had survived from the time of the endless forest, from a world that had not known the boundless ambition of Europeans.

Duncan again choked away his questions about Conawago, determined not to break the reverence of the place. At last they were ready to raise the dead man onto the platform. As they pulled the shroud from the body, Sagatchie seemed to grow more troubled. He looked to the sky and spoke something that sounded like an apology.

"Your friend," he suddenly said to Duncan. "The Nipmuc with the kind eyes."

"Conawago."

"Conawago," Sagatchie repeated with a nod. He spoke in a low voice, nearly a whisper. "He told me you were trusted by the dead. That you could read them. Why did he say that? What did he mean?"

"Sometimes the dead can leave behind questions they need to be answered. There were many questions left at Bethel Church."

"But you did not even know him."

Duncan recognized the invitation in the warrior's voice and saw the nervous way Sagatchie looked at the other dead, as if unsure they would approve. Duncan knelt beside Hickory John. "Did you?"

Sagatchie looked into the dead man's face as he spoke. "Towantha wandered through the towns of the Haudenosaunee when I was young, never staying more than a few weeks in one place, though my mother once asked him to live with us in our longhouse, with our clan. You could see he was lonely, but he always embraced life's joys. He would carve things, beautiful things. Bowls with stags leaping along their sides. Pipes for the old men, war clubs for the young ones. He was always looking for something. At first it was for a sign of his people, who had been forced long ago from their homes along the Hudson. Later it was sacred places. He knew about places no one else did. When I stood no higher than a yearling deer, he took me to a cave with paintings of bison and huge bears and told me it showed the lives of people from before time, from tribes who only live in the spirit world now."

Sagatchie walked slowly around the body. "They will take long to paint his life on the other side," he added, then gestured Duncan toward the dead Nipmuc and stepped away to gather cedar wood from the stream.

Duncan clenched his jaw and lifted the dead man's hands, both of which had been crushed, studying their ruin of broken bones and cuts.

He lifted away the shirt, noticing that someone had tried to wipe away the bloodstains. A cloth, which Duncan recognized as one of Conawago's precious linen handkerchiefs, had been placed over the hole in his chest. Duncan lifted the linen to probe the wound, then moved to the bruises and cuts that covered the dead man's face and shoulders. When he finished he gazed silently at the dead man, recollecting how he had been killed differently than the others, and separately. The others had died in a row, with Hickory John facing them. He had been forced to watch them die. Duncan looked up to find that Sagatchie had lit a small fire and was extending a piece of smoldering cedar wood around and under the scaffold. The fragrant smoke would attract the spirits.

"First he was bludgeoned," he explained when the Mohawk paused at his side.

"I know not this word."

"Beaten with something. I saw a bloody wheel spoke in his shop. They beat him, and then they broke his fingers, probably with the hammer that killed the others. The breaks don't line up, which means his killers broke his fingers one by one, probably laying each one on his anvil. They knew who he was, knew they were destroying his ability to work, to carve those animals and make his wheels."

Sagatchie considered Duncan's words for several heartbeats. He clenched his jaw. "You are saying they made sure he took long to die."

"He suffered long," Duncan agreed.

Sagatchie spoke to the dead man now. "Like a captured warrior who frightened his enemies."

The words caused Duncan to hesitate. The Nipmuc had indeed died a warrior's death. "I think he was tortured for some knowledge," Duncan continued, "some secret, and when he would not talk they lined up the others in front of him. I think the raiders meant to leave no witnesses in any event, but they made sure to kill the others in front of him, slowly, one at a time, meaning to break him. When they finished with the others and he still did not speak, they found another way to threaten him." Duncan touched the strange medallion he had found in front of the Nipmic's body, still in his pocket. "He finally spoke, and they finished him with a blade to his chest."

Sagatchie frowned, as if not certain he could accept Duncan's words. "You speak as though you were there with the killers, like Sergeant Hawley said."

"I was trained as a healer, to understand the many ways of the human body. I came with Conawago to celebrate with Hickory John, not to bury him."

Duncan returned Sagatchie's intense stare. It was the way Conawago had studied him when they had first met. It was as if certain members of the tribes could see into another human in ways unknown to others. Sagatchie took a beep breath and raised a hand to the sky. Duncan was not certain what had just happened, but the distrust was gone from Sagatchie's voice when he spoke.

"Your friend would not let go of this one when we found him," the Mohawk said. "He was wild in the eyes and frail in the body. I took him to a bed in one of the houses."

Relief washed over Duncan. Conawago was safe.

Sagatchie made one more solemn circuit around the body, holding the smoldering wood near it. "You are finished?"

When Duncan nodded, Sagatchie gestured for Duncan to help remove the dead Nipmuc's shirt. "They must see the greatness of the man who is coming to their door," the Mohawk declared, and he pointed to the intricate designs tattooed over much of Hickory John's upper torso. Each of the tattoos told a story, Duncan knew, stories of great achievements and spiritual victories, some no doubt lost in the fog of time. Some might well be from rituals no longer known by the tribes. Duncan found himself looking back at the trail. Conawago should be here, Conawago would recognize the stories.

Sagatchie touched the small amulet pouch hanging from his neck, which Duncan knew contained a token of his protector animal spirit, then lifted his face to the sky. "Hear me, oh great ones! I am Sagatchie of the Wolf clan, born of the Mohawk! I give you Towantha of the Nipmuc people! He knew how to release the spirits that live inside wood. He brought joy to the young of the tribes. As a boy he ran in forests that had been untouched by ax and saw." The Mohawk ran his fingers along the tattoos, gazing at them as if reading from a book. "He journeyed to the big water. He carried wampum belts to the Huron to seek peace between our peoples." A twig snapped, and they looked up to see several deer. The animals were not frightened, but seemed to be listening. Sagatchie raised a hand in their direction as if in respectful greeting then continued, studying another tattoo of wavy parallel lines and small horned animals. His brow furrowed for a moment then lit with surprise. "He journeyed long ago to the great Mississippi and saw bison that covered the land like blades of grass."

As he gazed upon the dead Nipmuc, Duncan regretted more than ever that he and Conawago had not met the man. Surely if Hickory John had kept up his search, the two men would have connected. But he had given up and settled in the little community of Indians who followed a god not his own, making implements for people not his own, so he could give young Ishmael a steady life.

As Sagatchie rose, Duncan silently followed his gestures and lifted Hickory John to the high platform. He knew some of the death chant from sitting at Conawago's side at all too many burials, and he joined in Sagatchie's singsong prayer as they set natural adornments around the body. A twig of crimson maple leaves. A turtle shell. A clump of star moss. The skull of a small mammal.

Duncan folded Hickory John's shirt and laid it under the dead man's head, then he reached into a pouch at his belt and extracted a handful of precious salt. He poured the salt into a small pile on the linen near one of the dead man's ears, then sifted a handful of loose soil into a pile by the other ear.

"It is one of the old ways of my tribe," Duncan explained, answering the query in the warrior's eyes. "Earth for the corruptible body, salt for the everlasting spirit."

Sagatchie slowly nodded. "I cannot read all the stories. Someone should be here to speak the full tale of his life," he said in a forlorn tone. "The women of his tribe should sing songs of lamentation all night. There should be a condolence of at least a week for one such as he."

"Conawago will have songs when he comes," Duncan offered.

The Mohawk cast a hesitant glance at Duncan. He seemed about to say something, but he turned to survey the forest floor and pointed to a fallen log. Duncan helped lift the log, and with a grunt of satisfaction Sagatchie swept up a small ring-necked snake. He held the snake close, whispering to it, then gently laid it on the dead man's breast. With an approving nod he watched the snake slither around his neck and disappear into the makeshift pillow.

The whicker of the horse broke the spell. It was late. They would have to hurry if they were to reach the settlement before nightfall. Sagatchie turned from the scaffold then hesitated and pulled a piece of paper from his belt and began to place it on the folded shirt. Duncan suddenly recognized it and put a restraining hand on the Mohawk's arm.

"That is Conawago's, a treasured letter sent by Hickory John."

"He said I was to leave it with the body. He said those on the other side had to see it."

Sagatchie did not resist when Duncan pulled the tattered paper from his hand. He, like Conawago, knew the elegant script and words by heart. The pain of the murder stabbed him anew as he read it one last time. When he finished his eyes were moist. "Surely this is something Conawago himself should do," Duncan said. "He can bring it here tomorrow."

"You do not understand, McCallum. Your friend is not coming."

"But he is in the village resting, you said. He will want to come here, to sing the Nipmuc songs."

"I said I took him to a house to rest. But he left after sleeping two hours. He had a wound on his shoulder that had bled through the bandage, so Madame Pritchard changed it. He was eating some stew brought by those farmers, and talking with them, walking around the room as if to get strength back in his legs. I was keeping watch outside so they would not be disturbed. He found something, then spoke urgently with them. Suddenly he picked up his pack and rifle and climbed out a window. He nodded his thanks to me as he climbed out, then ran across the pasture to the northwest. His face was like a storm."

Sagatchie took the letter, and Duncan watched in silence as the Mohawk reversed the fold so that the original address was on the outside. Duncan glimpsed words he had not seen before, scrawled along the back. He took the paper once more and held it in the sunlight. *Stay silent between the worlds*, the first sentence read, in Hickory John's hand though not as elegant as the words inscribed inside. They seemed to have been written hastily, as an urgent postscript, as if Hickory John had made a discovery just as he posted the letter. *Hasten*, it said at the end, *this is how we first die.*

"This is how we first die," Duncan did not realize he had repeated the words until he looked up and saw the Mohawk. Sagatchie had gone very still. "What does it mean?" Duncan asked.

Sagatchie stared at the dead man. The warrior reached out and held the scaffold as if he had suddenly grown weak. He looked mournful again, but also worried. "It means this old wheel builder was one of the few who could save us."

Suddenly the surly corporal shouted, complaining that they were losing daylight. Duncan stared at the Mohawk. The Mohawk stared at the dead Nipmuc. When the corporal threw a rock to get their attention, Sagatchie spun about as if he were going to attack the man. Duncan silently looped the prisoner strap over his head and handed the end to the Mohawk ranger, who reached up to touch the dead man one more time. The prisoner led his captor out of the grove of the dead.

The corporal, riding the horse now, led them back to the settlement at a fast pace through the lengthening shadows. Sagatchie remained in his melancholy mood. He remained silent even when the corporal paused as the buildings came into view and demanded the prisoner strap so he could force Duncan to follow at a half trot for their arrival in the village.

The dead in the churchyard had been buried. The band of rangers sat at the front of the barn by a campfire, finishing their evening meal. They stared at Duncan with venom in their eyes as he was tethered to one of the iron rings used to restrain livestock. None offered him any of the stew in their pot. Sagatchie silently accepted a steaming wooden bowl and disappeared. The corporal scraped all that was left into his own bowl, then greedily gobbled it up. As his men drifted toward the houses, Sergeant Hawley bound Duncan against one of the posts along the center aisle of the barn, hands behind him, then shoved him down against the packed earth and tied his feet together, warning him that a sentry would be patrolling the settlement while the others slept.

"I need to speak with that woman," Duncan said to Hawley as the sergeant turned to leave. "The one who identified the dead today. Just a word. I beg you."

Hawley seemed to relish the request. "Did ye not see her today?" he asked with a cruel grin. "Pointing and gesturing after painting those markers? She's a mute, you damned fool!"

THE VISIONS CAME again in the night, but this time Duncan's father stood atop a heap of bodies when he beckoned Duncan to death. Shades of the dead hovered near, urging Duncan forward. As he neared the pile of bodies, it was no longer his father but Conawago who summoned him, and the bodies were all the dead of Bethel Church, who rose and began pointing to him as well. Then one of the ghosts touched his foot.

He jerked awake with a sharp intake of breath. "Sagatchie!" he said as he recognized the silhouette of the tall Mohawk. The Indian held a ladle of water to his mouth. As Duncan gratefully drank, a second figure knelt at his side, cracking open the side of a baffled lantern. Her blond hair gleamed in the dim light.

"You wanted to see the woman from the farm," Sagatchie said as he lowered the ladle.

"But then I learned she is mute."

"Not mute," the Mohawk explained. "*Français.*"

"I am Madame Pritchard." As soon as the woman spoke, Duncan understood why she had deceived the soldiers. Although she obviously spoke English, her accent was unmistakable. She would be in danger of imprisonment if the English army knew a French woman was living along its chain of forts.

"You knew these people well?" Duncan asked. "You knew Hickory John?" He glanced nervously out onto the moonlit road, where a sentry was supposed to be patrolling.

Sagatchie sensed his worry. "The guard found a bottle of applejack. He will not be troubling us."

Duncan studied the Mohawk for a moment. Even rangers from the tribes had to observe discipline, had to follow orders. Sagatchie seemed unconcerned that he was likely to incur the sergeant's wrath.

Madame Pritchard spoke in slow, patient tones, first of her admiration for the little mission community and the Christian natives who had cleared the land near the church and built the first cabin, now the school, and then from that nucleus constructed a thriving settlement. Their priest, an Anglican, had been a woodworker before joining the clergy, and even as they built their houses he had insisted they also build items that could be purchased by the military, at first barrels and kegs, then later wagons and carts. Although the man had died of fever the year before, his dream had been fulfilled.

"Where were they from?" Duncan asked. "What tribe?"

The woman glanced at Sagatchie. "Iroquois. Mohawks I think. There are hundreds of Christian Iroquois in Quebec, where I was born, taught by the Jesuits and Dominicans. When the British pushed the Catholic missionaries out of their lands, the Anglicans arrived." She shrugged. "God is not jealous about whose Bible you read from."

"But Hickory John was never christened."

"Hickory John was as close to a saint as any of us ever knew. He openly admired the wisdom of the holy book, but his gods were in the trees and beasts of the forest. A reverent man, but not afraid to laugh. When he was not making his famous wheels, he would carve little things, useful things like spoons but also frivolous things likes toys for *les enfants.*"

"And his grandson?" Duncan asked.

The French woman found a milking stool and sat close to Duncan. "Ishmael was the center of his life. It is why he settled here, he told me once, because he knew the boy had to understand the European world. But he still kept the boy rooted to the old ways. They would go off in the forest, sometimes for days at a time, and the boy would come back with strange markings on his skin."

"They went to the church?"

"None sang louder than Hickory John. He loved the ritual. He wanted the boy to know how to speak to the European god, he told me once. He knew he would not have too many years left with the boy, and he wanted the people here to consider him part of their family when he was gone." The French woman sighed. "Now what will he do?"

Duncan's head snapped up. "He was not killed? He is safe?"

"Safe, never. Alive, yes, for now. I have prayed for him, for them all, and will do so everyday."

"Them? The other children? You know where they are?"

Madame Pritchard would not look him in the eye. "They came in the morning, before noon. Ishmael said he heard a wagon on the road and men's voices raised in greeting. He thought it was just another supply train. But it wasn't. We thought no raiders would dare strike this close to the forts, never on the main supply road where the army is always coming and going." She dabbed at her eyes with the hem of her long dress. "The boy had so many tears and sobs, hard to make sense of his story. There were ten or twelve of them. French Indians and European militia, he thought. They moved quickly, like raiders always do. They forced everyone into the smithy where Hickory John made his wheels. Some of the raiders went to the barn and some worked on his grandfather. That's what the boy said. Worked on him, with his own tools."

Duncan clenched his jaw, exchanging a knowing glance with Sagatchie. They had seen how the raiders had worked on the Nipmuc.

"They forgot the children at first. After he asked the two oldest to run to see if they could help their parents, the schoolmaster, Mr. Bedford, told the others to hide in the woodshed behind the school. But Ishmael ran out, looking for his grandfather. He was too late, for his grandfather was already a prisoner in the smithy. He hid in the rocks on the slope above. The shutter on the rear window was partly open, and he could see figures inside, though they were in shadow. Some raiders guarded those of the town while another tormented poor old John. Ishmael never saw his face, could not hear his voice, though sometimes the raiders laughed at things he said."

Duncan closed his eyes for a moment, remembering how the old Nipmuc's body had been savaged. "Why? Why would they break his fingers and beat him?"

The French woman no longer bothered to wipe at the tears that flowed down her cheeks. "They demanded something. He would not give it up. They beat him with a wheel spoke. They took each finger and pounded it on the anvil like it was some bent nail. Finally they began killing the others," she said with a sob. "The boy said they sang a hymn as they died, poor wretches. They were taught not to be violent, to accept the destiny the Lord had chosen for them. I suppose they thought it was just the way they were being called to heaven.

"Hickory John sang, too, the boy said, at first that hymn. But after a few died he switched to an old Indian song, a warrior's death song."

Duncan wanted to weep himself.

"Then they hitched the horses and left."

Duncan looked up in confusion. "Hitched them to what?"

"The new wagon in the barn."

"Raiders don't use wagons."

Madame Pritchard shrugged. "They must have had something to carry."

"Left in the direction of Quebec?"

"South."

"Surely not," Duncan said. "South is where the British troops are thickest. You saw them?"

She shrugged again. "We are a quarter mile off the road. We work hard. We don't take notice of every wagon or rider. The boy saw. Ishmael saw them drive the wagon south on the Albany road."

Duncan considered her words. It was so horrible, and so impossible. Raiders didn't use wagons. Raiders didn't leave settlements unburned. Raiders didn't commit such atrocities then continue deeper into enemy territory.

"The boy?" he asked, "the children?"

The French woman scrubbed away more tears. "They took the children. Brave Mr. Bedford tried to escape with them, and they were caught. The Huron have lost most of their people to sickness and war. A strong child will fetch many furs when they reach the slave market in the North."

Duncan's heart sank. "All the children? Ishmael is with the raiders too?"

"I fear he wants to be."

"I'm sorry?"

"He watched the raiders then ran to our house."

Duncan felt a flicker of hope. "He's there now?"

"He stayed with my older daughter when the rangers fetched us here. I went back for chores, to get my children to bed. But Ishmael wasn't there. It was someone else."

"Someone else?"

"I told your friend Conawago when I went to give him food and change the bandage on his shoulder. Somehow he knew I was no mute. He wanted to know everything. When I said he was in the very chamber where the Nipmucs lived, he rose and walked about, lifting things, even moving furniture. There was a loose board under a chest. Conawago pulled it up and extracted a knife wrapped in doeskin. A beautiful knife, with a long handle carved with forest images and a flint blade, very old, more like a ceremonial object than a weapon. He pressed the hilt to his heart then stared at it a long time and grew even more sad. He wiped his eyes, and when he looked up there was a terrible fire in them. He put the knife in his belt then grew calmer.

"He asked about the boy, about the boy's life here, and I told him what I knew, about the preacher who had helped look after him until he died last year, about the joyful songs the boy sang sometimes, about how he was able to call in butterflies and the vigil he kept with the dying when the smallpox hit the village three years ago, even how Hickory John sat with the boy for four days and nights without sleep when the pox then struck Ishmael.

"When he finally asked me where the boy was, if he was safe, I had to tell him I did not know. When I returned to my house, Ishmael had stripped off most of his clothes. He had leggings over his britches and had untied his long hair. I tried to stop him. *Mon Dieu*, he's only a boy. He had used soot and whitewash to paint his body like some savage warrior. He said—" the woman's voice broke and her hand went to her mouth.

"Said what?"

"He wasn't the boy anymore. The look in his eyes scared me as much as seeing those bodies today. It was like he had been possessed. He had the look of a wild beast."

"What did he say?" Duncan insisted.

"'Now is the time to shake with fear,' he declared, then he looked up as if speaking to something in the sky. 'The world breaker is here!' he shouted. Then he ran into the forest."

"World breaker!" Sagatchie repeated the word in alarm.

Duncan looked up at him.

"It is a monster from the old stories, a demon from the end of time when the world has to be destroyed to save the gods."

Madame Pritchard crossed herself. They remained silent for a long moment, the name of the spirit monster seeming to hang in the air. Then the French woman dipped the ladle in the water bucket again. She was lifting it to Duncan's lips when it was knocked out of her hand from behind.

"Who the hell gave you permission to visit with my prisoner?" Sergeant Hawley roared as he appeared out of the shadows. He spat a curt word in the Mohawk's tongue and Sagatchie backed away, his eyes remaining on Duncan until he disappeared into the shadows. Madame Pritchard rose from her stool, meekly bowed to the sergeant, and followed the Mohawk.

"If I didn't have to account to the colonel for that dead corporal of his I would string you up right now!" Hawley shouted at Duncan. He extended a small metal token on a neck strap toward Duncan, a familiar bronze circle with a tree etched on one side and a large W on the other. "If ye were a ranger on duty ye would have shown this to us! Which means ye'r a damned deserter! We beat deserters with halberds to break their bones before we hang them!"

Duncan's mouth went dry as he watched Hawley set the lantern on the stool then pick up a length of rope. "Captain Woolford," Duncan ventured as Hawley tied a heavy double knot into the end of the rope. "Woolford is my officer."

"A lie! Woolford and his men are in the North, with the others along the Saint Lawrence."

"He does special missions for the general in Albany."

"That don't include cold-blooded murder of the king's men!"

"I told you. I was trying to help."

"I believe yer actions, not yer words! We found what else ye had stowed in yer kit. The dead soldier has a name now." The sergeant flung two items onto the floor beside Duncan. The first was a tattered pasteboard rectangle printed with a large 42, bearing the handwritten name Jock MacLeod above blocks printed with the names of months. It was a pay chit, the record soldiers presented to receive the king's shillings. Beside it lay the small, finely worked dirk Duncan had taken from the drowned Scot.

Hawley seemed unable to contain his wrath. He furiously whipped the rope at Duncan. The knot was like a rock against his flesh. It hit his shoulders, his neck, his belly, then drew blood from his jaw. "You bastard! I'm going to drag you behind a horse all the way to the Highland garrison!" he shouted. "Colonel Cameron can decide whether to hang you as a deserter or just as a murderer!"

Chapter Three

This is how we first die. The words gnawed at Duncan. Conawago had never let Duncan hold Hickory John's letter, only listen to its message. He had not wanted Duncan to see the urgent postscript. *Stay silent between the worlds. This is how we first die.* Had Hickory John glimpsed the horror that was coming to Bethel Church? Duncan feared for his friend more than ever. Conawago had rushed into the wilderness after witnessing the work of demons at the settlement. He would not have done so in fear. Conawago had retrieved an artifact and had gone to confront the demons.

He tried to sleep, but every few minutes the nightmares returned. He worked at his bindings, but his twisting only seemed to make the ropes tighter. Finally he settled for staring at the rising moon out the rear door of the barn. The demons Conawago sought were creatures of the war. But Conawago hated the war, had warned Duncan again and again that they must not be drawn into it. It made no sense. Nothing of the day's events made sense.

Suddenly he sensed a presence beside him. Sagatchie held a muted lantern, which he set on the floor beside Duncan.

"Until today I had only met three men who wore the mark of the dawnchasers," the Mohawk said, referring to the tattoo worn by those who completed a treacherous, sometimes fatal, twenty-four-hour circuit that connected old forest shrines on a run from one sunrise to the next. It was a ritual of the old ones that Conawago had taught to Duncan, a ritual lost to most of the tribes. "They were all old men when I was young, long dead now. At first I could not believe my own eyes when I saw the mark on Conawago." Sagatchie looked into the shadows uncertainly. "There are those who still say the old ways do not have to be lost. But the cord that binds us to them is so frayed it could break at any moment. And when it does, we will never find our way back."

"Conawago says the old spirits are not lost, that we have just become blind to them."

"We? Do not mock my people by pretending you are one of us."

Duncan twisted, using his elbow to pull his collar tight against his shoulder. "When I was young no one dared to plant the first seed in the spring before one of our old women spent a night in the hills making offerings to the earth spirits. We would never launch a new boat without making an offering to the winds and sea."

"Those are just the habits of old—" the Mohawk's words died away as he glimpsed Duncan's shoulder. The stern warrior had the expression of a bewildered boy as he held the lantern closer. He muttered a low invective as he pulled away the fabric to study the pattern of the rising sun that had been tattooed over Duncan's shoulder and right chest. He was silent for a long time, his gaze fixed first on the tattoo, then on Duncan's eyes. "It is a grave sin to steal such markings," he finally said. "They are not for Europeans."

"Do you think Conawago would allow me to run the woods at his side if I had stolen such a thing? We opened the old shrines for the Turtle clan of the Onondaga. We brought the ritual back to life."

Sagatchie stared at Duncan intensely, fingering his war ax, his face clouded first with anger, then confusion. "There was an Englishman who helped the Turtle clan after his people executed the Skanawati chief." His hand moved to the sacred totem bag that hung from his neck.

Duncan returned his level stare. "Do not mock my people by pretending I am English. I am a Scot. The English burned my home and slaughtered my clan when I was a boy. I was imprisoned with Skanawati and was proud to name him a particular friend. The English hanged him for a murderer. He was not guilty but he chose to die for the honor of his people."

Sagatchie looked into the shadows again, then moved to the entry of the barn. He stood in pale light, looking up as if consulting the moon, then stepped back and knelt by the post to which Duncan was tied.

"The boy came back," the Mohawk declared, now in a hushed, hurried voice. "I saw him in the dusk. He climbed into the window at the back of the schoolhouse, then came out a few heartbeats later and darted into that house where Conawago was taken. He reappeared with a sack and rolled blanket before heading south." Sagatchie looked into the shadows for a long moment then slowly nodded. "I will leave your rifle and pack in the shadows behind the barn," he declared. "Be far from here by dawn."

"Not the barn," Duncan said. "The schoolhouse. At that window where you saw the boy. And I'll need your lantern there."

Sagatchie did not argue, only leaned behind Duncan for a moment, then rose, grabbed the lantern, and faded into the shadows. As he disappeared Duncan discovered his hands were free and his own knife was lying on his lap.

Minutes later Duncan inched around the corner of the schoolhouse. His pack and rifle leaned against the woodshed built along the back wall, the dim lantern on the ground beside them. He stooped to check the contents of his pack then quickly climbed into the window. He entered not the classroom but a small sparse chamber that served as quarters for the schoolmaster. A narrow cot with a straw pallet hugged the back wall. From a row of pegs hung a threadbare shirt, a bundle of turkey feathers, and a tattered green waistcoat. The boy could have just run after the wagon he had seen heading south but instead he had come back to the schoolhouse. He had been in the room for only a few heartbeats. He had known what he wanted, and where to find it.

A table was tucked into the corner at the far end of the chamber, on which lay books, slates, writing leads, two candles in pewter holders, and a wooden candle box. The sliding lid of the candle box was open, and it held not candles but letters, several of which were on the table beside it. Duncan slid up the baffle on the lantern and leaned over the table. They were all addressed to Henry Bedford, all in the same cramped hand, with the return address simply *Eldridge, Forsey's, Albany.*

Duncan stuffed one of the letters into his shirt. He hesitated as he turned toward the window, cautiously pushing the latch of the door into the classroom. With an aching heart he walked along the crude desks. Two of the older students had died from a hammer to their heads, and Ishmael had escaped, but the others had been taken. The raiders, who existed to disrupt the British war effort, had killed Christian Indians, taken a wagon, and kidnapped five children and their teacher.

He paused at the papers pinned to the wall, drawings of animals, trees, and people in different hands, each with a verse and with a student's name at the bottom. Lizzie Oaks was there, and Barnabas Wolf, the teenagers who had been buried behind the church. With a sudden impulse he pulled away a paper from each of the other students and pushed them inside his shirt beside the letter.

As he began to climb out a hand clenched his extended leg. His heart lurched, then he recognized the Mohawk ranger.

"You will need a writing stick," Sagatchie whispered.

Duncan did not question the Mohawk, just darted to the table and retrieved one of the sticks of lead before climbing out.

"I need you to help remember them."

Duncan still did not understand, but he knew he owed much to the quiet Mohawk and so followed him behind the church.

He glanced at the stars as they reached the burial yard. It was one or two hours past midnight. For any hope of evading Hawley's rangers, he needed a several-hour head start. He should be away, running in the woods. But then he saw Sagatchie standing with the lantern at the first cross.

"*Akenhakeh*," Sagatchie declared. *Summer*. Duncan looked up in surprise, returning the Mohawk's solemn gaze for a moment before kneeling in front of the cross to write under the English name of Rebecca Halftree.

They moved from cross to cross, Sagatchie mouthing the tribal names of the dead and Duncan rendering the Iroquois words as best he could into English letters. *Tigneni Ahta*, Two Moccasins. *Wayakwas,* She Picks Berries. *Yaweko Ogistok*, Sweet Star. *Skenadonah*, Little Deer. *Tehatkwayen*, Red Wings. *Odatschte*, Quiver Bearer. *Aionnesta*, Stag.

When they finished, Duncan swung his pack onto his back. "You said Conawago went north?"

Sagatchie, staring forlornly at the graves, seemed not to hear. He had known these people, members of his tribe who had done more to coexist with the European world than any natives Duncan had ever known. He quietly repeated the question.

The Mohawk nodded. "It is three or four days to the French lines."

"And two days to Albany, if I go straight as an arrow."

"Albany is in the opposite direction. You have no hope of finding one wagon on a road filled with wagons. You must not go that way, McCallum. They will run you to the ground, and they will hang you. You must find the old Nipmuc. He has ways of keeping us joined to the spirits. He is needed more than ever."

Duncan murmured his thanks and slipped into the shadows. Finding his way to a ledge above the settlement, he studied the landscape in the silver light, considering the battering events of the past two days. Conawago, shouldering a terrible grief and driven by a foreboding message, had rushed into the northern wilderness for a reason. The twelve-year-old who carried the last of the Nipmuc blood had shed his European clothes, put on the face of a savage, and gone south after taking something from his schoolmaster's chamber. Two phantoms, joined by blood, fleeing in opposite directions. South was where a hanging rope awaited Duncan. He raised a hand in a silent prayer toward the phantom in the North and then set out toward Albany.

A MILE BELOW the settlement, Duncan emerged from the forest and set out at a steady trot along the packed earth of the military road. He knew the risk he took as a fugitive on a route frequented by the army, but he dared not run in the forest at night, for fear of a twisted ankle or worse. A few minutes later he slowed at the sight of a cabin set back from the road in the center of cleared fields. It was where the terrified boy had run after seeing his grandfather tortured and murdered. It was where the gentle Christian boy described by Madame Pritchard had transformed into a vengeful warrior.

He paused for a moment, staring at the tranquil homestead in the moonlight, a silver thread rising out of its chimney. Once, in another life, he had lived in such a place, and their seaside croft had echoed with the laughter of his family. That life was gone, and the hope of ever achieving it again was as remote as the stars. He pulled himself away, shamed for the envy he felt for the simple farmers who lived there.

The road steadily unfolded before him. Deer grazing at roadside tufts bolted at his sudden approach. Something large, a bear or catamount, growled and sped into the shadows. He rounded a curve and discovered with momentary alarm that he was passing a camp of teamsters with circled wagons, their only guard a barking dog. Duncan hesitated a moment, futilely studying the wagons. Sagatchie was right. He had no hope of finding the wagon. He had to find the world breaker.

As dawn seeped into the eastern sky, he slipped into the forest to the west of the road, slowing, probing the rising landscape until he found the expected game trail running along the ridge, parallel to the road. When he paused on a bare ledge an hour later to tighten his moccasins and chew on venison jerky, he had an unobstructed view of the lake's shore, less than half a mile away.

He gazed at the lake absently, rubbing at the bruises left by Hawley's rope, and did not realize he was staring at the island he had visited at Conawago's request until an eagle crossed his vision. He knew it was there, not the settlement, where he should mark the beginning of their misery. There the eagle had shared with him its secret of death under the water, there in an unguarded instant when Conawago had revealed a dark foreboding in his eyes. With a terrible wrenching of his heart, Duncan realized that things might have gone very differently if he had not held back from his friend, had spoken of that first dead Scot. Conawago had a way of understanding things that extended beyond Duncan's senses. What if Duncan had spoken of the death and Conawago had decided to rush straight to the village? They may have arrived in time to stop the massacre. They may have missed the men on the boat who had accidentally wounded the old Nipmuc. But then he recalled the strange writing on the back of the letter from Bethel Church. *This is how we first die.* It had been an urgent summons, more important even than the long-awaited reunion, and something Conawago had found at Bethel Church gave it a sudden desperation, even perhaps a destination.

Duncan recalled how Conawago had prepared for his reunion with Hickory John. There had been joy on his face, but also reverence. Although his friend never spoke of it, Duncan had learned from others how the Nipmucs had been one of the most spiritual of all the woodland tribes, how their small tribe had evolved into keepers of sacred secrets, like the guardians of secret temples in ancient lore. If Conawago was such a guardian, then Hickory John must have been as well.

Duncan followed the shoreline with his eyes, noting the little coves, seeing now a solitary man rowing a boat in the open water a mile below the eagle's aerie, coming out from the shore near where a narrow track left the main road.

He descended to the road, then lingered to listen and watch. A northbound dispatch rider galloped by, then Duncan crossed the little intersection and followed the rutted track to the lake.

The pier of rough-hewn logs at the end of the track had been designed to accommodate wagons. Split logs laid lengthwise along the pier were splintered and torn where heavy wheels had rolled over them. Wagons were loaded here onto the bateaux used by the army for hauling supplies. The string of forts along the lakes had their own piers, but where he stood was in the longest gap between forts, a likely place to take on loads of supplies from the nearby farms and timber camps. He cast a nervous glance toward the main road then backed into the shadows. It was also a place where patrols might be off-loaded, or where they might rendezvous. He crouched beside a large boulder, watching the still waters for a moment, studying the little isles that speckled the lake, some of them barren mounds of rock, others sprouting pines and cedars. Around the bend in the northern shoreline was the isle of the eagle and the dead soldier. Around the bend after that was where the crew of the bateau had shot Conawago. Once again he struggled with the impulse to reverse direction, to run north to find the old Nipmuc. But he knew that Conawago cared about the boy more than life itself. The youth they had never met kept the blood of his people alive. Duncan could never face his friend if after all their struggles he had let the boy's trail grow cold.

Duncan dropped to a knee as a twig snapped and brush began shaking in the thicket nearby. He cocked his rifle and began inching toward the sound.

The riderless horse, a powerful bay wearing a light saddle, had snagged its reins in an alder. Its eyes grew wild as its efforts entangled the reins further. Duncan rose and moved slowly toward the animal, speaking in low, reassuring tones.

When he had freed the horse, he led it out onto the open track. The well-polished brass and leather of its tack marked it as army property as clearly as the broad arrow brand on its rear flank. He studied the animal as it grazed. Its legs were not built for hauling wagons or caissons, nor for carrying an officer into battle. It was built for speed. He found himself looking back to the north shoreline, toward the eagle's isle. The drowned soldier had been traveling light, with neither sword on his shoulder belt nor cartridge box at his waist. He walked around the animal and saw now the stiff leather cylinder tied to the saddle, sealed with a waxed string. The man had been a dispatch rider. He had been forced onto the lake from this very dock, and his horse was still waiting for him, not knowing he would never return.

Duncan's hand lingered on the dispatch box for a moment, but he resisted the temptation to open it. The man had not been killed for his dispatches, but for challenging something suspicious. Duncan tied his rifle and pack on the saddle and eased himself up. Taking a government horse was a hanging offense, but they could only hang him once, and with a mount he could be certain to leave the pursuing rangers behind.

The horse seemed to relish the open road and quickly settled into the long loping gait used by military messengers. As he emerged from each curve and crested each hill Duncan half expected to see the boy, but by late morning his hopes began to fade, and he realized Ishmael himself could have found a horse, or a ride on some carriage or wagon.

His strength, and that of the horse, began to flag by early afternoon, and as he approached the southern end of Lake George, he dismounted and led the horse off the road and up the ridge that ran parallel to it. He found a small high clearing overlooking the lake then removed the saddle and rubbed down the horse with dried grass before turning it loose to graze. He ate a meal of jerked meat and lay at the edge of a stream, filling his canteen before dipping his face in the cool water, then leaned back on a paper birch, listening to the songs of the thrushes, the hammering of woodpeckers, the screech of a hawk high overhead. He extracted the letter he had taken from the schoolhouse and read the return address once more. *Eldridge, Forsey's, Albany.* It had the sound of a commercial establishment. He unfolded the paper and for the first time read the message inside.

My dearest S, the crude, uneven handwriting began. The salutation was followed by a prosaic description of affairs in Albany.

> *The boatyard has been busier than ever making transports*
> *for the army. The hammers keep me awake long into the evening.*
> *An Oneida brought in the pelt of a snow-white catamount and*
> *declared it had magic healing powers. A Dutchman bought it*
> *for his sick infant. You would have laughed to see the moose that*
> *walked into the open door of the Reformed Church during services.*
> *There has been no word from New York town.*

The letter was signed with a simple *M*. Duncan hesitated and looked at the address again. Henry Bedford, it said, though the letter was directed to someone whose name began with an S.

He withdrew the papers he had taken from the wall of the classroom. The first had the drawing of a cat on it, followed by the simple verse

Great A, B, C and tumbledown D.

The Cat's a blind bluff. She cannot see.

Below it was the name Hannah Redfern. Under the drawing of a man with a fishing pole was the verse

The artful Angler baits his Hook

and throws it gently in the Brook.

Jacob Pine had signed the page. Next came a drawing signed by Abigail Hillwater of a tree with leaves falling, with the verse

Autumn succeeds in flame Yellow clad

With Fullness smiling and with Plenty glad.

A simpler drawing of a bird in a crude, younger hand, signed by Abraham Beaver, was over the verse

Fine Feathers make Fine Birds.

A boy named Noah Moss had signed a drawing of a fox staring at a long-necked bird, over the words

When the Fox preaches beware of the Geese.

Finally came a more refined drawing of a man looking up at a crescent moon over the words

Learn well the Motions of the Mind

Why you are made, for what designed.

It was signed Ishmael Ojiwa Nipmuc.

The verses, Duncan suspected, were from the popular book of children's verse by John Newbery, a fixture in many British schools. But Ishmael had scribed another verse in much smaller writing at the bottom of his paper. *The world's a bubble,* it said, *and the life of a man less than a span. Francis Bacon.* He extracted the oval medallion that had laid by Hickory John's body. It was an exquisite carving of a deer and a bear standing like sentinels on either side of a kneeling man.

He stared at the medallion, knowing it must have held important meaning for the murdered Nipmuc, then set the papers in the grass around him, trying to understand what about them nagged him. He recounted the names on the crosses at Bethel Church. The captured children did not share the names of the dead. The children who shared the names of the adults had been killed. The Nipmuc wheelwright who lived apart from the war had a secret the raiders desperately wanted. He had kept an ancient flint knife hidden in his room that had sent Conawago rushing north. Bethel Church was built upon layers of tribal mystery.

As he stuffed the papers back into his shirt, he heard a new hammering, a staccato beat in the distance. This was no woodpecker. He lifted his rifle and found one of the ledges that broke through the cover of the trees, quickly stepping to the edge and just as quickly stepping back. He dropped to the ground and inched forward on his belly.

Fort William Henry, at the end of Lake George, was much larger than he had anticipated. He recalled reading how it had been reinforced and strengthened after the British had reclaimed it following the terrible massacre by French Indians there three years before. The parade ground inside the palisade held ranks of soldiers being drilled. Two heavily laden bateaux were rowing away as another was being loaded. On a broad flat outside the palisade more soldiers were being trained, marching, stopping, pivoting, fixing bayonets, and charging at straw figures tied to posts. They were moving through stations, sprinting up an earthen mound at one position, leaping over a trench at another, then spreading out with mechanical precision into the treacherous double line of muskets that had wreaked havoc on so many European battlefields. With grim recognition he saw the final station, a hundred feet from the gate. Troops completing the circuit were drawn into tight formation and ordered to halt to gaze upon a scaffold where the body of a man swayed at the end of a rope.

DUNCAN TOSSED SEVERAL coins on the table as the innkeeper reached to remove his breakfast dishes. He had paused on his desperate ride from Fort William Henry for a few hours' sleep, rising before dawn to cover the last few miles to Albany before releasing his horse and stopping at the first tavern on the outskirts of the town. "I'm looking for a place called Forsey's," he ventured.

The old Dutchman eyed him in surprise. "Enlisting, are ye?"

"My brother's an officer," he replied warily. His brother Jamie had indeed been a captain before being court-martialed as a deserter.

The innkeeper didn't seem particularly convinced, but he shrugged and pointed out the window. "Down Water Street then turn at the old elm and head toward the river. Sign's out front."

By New World standards, Albany reeked of age and culture. For a few minutes as he walked down the cobbled street he felt he was back in Holland, where he had been a boarding school student. Stout brick houses with stepped roofs and smaller, brightly colored, tidy abodes with tall chimneys lined his passage. He reminded himself that the town had its start as the Dutch community of Fort Orange more than a century earlier. A woman tended asters in a cemetery beside a yellow building marked as the Dutch Reformed Church. A team of matched horses was being hitched to an elegant carriage before a stately house. A beefy, unshaven man led a procession of several weary-looking Indians bearing enormous bundles of furs on their shoulders. Heavy wagons loaded with barrels rumbled over the cobbles. An Indian woman sold baskets under a huge tree. He looked up, recognizing its fan-shaped branches, then turned down the cross street and descended toward the Hudson. Halfway down the street was a substantial brick building. With a sinking feeling he saw the soldiers, nearly all officers, idling near its entrance. He ventured close enough to read the sign over the front door before ducking into an alley. *Forsey Bros*, it said. *Clothiers to the Military.*

He waited in the shadow of a stable behind the building, watching women in plain work dresses carrying red and blue fabric out of a cellar door to hang on a rope stretched between two trees. When one of them inadvertently kicked over a basket of their split-stick clothespins, scattering them across the ground, Duncan emerged into the sunlight to help her collect the pins.

She looked at him suspiciously but offered a stiff nod of gratitude when he dropped the last pin in the basket. "I was looking for Mrs. Eldridge," he ventured.

The woman looked as if she had bitten something sour. "The old widow witch? Like as not cajoled some fool into trading a pint of rum for a fortune-telling and is passed out in her hut."

"Fie!" the second woman snapped. "That's no Christian way!"

"Christian don't exactly describe her," the first woman sneered.

"And thank God you have been spared the torment she has known," the older woman chided. Her companion gave an exaggerated grimace and retreated toward the cellar.

"Hetty's life has been harder than most," the woman explained to Duncan.

"She works here?" he asked.

"Most days. Sewing lace to officers' tunics, though I daresay she's never worn lace in her life. If she's in her way she'll not say a word to you."

"In her way?"

The woman winced. "Her hut lies beyond the yard where they build the bateaux. Not hers exactly, but no one had the spine to put her out when she squatted in it."

The shipyard at the bottom of the hill was a hive of activity. Wagons stacked with timber were lined up waiting to unload. Three separate boats were under construction, each braced within heavy pilings above the muddy bank down which they would slide upon completion. Mallets and hammers beat an unsteady rhythm. Rough-looking men working with planes and chisels glanced up at Duncan and seemed to dismiss him as one of the trappers or scouts who frequented Albany. Curses rose from a long deep trench in the ground where a man on the wrong end of a heavy sawblade spat out the wood dust constantly falling on him.

Duncan paused at the far edge of the yard near a massive dog with shaggy brown hair sitting on its haunches. It possessed a wild, noble air about it, and Duncan, who had befriended several such creatures in his youth, instinctively took a step closer.

"Wouldn't," came a terse voice behind him. The speaker was a burly bearded man covered in sawdust who had just climbed out of the sawpit.

"Just admiring your animal," Duncan offered. "I've seen many mastiffs and hunting hounds but few as magnificent as this beast."

"Not my animal, nor any man's here. It just appeared two days ago. Will have naught to do with us. Won't take meat, won't take a bone. I've got Iroquois here who say that warriors killed in battle sometimes come back as such creatures for unfinished business."

Duncan inched closer. The dog did not move its broad, heavy head, but a low rumble of warning rose in its throat. His expression was suddenly that of a fierce predator.

The man produced a rag from his pocket and began wiping his face. "It just stares like that. All day, all night as far as we know." The man, Duncan realized, was frightened of the animal. "A boy threw a stone at it. The dog just gave him its eye and the boy fell back into the pit, broke his damned ankle. My men are calling it the hell dog."

"Perhaps it waits for a boat, for some trapper to arrive," Duncan suggested.

The man snorted. "That's what I thought at first. But someone pointed out that the Welsh witch has been inside there ever since he arrived. Yesterday two of my men refused to come to work. Today four more. I said I was going to shoot the damned beast, and one of the Oneidas said my wife would be a widow by the next moon if I did."

With a chill Duncan now saw the dog stared not at the river but at a decrepit log hut near the bank.

The structure clearly survived from the town's early age, when Albany and before that Fort Orange had been centers for the fur trade. The logs at one corner were rotting, lending an unstable tilt to one side of the roof. The low roof had skulls scattered across it, of beaver, otter, hares, and other small mammals. Several of the willow hoops used for stretching skins lay rotting against one wall. From the low uneven eaves hung the black-and-white furs of polecats. From a pole near the door feathers fluttered in the breeze, all of them from crows or ravens.

Duncan ventured several steps closer to the cabin then turned uneasily. The sounds of the work in the yard had stopped. The eyes of every man in the yard seemed to be on him. The rumble of the dog grew louder. A sharp complaint from the man who had spoken to Duncan sent the men back to work.

He approached to within six feet of the dog then dropped onto one knee, holding his rifle upright like a staff. He collected himself, looking down at the grass for several moments before addressing the animal with soft, respectful words in the Mohawk tongue, words he had heard Conawago speak to a bear that had walked into their campsite one night. When the dog did not react he tried them in English. "I honor the tooth and claw of your spirit," he intoned. "I honor the beauty of your paw and know your greatest strength lies in not using it."

A low growl came from the creature's throat, but it slowly shifted his eyes to meet Duncan's gaze as he repeated the words, shifting between the tribal and English tongues. He steadily lowered his voice, until it was a faint whisper, but stopped only when the dog stopped growling. From a belt pouch he extracted a small yellow feather he had found in the forest and set it on the ground in front of the animal. As the dog cocked its head at the feather, he slowly rose and backed away, toward the hut.

The door of the structure was ajar. He called out the woman's name, then slowly pushed the door open when no response came. A strange translucent veil hung over the entry. He advanced a step then froze as he realized it consisted of the skins of huge rattlesnakes, the heads pinned inside the lintel, the rattles hanging to betray the passage of any who entered. He clenched his jaw, pushed the skins aside, and stepped into the single room of the decaying cabin.

The air was thick with the smoke of cedar, used by the tribes to summon spirits. He stood still, letting his eyes adjust to the dimness, surveying the strange chamber he found himself in. More animal skins, moth-eaten and tattered, hung on the walls. Woodcutting trestles supported rough planks for a low table, with a lopsided milk stool the only seat. The woman sat in a corner on a pallet of cedar boughs, her eyes fixed on the bottom of a green onion-shaped bottle she clenched in her hands. A piece of cedar wood smoldered in a bowl at her side.

Duncan leaned his rifle against the doorframe and settled onto the floor in front of her. Her hollow eyes slowly found him, and her lips curled into a lightless smile. When she turned the bottle he saw that her wrists were encircled with such heavy scars she seemed to be wearing bracelets of raised flesh.

"Poison snake take you home," she suddenly declared. Her voice was dry as sticks.

A chill crept down Duncan's spine. "I am here about Henry Bedford," he declared, and paused. He had made an assumption about the relationship of the woman who sent the letters and the schoolteacher, but it did not seem possible that this fearful crone could be the man's mother. "Mr. S.," he tried. "And a student of his who may have come looking for him."

She trapped some smoke inside the bottle and became so engrossed with it she seemed to have forgotten his presence. After several long moments her gaze shifted to Duncan's foot and slowly wound its way up his leg. She finally looked him in the face. Even then her only reaction was to cup some of the smoke in her hand and release it under his chin.

He noticed a crumpled paper that lay at her side, similar to the letter he had inside his shirt, and he fought the temptation to grab it. "The boy Ishmael. Has he been here?"

She leaned close to him, so close he could smell her sour breath. But she did not seem drunk. "You are one of them then."

He paused, noticing now a pattern drawn on the earthen floor beside her, a parallelogram with two dots and a slanted line inside. "One of them?"

"The dead of Bethel Church."

Duncan swallowed hard. "Madame, I am here, sitting in front of you in this world."

"Then you know nothing."

"On that much we agree," he muttered. He saw now a belt of beads on her lap, not the shiny glass beads of European traders but the plain wampum shell beads of the tribes. His head snapped up. It was a message belt, used in the wilderness for communication between native villages, even between separate tribes. He had not seen many, but he knew they always conveyed vital, solemn messages. Belts might warn of epidemics or summon members of tribal councils to meetings. Black belts, comprised solely of dark purple shells, were used as a declaration of war. This one held a complex pattern of stick figure humans and animals. It made no sense that the woman in front of him, a Welsh seamstress with a taste for rum, would have such a belt.

Duncan saw now more beads, a single strand of white wampum laying on the pallet. He lifted it and conspicuously draped it over his open hand. The white strand was a warrant of truth among the tribes. No man could hold such beads and lie, though he was not certain what they might connote to a Welsh widow living in Albany.

"My name is Duncan McCallum," he tried again, raising his hand with the beads. "I seek the boy named Ishmael, Ojiwa of the Nipmuc, who came here from Bethel Church after its people were massacred." His free hand extracted the letter he carried and held it in front of her. "You know the schoolteacher there. You are his mother," he ventured. When she did not object, he continued. "Ishmael was here because he believed you knew something of those who captured your son and his students."

Her cackle was like a rattle in her hollow chest. "If he is gone he needed to be gone. The half-king stands tall. White George stumbles. Not long now. When the dead walk the living tremble. How many times can you die?" As she laughed again, Duncan glanced toward the entry, fighting a compulsion to flee.

"Where do they go to?"

"Beyond, and beyond." The woman kept cackling, holding the bottle up to an eye and looking at Duncan through its bulbous translucent glass.

Duncan clenched his jaw in frustration. He gazed at the wampum belt, knowing that without Conawago he would never unlock the riddle of its beads. "Your son and his students. How do I find them?"

"People think there is forgiveness on the other side," the Welsh woman croaked. "But that is where payment is made."

"Damn it!" he snapped. "There's children to be saved, woman! Enough of your gibberish."

She cocked her head toward a bear skull he had not seen before, suspended from a roof beam so that it seemed to float in the air. She seemed not to see him now. As he watched uneasily, she began to unbutton her soiled linen blouse. "Enough of your gibberish," she echoed. With one quick movement she pulled the blouse down, below her small, pinched breasts. "Here is where they go!"

Her chest was covered with scars and tattoos, a maze of small deliberately inflicted scars and ink depicting stick figures of humans, a tree, and a bear. Around and through it all was a tattoo of a long snake, its head facing a sun rising over a vertical line. Her torso began to undulate, and the snake began to move. A small, fearful cry escaped Duncan's throat. She was a witch after all.

"You won't even know what to say when he finally speaks to you," she said in a surprisingly level voice. It had the sound of an accusation.

As Duncan gazed at her hideous disfigured torso, his jaw moved up and down but no sound came out. "Whom must I speak to?" he finally asked.

"The Revelator," she replied, her eyes wild again. As she laughed the snake writhed on her naked flesh. "The Revelator summons you! He will seize the heart from your chest and wring the truth out of your miserable life!"

He dropped the beads, grabbed the crumpled paper, and fled.

Chapter Four

"People say Albany is at the edge of the world," the man in the brown waistcoat observed. "But they're wrong. We live between the edges of two worlds. The pressing blade of European settlement and the sharper edge of the tribes."

Duncan had found Thomas Forsey, one of the two brothers who owned the clothier, smoking a long-stemmed pipe on the back step of the big brick building. He nodded to his workers as they filed out, murmuring polite farewells, at the end of their workday. Duncan had told him he was a scout, looking for Mrs. Eldridge. "Her son is a schoolmaster. He and his students are missing."

Forsey tilted his head and studied Duncan as if deciding whether to believe him. "Who did you find?"

"She was there, in that hut with the skins and skulls."

"There is a fortune-teller who lives there," Forsey said, taking another puff on his pipe. "'The Welsh Oracle,' some in the taverns call her. People buy her a drink and ask when to plant their grain. For a whole bottle she'll tell you what to name your child and how you will die."

"I thought I was going to meet Mrs. Eldridge."

"When she is here, the meek Hetty Eldridge is the best seamstress we have. There is also a drunk who lives in that hut, though thank God no man's ever been drunk like her. And there is the ghostwalker."

A ghostwalker. It would explain much, Duncan realized. Inhabitants of the settlements used the term to refer to the uncertain souls who had been captured by the tribes and later released, usually after many years of living as a member of a tribe. "How long?"

"Who knows. Long enough. I remember Mr. Conrad Weiser of the Pennsylvania colony coming here many years ago, looking for signs of her. She had been taken in a raid on a farm in the Tulpehocken country long before, just after being married. There was a deal struck with some Mingoes ten or twelve years ago. They agreed to return captives to the army in exchange for some guns and blankets. She came back dragging a half-blood son with her." For many captives the return to European society was more difficult than their original capture. It was why they were called ghostwalkers, for the way many never fit back in, for the way they stayed between worlds, often wandering aimlessly.

"She has her job here," Duncan observed. "Why does she live in such squalor?"

"Hetty and I have a game we play. Every time she collects her monthly wage, I offer her a room in our attic. Every month she thanks me but refuses. She wants full wages, nothing deducted for room and board. But she never collects them. She worked hard to educate her son, but after he left her nest he went back out among the Mingoes for a few years. A month after he finally returned, he murdered some Dutch patroon's son over a card game. He escaped custody but he was still found guilty. She is convinced of his innocence and has me send every shilling to a barrister in New York town who is petitioning the crown for a pardon."

"But she has two sons? There is one who is a schoolmaster."

Forsey held up a hand, as if he did not want to hear more. "One son. You must be thinking of someone else," he said pointedly.

Duncan was more confused than ever about the woman and the hell dog that had watched him so ravenously when he had retreated from her hut. "She smelled like she was drunk but . . ." he searched futilely for words, "but she wasn't."

"The rum doesn't go into Hetty like it does other humans. It's like it becomes a spirit of another kind, a spirit of the other side, some say, that possesses her at such times." Forsey seemed to try to grin but the effort became a grimace, which quickly faded as he looked over Duncan's shoulder. He dipped his head in greeting to someone and slipped back into his building.

"Christ's Blood, Duncan!" a man behind him snapped, then pulled him off the step. "You must have a death wish!"

Captain Patrick Woolford was a man who looked elegant in any uniform, even the roughspun ranger tunic he often wore, but the man before Duncan was haggard and nervous. A pistol was stuffed in his belt, and the pan of his rifle was primed as if he expected an attack at any moment. He spoke no more until he had led Duncan into the shadows of the stable at the rear of the property.

"My God, man! They are searching for you up and down the lakes!" Woolford exclaimed. "Murder of a corporal in the 42nd they say."

"They are wrong, Patrick."

"Of course they are. But this army is in a hanging mood. You have to flee. Come back to my room above the old tavern, then tonight slip into the forest with Conawago for a month or two. Go to the Iroquois towns. Go to Sarah Ramsey. Anywhere but here."

"And what are you doing here? You are supposed to be in the North striking the coup de grâce on the French."

"I am in the North, in the West, even in New York town. My men are scattered. General Calder says rangers are good at operating in the shadows, and he has taken to using my company for shadow errands. I was heading for the fort at Oswego when he summoned me back."

"Because of the murders?"

"Not exactly." Woolford cocked his head. "I heard of but one murder."

Duncan gestured him toward two thick cut logs used as splitting blocks. They sat among the woodchips, and he explained the journey he and Conawago had taken to find Conawago's long-lost kinsman and the horror that had awaited them when they finally reached Bethel Church.

"I know Bethel Church," Woolford said in a hollow voice. "A village of Christian Mohawks."

"Who were forced to stand in a line and wait for a hammer to their skulls. Women and men in the full of life. A young maiden. And one Nipmuc, tortured as if he were the object of the raid."

Woolford clenched his jaw. "A Nipmuc?"

"Conawago was with me. But he fled. There was something he recognized, something that caused him to run north after my arrest."

"But you came south."

"His great nephew, the very last of his blood, escaped, and seeks revenge. The boy came here. He spoke with the mother of his schoolmaster, though I can't fathom why."

"The provosts had word there was a stranger seeking the witch of the boatyard."

Provosts. The mention of the army's brutal enforcers caused Duncan to cast a nervous glance toward the street. "Forsey says she is a ghostwalker."

Woolford pushed back his long black hair and nodded. "She had been taken as a teenage bride by the Iroquois who migrated west, the Mingoes. Twenty-five years ago, or more. Settlers say she was rescued in a negotiation to free captives. But the tribes say she was forced out, for being a witch. They were terrified of her."

"But she had a family among them."

"She married a great Mingo warrior, a subchief. He died in battle with a western tribe, and she was taken in by his clan for a few years. But she scared them. They turned her out, sent her to the settlements, though for half a shilling most in Albany would run her out of here as well." Woolford studied Duncan and shook his head. "You have to leave, Duncan. I don't know if—"

"Not without Conawago's nephew."

"You can't know he is here."

"He was with her, only hours ago."

"You don't understand, Duncan. There's dark things afoot. I've never seen the general so worked up. The provosts are like mad dogs. They'd as likely skewer you on their bayonets as arrest you."

Duncan studied Woolford's worried countenance. "You mean there's more than murders hanging over the army. What else happened?"

Woolford stared at him in silence. There was a reason the general trusted him for clandestine missions. "Most think the war is almost won," he said in a lower voice. "But our successes have been built on sand." Suddenly the captain's eyes went round with surprise as he looked over Duncan's shoulder and cursed. Duncan heard the running footsteps behind him and was about to turn when Woolford spoke.

"I'm sorry," the ranger captain said, and he slammed a fist into Duncan's jaw. Duncan staggered and dropped onto his knees. "Stay down, damnit," Woolford pleaded.

As Duncan tried to shake the pain from his head, a second blow came, a glancing strike of Woolford's rifle butt onto the side of his head. Duncan sank into darkness.

HIS SENSE OF smell woke first. Wood smoke. Tea. Candle tallow. The talcum used on wigs. His eyes fluttered open to see burning logs in a huge hearth at the far side of a spacious chamber and candles on a long table near the fire. He lifted his head and shook the fog from his eyes.

Woolford sat at the table with three other men, conferring urgently over a large map. More maps were pinned to the walls of the room. The bronze glow of dusk filtered through two windows along one wall. Between the windows stood a heavy desk on which papers and quills were strewn. The door opening into a corridor was blocked by a stern guard in a scarlet coat holding one of the army's deadly Brown Bess muskets. Outside the windows the sound of heavy boots marching in unison echoed off stone walls.

Duncan stirred, trying to rise, and discovered that his feet were bound with chains, his arms tied to the chair with sashes. The rattle of his manacles caused the men at the table to turn toward him.

With relief Duncan recognized the man who stood and approached him. He had met General Calder on his first day in the New World, and he knew him to be a fair man of moderate temper. He had been tied to a chair on that day as well, and Calder had called off the officer who had been assaulting him with a horse crop.

Duncan forced a respectful nod as Calder approached. "Good evening, General," he offered.

The general slammed the back of his hand across Duncan's jaw. "I should have kept you in chains that first hour I met you, McCallum!" Calder snarled. "I will not have you destroy my army!"

Duncan looked in desperation at Woolford, who hesitantly rose from the table. "I have always found McCallum to be a man of integrity, sir," the ranger captain ventured. "He states that all the killings occurred before he arrived at Bethel Church."

"The word of a murderer and traitor means nothing!" Calder snapped.

"It will be for a magistrate's court to decide if he is a murderer," Woolford said in a level voice.

Calder's face flared with anger. He stepped to the desk and lifted a bronze disc dangling from a leather strap. "Did you not issue this to McCallum, Captain Woolford?" the general demanded.

Woolford glanced at Duncan apologetically. This was treacherous ground. If he lied, Duncan would be guilty of falsely claiming to be a ranger, the act of a spy and traitor. But they both knew what it meant for him to admit the truth.

"For safe passage through the frontier. He assisted us, as a scout. He never received a farthing of the king's pay."

One of the other officers, an elegant middle-aged man with eyes like two black pebbles, rose from the table. "Answer the general, Captain," he growled. "Did you issue a ranger's badge?"

"Yes, Colonel Cameron, I did."

"Which means he will not be subject to a civilian court proceeding." Cameron approached Duncan as he spoke, walking around his chair. "He will be prosecuted by the army, in a closed chamber. We can spare an hour tomorrow morning. The witness statement will suffice for the court-martial. We can have him strung up before lunch. A least we can bring one of the McCallums to the king's justice."

"Witness?" Duncan asked.

The colonel's eyes flared at being interrupted. "Sergeant Hawley signed an affidavit attesting that he saw you stabbing the poor man." He leaned over Duncan as if about to strike him. "The soldier you killed was well-liked in the 42nd. We should turn you over to them. They would pull off your limbs before they strung you up."

"Hawley lies!" Duncan spat. "I had no connection to Bethel Church. They were all dead before we arrived."

Colonel Cameron raised an eyebrow. "We?" He turned to Woolford. "Who else was with him? Where is his accomplice?"

When neither Woolford nor Duncan replied, Cameron raised a crumpled piece of paper. "You would have us believe you were a stranger to those at Bethel Church! Yet you walk around with a letter addressed to Bethel Church!"

Duncan swallowed hard. "It was raiders! The enemy!"

"Raiders who didn't steal anything. Raiders who left without burning a single building or destroying any stores."

"They took horses and a wagon," Duncan explained. "They took children. They killed nine settlers."

Cameron sneered. "If there had been—"

The general looked up from the desk. "Children?" he interrupted.

"There were eight children in the settlement. Two were killed with the others in the smithy. One escaped. The others were taken."

"French raiders don't risk such a deep penetration into our lands to take children," Cameron declared icily.

"I didn't say they were all French. There were natives too. The Hurons and Abenaki who run with the French take children. They sell them as slaves in the North."

General Calder studied Duncan in silence then lifted two more objects from the desk. Duncan shuddered as he recognized the little dirk and the pay chit that Hawley had claimed to take from his kit. He extended the dirk to make sure Duncan saw it, then dropped it on the desk and approached Duncan with the chit raised before him. "Why take this?" Calder demanded.

"I did not steal it. Hawley planted it in my pack. He found me bent over MacLeod trying to render aid. I had medical training."

"You said they had been dead for hours," Cameron snapped.

Duncan looked at the floor. "The residents of the town, yes. But he was not a resident. I was hoping it might be different for him, that he may have just been left wounded by the raiders. There was yet warmth in his body."

The general did not seem to hear. He paced across the room, staring forlornly at the little piece of pasteboard. As he approached the hearth he spat a bitter curse and flung it into the fire.

"There was another dead soldier. That was his dirk. A dispatch rider," Duncan said to his back. "In the lake. Tied to a wheel. Hickory John made wheels for the army." He realized the others were all staring at him as if he were mad. Duncan himself did not know why he had spoken the words. Even to him they sounded like the ravings of a desperate man.

The fourth man at the table, a wan junior officer wearing lace cuffs and a stiff collar, had kept busy with his quill but now looked up. Cameron hastened to his side and looked over his shoulder. He gasped and hung his head.

"Marston?" Calder called.

The young officer looked up. "Uncle, I don't think that—" he began, gazing pointedly at Duncan.

"Just tell me!" Calder snapped.

"Seven five three two, sir," Marston stated morosely. The pronouncement had the sound of more raving.

But the general seemed to make sense of it. The words struck him like a physical blow. He sagged and sank into a chair at the end of the table. "We can deal with mere murder tomorrow," he declared in a voice that was suddenly weary.

Colonel Cameron spoke into the ear of the guard at the door, who leaned his musket on the wall and marched to Duncan's chair. Cameron fixed Duncan with a cruel grin as the soldier tied a piece of twine around Duncan's upper arm before releasing his arm restraints. "The iron hole," Cameron barked.

Woolford gasped. The color drained from the ranger's face as Duncan was led out.

Chapter Five

The iron hole. Duncan could not fathom what the reference meant, but the provosts who escorted him clearly were pleased with the prospect. They shoved him out of the fortress, not reacting when a handful of men in kilts threw stones at him. When the last stone, a sharp blow to his knee, caused him to stumble, his guards simply swung down their muskets, bayonets at the ready. He struggled to his feet with a clanking of chains. As they passed a stable, a man pitched a forkful of manure at him, eliciting a growl from a provost only when some landed on his boot.

They marched to the edge of town then onto a rough road before turning into a narrow gully through a gate of timbers where another squad of provosts stood guard. The twisting gully quickly darkened as they descended, the walls growing close together, until they suddenly rounded a turn and faced a large opening in the rock wall.

A shiver ran down Duncan's spine as he saw the gate of stout iron bars. A guard stepped out of the gloom to open the gate, casting a glance of contempt at Duncan, then shoved him into the cave so hard he fell onto his knees.

As the gate slammed behind him, a soldier with a hard, sour face appeared from a side chamber and pointed Duncan to a low stool. He set a lantern on the ground as Duncan sat down, then lifted a hammer and a short iron punch. With two quick taps he released the pins from Duncan's manacles and hung the chains on a peg.

Duncan's relief at having the chafing metal off his ankles quickly faded as the guard gestured him into the murk of the descending tunnel. Lanterns hung from support beams every ten paces. After ten lanterns, the tunnel made a sharp turn and the guard paused to stuff two pieces of what looked like raw wool up his nostrils. As they rounded the corner the stench of human filth struck Duncan like a physical blow.

"Two levels," the guard explained as he pushed Duncan forward. "No one goes into the main tunnel without permission. No one disturbs the candles, no one upends the pisspots, no one fights with another prisoner. Break those rules and ye get sent to the bottom level. Half the men there get carried out in shrouds. The stench be so thick in the bottom ye can carve a slice and eat it for breakfast. And try to go into the old mine beyond the second level and the mountain will kill ye," he added as he halted at the low entrance to a side chamber. "Took three bodies out of here last week," the guard added. "Which means ye might be able to find a blanket." He gestured Duncan through the low arch. "God save the king," he said with a mock salute.

A dozen specters looked up as Duncan entered the dimly lit chamber, the pale, hollow faces of emaciated prisoners. He had seen such faces before, when he had been imprisoned in Edinburgh and on the prison ship that had transported him to America. They were drained of strength, drained of hope. Some wore vestiges of uniforms, others just filthy grey tunics. This was no holding cell, no simple brig where soldiers were disciplined. This dungeon was of a kind Duncan did not know existed in America.

The chamber, at least twenty paces long and ten wide, was lit by only three stout candles resting on squarish boulders evenly placed along the center. The prisoners sat in small groups on filthy straw pallets along the near end. They offered no greeting, just watched Duncan with empty eyes as he retrieved a moth-eaten blanket from a pile inside the entrance. Nearby, two men eyed him, muttering to one another, then each tossed a button on the floor between them. He carried the blanket to an empty place along the far wall and was beginning to fold it into a cushion when it seemed to move. He dropped it. The blanket was crawling with lice.

One of the two prisoners at the entry gave a victorious guffaw and swept up the buttons.

Duncan kicked the blanket away and moved farther down the chamber, settling down against the cold wall near the third candle. He could see now the small alcoves at the end of the cavern where miners had once chiseled out iron, and the waste buckets in them, and he understood why the prisoners gathered at the far end.

His head sagged. It felt like he hadn't had real sleep in days. The despair that seized him seemed to block all conscious thought, but it fought a losing battle with his exhaustion. He touched his belt and realized that in their haste the provosts had not searched him thoroughly, seizing only his obvious weapons. In a pouch on his belt he found one of the fragrant chips of cedar wood he kept for Conawago's spirit fires. He pulled up his knees, crossed his arms over them, and cupped the cedar under his nose as he surrendered to his fatigue.

He was a young boy again, running over the hills in defiance of his father's stern command to stay at home. His mother had sent him to his room, saying it was no business for children, but she had not known that Duncan had learned to drop out of the upstairs window. As he peered around a tree trunk, he was filled with pride at having reached the men at the grove of trees undetected, and he was about to race to his father's side when the company suddenly went silent. A terrible inhuman cry rose from the tallest tree, then a riderless horse galloped away. As the company parted for it, Duncan saw the man swinging from the limb, struggling with his noose as his face turned blue. The cattle thief had taken a long time to die.

A low, steady voice crept into his consciousness, a new voice singing one of the net hauling shanties of his youth. He lifted his head, his eyelids heavy, to see another gentle old Scot cleaning his net on a twilit beach. He shook his head to clear his vision. He wanted to be asleep. His waking world was nothing but nightmare.

He paused, studying the figure before him, and realized he was no longer dreaming. The man was not as old as he had imagined, but he wore the kilt of a Scottish regiment over his brawny legs. He was holding the corner of the blanket Duncan had cast away over the naked flame of the candle. The other prisoners lay on their pallets at the far end of the cell, most of them snoring.

The soldier glanced at him. "I do me best work at night," he said, as if to explain himself.

Duncan's throat felt dry as a bone. "How—how do you know it's night?" he asked as he rose to approach the man. The scent of singed wool hung about him.

"The wee ones tell us," the big man answered good-naturedly, with a vague gesture toward the cell's entry. "Y'er going to get cold, lad," he declared, and stooped over his task. He was slowly passing the fabric of the blanket over the flame. Duncan heard tiny popping sounds as the lice were burnt away.

"*Tapadh leat*," Duncan said, thanking the man in Gaelic.

The prisoner looked up with a grin. "*Se do bheatha*," he replied. "I love to hear the little buggers pop."

Through his pain and despair, Duncan recognized the man's accent. "My grandfather would say those of the outer isles had salt and peat in their voice. Never in my wildest imagination would I have thought to meet a man from Stornaway."

The man's face brightened. "Be that an echo of the western coast on yer own tongue?"

"My clan is McCallum, of the western coast and the Hebrides. My grandfather and I used to fish the waters of the Minch off Lewis when the weather was fair," Duncan replied, referring to the western isle for which Stornaway was the main port.

"Macaulay," the man offered. "Corporal William Macaulay of the 78th. Fraser's Highlanders." He finished at a corner of the blanket, then rose to hand it to Duncan. "Free of the wee beasties for a day or two."

"Long enough then," Duncan replied, trying to keep his voice level.

Macaulay hesitated, then noticed the twine around Duncan's upper arm. "By the blessed saints," he muttered. "I'm sorry, lad."

Duncan followed his gaze. "I didn't ask what it meant."

"T'is the mark of the king's rope, son. Surely the provosts mentioned the gallows."

"It was a colonel named Cameron who did most of the talking. There is supposed to be a trial."

Macaulay cocked his head. "But the army don't hang civilians. Ye need a magistrate for that."

"I've done tasks now and again for Woolford's rangers. It was enough for them."

The big Scot sighed and shook his head heavily. "So what was it? Spilled your ale on our priggish colonel's boots?"

Duncan met Macaulay's level gaze. "They claim I killed a corporal of the 42nd."

The soldier's eyes narrowed.

"I found him in a pool of blood. I was hoping to help him, but he was already gone. It was just my bad fortune that a patrol happened by."

"What corporal?" The warmth had gone out the big Scot's voice.

"His name was MacLeod."

Macaulay muttered a curse. "Jock MacLeod of the 42nd? The barefisted champion of the regiment? Not likely." He shrugged. "He'd never be taken by a child like ye. No offense lad."

"None taken. It's welcome to find at least one man in Albany who believes me."

"And my testimony will count like Bibles before the bastards who will judge ye."

Duncan fingered the piece of twine. The vow to hang him the next day had seemed so remote, just another of his terrible dreams. But the twine made it real. The pain of his beating, the desolate cavern prison, the promised noose. He had come to Albany in search of the truth and a boy he had never met. But he had really come to die. His father had been summoning him to the gibbet, to join the rest of the clan. This was the ending of his short and tormented days. He had to find a way to write a letter to Sarah Ramsey, to let her know she should wait no more.

Macaulay, seeming to sense his strange paralysis, took the blanket out of Duncan's hands and draped it over his back. Then he settled onto the floor on the opposite side of the candle, holding his open hands toward the flame as if it were some comforting hearth.

"Jock was a Lewis man too. He loved the war," Macaulay said in a soft voice. "He was fond of reminding me that the men of Lewis were descended from Vikings, that we were meant to die in battle, with a weapon in our hands."

"He had a sword in his hand when I found him. His fists were bloody."

"Amen," Macaulay said with a satisfied nod. "Tell me about it lad. Tell me all."

Duncan began with the morning of the terrible day of death, speaking of his discovery of the dead dispatch rider in the water.

The big Scot spat a curse when he heard it was another trooper wearing the plaid. "A sad waste of life. Always the Highlanders, eh?"

"I'm sorry?"

"'Tis always the Highlanders who pay the butcher's bill in this army." He shook his head and stared into the flame for a moment. "But what of Jock? Where was this settlement he fell in?"

Duncan continued his story, telling how an entire village was slain, even how he had come searching for the Nipmuc orphan who had gone to the river witch.

"Hetty the Welsh sorceress," Macaulay said. "When I was young ye wouldn't go near such a fearful hag without clutching a piece of iron in your hand." Superstitions ran deep in the Hebrides.

Both men remained silent, staring into the solitary flame. A moth appeared and circled over the candle.

"The Highland troops," Duncan asked at last. "They are all supposed to be in the North."

"One company from each regiment was held back for the western campaign up the great lake to the Saint Lawrence to steady the fresh troops coming up the Hudson, called up from the Indies. Orders are expected to go west with Cameron to Oswego any day."

Duncan gestured to the other prisoners, several of whom wore kilts. "Some of them sit in the iron hole."

Macaulay spat a curse. "Some don't lick the boots of English officers quick enough."

Duncan tried to clear his mind, to consider what had transpired in the general's office. "A soldier works hard for his shillings," he observed. He had not forgotten the general's despairing gaze upon the dead man's pay chit, nor how he had angrily flung it into the fire despite it being presented as evidence against Duncan.

"Not in this man's army," Macaulay rejoined. "Nigh a year without pay." His face darkened. "We didn't come all this way to be English slaves."

Duncan shivered again and glanced about the cold, dark chamber. "This place is a chamber of torture. How do you stand it?"

"I was raised in a black house, lad," the soldier said, referring to the houses of unmortared black stone common in Scotland's western isles, known for their cold and damp.

"How long have you been in here?"

"Just yesterday. But I've been a guest before."

"For insubordination?"

"This time for taking a sick friend's place on sentry duty without asking permission. Then not groveling when an English officer expressed his disapproval." Macaulay shrugged, then stood, stretching. "Get some sleep. Ye'll need your wits about ye tomorrow. Tell them ye want a rasher of bacon and a piece of apple pie from the officer's mess."

"I'm sorry?"

"They'll come a couple hours before yer trial. They'll clean ye up, make ye presentable for the English prigs who will condemn ye. They always give a man his request for a meal before . . ." Macaulay hesitated. "Before such things," he finished awkwardly, then moved away.

Before his hanging. The prisoner was given his choice for his last meal on earth.

Duncan sat against the wall again, huddled in his blanket, futilely trying not to stare at the twine around his sleeve. He was strangely scared to touch it. He desperately tried, but failed, to summon visions of his youth or memories of his days learning of the forest from Conawago. All that came were visions of the many McCallum clansmen who had swung from the king's gibbet.

Death was a beast that had to eat its fill, his grandmother used to say of the epidemics that sometimes swept the Highland towns. The deaths at Bethel Church were no mystery for him to resolve, they were just another sign that death was calling him.

He woke to a hand gripping his shoulder. Macaulay hovered over him, holding a wooden bowl of porridge under his nose. "Better when it's warm, lad," the big Scot offered.

The other prisoners sat on their pallets, scooping porridge from bowls with their fingers. Duncan dipped a finger into the lukewarm gruel and hesitantly touched it to his lips before ravenously scooping it into his mouth.

"I thought I was to have mounds of bacon and pie," he said when he had finished.

"Don't tempt the fates, lad. They do their trials and hangings in the morning. If they ain't come for ye by now then ye have another day. But they'll ne'er forget a prisoner with the twine on his arm. There's no . . ." Macaulay's words faded as a man with a bloody face was shoved into the cell, followed an instant later by two more prisoners. Macaulay sighed. "There be the reason. The hounds have been busy chewing up others this morn."

The three men all fell to the floor of the cavern, holding wounds that oozed blood. They all wore the kilts of the Highland regiments. The forearm of the youngest hung at an unnatural angle. He clutched it in obvious pain.

Duncan shot up and went to the young soldier's side. When he reached for the arm the man pulled it away. "It's broken," Duncan said.

"Goddamned right it's broken," one of the other newcomers spat. "Didn't it sound like a snapped spoke when that provost bastard pounded it with his halberd!"

"I attended medical college in Edinburgh," Duncan explained.

"You're a doctor?" the young asked with a grimace.

"Close enough. They arrested me for aiding my old Jacobite uncle before I got the robe." He nodded at the arm. "If you don't let me splint it, it will never heal straight."

He became aware of Macaulay at his side. "He's one of us, lads," the corporal explained, and he gestured to the twine on Duncan's arms. The anger left the eyes of the new prisoners. The young Highlander gritted his teeth but did not resist when Duncan touched his arm again. Duncan frowned, then looked around the dim chamber. As the others silently watched, he stepped to the empty porridge bucket and slammed it against the wall, extracting two of the grooved, slightly bowed slats from its loosened hoops. Macaulay, quickly understanding, pulled out his shirttail and began tearing away a strip. Duncan nodded, then gestured to his patient's shoulder. The corporal planted himself behind the man and gripped his upper arm tightly as Duncan lifted the broken forearm. "What was the name your mother gave you?" he asked the man.

The young soldier looked up in confusion. "Colin," he murmured.

"I can't hear you, trooper," Duncan taunted loudly.

Anger swirled on the man's face for a moment then he shouted, "Colin Mc—" The words died away with a wince as with a quick pulling motion Duncan snapped the bones back into place.

The onlookers laughed. His patient looked at him sheepishly and nodded his thanks as Duncan placed the makeshift splints on the arm and began wrapping it tightly with Macaulay's strip of linen.

The two other new arrivals quickly warmed to Duncan, letting him look at their bloody cuts and bruises, none of which were severe.

"Damn the provosts and damn the officers who unleash them," growled Macaulay. "What happened, lads?" he asked.

"On the parade ground, standing in ranks," explained the oldest of the newcomers. "Colin called out to ask where our pay was. The major didn't take to men speaking without permission. He demanded that the man who spoke step forward. He was even less pleased when all three of us stepped out of the ranks." The man paused to push at a bloody tooth, which was obviously loose. "He said the paymaster waited for the others in the North but that we three would learn a hard lesson for our rudeness."

"That ain't why we're here," Colin interjected. "We would have just gone to the brig in the fort for a few days, but we were being held by the stables when the major met Colonel Cameron around the corner from us. They didn't know we were listening until the provost shouted a warning to the colonel. But it was too late. We heard the report, that the king's payroll never made it to the northern troops, that the paywagon was empty when it arrived. As the Colonel walked away, the major shouted that it was impossible, that no one could steal from such a wagon, that the report had to be a mistake. When he realized we had heard, he was furious, and he ordered the provosts to send us to the iron hole. We put up a wee protest," Colin said, nodding to his arm. "We'll be down here until they find that chest of coins."

Duncan considered the words. "What kind of wagon would it have been?"

"Purpose built. One-of-a-kind. I've been a guard on it more than once on runs to Ticonderoga and Crown Point. Like a heavy coach, but it has a special box bound with iron, built into the inside where the seats would be. Like a rolling safebox."

"Jock MacLeod was one of the escorts?"

"Colin!" Macaulay barked in warning.

"They have shit for honor!" the young soldier shot back. "You think I care about their damned secrets?" He nodded to Duncan. "Jock was with it."

"Ye don't know that, son," Macaulay interjected. "The escorts don't know their assignment until they report to duty."

"But I was on sentry duty at the gate when the wagon pulled out. Jock waved at me, from the top of the wagon."

"He died at Bethel Church," Duncan said, "when the wagon passed through."

Macaulay frowned. "Then the poor lad must have seen sign of those raiders and stayed behind to make sure the wagon was safe. He was always bigger than life, our Jock, probably thought he could take them single-handed. He died a hero to be sure."

Duncan looked at him in confusion. It made no sense. A missing escort would have been noted, would have been reported at the next fort. But the wagon had gone all the way to its destination with neither the missing guard nor the missing payroll noticed.

A man in a torn and soiled red jacket muttered a curse. "The world's a bubble for sure, and the life of a man less than a span."

The English infantryman who had spoken extended his arm, which was swollen with boils. The other prisoners soon followed, seeking Duncan's medical advice. He reached for his pouch and did what he could, applying the healing powder Conawago mixed from forest herbs, washing dirty wounds and applying more makeshift bandages.

As he worked something nagged at him, plucking at the back of his mind until suddenly he shot up and returned to the infantryman with the boils. "Why did you say that?" he asked the soldier. "Why speak the words of Francis Bacon just then?"

The soldier shrugged. "Never met any Francis Bacon. Just on my mind I guess. That boy recited things in the dark as he sat by the entry, is all. He said some over and over, like a chant. That was one."

Duncan knelt by the man and gripped his shoulder. "A boy?"

"The savage choir boy we called him." The grin on the man's face faded as he saw Duncan's stern, intense expression. "Just a lad of eleven or twelve. Acted like one of those ghostwalkers, clutching his hands in Christian prayer one minute, drawing pagan images in the dirt the next. He looked like he had painted his face, but most of the color had rubbed away. He had been weeping. Wouldn't let us comfort him. Took to watching the clock birds. Sat in the entry singing his forlorn songs, staring into the shadows of the tunnel like he expected some beast to rise up out of the earth below."

"Surely a mere boy would not be sent into this pit."

The trooper with the broken arm looked up. "I reckon it was the lad who interrupted the assembly yesterday, slipped right through the front gate and when the officer on duty wouldn't hear his story he ran out on the parade ground, dodging those who chased him, shouting out that there were French Indians in the woods, like the attack everyone fears had started. Troops were sent running to the palisades. Some fool in town began ringing an alarm bell. Colonel Cameron came out and put an end to it right quick. The provosts dragged the boy away, though I figured it would be for a caning in the stable."

A dozen questions leapt into his mind, but Duncan knew he could not risk betraying too much interest in Ishmael. "Clock birds?"

"The mice with wings." The soldier with the boils gestured again toward the far end of the cavern where the waste buckets sat. "They go out and we know it's dusk. They come back and we know it's dawn."

Duncan glanced around the cave once more, trying to make sense of the words. "But he was released?"

"Released of his earthly bounds, more like it. He finally ran deeper down the tunnel, toward the oblivion. Lunacy. Naught but blackness and death down there."

A new weight bore down on Duncan. The one glimmer of hope he had nourished was that the boy yet lived, running free in the forest.

"There's smallpox below," the prisoner added. "The guards stopped going inside, just leave their gruel in the tunnel." The man shrugged. "The pox takes what? Three, maybe five days to kill ye? Could be he's still alive. But he has damned little time left, and a wretched time it will be. The monster below has swallowed him, and that's the end of it."

Duncan suddenly felt weak again. He stumbled back toward his blanket. He sat in a silent, numb state, sometimes on the verge of sleep, mostly just staring into the shadows. At last he rose and stepped toward the deeper shadows near the slop buckets and found the little mounds of fur tucked along the cracks in the stone. Below them he saw the drawings in the dirt of the floor: stick figures of men were falling over two lines drawn at a right angle, with stick-figure bodies below, as if it were men falling off a cliff. The image had been at the center of the wampum belt Duncan had seen at the witch's hut. He pulled out the paper he had taken from the schoolhouse wall and found the one that bore the boy's name, with the quote from Bacon. He began to piece together the description of the boy he had heard from Madame Pritchard and felt a tiny flicker of hope.

He sat inside the entry, waiting for the flying shadows. Finally they began flapping. The bats cast a spell over the prisoners, the men watching them with something like envy. Duncan studied them as they swooped out of the low arch. Most went right, up the tunnel, but several went left. He grinned. He understood the boy's lunacy.

The evening meal came, a watery oxtail broth with bread that was as hard as naval biscuit. Duncan checked the condition of his patients and listened as the other prisoners complained of the provosts, the army, the French, and the bloodthirsty Hurons who were allied with the enemy. The army seemed to be in worse shape than Duncan would have thought, with regiments depleted and morale low despite the recent string of English victories. Several of the men had been in the Americas for years. Some had suffered the fevers of the Indies, one had survived the terrible massacre in which General Braddock and much of his army had been destroyed near Fort Duquesne. Most had been in the horrible bloodbath of the first battle at Ticonderoga in which the Black Watch had lost two thirds of their men.

Duncan retired to his blanket and tried to sleep but spent much of his time drawing a map in his mind of the region around Albany and the Iroquois towns beyond. He found his gaze drifting toward the arch that led to the tunnel. His life hung by a thread. When the bats returned, the provosts would come for him soon after. A handful of officers would be rising, their orderlies adorning them with stiff collars and lace cuffs for the solemn words that would mean his death.

He waited until every man was sleeping, then rose and stepped into the forbidden corridor. There was no sound, no movement from the guard station at the top of the tunnel. He turned and slipped into the gloom below.

The tunnel narrowed and turned as it descended, the slow-burning pitch torches spread far apart now so that he could barely see where he placed his feet. He had grown to tolerate the fetid odor of the first cell, but that in no way prepared him for the reek that reached him. It was the smell of decay, of suffering, of death. For a moment he gazed back up the tunnel. Nothing but the king's noose waited in that direction. He turned toward the death he did not know.

Dante's hell needed nine levels to capture all the aspects of human suffering. The iron hole of the English only needed two. The chamber he stepped into echoed not with the sounds of slumber but of misery. Five men lay on filthy straw. Two were moaning and clutching their bellies. A man with a filthy bandage over his shoulder stared at the floor and murmured the same short prayer, over and over. A man who looked more like a skeleton than a living creature stared with vacant eyes at one of the cell's two candles.

With a sinking heart Duncan saw there was no one else in the cell, no boy, no refugee from the massacre of Bethel Church.

He retreated a step, reflexively wanting to be away from the squalor and suffering, then looked again, more slowly, at the prisoners. For a moment he sensed Conawago at his side, so intensely that he thought he smelled the sweetfern sprigs the Nipmuc kept in his pockets, and he saw in his mind's eye the opened, extended hand that always meant he expected something of Duncan. He clenched his jaw then knelt by the first of the prostrate figures. The man was ghostly pale and hot to the touch despite the chill of the air. Duncan saw a rag hanging on a bucket of water and made a compress for his forehead. The next man was much the same but did not even respond to his touch. Duncan gazed in horror at the black splotches on the face of the third. The fourth man, a soldier with long blond locks not much older than Duncan, gazed at the candle but did not see. He had been dead for hours.

Duncan studied the pathetic souls of the cell. There was almost nothing he could do for them. He approached the man with the bandaged shoulder, whose gaze was now fixed on the shadows at the back of the cell. The prisoner winced when Duncan pulled at the bandage but did not stop him from unwinding it. The long piece of linen had been applied by an experienced hand, probably by a regimental surgeon, but it should have been replaced long before. Duncan threw the foul cloth into the shadows and examined the long ragged wound. It was dirty but not festering. He retrieved the bucket with its wooden ladle and sluiced water over it.

"Huron tomahawk," the prisoner declared in a hoarse voice. "I killed the bastard. Now he kills me."

"The flesh is not mortified," Duncan replied. "You just need to keep it clean."

The man glanced at the prisoners on the straw and cast a bitter grin at Duncan, seeming to indicate that Duncan was only saving him for a worse fate. Duncan began ripping a strip from his shirttail. When he had the bandage ready, he took a cartridge-like container from a belt pouch and poured out its contents, a dark brown powder, over the wound. "A wise old healer makes this," he explained. "He speaks words over it which his people think give it great power."

"You mean a witch or an Indian?" The man asked, wincing as Duncan tightened the bandage over the wound.

"They say the people of the forest hold secrets that go back to the beginning of the earth."

"And they send their lads deep into the earth to dig more secrets out," the man said. He gazed again into the deepest shadows.

With a rush of hope Duncan called out toward the darkness. "Ishmael?"

There was no response. "*Shay kon*," he said, trying the greeting of the Mohawks, then added, "Ojiwa of the Nipmucs? I come from your uncle."

The movement was barely noticeable at first, a shadow moving across darker shadow.

Duncan straightened and repeated the Iroquois greeting, in a near whisper. When Ishmael stepped forward, he wanted to embrace the boy but instead stood still very still, as he might before a wild creature of the forest.

"They would never put children in here, so I was sure he had to be a ghost when I first saw him," the wounded soldier said. "Suddenly he was just standing there, all pale and silent, staring at us like he had come to escort one of us across to the other side."

Although the boy wore a shirt, it was unbuttoned. Duncan could see the traces of whitewash on his skin. But this was not the angry world breaker who had left the Pritchard farm, this was just another forlorn prisoner.

The boy studied Duncan warily, keeping himself slightly bent, as if ready to leap away at any second.

"I am the particular friend of Conawago, elder of the Nipmuc tribe," Duncan declared, and he reached into his waistcoat pocket. "Kinsman of Hickory John."

"Towantha," the boy replied, using his grandfather's tribal name.

"Towantha," Duncan repeated, and he pulled out the wooden medallion he had found in front of the dead Nipmuc.

The boy's eyes went wide. He took one step forward, then another.

"A twine?" the soldier interrupted, pointing at Duncan's sleeve. "You've been marked with a damned twine? You're bound for the gallows?"

Duncan just nodded, not taking his gaze off the boy. "I've been looking for you, Ishmael," he said.

The youth darted forward and grabbed the medallion, clutching it against his heart. After a moment he looked up and studied Duncan with uncertain but intelligent eyes. "They would hang you for looking for me?" His English was slow but fluent, his voice heavy with fear.

"They would hang me for a killing at Bethel Church."

"But you were not one of the killers. I did not see all their faces, but none had yellow hair." The boy draped the medallion around his neck.

"We arrived not long after, seeking you and your grandfather. A patrol found me and Conawago with the bodies."

"Conawago." The youth mouthed the name in a reverent tone. "My grandfather spoke the name in the way he spoke of the old gods. He was waiting, praying Conawago would come. One last letter, he said."

"I thought he sent letters every year."

Ishmael turned to look into the flame. "He was making plans to leave. He didn't want me to know, but my friend Lizzie heard him speaking with her father about taking me into their home. They were cleaning out a storage room for me to sleep in. I could see the pain in his eyes. He was trying to find a way to tell me. Instead he would just recite old tales of Nipmucs who were called away to help the spirits when there was trouble on the other side."

"Away to where?"

"One night I found him gone from his bed. He was in his shop. He had made a ring of fire, and in the center of the ring was an old knife with a flint blade. I thought he was going to complain that I should be in bed, but he just gestured for me to sit beside him. He was disturbed, and solemn. More than solemn. It was like he was stretched very thin, like something of him was somewhere else. He spoke to the spirits with old words, and then he was silent for a long time, his eyes not seeing, like his own spirit had gone away." Ishmael glanced up at Duncan, confirming he still listened. That he still believed.

Duncan nodded. He had seen Conawago go away in such a fashion at fragrant fires on moonlit mountaintops.

"When he came back he shook me and said terrible things were happening on the other side, that if someone didn't go and fix them it would mean the end of all things."

Duncan stared into the candle, silently cursing a world that had to burden a young boy with such thoughts.

"The end of all things," the boy repeated. "The next day I asked him what he meant, thinking I hadn't heard right. He wouldn't tell me, but he didn't deny saying the words."

"Ishmael, why did you seek out the schoolmaster's mother?" Duncan asked.

He had pushed too far. The boy's face took on a stony expression and he glanced toward the shadows from which he had come.

"I could have gone north, disappeared into the woods," Duncan tried. "But there is a bond between my clan and Conawago's clan. Your clan."

"You are not of the forest."

"I am of the mountain and sea, from the land called Scotland. The English killed my clan." He looked back to the other prisoners on the pallets, toward the disease and death. They were all asleep, or unconscious. He had done all he could for them. "We will need some kind of light," he whispered to the Nipmuc boy.

Ishmael stared at him for several breaths then with a quick nod gestured Duncan toward the deeper shadows. Duncan freed the nearest candle from the wax droppings that sealed it to its rock and followed.

The boy had lowered himself onto a blanket. In his hand was a snakelike piece of wax. As Duncan held his candle closer, he saw that Ishmael had braided together several heavy threads from the blanket and had been pressing wax around the braids, using it as a wick, rubbing the wax in his hands to make it pliable. Duncan lowered the candle and with gestures showed the boy how to hold his makeshift light so he could drip more wax onto it, sealing the wick then dipping the threads into the wax pooled at the top.

Duncan fought a terrible foreboding about what they were about to do. "These passages have many forks," he said, struggling to keep his voice calm. "How will we choose the route?"

The Nipmuc boy extended a makeshift pouch made from a cloth torn from the blanket. He nudged it, and shapes inside it began to stir. Duncan's grin was hollow. The hope was as thin as a thread, but it was the only one they had.

They worked for another hour on the little candle, then Duncan warned they could not risk waiting much longer. Their guides would only serve at night, and judging by the flight of the other bats, it was already hours after sunset. As he returned the bigger candle to its base, a big hand appeared on his shoulder.

"Macaulay!" Duncan gasped as he turned toward the man. "You fool!"

"I'm in this with ye, McCallum."

Duncan made a frustrated gesture toward the pallets. "It's smallpox! You've come to the smallpox!"

"As ye and the boy did."

Duncan pulled Ishmael closer to the light. "Look at his face." He had not forgotten the words of Madame Pritchard. The boy had had the pox and carried the marks on his cheeks. "He won't get it again. And I took the inoculation in Edinburgh." Duncan's professors had insisted all the medical students receive the controversial treatment, both to experience the mild course of the disease it caused and to protect the population of the college.

Macaulay eyed the men on the pallets uneasily, then shrugged. "And didn't I serve a year in the Indies and never once sick? I'm as healthy as a horse. I am fated to die charging at the enemy with a sword in me hand."

"Healthy as a horse and as big as one," Duncan added. "You might not be able to follow where we are going."

Macaulay saw now how the boy lingered impatiently at the entry, the makeshift candle now lit in his hand, and seemed to finally comprehend. "There be only death waiting farther inside this mountain, McCallum."

"Not if we follow our guides," Duncan replied and was about to join the boy when one of the prisoners moaned. He was kneeling at the last pallet, shaking the blond-haired man.

"He's gone," Duncan said as he pulled the soldier away and led him back to his pallet. He turned and watched in confusion as Macaulay unfastened the twine around his arm. The big Scot murmured a prayer over the corpse then tied the twine around the dead man's arm. "Your age, same color hair," Macaulay pointed out. "They'll take time to work up the courage to look down here for you. Then when they do, this will confuse them all the more."

Duncan slowly nodded then mouthed his own silent prayer for the dead man and turned to Ishmael.

Moments later they were hurrying down the tunnel, past the last trace of light from the torches above, not stopping until they reached the first intersection of two passages.

Macaulay cursed. "Surely this is folly. We have no idea—"

"Most of the bats fly up the tunnel," Duncan interrupted. "But not all of them."

The boy reached into his makeshift pouch and pulled out one of his captive creatures. He held the bat gently near his lips, whispering to it, then released it. The bat flew back and forth as if to get its bearings then shot down the left-hand tunnel. Ishmael followed so quickly that he was nearly out of sight before Duncan and Macaulay sprang after him.

The boy set a fast pace and muttered a syllable of glee when the tunnel began to ascend. No one gave voice to the fears Duncan knew they all shared. Their little candle would last no more than an hour.

They reached another fork, and another, each time releasing one of Ishmael's bats and following its chosen path. Several times they had to bend to their knees to crawl, the boy surrendering the candle to Duncan, who managed an awkward gait while holding the rapidly diminishing light. Macaulay began murmuring a prayer.

Suddenly they arrived in a cavern that had been heavily worked with pick and chisel, opening into three more tunnels. "One more," the boy declared uneasily as he produced the last bat, spoke to it in his native tongue, and released it. It circled about then shot straight upward. As Duncan extended the candle over his head, the flame bent.

"Wind!" Ishmael exclaimed.

"God be praised!" Macaulay exclaimed, then he quickly quieted as the flame revealed that the ceiling was several feet over their heads. As they stared hopelessly upward, the candle sputtered out, leaving them in a cold empty blackness.

A long dreadful moment passed before anyone spoke.

"Jesus wept!" groaned Macaulay. "We'll never find our way back. T'is our grave for certain."

Duncan reached out in the darkness, searching for Ishmael, but touching only the cold rock wall. "It's still night. The returning bats will tell us when the sun approaches. Then we just find a way to follow the daylight coming through their hole." He shifted a few feet and reached out again, finding the boy's shoulder, which he gripped firmly. "A few hours, no more."

A nervous prayer left Macaulay's lips.

"Ishmael?" Duncan said. When no response came, he repeated the boy's name and shook his shoulder.

The boy's response came out like a moan. "The blackness," he said, and nothing more.

"We're going to sit here and be blind men for a few hours," Duncan explained, working hard to keep his own fear out of his voice. "A small price for our freedom." But as soon as he stopped speaking, the fear rose up, gripping his belly. He pulled the boy closer, and they settled onto the floor of the cave, backs against the wall.

"It was a fearless thing you did, Ishmael," Duncan said, trying to keep the boy from thinking of the darkness, "to visit the witch who frightened grown men."

"Mr. Bedford had a rhyme on his wall. 'For the little bent squaw laughter he makes. Until she begins to throw off her snakes.' I asked him about it, said it was different from all the others. He said it was a reminder for us to keep people surprised, so we won't be taken for granted. He said his mother used to carry snakes in her pockets and would throw them at people who irritated her. I thought it was some kind of joke. But when I saw that hut I knew it was no joke. Snakes are servants of the gods, and someone who throws them would be . . ." he paused, searching for a word.

"A witch, to some," Duncan offered.

"If there is such a thing as a witch," Ishmael said, "then wouldn't she be a servant of the gods too?"

The question hung in the black silence. He sensed motion nearby and knew Macaulay was crossing himself.

He had no notion of how much time had passed before he heard the murmur. Macaulay was singing, his words barely audible at first, but soon the tune grew louder. "Who will take the cow to grass?" the Scot sang. "And who will fill the kettle?"

"It's a ballad from Scotland," Duncan explained to the boy, "about a fisherman lost in a storm." Soon he joined in the familiar song, keeping his arm linked through the boy's as he sang.

They sang one ballad after another, sang for what seemed hours, until their voices were only hoarse, fading whispers.

The vestiges of Duncan's remaining strength seemed to be sucked out by the cold rock at his back. Although he could not remember ever feeling so weary, sleep would not come. Images as black as the cave swirled about him. Conawago was being tortured, singing his death song. The dead of Bethel Church stood around him, pointing accusing fingers. A noose was being tightened around his neck by a mocking Colonel Cameron. He became aware of Ishmael squeezing his arm. The boy made a low clucking sound with his tongue, the kind of sound woodland hunters made to acknowledge each other's presence. Duncan realized that he had been moaning and, like Conawago, the boy was trying to stir him from his nightmares.

The silence seemed to endure forever, a palpable thing that ebbed and flowed, interrupted by the occasional rustling of clothing. It bore down on

Duncan like a dark ocean, nearly drowning him, sometimes making him struggle even to breathe. He knew his companions felt the same. He could tell by the big man's irregular breathing that Macaulay was not sleeping. A new, desperate murmuring came through the blackness. The big Scot was whispering the Hail Mary.

When the sounds of movement overhead finally came, they were like distant leaves rustling in the wind. Then came a tiny peeping, and another, starting above them before quickly fading down the tunnel. The winged mice were returning. Waiting for the light seemed almost unbearable now. Duncan found himself holding his breath for long moments. If the blackness did not abate, they would surely die.

At last came the barest hint of greyness above darker shadow. Minutes later he could distinguish nearby boulders, then the shape of Ishmael beside him. A small patch in the ceiling began to glow.

"God, no!" Macaulay cried as he leapt up, his arms extended in desperation. The hole, rapidly filling with light now, was at the end of a narrow slanting ten-foot long chimney that started several feet over their heads. Even if they could reach the hole it looked too small for the two grown men.

Macaulay cursed, again and again. Ishmael attempted to scramble up the rough slanting wall toward the chimney, again and again, but he fell back each time.

Duncan paced around the chamber, studying the walls and the chimney. "If I am not mistaken that is a *feileadh mor* you wear, Macaulay," he said at last. The army had begun to issue short field kilts, worn like skirts, but many of the Highland soldiers still wore the traditional long kilt, which was nothing but a swath of wool several yards long carefully folded and pinned around the body.

"Aye," Macaulay replied with an uncertain gaze, but he slowly grinned as Duncan explained his plan. The big Scot began to unwrap his plaid.

After several awkward efforts, Ishmael finally succeeded in climbing up the human ladder made by Duncan sitting on Macaulay's broad shoulders. The length of wool wrapped around the boy's waist made his passage up the chimney more difficult, but gradually he levered himself up, back against one side, feet pressed against the other.

"It's morning here!" the boy cried out as he climbed through the opening into the daylight.

Duncan grinned, then reminded Ishmael to tie one end of the cloth around a sturdy tree before tossing the other end back down the chimney. He let it slide past him, the end stopping at Macaulay's waist, then gripped it tightly and began climbing.

Ishmael was already prying stones from the edge of the opening when Duncan's hand reached out into the daylight. His shoulders would not fit through, but the stone at the surface was brittle shale, and as he pushed and Ishmael pulled they broke enough away for him to slide out.

He found himself gulping the fresh air, the drowning man pulled from the black sea, then he saw the cloth pull tight and he rolled to the side. With a string of Gaelic curses Macaulay began to climb. The big man, clad only in the long shirt worn under his kilt, had trouble finding purchase in the chimney. "Heave up ye slaggards!" he shouted. Duncan and the boy grinned at each other then began hauling up the brawny Scot. He had to wait, braced in the chimney, as they pried more stone from the hole, but soon he was out. Minutes later they knelt at a stream, sluicing water over their filthy arms and faces.

"Dear Lord!" Macaulay called up to the sky, "may ye strike me down if ever I think an unkind thought about a bat again!"

Ishmael laughed then laughed again as he watched Macaulay go through the ungainly process of lying on the ground to wrap his kilt around him. Duncan tied his hair back and began brushing the grime from his clothes. When he finished he pointed to an overhang of rocks half hidden behind alder bushes. "I will be back. We have to find Conawago," he said to the boy. "And we have to find the children. You can hide in there until I return. Get some sleep."

"Late for an appointment are ye?" Macaulay quipped.

"I won't put Albany behind me without my kit."

"Ye mean ye need yer gun."

"I mean I need what was handed down to me by my father and his father before him. I'll be back before noon," he promised Ishmael, then he eyed the big Scot uncertainly. "You're not bound to stay."

"The second I left that hole I broke with the army," Macaulay pointed out. He gestured toward the North. "A new life beckons."

Duncan lifted the boy's hand and gripped it tightly before leaving, but Ishmael only fixed Duncan with a reproachful gaze and clutched the medallion and protective amulet around his neck. The boy had been abandoned too many times in his short life.

Chapter Six

Woolford entered his room above the tavern in a great hurry, quickly closing the door and locking the latch as though he were worried about being followed. The ranger captain pressed his head against the door then splashed water on his face from the basin on the nightstand. As he reached for a towel he froze, at last spying Duncan's rifle on his bed.

"His majesty's army has misplaced a payroll," Duncan declared from the shadows.

Woolford forced a small smile of greeting. "There are those who would kill you just for knowing that. Personally I am inclined to praise God that you still live. Your pack is under the bed."

Duncan rose to retrieve his kit. "I kept wondering what might distract the general from hanging a hated murderer. But then I began counting all the Scots in the iron hole. They give the impression that their biggest crime was complaining about not being paid for months. They were promised hard coin last month, then again this month. A dangerous thing, not to pay the units that anchor your line of battle. It's what you meant when you said the army's victories are built on sand. The army itself is about to collapse."

"The last units of the Highlanders are heading north soon," Woolford replied in a worried voice. "General Amherst has promised them great glory in Canada. And their pay."

"But now all his coins are gone. What are you doing in Albany without your men?" he asked when Woolford did not reply.

With careful disinterest the ranger wiped his brow.

"Seven thousand five hundred thirty-two was the number the general's nephew recited. I thought it was supplies of some kind. Cartridges perhaps."

"I am sorry Duncan. For hitting you. If I hadn't the provosts would have used their halberds on you."

Duncan ignored him. "But it was pounds sterling. A veritable fortune. Enough to finance the war for months."

Woolford stepped to the smoldering fireplace and eyed Duncan in silence. "It would be irresponsible to speculate on such matters. Traitorous even."

"It's remarkable how easily speculation comes when your neck is to be stretched." Duncan knelt and pulled his pack from under the bed. "Especially when so many seem so hell-bent on hiding the truth. Maybe that is my real crime, being the only one outside the general's circle who knew enough to sense the disaster about to strike. Do you have a map?" he asked.

"Not here."

Duncan glanced at the table by the window, where a quill lay by a pewter inkpot. "Paper then." When Woolford gestured toward a drawer, Duncan extracted a sheet of paper, dipped the quill, and began drawing. "About ten miles below Bethel Church is a dock where bateaux call. Off this point of land," he explained as he kept drawing, "is this small island with an aerie, just a few trees and rocks. The eagle is still on the nest." He placed an X to the southeast of it.

"Get a swimmer. The bottom is about fifteen feet. Another soldier was killed there. Tied to a wheel and dumped into the water while still alive. Bring up the body. He was a dispatch rider. He confronted the thieves as they used that dock and paid for it with his life. Conawago and I saw a bateau going north above that dock. They shot at us. I think they were the ones who beat the rider and dropped him in the water."

Woolford's eyes narrowed. "One of the thoroughbreds reserved for dispatches showed up at the stables without her rider two days ago." It was Duncan's turn to stay silent. "It was you. You rode her here."

"The raiders at Bethel Church stole the payroll and escaped in that bateau."

The ranger captain slowly shook his head. "Impossible. If they had tried to open the strongbox there would have been evidence of it. It had not been tampered with. It was only that . . ." he frowned, then lowered his voice. "The keys to its two locks did not work. They had to chisel the box open, then found it empty. The provosts were heard to speak of magic being used."

"Is that the official explanation? Sorcery? The provosts don't deal well with subtlety."

"The money was loaded into that wagon in Albany. Thousands of coins. Shillings, crowns, guineas, though most of it Spanish dollars with the army's broad arrow mark stamped on them. The wagon was not disturbed en route. But there was not a coin left when it arrived in Quebec."

"Arrived without all its escort."

Woolford cocked his head at Duncan. "A Scot was missing. At the time he was treated as another deserter."

"Jock MacLeod. The escorts were participants in the theft, except for him. He confronted them in the barn at Bethel Church, and they killed him."

"Impossible. None of them knew anything about the treasure. They were assigned to the escort only an hour before its departure from Albany. And this morning Colonel Cameron ordered you brought back for interrogation. He is better with subtlety. They have indeed realized the man you are accused of killing was with the missing payroll. Right now you are more important to the Colonel and General Calder than any number of French raiders."

Duncan looped the straps of the pack around his shoulders and began to tighten them. "You're not normally so blind, Captain. Bring the body up out of the lake. There was a reason so many died at Bethel Church the day the pay wagon rolled through, a reason why a young Scot was drowned and another stabbed to death."

"We're at war. Our enemy is desperate but very clever."

"That's it? The citizens of Bethel Church slaughtered like animals, their children kidnapped because of the war? This wasn't the war, Patrick, this was something else, something that so unsettled Conawago he disappeared into the forest without even trying to account for his long lost nephew."

Duncan finally had Woolford's attention. "Conawago wouldn't run from—"

"Exactly. He wasn't running away. He was running *to* something, somewhere in the wilderness north and west of here. His kinsman Hickory John was tortured for a secret then killed. There was a message sent by Hickory John to summon Conawago. *This is how we first die,* he wrote. Conawago and Hickory John were guardians of ancient secrets. The others may have died because they witnessed the theft. But not Hickory John. He was tortured for one of those secrets."

Woolford lowered himself onto the bed, as if suddenly weak. "Not Conawago," he said in an anguished tone.

"I must find him," Duncan said, not certain how to read the alarm in Woolford's voice.

"The war hangs in the balance, Duncan. If the French have the treasure they will turn the tide. The generals will no longer be able to rely on the Highland troops. The French can buy every Canadian who can hold a rifle and arm every Indian north of the Saint Lawrence. This damnable war will go on another five years, and thousands more will die."

"I'm talking about Conawago and captured children. But you are more concerned about the king missing some coins."

"You are the one who suggests they are connected."

"The army can't have it both ways, Captain."

"Both ways?"

"It either has to treat me as a murderer or treat me like the one man who glimpses the truth about the killings and the theft."

"The court-martial will clear your name."

"Then you're a bigger fool than I thought."

"Come with me to the general."

"You can't be the dutiful soldier and still seek the truth." Duncan opened the window onto the rear porch roof.

"Damn you, McCallum. You don't understand."

Duncan handed the paper to Woolford. "Find the drowned man. Even the general would have to admit that I could not have left a body strapped to a heavy wheel a hundred yards offshore. And the Forseys know of a lawyer in New York town who represents a man named Eldridge who was convicted of killing a Dutchman in Albany a few years ago. Find a way to ask him about the murder." He lifted his rifle and moments later dropped from the roof onto the grass below.

As he stepped into the shadows of the trees behind the inn, a twig broke behind him.

"You would leave them to die then, all those Scots," Woolford said to his back.

Duncan looked to the ground, not turning around. "What goes on in that prison is on the conscience of the general."

"Not them. The dozens who will be executed because you have run away."

Duncan slowly turned.

"The Highland regiments are going to mutiny. Any day now. Colonel Cameron has nearly lost control of them. Dozens of provosts have been brought up from New York town. Orders have been sent by General Amherst, commander of all the British armies in America. At the first sign of rebellion the provosts are to disarm every Highlander. They are to line them up. Every tenth man will be taken to the wall and shot."

The color drained from Duncan's face. "Surely Amherst would never—"

"He can endure one more setback on the battlefield. But a mutiny will ruin him forever. No chance of the king's honors every general aches for."

"There's nothing I can do. You know I have to find Conawago and the missing children."

Woolford surveyed the empty yard then pushed Duncan deeper into the shadows. "I am ordered to secretly recover the payroll. By any means possible. Good men have already died for it. How many more will there be?"

"I can understand why you are an agent of the empire. Surely you can understand why I will not be."

The words struck a nerve. Woolford was a man who knew much more about the workings of the empire in America than Duncan. The ranger frowned. "I am an agent for the king's justice," he said, as if correcting Duncan. "I accept that what happened to those at Bethel Church is connected to the theft. Help me so I can help you. I will send one of my best men with you. There still may be time to keep the treasure from the French. Conawago must have understood. It is why he went north."

"No. He does not trouble himself with the affairs of distant kings. He raced north for something far more important to him, something to do with a breach in the spirit world."

As Woolford stared at him Duncan reminded himself that the ranger captain knew the tribes better than Duncan himself. When he finally spoke there was new worry in his voice. "You mean because of something he found at Bethel Church."

Duncan glanced back at the forest, aware that the provosts had patrols out. If he was taken again he would be chained to the prison wall with no chance of escape. "Because there was a desperate plea in a letter. Because the only other old Nipmuc was tortured and murdered. Because he found an old flint knife secretly kept by that dead man. Because he does not believe it is inevitable that the tribes must submit to the Europeans."

Duncan's words seemed to cause his friend more pain. "A flint knife?"

When Duncan nodded, Woolford sagged. "There are old legends of how flint knives were used by the gods to carve the first human out of sacred wood and cut openings from the next world to earth." The ranger gazed into the forest a moment before continuing, now in a despairing tone. "There's a native rising, Duncan. I've reported the signs to General Calder but he doesn't want to hear. Colonel Johnson, the superintendent of Indian Affairs, sends disturbing reports, which Calder shows only to me, and forbids me speaking of it with the other officers. His eminence General Amherst ridicules any officer who shows concern for the tribes, or about the tribes. An Iroquois is just another savage creature of the forest, the supreme commander told me last time I saw him, not worth the time of a true king's man."

Woolford looked nervously about. "There's a new cult among the western tribes, spreading like wildfire. Its leader says he has been given a sacred charge, that he is connected to the spirits on the other side and speaks for the old gods, that there is a terrible war beginning on the other side, in the spirit world, and only he knows how to stop it. At their camp-fires they shout for a war of extermination. Their leader makes overtures to the French while his warriors take vows to drive the settlers back to the sea. The beast he spawns will have an insatiable hunger for European flesh."

"What tribe?"

"That's the point. If their leader has his way, all the tribes. He is becoming like a god to them."

"An Iroquois?"

"Bands of Iroquois left for the West a generation ago, tribesmen who considered the federation to have grown too soft and weak. They call them-selves Mingoes. He is a Mingo, a self-proclaimed half-king, one who reigns over the lesser tribes. In English he calls himself the Revelator."

He had never seen Woolford look so despondent. "It could change the war, change the balance of power in the colonies," the ranger said.

Duncan looked back toward the river, where he had first heard the name of the Revelator, and took a step away.

Woolford reached to his belt and extended his black leather ranger's cap to Duncan. "Wear this. It will make you less conspicuous to soldiers." Duncan settled it over his crown, gave a mock salute to the officer, and slipped into the shadows.

Skirting the main streets, staying in the shadows, he followed the sound of the hammers and saws in the boatyard. The Welsh woman haunted him. He had unfinished business with her. He moved from tree to tree as he approached the river, not knowing if the workers would have heard of his arrest. He pushed the cap squarely on his head, stepped to the last tree before the open bank of the river, and froze.

Half the workers stood in a line as though at the edge of an invisible circle, staring at smoke and burning timbers. The cabin was gone. As he watched, the last of its walls collapsed into the fire, sending a shower of sparks and embers into the air. The men watched it somberly, some fearfully. No one made any effort to extinguish the blaze.

Duncan dropped his pack, leaned his gun against the tree, and approached the burning ruins. He paused when he reached it, studying the onlookers. Most kept gazing uneasily at the fire, as if expecting something to rise up out of it. One man repeatedly made the sign of the cross on his chest. Duncan paced around the ruins, looking for any sign of Hetty Eldridge. There was no hope she had survived. The old dry wood would have burned like an inferno.

Duncan knelt and picked up a rattlesnake skin that had escaped the flames.

"It started from the roof." The deep voice came from over his shoulder. He turned to see the bearded foreman.

"The roof?" Duncan asked absently. With a strange impulse he wrapped the long skin around his fingers and thrust it into his belt.

"A dozen of my men ran to their families this morning when the arrows started falling," the foreman explained. "The garrison went on alert. There have been rumors of the French mounting an attack on Albany these past months."

Duncan's head snapped up. "You're saying Hurons did this?"

The bearded man shrugged. "French Indians, sure. Like ghosts. They could have as easily fired the whole town but they chose the witch's hut, as if she scared them more than our troops. Poor woman never even tried to escape. One of my men said he heard hideous laughing as the flames leapt up. The walls may as well have been soaked in lamp oil, the way they burst into fire."

The heat of the old wood would have been like a furnace, searing Hetty's flesh from her bones. Duncan picked up a long stick and poked the embers at the edge of the fire. There were shards of rum bottles. He pushed further, raking out fragments of bone. With a sudden chill he saw the skull of a large dog, with a shriveled skeletal hand reaching out of its jaw.

"God's breath!" the foreman exclaimed. He grabbed the stick and shoved the skull deeper into the ashes. "If my men see that they won't be back for a month."

Duncan turned to the man in confusion.

"Yesterday at sundown the beast went inside her hut after watching it all these days. The woman began chanting, loud enough for us to hear. Words of the savages. Some of my men said she was taking control of the animal. Some said she was entering the body of the beast. Might be we could have stopped the flames at the outset, but my men . . ." the foreman shrugged. "No one wanted to."

A sudden wind kicked up the pieces of charred snakeskin around the edge of the hut, stirring them into the air. They swirled over the ruins, several lighting on fire then rising up into the sky.

"Snakes are the messengers to the spirit world," Duncan heard himself say. "Go-betweens, between us and the other side."

The foreman took a step back, his worried expression now fixed on Duncan. He glanced at his men, half of whom had fled, then shook his head. "I'll never get them back to work until I push these damned ruins into the river."

THERE WAS NO sign of Macaulay at the stream where Duncan had last seen him. Ishmael waited by the overhanging ledge holding a crude spear fashioned from a hickory pole and a sharp stone.

"The woman Hetty," Duncan announced. "The mother of your schoolmaster. She's dead, Ishmael."

The boy cocked his head and seemed about to ask a question but remained silent, touching the amulet that hung from his neck and turning his gaze to the northwest.

"Where is it?" Duncan asked. "Did she tell you where the raiders were going?"

When the boy looked back there was worry in his eyes. "She would not speak but I saw that message belt. The old ones are ending all ties with this world, it said. There were symbols of lightning I did not understand." He shook his head in despair. "Once the Nipmucs would have known how to stop such things." He turned away as if he did not want Duncan to see his face, and he spoke into the wind. "But there are only two Nipmucs left in all the world." When he turned to Duncan there was a new determination in his eyes. "The witch knew more. If she is dead, then there's a place where witches are made," Ishmael declared matter-of-factly. "If they are made then surely they can be remade." He set off at a trot, spear in hand.

Minutes later they joined a game trail that led north, and as they crossed a ridge they began to glimpse a broad river in the distance below, the traditional path into the western wilderness. Ishmael pointed to it and set off with renewed energy. They had reached a fork in the trail at the bottom of the ridge when a burly man appeared from behind a tree.

"Macaulay!" Duncan exclaimed. "I thought you had second thoughts about leaving the regiment."

"Naught left for me there."

"It goes hard for deserters."

The big Scot grinned. "Way I figure it, the army deserted me. And it only goes hard for those foolish enough to be caught."

Duncan saw now the pack hanging from the man's shoulder. "You've been busy yourself."

Macaulay grinned. "Sometimes the quartermaster is careless with supplies." He lifted the pack to his shoulder. "If we be going west, I know where the army scouts leave their canoes."

TENONANATCHE HAD BEEN the great east–west thorough-fare of the Iroquois people long before Europeans had arrived and renamed it the Mohawk River. As they paddled upstream Ishmael offered the names of the decaying palisade towns they passed, abandoned in search of fresher soil for crops, and pointed out spirit sites on low overgrown mounds or huge trees that were said to harbor lesser gods of the forest. Duncan studied the boy with the strong face and penetrating eyes, realizing that Hickory John had shown him the sites just as Conawago had shown Duncan similar sites, and regretting the cruel turns of fate that had kept the last three Nipmucs from making such pilgrimages together.

The river was used by both the Iroquois and the soldiers who traveled between Albany and the western forts. Four times approaching canoes forced them to hide in overhanging alders. Once, six canoes loaded with scarlet-coated British infantry glided past going west. The others proved to be natives hurrying by as if on urgent business.

By late afternoon dark clouds began rolling toward them from the west. The storm moved quickly, flinging lightning into the steep hills. The wind rose, bending the grass along the banks, pushing the alders and willows, then with a sudden blast it jerked the bow of the canoe toward the bank.

Ishmael, clutching his spear, jumped off as they reached the shallows and pulled the canoe onto the muddy shore. There was no chance of maneuvering their light craft into such a wind, and the lightning was getting closer. Duncan called out for the boy to help haul the canoe higher up the bank, but suddenly Ishmael seemed to forget his companions. He stood staring into the woods.

Duncan leapt into the water, steadying the canoe for Macaulay as he climbed out. The sky was darkening rapidly, giving new brilliance to the violent flashes of lightning. Macaulay shouted at the boy to help carry their packs, but still Ishmael did not respond, and now Duncan saw that the boy was gazing down a tunnel of foliage, created by dense trees arching over a trail leading to a solitary bark lodge that appeared to have been abandoned many years before.

Macaulay gave a yelp as lightning struck across the river. Rain began slanting downward. He grabbed his pack and ran past them toward the lodge, Duncan at his heels.

They glanced at each other as they reached the sturdy structure, grinning at their luck at finding shelter, but Duncan paused. Ishmael still had not moved. The boy was already soaked by the heavy rain, and as a massive strike of lightning crashed behind him, Duncan darted back and pulled the boy to the lodge. He called the boy's name repeatedly when he got him under the cover of the old bark roof, but Ishmael just kept staring, now into the shadows at the back of the longhouse. The wind was blowing even harder, the temperature dropping steadily. The river was barely visible through the sheets of rain.

Duncan saw that Macaulay too was staring, though it was at Ishmael. In his hand the big Scot clutched the iron nail many soldiers kept to clean their weapons. In the Highlands iron had always been a charm against evil.

"He's soaked," Duncan said. "We need a fire."

Macaulay gave no sign of hearing until Duncan shook his arm and pointed to the pile of dry wood along one wall. "We're not going anywhere the rest of this day," he said. "You tend to the fire." He gestured to the water dripping through the old bark roof. "I'll make a dry place."

Longhouses had a framework of beams overhead, where smaller logs provided shelves for storage and from which blankets or skins were hung to divide the dwellings into family compartments. Duncan found several old skins lying on the ground and draped them over a section of overhead beams above Macaulay's sputtering flames.

Only when Duncan led Ishmael to the flames did the boy acknowledge his presence. "This is the place I sought," the youth said. "But I never would have found it. The storm brought us here."

Macaulay muttered a curse.

"It's just an old Iroquois lodge," Duncan assured him, but he recalled the boy's earlier description of their destination: the place where witches were made. The tribes had their own lore of supernatural creatures. Hetty Eldridge had come out of the wilderness under the guise of a treaty, but in fact the tribes had forced her out because they preferred the witch to work her spells in the European world.

"There's a tale of a magic trickster who travels in and out of the spirit world," Ishmael said. "Sometimes she traps travelers to make them her slaves on the other side."

"Traps them?" Duncan asked.

"Entices them with what they want. If you are hungry after a long day she will have pots of maize and strawberries waiting. If you need shelter a lodge appears."

Macaulay eyed the boy uneasily before quickly laying more wood on the fire.

"Surely not a decaying one with a leaky roof," Duncan pointed out, forcing a grin.

"A new one would make you suspicious," came Ishmael's sober reply. The boy's hand gripped the amulet that hung from his neck.

Duncan left his companions to stand at the entry, surveying the landscape. Iroquois lodges were built in bottomlands and were abandoned when the soil in their maize and squash fields was depleted. The lodge should have overgrown fields nearby, but there were none.

As the daylight faded Duncan went to search for more firewood, leaving Macaulay to coax heat into their little pot of corn mush and berries as Ishmael absently drew with a stick on the dirt floor. The rain had subsided to a soft drizzle.

He carried an armful of wood into the lodge and left again, slipping

into the thick growth at the edge of the clearing. Duncan kept telling himself that the uneasiness he felt was because of Ishmael's strange behavior,
nothing more, but he also remembered now a night on a mountaintop
with Conawago when the northern lights had been eerily dancing across
the sky. The old Nipmuc sage had spoken of places where the spirit world
intersected with this world, where beings from the other side might slip
across on missions from the spirits. He was angry at himself for letting the
skittishness of his companions affect him, but he had also learned such
things, and such places, were often metaphors for Conawago, that they
were ways of speaking of things that otherwise would be too painful to
discuss directly.

The forest around the lodge was unnaturally quiet. The air seemed
unsettled, and he suspected more severe weather was coming. He would
have expected that birds would be flying in the lull between storms, that
in the dusk deer and other small mammals would be active. But there were
no birds, no deer, no fox, no squirrels. He circuited the site in increasingly
wide circles, walking along the riverbank then stealthily cutting back into
the forest. On his third circuit he halted above a low open swale overgrown
with brush and small trees along its sides. He realized that it was a less used
continuation of the path from the river. The lodge had not been the original
focus of the path, only a waypoint, as though it had been built after the
passageway. He followed it toward a waist-high mound, perhaps ten paces
in diameter, built in a circle of trees. In its center was a post with leather
straps. Some were old and rotting, others were fresh. He backed away as he
realized he had seen such a post before, in Pennsylvania. It was a *gaondote*, a
prisoner's post, where captives were tormented and sometimes put to death.
As his spine pressed against a tree, he turned to look into the eye sockets of
a human skull embedded in the wood. He clenched his jaw, forcing himself
to study the adjoining trees despite his pounding heart. Half a dozen held
skulls of large forest creatures. The mound was a place of ritual, and of death.

He continued to scout until he found a campsite near the riverbank
that had been used only a week or two earlier by a party that had chosen

not to sleep in the old lodge. Crude hoops made from branches tied in circles with leather straps hung along the edge of the clearing. He lifted one and smelled the wood, noting the leaves and bundles of berries. Mountain ash, or rowan in the Old World. There were several hoops of ash, but also oak and alder. They were not skin-stretching hoops as he first thought, they were charms against evil spirits, charms he had seen as a child. They were not made by Iroquois but by those who had learned to fear demons in the wild and ageless Highlands.

He paced about the campsite, noting how close it was to the water. Soldiers of the northern campaigns had been trained by American rangers not to camp so close to bodies of water for fear of being trapped against them. The Scots who had been here had not been under the discipline of an officer. A small patch of red in a bush caught his eye, and he plucked it from the branches. It was a crude human figure, made of dried corn husks in the fashion of the dolls he had seen in Iroquois villages. But as he lifted it he saw it was no doll. It wore a little red coat and sported a tuft of grey squirrel fur gathered at the back with a length of red thread like a miniature wig. It was a British officer. Jammed between its eyes was a little arrow. It was a campsite of deserters.

As Duncan threw the figure down, more thunder rumbled in the west. He began picking up dried branches. They would need a lot of firewood that night.

Ishmael was attentive but subdued when Duncan returned, and he joined without argument when Duncan asked him to help retrieve more wood. It was Macaulay now who was withdrawn, silently eating his hot mush, then standing at the entry to look into the falling night. As he turned to retire to his blankets, he made the sign of the cross on his chest.

Later, after Duncan made a sentinel's circuit around the lodge, Ishmael sat with him across the fire, studying Macaulay's now sleeping form. "The way he marked his chest," Ishmael said, "it is the way of the black robes. But the British do not follow those ways."

Duncan   hesitated.   Calvin's   reformers   had   ravaged   the monasteries and cathedrals of the lowlands, but the Church of Rome had a centuries-old grip in the Highlands and the Hebrides. The sign of the cross had been so common in his boyhood he had thought nothing of the Scot's gesture. But the boy was right. The British had driven out all the vestiges of Catholicism, banned priests from serving with the army, banned mass among the troops. "It is a thing from western Scotland," he offered, staring at the big infantryman. The Jacobites, the Scottish rebels who supported the exiled Stewart prince, were ardent Catholics, but the army dealt severely with anything hinting of their old enemies.

"They do it against devils," Ishmael said.

"An invocation of God."

"Against devils," Ishmael repeated. "Dark things of the night. My grandfather helped me join with my protector," he explained, touching the little amulet pouch that hung around his neck over the medallion that was now inside his shirt. "Also against devils."

"You have been raised an Anglican," Duncan reminded him.

"Grandfather said I would never understand Europeans if I did not understand their god, that I would never be able to truly speak with some Europeans unless I know how to speak to their god." He fixed Duncan with a challenging stare. "But when my grandfather took me alone into the woods, to the old worship trees, to the boneyards of our people, he would tell me never to forget I had no cross in my blood."

Duncan chewed on the words. "He meant all your blood is Nipmuc."

"The only young one left in all the world, he told me. Once we watched a newborn fawn taking its first steps. If that was the last fawn ever to live, he asked, what should the life of that fawn be?" Ishmael fell silent. The boy clearly struggled for an answer.

"It would be for the fawn to keep alive the essence of the deer," Duncan suggested, knowing that they were not speaking of deer but of Nipmucs, and that words would never be enough.

Ishmael gazed into the flames. "It is for me to keep the stories and the prayers of our people alive. When I was only six he began telling me them in cycles, different ones every night for a month, then when the moon shifted we would start over, until I could repeat them all."

Duncan too stared at the fire. He knew it was irresponsible at a camp in the wilderness, that doing so would hurt his night vision should trouble come, but somehow he could not leave the boy, could not stop from trying to see what the boy saw in the flames. "We went to a burial ground in the mountains above Bethel Church," he said softly. "The maples around it were all bloodred even though other trees had no color yet. A stream flowed by with silver water. A Mohawk named Sagatchie was with me, who read the stories on his skin. The animals of the forest paused to watch when we lifted Towantha onto his burial platform."

As the boy studied Duncan with his bright intelligent eyes, something seemed to fall away between them. He leaned forward and listened as Duncan described every detail of the death rites for his grandfather, nodding as if in gratitude when Duncan described how they had found a snake and how he had left salt in the Highland tradition. When he finished Duncan tossed more wood on the fire, and they both stared into the flames again.

"Why did we come to this place, Ishmael?" he finally asked.

"You saw the canoe turned into the bank on its own. The spirit wind made us come here," Ishmael stated, then shrugged. "My grandfather taught me that there are places that attract spirits and radiate great power, just like Christian places where saints performed miracles." When the boy turned to Duncan he spoke in the somber tones of confession. "A witch can speak to the other side without a messenger." He reached back into the shadows and produced his spear, then threw it into the fire.

Duncan did not speak for several minutes. "Why did the dead woman's son have a different name?"

"She is dead and she is not dead."

Duncan tried to ignore the unsettling words. "But what did she know, why did you go see her?"

"She knew and did not know."

"She lived among the Ohio tribes. She had a message belt. They had banished her as a witch, but someone in the tribes needed her. Why? What did she know?" Duncan asked again.

"I think what she knew," he continued when Ishmael did not reply, "hurt too much for her to speak it." Somehow the image of the raving woman in the hut was no longer fearful to Duncan. She had become in his mind the tormented Welsh ghostwalker who had something vital to tell the world but had not known how to say it.

Ishmael turned back to the flames. "My grandfather explained to me about witches. They are humans turned inside out. Once when he was out showing us the stars, Mr. Bedford said witches like his mother wound up as constellations. The others laughed but I remembered he talked about throwing snakes. I thought she could tell me about the flint knife."

The air seemed to take a sudden chill. Duncan threw another log on the fire. "Who is the Revelator, Ishmael?" he asked.

The boy looked out into the dark night. "A shaman," he said, "A warrior chieftain. A sorcerer. A saint."

Duncan shook his head in frustration and threw a stick on the fire, sending sparks into the air. "Why, when I go in search of murderers, do I hear the name of a saint?"

"Terrible things may be done in the name of terrible truths." The boy sounded like an old, tired man.

"Like the killing of your grandfather?" Duncan said. "Like the massacre of the men and women of Bethel Church?" The boy looked back into the flames without reply. He was fingering the medallion Duncan had recovered from Hickory John. "Did your grandfather know of the Revelator?"

Ishmael spoke toward the medallion. "People came to my grandfather to tell him things they would not tell others. There were stories from the West, more stories each time a new traveler from the tribes stopped at the smithy. Grandfather asked me not to spread the tales, not to tell the others in our village. They disturbed him, even frightened him, though I had never seen him frightened before. He asked Mr. Bedford to stop speaking of him."

"The schoolmaster spoke of the Revelator?"

"He drew an image of a warrior with angel wings on a slate and propped it against the wall. He said it was no sin to be proud of who we were and only weakness to let others tell us who we must be. When my grandfather found it, he wiped the slate clean and shouted at Mr. Bedford, told him no more, told him not to meddle in affairs of the tribes. In all my life I think it was the only time I heard him raise his voice."

Frogs sang. An owl called. "John the Apostle was the first revelator," Ishmael said, nearly in a whisper. "Who was he?"

"A man who spoke for God." Duncan replied.

"Have you read the book of Revelation? It is full of terrible things."

"It was his particular vision," Duncan offered uncertainly.

"Of the end of the world?"

It was Duncan's turn to remain silent.

"And what if Saint John was born in the forests of this world?" the boy with the deep, wise eyes pressed. "What if he grew up with his people always offering the pipe of peace to outsiders from another world but the outsiders always mocked them, bringing them disease, killing them, taking the animals and lands given them by their gods? What would his particular vision be then?"

Ishmael seemed to forget Duncan. He cupped the wooden medallion in his hands and pressed it close to his mouth as if whispering to it.

"Your grandfather was an artist with wood," Duncan observed. He was not sure the boy heard him.

"You found this in the schoolhouse, on my bench?" Ishmael eventually asked. "It is where I left it that morning."

"Not in the school. In the dirt in front of your grandfather. He was staring at it when . . ." Duncan's voice faded.

Ishmael looked up in confusion. "You mean in the smithy, where they tortured him." Tears suddenly welled in his eyes.

At first Duncan thought the boy was just grieving for his grandfather. Then the realization stabbed like a cold blade. They had broken his fingers and beat him, then killed his friends, and still Hickory John had not yielded his secret. The medallion had broken him. Ishmael had seen the truth first, and Duncan hated himself for inflicting new pain on the boy. Hickory John had finally revealed his secret because his captors had made him believe they had Ishmael and would kill him next.

AS HIS COMPANIONS slept, Duncan sat against the center post at the front of the lodge, watching as the new wave of storms reached them. Lightning shivered across the sky. The wind snapped at the trees, tearing leaves from their limbs. Duncan knew storms well, and from an early age he had taken a solemn joy in experiencing them closely, yet this one was somehow different. Macaulay's unnatural fear and the boy's strange talk had unsettled him. He could not escape the sense that they were being watched by someone, or something. Several times he rose and checked the powder in his rifle, which he had left close to the fire, until finally he blew out the powder in the pan and freshened it against the damp.

He was eager for first light, and he prayed the storms would be finished so they could leave the uneasy place behind. If indeed it was a place of the forest gods, the gods did not want him there.

Duncan was not aware of falling asleep, only of abruptly awakening, his heart thumping. There had been a terrible screeching sound, an unnatural sound. Or had it been in one of his nightmares? Wide awake now, he stood. There was an ebb in the storm, even a patch of stars high overhead. He lifted one of the branches gnarled with knots of pitch and lit it, then picked up his rifle and stepped out of the longhouse.

He had made another complete circuit of the lodge, watching warily, when he heard the wrenching sound again. It could have been a dying animal. It could have been an anguished human. He followed the sound, finding himself in the tunnel of trees that led toward the ring of skulls. The wind began to rise. Rain began to fall again. He forced himself forward, thrusting his torch ahead.

He was nearly at the mound when a massive stroke of lightning lit the sky. He gasped and stepped backward, dropping the torch. Sitting on the mound, staring straight at him, lit by the jagged flashes, was the massive brown dog that had died with the witch in Albany.

Chapter Seven

"We must go and present ourselves to him," Ishmael insisted as soon as Duncan told him of the dog. It was dawn and the storms had blown themselves out, bringing cool autumn air to the river valley.

Duncan was not certain why he felt so compelled to take the boy's lead, but he picked up his rifle again and gestured Ishmael toward the tunnel of trees. Macaulay grabbed a sturdy branch, brandishing it like a club, and followed.

Ishmael was standing on the mound when Duncan arrived. There was no sign of the dog, but the top of the prisoner post was split and charred from a lightning strike. Ishmael warily touched the post then looked back at Duncan and slowly nodded, as if it confirmed his expectation. His hand still on the post, the boy spoke solemnly to the skulls in the trees, then tilted his head toward the side of the hill beyond.

At first Duncan thought the object the boy stared at was just another log. Then the end of the log rose up, and two black eyes stared at them.

Ishmael leapt toward the dog but abruptly stopped, tottering as if off balance. A moment later Duncan was at his side, pulling the boy back from the edge of a small crevasse concealed by undergrowth.

"It is one of the places where they come across!" the boy declared. "Just as my grandfather said! A crack in the earth where lightning dwells."

Duncan's breath caught as he followed the boy's gaze. At the bottom lay the body of a woman smeared with mud. On her breast was coiled a rattlesnake.

"Jesus, Mary, and Joseph," Macaulay said at Duncan's shoulder. "It's the witch! The viper has taken the witch!"

Duncan was about to tell his companions that the woman had died in a fire in Albany, but as he studied the frail body, the ragged greying hair, and the square chin that jutted out from mud and hair, he realized it was indeed Hetty Eldridge. It could not be. Duncan had seen the ruins of her cabin, had seen the bones. A witness had insisted she had been inside when it burned, that she had laughed as the flames consumed her.

Ishmael knelt at the edge of the deep crack in the slope. There was no fear on his face, only fascination.

"Why should she come here to die?" Macaulay asked in a tight voice.

"She had already died in Albany." Duncan did not realize he had spoken the thought aloud until he saw the alarmed way Macaulay stared at him.

"It explains the storms," Ishmael solemnly stated. "It explains the mound and the strange lodge and the lightning."

Duncan looked at the boy, once again unsettled by his words. He watched in silence as Ishmael retrieved a long stick and then bent to gently tap the snake. The serpent slithered away to a pool of sunlight at the opposite end of the crevasse.

The dead witch sat up.

"God protect us!" Macaulay cried as he stumbled backward, desperately crossing himself.

Ishmael's face glowed with excitement.

"The snake was just there for the warmth of her body," Duncan explained, though there was no certainty in his voice. "She must have fallen into the pit during the storm." He followed Ishmael as he climbed down to help the woman.

HER EMPLOYER IN Albany had spoken of Hetty the witch, Hetty the rum-soaked ghostwalker, Hetty the exceptional seamstress. Duncan had no idea who was with them now. The woman who sat before them in the lodge was more of an old Welsh grandmother. Ishmael tended to the woman with surprising gentleness, spooning hot broth into her mouth as Macaulay watched from ten feet away. The big Scot seemed not so much scared of Hetty now as resentful of her.

Duncan slipped away from the lodge and returned to the clearing where they had found her. The snake basked in the sun at the head of the little gully. There was no sign of the woman's presence, no camp, no blanket, no gathered firewood. It seemed impossible that she could have arrived by herself, even more impossible that she could have traveled so far upriver, against the current, except in a canoe propelled by powerful arms.

He covered the grounds systematically, searching for something, anything, that might lend sense to the events, and finally he paused at the post. Something had been added since the day before, a small mud-spattered grey bundle lashed to the bottom. He knelt, pushing the bundle with a tentative finger. He was loath to disturb what may have been placed as an offering for the gods. For a long moment he looked up at the human skull that gazed from the trees. "Forgive me," he murmured to the skull, then cut the straps around the bundle.

He should have known better than to try to make sense of anything found at such a place. First he saw a short straight stick like a baton painted with stick figures of men and animals, then a heavily worn silver Spanish coin pockmarked with little indentations. A square piece of thin, finely worked doeskin folded in a square. A worn linen handkerchief folded over a ring made of bone carved with leaping animals. He lifted the ring on his palm and studied it, realizing it was not bone but ivory and the figures were elaborately carved dragons. It was not an object of the tribes, it was European, something that the Welsh traders who called on the ports of his youth would have sold to local nobility.

To his surprise the doeskin contained nothing inside its folds. The

treasure was the skin itself. Its inside surface was covered with faded drawings, images like those of tribal chronicles that told of battles and great
chieftains. But these were no stick figure characters of warriors and bears.
The images had been done with an artful hand in a European style. A
little girl stood at the rail of a great sailing ship, watching whales frolic
in the ocean. A young woman stood hand in hand with a man before a
prosperous-looking farmhouse. In the next panel the house was burning,
the man lay with an arrow in his chest, and the woman was being led away
by a neckstrap. Next the woman was at a bark house of the tribes, grinding
corn on a stone, then with a tall warrior under a crescent moon. She carried
an infant in the next, then stood beside a young boy at a burial scaffold.
The next was a scene of Indians casting stones and sticks at the two. In the
last the woman and child clung to each other in the night, looking up at a
wolf silhouetted by the moon. He thought of the frail woman in the lodge.
Maybe Ishmael was right. Maybe Hetty had died and had been called back
for one last task on earth.

He spun about, suddenly aware of eyes on his back. The great brown
mastiff sat only three paces away, watching him. But there was no anger or
challenge in his eyes this time. What Duncan saw there was sadness. He
looked back at the last image on the doeskin. It could have been a wolf in
the scene. Or it could have been a great dog.

Without knowing why he bowed to the animal, then shifted so the dog
too could see the objects. It approached warily, sniffing them attentively. As
it did so, a memory stirred unexpectedly. He had seen an old silver coin like
that, a precious heirloom preserved by his mother. It was a teething coin,
passed down through families for the infants of each new generation. The
sad, drunken, angry witch had had a human life once, had been part of a
proud family. But she had decided that here, after the massacre at Bethel
Church, after receiving a message belt from visitors from the West and
destroying her existence in Albany, here she would finally abandon it.

He stayed very still as the dog studied him, pushing its muzzle against
his chest as if taking the scent of his heart. When it backed away, Duncan

wrapped the ring in the doeskin, stuffed the skin inside his waistcoat, then packed the other objects in their grey cloth and refastened the bundle to the prisoner post.

As he walked back to the longhouse, the dog followed. By the time he reached the entry it was walking quietly at Duncan's side, as if they were old companions.

The appearance of the creature seemed to awaken something in the Welsh woman. A new light entered her eyes. As her gaze shifted back and forth from the dog to Duncan, he realized it was not so much the arrival of the animal that stirred her as its choice to stand at Duncan's side. It was as if Ishmael, and now the dog, were reconnecting her to the world. She seemed to become aware of her surroundings, and she studied the lodge and then Ishmael and Macaulay as if seeing them for the first time. She touched the boy's hand and ran her fingertips along his forearm with a strangely affectionate motion. "The tribes sometimes call this place the fount of thunder from the way the storms like to settle here," she said in the voice of a tired old matron. "I hope it did not frighten you."

Ishmael glanced at Duncan then turned uneasily toward the woman. "I was not scared, Mother," he said hesitantly. "I was listening. My grandfather thought lightning bolts must be words spoken between the spirits of the sky and spirits of the land. He used to take me out in the storms and listen, marking the differences in the sounds. He taught me how there were different kinds of thunder, whispering thunder and angry thunder, patient thunder and warning thunder."

Before the boy could react, the woman reached out and pressed him to her breast. The hell dog sniffed Ishmael, then turned to the front of the lodge and sat facing outward, as if protecting them all now.

The woman held the boy for a long time. It was not clear who was comforting whom.

"The dog," Duncan ventured. "Is he yours?"

Hetty cocked her head. "A warrior belongs to no one. Sometimes he disappears for weeks at a time. But the day that belt came, he was back."

"In Albany they called him the hell dog."

The Welsh woman considered his words in silence then nodded, as if approving of the name.

Suddenly Ishmael reached inside his shirt and produced the fletched end of an arrow and tossed it on the ground by the fire. At first Duncan thought he was showing it to Hetty, but then he saw in her face that she had seen it before. He had used the letters, as Duncan had, to find the woman, but then he had shown her the arrow. Duncan picked it up and studied the long stiff feathers of its fletching. The coloring was of a bird unfamiliar to Duncan in a distinctive uniform pattern, each dark grey feather bearing two circles of white. He realized he too had seen the pattern before, drawn in the dirt floor of Hetty's hut beside the crumbled letter Ishmael had left there. It meant something to the woman.

"I stole it from a raider's quiver when he set it down," Ishmael explained to Duncan, "and broke off the end to show my grandfather afterwards. He knew the fletching of every arrow made on this side of the Mississippi." He looked up with a melancholy glance at Duncan. "But now I know. It was Mingo," Ishmael said to Hetty in a questioning tone. "Because you went west, not north, to find your captured son."

When she did not disagree, he turned to Duncan. "I thought she would give me some notion of where the raiders would go. Then I saw that belt. A Mingo delivered that belt to her."

"But you raised the alarm in the fort by crying out that Hurons had attacked."

A spark of mischief flashed in Ishmael's eyes. "Because they would never react if I said they were Mingoes. I thought there was a chance the troops could trap the Mingoes close to town and maybe I could speak with them. I never expected to be arrested." He paused as he saw the uncertainty still on Duncan's face. "No Mingo would come so far east as Champlain except for his war."

"His war?" Duncan asked. He glanced at Hetty, suddenly remembering that she had lived with the Mingoes, that they had been the tribe that had banished her.

"The half-king's," Ishmael said in a near whisper. "The one who spills blood for the old gods."

Duncan weighed the boy's words and began to glimpse the depth of his pain. "Why," he asked Hetty, "would his grandfather and the others of Bethel Church have to die to protect the old gods? Why would the old gods need the king's coins? Why take the other children?" Why, he wanted to ask, would a feather and belt of beads cause you to leave your life behind?

Her eyes filled with challenge, as if she resented his questions. "You will have to ask him," Hetty replied. "If he lets you keep your tongue."

No, Duncan meant to protest, I have to find Conawago and the children. "We will never find him in the wilderness," he said instead.

"The white sachem will know where to find him," she declared, and she began packing for travel.

THEY PADDLED FOR hours, making steady but slow progress, the current against them having strengthened from the rains, with Hetty and Ishmael in the center of their canoe, the old woman fast asleep. The dog had made no effort to climb into their crowded vessel but followed the trail that hugged the bank, keeping pace with long, effortless strides.

They had rounded a big bend in the river when Hetty pointed to a landing where a score of canoes were pulled up on the bank. Macaulay nodded at Duncan's suggestion that he stay hidden near the canoe, then they followed Hetty up a trail that wound through huge sycamore trees.

When the thick trees opened onto a broad field, Duncan expected to find a palisaded fort, and he halted in surprise. A European estate had been transported into the wilderness. The tall three-story house in the center of the sprawling yard was of cut stone, as was a sturdy blockhouse on the hill overlooking the compound. A hundred paces beyond the great house was a mill, its wheel turning against the water of the brook beside it, and a large barn that seemed to be in use as a lodging for native visitors. Several of the Indians could be seen bending over steaming pots at half a dozen fires, while others worked butter churns and still another group butchered a deer hanging from a tree. He looked back at the house, noticing now its heavy shutters and the narrow slotted windows on the upper floors. The house itself was a fortress.

It had been Macaulay who had revealed the identity of the white sachem, explaining that the taverns of Albany echoed with tales of the legendary William Johnson, who reigned over the colonial and tribal troops in the region, the hot-blooded Irishman who had been awarded a baronetcy after leading the famed victory at Lake George three years before. Duncan tried to recollect what he had read about the man, who often figured in the New York and Philadelphia journals. William Johnson had been an impoverished teenager when he had arrived from Ireland to set up a trading post along the river. No European had been more adept at forming bonds with the Iroquois, and he had quickly risen to become not only the senior emissary between Britain and the tribes but also senior officer of the peculiar militia of the region, which combined tribal warriors with Dutch, German, and English settlers. The Hero of Lake George, the journals had labeled him after he and his irregulars had won the first significant victory for the British at the long lake. He had been lauded not only for defeating the French with his largely Iroquois force but also for saving many French captives when the tribesmen had tried to put them to the knife.

They had arrived amidst the preparation of a feast. Planks were being laid on trestles along the broad front of the house. Several tribal women wearing calico dresses seemed in charge of the household and were directing a small army of younger natives, German settlers, and even several Africans.

Hetty seemed uneasy around so many strangers, but Duncan saw the bright curiosity in Ishmael's eyes, and, leaving his pack and rifle with Hetty as she settled onto a log in the shadows, he led the boy into the throng. The long table was quickly being transformed as tankards and chargers of wood, pewter, and even china materialized on its planks. No one objected when Duncan guided the wide-eyed boy into the huge house. The wide central hallway held several small paintings on its yellow plaster walls, framed landscapes of mountains and lakes, but otherwise the hall had the air of an arsenal. Racks of muskets lined one side, racks of spear-like spontoons and halberds the other. The walls of the sitting room, however, offered neither signs of war nor of European opulence. They were adorned with the trappings of an Iroquois chief, including a half circle of tribal arrows radiating like the rays of a rising sun from an orange hub. An elegant robe of fur and feathers hung on another wall, under a long ceremonial pipe. Beautifully worked tomahawks and clay bowls with crenulated patterns along their lips lay across the mantle of the fireplace.

"You are welcome in our house," came a soft, refined voice behind him.

Turning to greet the European woman who spoke, Duncan could not hide his surprise at seeing instead a comely Iroquois woman dressed in a simple vermilion dress. She smiled at his reaction. "Although the anniversary of my birth is not for some weeks, William will soon be off to war once more and has decided to celebrate today. He likes to call our little settlement Fort Johnson, but I prefer to think of it in more hospitable terms. All travelers are welcome in our humble home. Let us pull the thorns from your feet and wipe the dust from your eyes so we may speak as friends."

The woman in the European clothes, in her very European house, was offering the Iroquois words for welcoming travelers. Duncan grinned but was suddenly very conscious of his unkempt appearance. She smiled again as he pushed back the long strands of hair that had escaped from the tail at his neck. "We have no call on your hospitality, ma'am," he said awkwardly.

"Of course you do, and I am no madame. I am Molly Brant, and we welcome all visitors, of all nations," she said and cocked her head at Ishmael in curiosity for a moment before gesturing to the tall, lithe woman who had appeared at her side. "Kass will see to you," Molly said, then hurried to a group of men carrying chairs from the dining room.

They followed the woman named Kass out the rear door to a bench set by a hand pump where buckets of water and towels lay waiting. Ishmael could not take his eyes off the woman. "You are Mohawk?" the boy blurted out.

"Molly is Mohawk. I am Kassawaya of an Oneida clan." A gentle smile lifted her high cheekbones. "Many Mohawk and Oneida reside in the household of Colonel Johnson. When the last of my family was sent by the Council to fight in the North, Molly and the Colonel asked me to stay with them." As she glanced toward the river, Duncan saw the little tattoo of a fish on the woman's neck, above her necklace of glass beads.

"You can bring the big Scot who hides by the canoes. He has nothing to fear from us."

"He is shy," Duncan replied, realizing she suspected he was a deserter. "If he smells the ale he may come yet."

Kass's dark eyes flickered with amusement, then she grew serious. "It is dangerous to travel on the river alone. You will have to choose a binding or one will be forced on you."

"Binding?" Duncan asked.

"Will you be bound to the king's army? To the French? To the tribes? To the rebels in the West?" With a quick deft motion her hand went to Duncan's belt and pulled away the leather cap Woolford had given him. "Or perhaps to the half-wild rangers?"

"We are bound to an old Nipmuc who protects the old spirits in the wilderness. And to five children captured by Mingoes."

Kass seemed unhappy with his words. "That is no binding at all. That is a wish for death," she declared, and without another word she stepped away, the ranger cap still in her hand.

"Mind your feet!" a good-natured voice called out, and a bucket of water was tossed onto their hands. Duncan looked up into the broad walnut-colored face of the man who handed him a towel. He smiled at the African and nodded toward Kass's departing figure. "Colonel Johnson seems to enjoy the company of Iroquois women."

The servant laughed. "The Colonel, he enjoys the company of all women, but Mohawk and Oneida most of all. Miss Kass, she's just a friend. Miss Molly, she's the mother of two of his children. They play and learn alongside those of his first wife, a good German who was taken by a brain fever."

By midafternoon, the banquet was underway. Colonel Johnson, seated with Molly at the head of the table, was a man who laughed much and deeply enjoyed the motley assembly of neighbors, Iroquois, militiamen, and traders who were perched around the table on stools, kegs, and upended logs. Molly had brought the Colonel to Duncan for a hasty introduction before the meal. His greeting to Duncan had been cordial if perfunctory, but he had turned back as if in afterthought. "There was a young Scot who visited that Welsh woman who kept dying. But he was imprisoned so that cannot be you," he observed pointedly. "I'd like to chat with someone who met the witch of Albany. Mingo runners came through here urgently looking for her. Now people say enemy tribesmen attacked her cabin there," Johnson added.

Duncan studied the man with new interest. It was too early for the colonel to have picked up casual rumors. Johnson had specific intelligence sent by courier from Albany. He had to remind himself that the affable head of the household was also the most important military figure on the frontier. "People?" he asked.

The big Irishman shrugged. "The king looks to me in matters of the tribes. Reports of Huron raiders in Albany would not only be inaccurate but irresponsible."

"I agree. They were Mingo. At Albany and at Bethel Church."

"That, sir, is not possible."

As if on cue Ishmael pulled the stub of the Mingo arrow from inside his shirt. Johnson's brow furrowed, and he reached out for the arrow. The white chieftain studied the fletching with intense interest. "You could have gotten this anywhere."

"We have not come for your food, sir, nor to ask for men at arms," Duncan said. "We only seek information and will be on our way. The Mingo half-king is approaching from the west. Where is he now?"

"You speak of matters that are the concern of the government."

"Our concerns with the half-king are private."

Johnson grimaced. "Lad, there is no private business with that damned renegade, and you will never reach him alive. There was only one who had a chance of acting as intermediary, and I was about to send for her when I learned she had burned alive in her cabin. I've heard half a dozen stories about her deaths through the years. She turned into a skeleton when Shawnees were chasing her, got eaten by a bear another time. This time witnesses swear she burnt alive."

"And didn't we see the earth give her up again last night at the witch's hole!" Ishmael shot back.

Johnson's breath seemed to catch in his throat. He quickly looked about as though to be sure no one else had heard then put a hand on the boy's shoulder and seemed about to usher them back inside the house when Molly pulled him away, declaring that forty hungry guests waited his arrival at the table.

Duncan stayed at the feast for Ishmael's sake, but he watched with interest as the tribesmen listened with rapt attention to the colonel's flowery speech about the covenant chain that bound the Iroquois and British peoples. For the first time he saw the boy relax, enjoying himself as an adolescent should. Duncan knew the young Nipmuc was in sore need of good food, and he grinned with pleasure as the boy consumed huge servings of mashed pumpkin, succotash, roasted venison, and corncakes.

One of Johnson's sons, who was nearly of an age with Ishmael, struck up a conversation with the Nipmuc boy, and when the young Johnson announced he had an albino raccoon in the barn, Ishmael looked up at Duncan, who nodded his consent. As the boys scampered away, Duncan too rose, grateful for the chance to explore the estate. Soon he found himself at the mill, first admiring the big waterwheel then following the sounds of the great gears through the open door.

As he opened the shuttered window to admit the fading light, a thick timber materialized from the shadows and slammed into his belly. He lost his wind, lost part of his meal, and was on his hands and knees when his assailant flattened him with a kick to the ribs and a knee on his chest.

Duncan's raised fist froze as a blade touched his throat.

"I could save the king a lot of trouble," the man snarled.

"Hawley!" Duncan gasped.

"Slowly lad," Sergeant Hawley instructed as he pulled Duncan up by his collar. "General Amherst needs yer tongue to work, but he won't mind at all if the rest of ye be in pieces."

Duncan staggered to his feet, the blade pressed against his chest. "I didn't—"

Hawley pushed the knife, the tip stinging his flesh. "We know ye killed that escort to the payroll. They have my sworn statement to prove it. But ye know much more, we're thinking. Amherst will pay me richly to have ye in chains before his lordship. Now pick up that rope by the gears and—"

Duncan twisted out of the sergeant's grip, threw out his foot, and shoved him backwards onto the rolling grist stone. Hawley gasped as he saw the heavy stone roller advancing toward his head, then rolled onto the floor. As he rose, his knife was in his hand, aimed at Duncan's belly. He swung, Duncan ducked, he swung again, and then he froze at the sound of a gun being cocked.

"Fort Johnson is a sanctuary, sir," Molly Brant declared as she stepped through the entry, holding a heavy pistol. Ishmael and his new friend were at her side.

"I am on General Amherst's business, woman!" Hawley hissed and ventured a step closer to Duncan.

Molly ignored him. "William will be so disappointed when I tell him I had to kill a man at my own birthday celebration." She moved the pistol up and down as if deciding where to aim. "I am a crack shot, sir. Shall I just take an ear for now?"

"One shot is all ye'll have," Hawley growled. "I'll have my knife in both of ye before ye can reload."

Molly sighed and aimed at Hawley's groin. "Be gone, sir. If I see you again I will call some Mohawk friends who will not be nearly so gentle with you."

For an instant Duncan thought Hawley was going to test her skill, but the ranger thought better and lowered his blade. He cursed and slipped out into the dark.

"Once more, I appreciate the hospitality," Duncan offered.

Molly smiled and handed the gun to her son. "Thank the boys. They saw him lurking about like a thief," she said, and she rubbed Ishmael's head.

As the sun set, they took food to Hetty and Macaulay at the landing, and as their companions ate, Ishmael helped Duncan make pine bough beds near their fire. Duncan lay down beside Ishmael but knew he had unfinished business at Fort Johnson. He waited until slumber overtook the boy before rising to study the grounds for any sign of Hawley, then he warily worked his way along the path to the blockhouse on the hill.

He soon found himself at a ledge overlooking the river where a log bench had been erected. Behind, he had a clear view of the compound of Fort Johnson, lit by lanterns and pitch torches. To the front, a long expanse of rolling hills glowed under a purple and golden sky.

"This is the way Eden dies," a deep, contemplative voice said over his shoulder.

Duncan could not hide his surprise at finding William Johnson standing beside him. He offered a respectful nod to the Irish baronet, then he turned back toward the spectacular landscape. "I can't but wonder if Eden was so beautiful."

Johnson lifted a pipe to his lips, coaxing smoke out of the smoldering tobacco. "I was a year or two younger than you, McCallum, when I first traveled up this river. My knees trembled like a frightened child's. I was terrified of its beauty. It was so majestic, so powerful, so untamed. A world different from any I had ever known."

"Inhabited by a very different people."

Johnson looked at Duncan in surprise, then nodded. "Aye. I fear we are the Romans, and the ancient tribes crumble before us. We want to treat the land like it is just one more little vale off the Thames. But the biggest mistake is that we treat the natives as if they were just cruder versions of ourselves. It took me years to understand how wrong that was. The more I understand the people of the woods the more time I want to spend with them." Johnson bent and picked up a feather from the ground. He studied it as if it might hold some secret message. "I've been given royal gifts, anointed as a baronet, installed as a colonel. But all of that is as dust compared to the day the Haudenosaunee adopted me as a chief of their longhouse."

A flock of geese flew past, so low and close the two men could hear the wingbeats.

Duncan broke the silence. "From the day the English destroyed my clan nearly fifteen years ago," he said, "my heart was in a shadow. Then I learned to walk at the side of an old Nipmuc."

The man beside him had none of the airs of the loquacious baronet who had lorded over the feast. He spun the delicate feather between his fingers, then looked out toward the setting sun.

"I owe you an apology, McCallum. It was only in the past hour that an Onondaga friend found me. I had no idea you were the Scot who stands with Conawago. You would have sat at my right hand today had I known. I envy you. He is one of the last of his kind."

"Last of the Nipmucs."

"Not just that, but yes."

"So you are acquainted with him?"

"He has dined at my table more times than I can count. We have passed happy hours together in my library debating the Greek philosophers while blizzards howled outside. He and my wife played scenes of Molière in our pavilion one summer. A lifetime ago." Johnson spoke toward the feather now. "I would give much to spend a week or two at his side in the woods." He looked up at Duncan with a sad, sheepish grin.

"I lost my chance fifteen years ago," he continued. "He had spent some nights under my roof, reading my books, then announced he was leaving for Lake Champlain, on a straight path through the mountains instead of along the rivers. I had never seen that high country. He wanted to borrow a volume of Aristotle. I said I would gladly give him the book if I could travel with him. He agreed, though he insisted we must leave before dawn. But I encountered a coppery lass under the moonlight. Iroquois women are formidable, lad. They know their own skin. She grew amorous. The women have a saying on such nights: The moon will not be refused. I woke up midmorning and Conawago was gone. He had left the book on the table, open, with a feather pointing to a passage. 'A man is the origin of his action,' it said. I wanted to weep."

Johnson paused and looked out over the glowing hills. "I have often thought of that lost journey. It's strange, but I think I would have been a different man if I had chosen differently that night. A better man. It's preyed on me all these years, though I've never spoken of it to another soul until now."

"Why do so now?"

"Maybe because I see so much of myself in you. Because you still have choices ahead of you. Because Conawago is in grave danger, and you and the Welsh witch are his only chance of staying alive. We think she may know the half-king, think he may have even summoned her."

Duncan's heart seemed to stop beating for a moment. "What danger?"

"Conawago met one of my scouts in the North, an old acquaintance of his. Conawago gave him a message for the Council of elders at Onondaga Castle. He told them they must protect the old shrines, that nothing was more important than protecting the old shrines. Why would he say that?"

Duncan studied the Irishman for a moment, wondering how much he knew about the Nipmucs. "Old shrines are where the tribes speak with the old gods."

"I think the half-king wants the gods for himself."

"I don't understand," Duncan said.

"He claims to be the voice of the old gods, and that the old gods want him to lead a new nation of tribes."

"But that has nothing to do with Conawago."

"I wish you were right." Johnson nursed his pipe for a long moment.

"Old legends of the Haudenosaunee speak of a place in the North where there's a passage to the other side, where men and tribes were taken for judgment in another time. The Lodge of Lightning, it is called in the old tales, for they say it is where lightning gathers out of the sky. The elders speak of it as the most sacred of places, so sacred it is kept a close secret. Only a handful of the old ones are said to know where it is and how to open the passage. The Council has been debating these months whether to reopen the shrine, and they have finally sent warriors to protect it. If that damned Revelator took it for his own use, he would become the most powerful chieftain for hundreds of miles."

Duncan closed his eyes a moment, knowing Johnson had just answered the question that had been haunting him. "It is where Conawago is going."

The words seemed to stab at Johnson. He sighed and lowered his pipe then stepped closer to the river. He raised his hand with what seemed great effort and released the little feather into the wind and watched it fly into the darkening sky before turning back to Duncan. "The half-king seeks its location so he can go there. He knows it lies near an abandoned Iroquois village, but there are dozens of those."

Duncan's throat went very dry. "If the half-king finds it and discovers Conawago there . . ."

"The half-king will just see him as another Indian in European clothes. He reviles such men, says they are abominations, the means by which the poison that is killing the tribes spreads. He is said to have roasted one alive last month."

"How would you know this?"

"I may have been born in County Meath, but I have become more Mohawk than Irish."

"This is no time to speak in riddles, sir."

"I have couriers who keep me connected with the Council at Onondaga Castle. The Council has ways of knowing all that happens in their lands. I have never seen the sachems of the Council more disturbed.

The half-king seeks to force them into an alliance with him. He says the old spirits are angry at them, that if they do not join, the spirits will abandon them. Without the spirits he says the Iroquois will become hollow men and will be destroyed alongside their British friends."

"Conawago thinks there has been a break in the path to the other side. He believes he has ways to patch such rifts," Duncan offered uncertainly.

"The half-king," Johnson said, "the Revelator. It is how he rallies so many of the lesser tribes, how he believes he will subjugate the Iroquois. He himself will cross over and fix the rift. When he finds the most ancient of shrines, he says he will have the power to vanquish the renegade European spirits. The tribes can then follow him into a glorious world of his making."

Duncan had a hard time speaking. "This place. Conawago has kept its location a secret all these years."

"The Nipmucs were the monks of the woodland tribes. The Nipmuc elders always knew."

"The raiders at Bethel Church tortured a Nipmuc elder."

Johnson's eyes went wide. "A Nipmuc lived at Bethel Church?"

"He lived out of sight, with an English name. Conawago and I arrived to meet him, but he had been killed just hours before. He had sent a message to Conawago. *This is how we first die*, it said."

Johnson seemed to stagger. He put a hand on a tree to steady himself. "My God. He was talking about the end of time for the tribes. When they lose the spirits on the other side, they will wither and die. The Nipmuc at Bethel Church was tortured for the location of the Lightning Lodge. Now the half-king knows where it is. The Council already sent some of its best warriors to protect it, Kass's brother and father among them. It is the Council's last desperate chance. But he will be unforgiving of any who interfere with him."

Duncan's mouth was dry as sand. "You're saying Conawago . . ."

"You know damned well what I am saying. Conawago and the half-king are racing to the same place, and when the half-king arrives he will shred Conawago's flesh from his bones."

DUNCAN DID NOT know how long he sat gazing in anguish across the rolling landscape. *Run,* a voice inside shouted. *Save Conawago.* But he suspected having a European at his side would make things no better for the old Nipmuc.

When he looked back, Johnson was gone. Kass was standing there, as if she had been patiently waiting for him.

"There is someone from the war," she announced. The role of demure hostess at Molly Brant's side seemed be wearing on her. Her hair was loose. She had pinned a piece of sweetfern to her bodice, in the fashion of maids Duncan had seen in the Iroquois towns. Hanging from her neck was no longer her beaded necklace but a small pouch for the amulet of her protective spirit.

"You have a brother and father in the war," Duncan observed.

Kass nodded. "They have been given a sacred duty, yes. The Council is used to solving its problems with words, but words will not be enough this time."

She gestured him to follow her.

As they reached the blockhouse on the hill above the compound, Duncan hesitated. Two stern warriors stood guard at the door, and he now saw the iron bars on the windows of the squat building. The building was as much a prison as a defensive post.

Kass sensed his discomfort. With a small silent motion, she clapped a hand over her heart and then extended it, opening her palm toward him, in a sign that he could trust her. "Please," was all she said. Duncan followed her inside, to the base of a steep ladder stair that led to the upper floor. She gestured upward and backed away. He climbed the steps warily, realizing how little he really knew of William Johnson. If Johnson truly answered to the commanders in Albany, he could be walking into a trap. Officers in Albany still wanted to hang him. He scanned the candlelit chamber at floor level when his head cleared the opening. Along each wall was a cot, with a table and chairs at the center. A man slept on the farthest cot. He ascended and approached the cot cautiously.

As a board creaked under Duncan's foot, the sleeping man sprang to life, rolling off the bed and dropping into a fighting crouch.

"Sagatchie!" Duncan gasped.

The Mohawk ranger appeared to have come from a battlefield. His face was bruised, one cheek swollen, his hair matted from a wound bleeding on his crown. As he straightened, holding his belly, he was almost too weak to stand. He stepped to the table and dropped into one of the chairs.

When Duncan hastened to examine Sagatchie, the ranger held up a restraining hand. "A few blows, no more. No bullets touched me," he said, and he touched his amulet as if in explanation.

"But why are you a prisoner?"

His question brought a bitter grin to the Mohawk's face. "The guards do not keep me in, McCallum. They are to keep others out."

A dozen questions leapt to Duncan's mind. The Mohawk had been at Bethel Church the last time Duncan had seen him. He was supposed to be on patrol along the lakes, where the murderers had escaped. But his questions died on his tongue when Sagatchie spoke again.

"Hawley will seek you out," the Mohawk declared. "Beware of every shadow."

Duncan lowered himself into a chair. "He attacked me this very evening. Molly Brant persuaded him to leave." He hesitated. "How would you know that? You were one of his men," he said a moment later, as if answering his own question.

The Mohawk shook his head. "I was a guide. A watcher."

"A watcher?" Duncan asked. "Watching for what, exactly?" Duncan saw Sagatchie's stony expression and knew the ranger was a man who kept many secrets. "Watching him come for me?" he asked bitterly.

"I told you," came a weary voice from behind Duncan. Patrick Woolford stood on the stairs, mud on his sleeves and grime on his face. "I was sending my best man to help you." The ranger captain turned on the stairs, motioning to someone below. One of the guards followed him up, carrying a body on his shoulder, which he lowered onto the floor.

Sergeant Hawley would stalk Duncan no more.

Duncan found no sign of a wound on the sergeant until he rolled him over. The oozing gash in his back was over his heart. Duncan looked up at Sagatchie and Woolford.

"Rangers don't stab other rangers in the back, Duncan," Woolford said, sensing the suspicion in his gaze. "Not even one who deserves it." He seemed about to explain further when he saw Sagatchie's injuries and darted to the table.

The questions all came from Woolford now, in the Iroquois tongue, and so fast Duncan could not follow. After a few minutes of hushed exchange between the two rangers, Woolford looked up.

"Who else knows you came this way?" Woolford asked Duncan.

"No one."

"Sagatchie is known in some circles as one who performs dangerous assignments for me, assignments in the shadows of the war. He was following Hawley because we suspected Hawley meant to do you harm. And with luck he might have taken us to the half-king's messengers."

"Messengers?"

"I have had men patrolling trying to discover how the half-king communicates with the French. If we can cut off his line of communication, we will cripple his plans for alliance."

"But surely that is impossible. They could be anywhere in thousands of miles of wilderness."

"Difficult, but not impossible." Woolford dipped a finger in a mug of water on the table and hastily drew an irregular oval. "This is the great lake, Ontario." He traced a dotted line of moisture inside the top of he oval and continued, "There is a water route along the northern shore that is used by the Jesuits and French trappers. The Jesuits rule it with an iron hand and surely would not condone an alliance with tribes who butcher women and children. The half-king would keep his distance from that path. No canoes would ever dare the waters in the center of the lake. And the half-king would not move openly through the heart of the Iroquois country south of the lake. That leaves the southern shore and a corridor of perhaps twenty miles south of it. My men have been watching there these past weeks."

"It was just Sagatchie's bad luck that he met raiders on the river," Duncan surmised.

Woolford settled into one of the chairs. "Not raiders. Deserters. He found your signs at the old spirit lodge by the river. Someone had been lying in a narrow gully by that mound with that prisoner post. He went down in it to investigate, and when he climbed out they jumped him, began beating him. When he broke away they shot at him."

Duncan shrugged. "Deserters are desperate men."

"These were a special kind of deserters. Very savvy about the workings of the army, and the rangers. Sagatchie says they all had bare legs."

"Highlanders?"

"There is no better cover for murder then war. It's always happened. A hated officer is found with a bullet in the back of his head. Who's to say it wasn't an accident, or that he turned to rally his men and was hit by the enemy? The general asked me to look for patterns. The Highland units were thrown together quickly, sometimes with only a few weeks' training before shipping out from Scotland. That meant a number of the key administrative billets were not necessarily Highlanders. I found five suspicious deaths among the Highland troops. Four were Englishmen. One of those was a quartermaster, another a provost who arranged guards for the paywagons. General Calder and I were watching some of the Scots. There was talk of secret meetings with French agents in the forest. That's why Sagatchie was with Hawley's patrol at Bethel Church."

"Hawley wasn't Scottish."

"Hawley's company reported to General Amherst, in the North. And Hawley was on patrol with two of the four English officers when they were murdered."

Duncan hesitated. "You mean Hawley was a suspect."

"He was a man of expensive habits, known for immoderate gambling and wenching whenever he came to town. Last month he came into a lot of money, which he spread in taverns all along the Hudson. We were more interested in finding a way to negotiate with him, to let him trade information for his life. General Calder and I were about to have that discussion with him when he slipped out of Albany."

Duncan spoke slowly, weighing Woolford's words. "Hawley wasn't working for Calder, but for Calder's commander. And someone betrayed your plans."

Woolford shrugged. "Hawley's dead and Sagatchie's nearly killed. There's rot in the regiments and men are dying of it. Funny thing about these recent deserters. Deserters in the Scottish regiments always leave their paychits behind in some conspicuous way, like a matter of honor, a renunciation of the king. And they always go south, to the Scottish settlements in the Carolinas. But not these. They are keeping their paychits and going west. We are desperate to learn why."

Duncan did not like the pointed way Woolford gazed at him.

"You are a Highland outlaw, McCallum."

Duncan's heart sagged. "Do not ask me to act against the clans." He stared into his folded hands. "Go win the war in Canada and we can be done with this."

"Would that it were so simple," came a new voice. William Johnson was climbing the stairs. "The fight we worry about is not in Canada. We win all the battles but are on the verge of losing the war in the forests between here and Montreal." The colonel scowled at Hawley's body then called for the guards to take it away. When they were gone, he scraped at the bloodstain on the floor with his boot. "The body will disappear," he assured Woolford, then he paced around the table, silently studying the three men who sat there. "I will ask no questions except why would a ranger reporting to General Amherst be secretly stalking my guests?" His gaze lingered on Duncan. "Without General Calder or me knowing about it? A few French raiders roaming our lands, that's just war. But for Amherst to disrupt my Molly's festivities, that is downright rude."

"General Amherst doesn't consult with me, sir," Woolford replied.

"But your conjecture would be better informed than mine."

Woolford sighed. "Amherst doesn't trust my rangers, doesn't trust the tribal troops, hates the colonials, and curses every time he hears a Highland name. Take your pick."

As he spoke, Kass appeared carrying a large basket covered with a linen cloth. She silently set it on the table and extracted a wooden plate of sweet biscuits, several chipped china cups, and a copper teapot with steam rising from the spout.

Woolford gave a satisfied sigh. "If I had the strength I would hug you for this, Kassawaya," he said. She offered a silent smile in reply as she filled the cups.

Sagatchie sipped at his cup with surprising relish.

Woolford grinned at his Mohawk ranger. "I am afraid the baronet has corrupted our friends' simple tastes," the captain announced with a glance to Johnson. "I saw the list of the first supplies you ordered, Colonel, when you were asked to organize the tribes into auxiliary forces: two hundred blankets, two hundred axes, forty teapots, and four hundred pounds of tealeaf. It sells as dear as bullets in many villages." He grinned more broadly as Sagatchie drained his cup and refilled it.

Kass poured herself a cup and sat on the edge of a cot, gazing expectantly at Woolford, who shrugged when he met her gaze. "I have no news, Kass. All I know is that the half-king's army is moving with lightning speed. Scores of canoes passed the fort at Oswego in the dark three nights ago."

They were interrupted by a low whistle from below. Johnson leapt to his feet and shot down the stairs. When he came back up, he moved much more slowly.

"A messenger," he announced in a grim tone.

Before explaining he stepped to Kass and bent over her, whispering. The woman's face tightened, her eyes flared. She threw her cup against the wall, shattering it into tiny fragments, then dropped her head into her hands.

"It was only a small force the Iroquois Council sent to the Lightning Lodge," Johnson explained to the others. "The Council has to be careful not to start a whole new war. They tried to defend it. Hurons came from the North and Mingoes from the South. Waves of them, like locusts on trees." He looked back at Kass with pain in his eyes. "The Iroquois all died, except one taken captive to serve as a messenger. The half-king sent word that the Iroquois must either come to ally with him or come to die."

Duncan drained his cup and rose. "I would ask that you keep the boy safe here," he said to Johnson.

"You leave so soon?"

"You said it already. Hetty may be the best intermediary. If Conawago still lives I have to—"

Johnson held up a hand to interrupt. "I'm sorry lad. There's more. The messenger talked with those at the landing. As soon as they heard the news they threw their bags in the canoe. Hetty and the boy left with that big Highlander."

Chapter Eight

The river fought them as they paddled, throwing a constant wind in their faces, as if it did not want the canoe to go deeper into the tribal lands. Duncan dug into the dark water, doing his best to match the strokes of the figure in front of him. He had not at first recognized the woman when she had appeared by the canoe Sagatchie readied. The Oneida maid wore no more calico, only a sleeveless green waistcoat over a long dun-colored shirt and doeskin leggings with strips of fur for garters. Her protective amulet hung between her long black braids. This was not the gentile courtesan of Johnson's household. She was Kassawaya, the untamed Oneida, and she had been transformed by the news of the deaths of her father and brother. On her forehead she had painted two wavy blue lines, the sign of the river, under an arrow, the sign of a warrior. On her back had been a quiver of arrows, in her hand a well-crafted bow.

Sagatchie had stared in confusion when he first saw her. Duncan had been unable to read the flood of emotion that had risen on the Mohawk's face, but he could not mistake the angry tone of his words as he approached the woman, stepping between her and the canoe. The ranger had quickly recovered from his injuries and stood strong and straight, firing questions at her, pointing toward Fort Johnson. The woman had replied to each with firm, short syllables. Whatever she intended, she would not be dissuaded. Sagatchie's tone had changed from anger to worry, then finally resignation, and he had stepped aside. Kassawaya had helped finish loading the canoe and then settled into the bow.

They had left just after dawn, and there had been no words spoken among them for hours. The three paddled with grim determination, the Oneida woman making no acknowledgement of her companions except to point out an otter that chose to follow them. The creature moved lithely along the canoe, its sleek form often visible just under the surface, effortlessly keeping up with them, finally speeding ahead then rolling over and flipping its tail as though to mock their slowness before diving into the deeps. When it reappeared beside Duncan half an hour later, Kass paused and gazed at it intently as if reading something in the animal's actions, then she cast a long, impatient glance at Duncan, which he could make no sense of.

"You knew her once," Duncan suggested to Sagatchie as they gathered firewood at their evening camp.

"Her father was the greatest war chief of their clan. Her family would often visit our village. Kassawaya and I would run in the woods together. She still knew how to laugh then. She had four brothers, all fierce warriors. Like my clan, they have a particular feud with the Hurons. Her mother was captured years ago by Hurons and died before they could rescue her. One brother died of a Huron ax blow at the battle of Lake George. Two were killed by Hurons at Fort Niagara. Her father and last brother left her with Johnson for her safety. She was supposed to be married to some Seneca chief." Sagatchie paused and looked back at the fire where Kass sat cleaning fish they had caught. "It is not for a woman to be a warrior, I told her. It is not the way of our people, I said. We need our women to be safe, in our lodges and at our councils. She told me all her people were dead now, and she would decide her own way."

When they finally returned to the fire carrying wood, three small trout were spitted over the flames, scant fare for their empty bellies.

Duncan saw no sign of the woman until Sagatchie betrayed her with a small gesture. The Oneida woman stood motionless in a cluster of reeds. As Duncan took a step forward, a duck flushed from the reeds. Kass lifted her bow and loosed an arrow before Duncan even grasped her intentions. The duck fell, an arrow through its neck. The woman turned toward them with a gloating smile, making no effort to retrieve her prey. Sagatchie remained motionless, frowning, in obvious disapproval as the duck floated downstream. In the tribal world she had done the man's work and she now expected Sagatchie to do the woman's. Duncan looked from one to the other in frustration then leapt into the water to fetch the rest of their supper.

FORT STANWICK WAS a hulking shadow as they drifted by in the moonlight. Sagatchie had shaken Duncan awake at midnight and pointed to the canoe, where Kass waited. "If we go before the moon rises high, we will not be seen by the fort," the Mohawk ranger explained.

Now, as they passed it, the last of the garrisons protecting the settlements, Duncan reconsidered Sagatchie's words. They had not just been an acknowledgment that Duncan was a fugitive. Sagatchie himself did not want to be seen. Sagatchie did not trust the army. There was rot in the regiments, Woolford had said, and men were dying from it.

He found himself watching the outpost, forgetting to paddle. The lanterns hanging at its corners seemed feeble sparks against the dark wilderness beyond. In such moments the grip of the Europeans on the land seemed so frail, an impossible overreaching, an overreaching that Duncan increasingly hoped would fail. Duncan had barely begun to glimpse the depth of the woodland people, but he understood enough to know the Europeans grasped so very little of the wildness and its nations. He recalled Johnson's words: Our mistake is to think of the tribes as cruder forms of ourselves.

THE TRADITIONAL ROUTE into the heartland of the tribes lay over the portage known as the Carrying Place and on through Lake Oneida, but Sagatchie ignored the well-worn landing at the portage, pointing them into the northern arm of the river. The Revelator was in the North. Hetty and Ishmael were going north. Conawago was going north. They were converging on the secret place where spirits died.

The once mighty river became a narrow stream. Several times they portaged around falls, Sagatchie moving quickly each time to see that he and Duncan did the work of carrying the canoe, leaving Kass to bring the packs and rifles, ignoring her when she suggested loading all the equipment in the boat so they could all three carry the load.

At first she seemed amused at being shunned by the Mohawk warrior, but as the day wore on Kass grew sullen. Finally, at the fifth of their portages, she hastened forward to grab the canoe, lifting the vessel with Duncan and leaving Sagatchie to carry the remaining gear. When she dropped her arrow quiver, Sagatchie ignored it. The woman made a low growling sound, and when Sagatchie stepped away from her quiver, she abruptly dropped her end of the canoe and leapt at him with an angry snarl. The packs he carried went flying as she collided with him, knocking him into knee-deep water.

They fought like two angry bears, Kass clearly expecting no quarter because of her sex and Sagatchie giving her none. They disappeared under the water so long Duncan was about to leap after them when Sagatchie emerged coughing up water, dragging a limp Kassawaya onto the bank. But as the tall warrior turned his back, the woman rose and leapt onto him again. They went down on the bank, rolling in the mud, spitting epithets in their native tongue, pausing only for one quick silent moment to gauge each other before Kass flung mud and took up the fight again. Finally Duncan tried to intervene. But as soon as he pulled Kass away, she rolled and jerked him downward so that all three lay in the mud. As Duncan pulled himself up onto his hands and knees, he realized his companions had gone quiet.

He lifted his head to see a moccasined foot before him. Duncan turned over and looked up into the face of a fierce warrior. Then he saw another, then half a dozen more, all with rifles or war axes raised. They were not Iroquois.

Kass snapped a hostile greeting. "*Huron agaya!*" Huron dog! She eyed the quiver laying on the bank. More figures appeared, the last of them two fair-skinned men in kilts.

"I regret to say you are prisoner of the half-king," the nearest of the deserters declared with a Highland accent. "Though I daresay," he added with a grin, "you might be better off if we just let you kill yourselves in peace." His hearty laugh was echoed by the man beside him, then by others, until the entire company was laughing at their mud-covered, helpless prisoners.

THE DELAWARE, A muscular man with a strong, handsome face, had been dying for days. The Huron women who brought them their food made sure Duncan and his companions, tied to posts across from the Delaware, understood the penalty for those who opposed the Revelator. With cruel glee they explained that the man had come from the West with a load of furs, defying the half-king's decree that no more animals of the Ohio lands would be sacrificed for the enrichment of Europeans. The Christian Indian had been given a hearing before the Revelator and had chosen to loudly denounce the Revelator as a false god. He had been condemned to what the half-king's followers called the death of five days.

"Scar!" a woman hissed. The women quickly retreated at the approach of a huge Huron warrior with a face covered with hash marks of deliberately inflicted scars. The hideous pattern twisted with a sneer as the man called Scar declared himself to be the lieutenant of the half-king, then kicked dirt in the Delaware's face and boasted of the man's torture. On the first day the man's knees and ankles had been shattered with stone hammers. On the second children had been allowed to work on his extremities with knives, slicing away small pieces of flesh, which they fed to the gathering dogs. On the third his toes and ears had been sliced away. On the fourth his fingers had been taken. On the fifth, that very morning, long splinters of wood had been thrust into his body. If he survived to the next dawn, he would be roasted alive. The Huron grinned then kicked the man before marching away.

Such cruelty was the way of some tribes, Duncan knew, but his heart wrenched as he realized the tortured man gazed at him. The post he was tied to was no more than five paces from that of the Delaware, close enough for him to hear the labored breathing and to see that a deep intelligence endured behind the torment in the man's eyes.

"He is a Delaware," Sagatchie said, as if that explained much. "His tribe has lost its hearth. He is brave, but a stick standing by itself will always break."

The tale of the Lenni Lenape, the Delaware tribe, was often told at wilderness campfires. They had once been a mighty foe of the Haudenosaunee, ruling the lands of the mighty river for which they were named, but in the last century they had been decimated by disease and colonial encroachment on their traditional lands. When a few drunken subchiefs had signed away huge tracts of land to settlers, the Haudenosaunee had been furious, claiming the lands lay within their federation and threatened to exterminate the remaining Lenape if they did not acknowledge the supremacy of the Council and settle in towns under Iroquois rule like Shamokin.

Some of the Delaware had left their clans, choosing independent lives along the fringes of settlement. They were powerless against the tribes, for alone they had no strength. Tribal orators were fond of holding bundles of sticks as they spoke of how warriors standing alone were like single sticks that could be shattered but those who acted together, bound like a bundle, were unbreakable.

Duncan watched in torment as a spasm of pain shook the Delaware's body, triggering new trickles of blood from half a dozen wounds on his torso. With a deep groan the man lost consciousness.

"I'm sorry," Duncan said, turning to Sagatchie. "I didn't mean for you to—"

Sagatchie interrupted. "You wanted to get to the half-king's camp." There was not even a hint of fear in his voice. "Kassawaya made certain we did."

"Kassawaya?" Duncan asked, straining at his bindings to look at the woman, tied to a post on the other side of the ranger. She did not return his gaze, but he did not miss the tiny grin that flickered on her face.

Sagatchie waited for a guard to walk by before replying. "If they found us coming by stealth, we would have been attacked and overwhelmed, killed in the forest. We survived because we were seen as harmless. The young girl I knew was ever the prankster. They had been following us for nearly an hour."

Duncan stared at the Mohawk in disbelief. Ever the prankster. They were facing hideous deaths, but Sagatchie wanted him to know he had forgotten his disapproval of Kass the warrior and was getting reacquainted with the girl he had run with in the forest as a boy. The fight in the mud had been staged.

It was early evening when the straps that bound Duncan and his companions were loosened, and they were escorted by half a dozen warriors to a stream to wash away the dried mud that still clung to them. They were being prepared for something, Duncan knew. Most likely it was the gauntlet, the alley of torture in which prisoners were shoved down a path lined with enemy warriors who lashed at them with their weapons. Prisoners did not always reach the end alive.

As Sagatchie straightened, still standing in the stream, the tall Huron named Scar appeared, studying the Mohawk with a sneer then flinging more mud on him, striking his face. Sagatchie snarled a curse, and Duncan was certain he would have leapt at the well-armed man had Kass not put a restraining hand on his arm. Scar laughed and lifted his necklace into the faces of his prisoners, shaking the sticks that hung on it. With a gasp Duncan realized they were not sticks but human fingers, freshly amputated.

"Take our hands and we will hit you with our arms! Take our arms and we will kick you with our legs!" It took a moment for Duncan to realize Kass had spoken the defiant words.

The Hurons laughed. Some made lewd gestures at the woman, others smiled coolly and looked in the direction of a small raised flat at the edge of the abandoned town. The tent that had been raised on the flat was unlike any of the others scattered around the old town site. It was a large white canvas box of a tent with scalloped flaps, the kind used by the French military for high officers. Its white canvas had been painted with a grey pattern to give it the appearance of a stone cabin.

They were being prepared for an audience. He watched in alarm as Sagatchie again seemed about to leap at his captors. The Mohawk had been beaten with a spear shaft on their journey to the camp. His ribs would crack with more blows. Duncan moved to step between him and the Huron who goaded him, but Kass was there first, drawing up her body in a way that seemed to unsettle their captors.

They motioned their prisoners forward, not toward the ornate tent but up a worn trail that led out the far side of the abandoned town. After a quarter hour of steady climbing, they passed between two nearly symmetrical conical hills that were strangely devoid of trees. As they reached the shadows between the hills, they were met by half a dozen somber warriors in fur robes who carried heavy spears as their only weapons.

"Follow," the tallest of the warriors commanded. Duncan realized he had spoken in the Haudenosaunee tongue. The Hurons had given them to Mingos, the western Iroquois.

They ascended the narrow cleft and emerged into an eerie, otherworldly scene. The wide bowl they entered was scorched and charred, its only trees the twisted burnt offspring of the huge oaks that grew on the slopes below. There was still enough light left for Duncan to see that the high barren bowl was pockmarked with lightning strikes. They were at the place where lightning gathered, the ancient shrine whose secret Hickory John had been tortured for. Bizarre rock formations, most scorched and cracked by heat, surrounded a central formation lit by torches. Their escort had the air of robed monks, the torchlit bowl that of a pagan temple. The long rounded formation at the center of the bowl, covering what appeared to be a cavern, had the appearance of a stone lodge.

A solitary man wrapped in a blanket sat before a smoldering fire at the entrance to the Lightning Lodge. As they were taken closer, stopping a hundred feet away, Duncan made out other figures, perhaps twenty in all, sitting against rocks arranged in a half circle around the man as if paying homage to him.

As he took another step closer and saw the arrows in several of the figures, realization stabbed Duncan like a cold blade. He sprang forward to grab Kass's arm as she gasped. She too now understood, and he was terrified she would react. Those against the boulders were dead. The Iroquois Council had sent its best warriors to protect the old spirits, and they had been killed by the half-king. Among the dead in front of them were Kass's father and brother.

The seated man spread his arms to point out his handiwork.

Duncan felt Kass tense, sensing her anguished fury. Then Sagatchie appeared on her other side, pulling her backward, and she relented, a sob escaping her throat as her gaze settled on two bodies at the near edge of the half-circle. Duncan stood at the front alone, straining his eyes, desperately searching for, and just as desperately hoping not to see, the body of Conawago.

Their robed escorts signaled for them to turn around. This was all the audience they had intended. The prisoners had seen the dead, had seen the sacred shrine, and, Duncan suspected, they had seen the Revelator.

They were taken back to their posts, but when the guards had finished tying Sagatchie and Kass, they led Duncan away, toward the flat with the stone-painted tent, and they ordered him to stand alone by a smoldering fire. He sensed many eyes watching him from the darkness. After several minutes, a familiar figure approached. Macaulay acknowledged Duncan with a silent, chagrined nod then offered him a gourd of water.

"Do whatever he asks, lad," the big Scot advised. "Say ye want to be one of his Highland warriors and he may let ye live."

"There's an old man named Conawago," Duncan said. "Do you know where he is?"

Macaulay cocked his head toward the elevated flat at the center of the village and seemed about to speak when a stone struck his shoulder. He retreated into the shadows, where guards were watching.

Duncan watched the constellations rise, losing track of time but not daring to move. Finally a tiny ringing sound rose from the darkness. Something small and metallic jingled and stopped, jingled and stopped, the sound gradually getting louder.

"In the Ohio country my people were fascinated when a British trader first introduced these," came a voice from the shadows. Had Duncan not known better he would have thought a well-educated European was addressing him. "They would pay a full beaver pelt for just one."

The silhouette of a tall, lean man moved toward him, not from the tent but from the direction of the sacred place above the town. The low flames reflected off a small silvery bell that the man tossed from one hand to the other. "Women and men alike braided them into their hair. One of our women traded her daughter for ten such bells." More shapes became visible, guards holding spears and muskets. A woman slipped out of the shadows to dump an armload of wood onto the dying fire.

"Later I discovered they were called hawk bells." The man's precise, articulate words held the faint trace of a French accent. "They tie them to their hawks and falcons in your world."

"Not in my world," Duncan said, his voice calmer than he felt.

"The ones who rule your world do so."

Duncan offered no disagreement.

"At first that discovery made me sad. But later it made me angry. A man has no right to do such a thing. It is an insult to hawks. It spits in the eyes of the hawks and the gods they serve. These are the same people who take our land. These are the people who would destroy our tribes and put bells on the few who survive."

The dry wood burst into flame so abruptly that the man in front of him seemed to have taken shape out of thin air. He wore a sleeveless waistcoat over his painted torso and one of the army's new shorter field kilts over deerskin leggings. The Revelator's strong chiseled face might have seemed handsome were it not for the line of tattooed snakes that ran up from his neck over his cheek and onto his scalp, disappearing into long brown hair that was bound at the back into the kind of tight braided knot favored by British seamen. The fur of a fisher fox was draped over one arm, the head of the animal perched on his shoulder. The white beads that had been sewn into the eye sockets gave it the look of a beast from the other side. The half-king extended his hand over the fire and let the bell fall into the flames. "What do you desire of us?"

"You make it sound as if we came willingly."

The Revelator sighed disappointedly. "Your name is Duncan McCallum, chieftain of one of the Highland clans that have been so sorely tested by fate." He paused as he realized Duncan was pointedly gazing past his shoulder. "You wait for someone else perhaps?"

Duncan looked into the man's deep eyes. "The Revelator is a great Mingo warrior who strikes terror in all he approaches. But you speak like one of the Presbyterian ministers who used to troll for souls along the coast where I was raised." Duncan was indeed confused by the European affectation of the man.

The man's smile was as cold as ice. "My father left me at a Jesuit mission when I was young." As he took another step forward, the fire lit his face. His eyes glowed like black jewels.

"Jesuits teach in French."

The man shrugged. "I can always *parle français* with a new friend."

"I come because I am a friend of Conawago of the Nipmucs," he said. "I chose my friends based on who they are, not what they are."

"Which makes you a very bad soldier."

"I am no soldier."

"But we are all soldiers," the half-king said, taking in the camp with a sweep of his hand. "It is the great mistake of the tribes. They have been bears, slumbering in caves, roaming aimlessly in the forests. Now is the time for wolves. Wolves reign supreme in their lands because they stand together. The bigger the pack, the greater their power. Their world is absolute. Once they choose a prey, it must always die."

"We had wolves in the hills where I grew up," Duncan replied. "Men with guns would bait them with raw meat then shoot them while they ate. They died because they were so predictable."

The Revelator shrugged. "I thought Scar had showed you what we do with those who oppose us. And you would be hard pressed to predict what I am capable of."

Duncan became aware of others beyond the half-king's guard, figures arriving to sit in the shadows as if in hope of hearing the half-king's words. "I was told the Revelator was a visionary who spoke for the gods. Instead I find just another savage who plays with knives. A whole camp of your soldiers against a single Delaware tied to a post."

The Revelator's cool smile did not dim as he produced a clay pipe from a pouch and bent to light it from a flaming stick. "You are indeed from the Highlands?" he asked as he coaxed smoke out of the tobacco.

Duncan nodded slowly, more confused than ever about this Mingo from the West who spoke like an educated European yet behaved like the most violent of savages.

"The English tried to extinguish the clans there. What would you do if certain English soldiers tortured and killed your family and you found those same foul creatures under your control years later?"

The words stabbed at Duncan's heart so painfully that several moments passed before he could speak. "This is not about Scottish tribes. It is about the woodland tribes."

The man's eyes flared. "Then you know nothing! It is about the Mingoes and the Mohawks and the Hurons and the Onondaga and the

Scots and the French *métis* of the north country! It is about the deaths of all our people, here and on the other side!"

Duncan went still. "What do you know of death on the other side?"

The leader of the rebel tribes grew solemn. "I have walked on the other side," he declared, stirring murmured chants among those who sat behind him. "I know everything about death. My people are the blessed guardians of death."

"We have the oracles!" a woman in the shadows cried out. "We know we are the true humans because the oracles have come to say so!"

The Revelator paced around the fire, working his pipe, pausing by his guards, who began clearing away the onlookers, then stepped in front of Duncan. "You will carry messages back to the general," he stated. The spiritual leader seemed to have disappeared. The half-king had become a military tactician.

"The general will not listen to me. I am done with generals," Duncan replied.

"We are the true humans!" an acolyte cried out, as if the words were part of a liturgy.

The Revelator ignored the woman. "The general will be certain to listen to you. Such a man may not believe what he is given, but he always believes what he takes."

"I am too weary for riddles."

"You are going to be taken to Albany as a prisoner. The general will have received an intercepted letter in which it is revealed that the murder committed by the fugitive McCallum was just part of a greater effort to assist the French army. He will interrogate you and discover from you that a large French army is making its way for a surprise attack on Albany along the west side of the mountains."

"I never wrote such a letter!"

The Revelator shrugged. "Your name is signed to it. I believe that is all that matters. The general so wants to believe you are a traitor. But you must take a beating first, so he believes you."

"I refuse."

"Of course you do. But if you do not agree, you will all die. If you agree but don't play your part satisfactorily, your friends will die in exquisite pain," he said. "I will crush every bone in their bodies like shells under my feet, and the old Nipmuc will be sent to the other side permanently," the Revelator declared, then he turned away from the fire.

Strong hands seized Duncan, pulling him toward the retreating figure of the half-king.

They arrived at a small lodge on the knoll at the center of the former tribal town, past two dozen fires, each a camp for fifteen or twenty figures. The half-king's force was far larger than Duncan had realized. The structure was set apart, on the highest point of the town, with small smoky fires outside each corner and torches flanking its entrance. Garlands of small skulls reached to the ground from either side of the entry. The Revelator disappeared inside, and his guards shoved Duncan after him.

The long low platform in the center was surrounded by tallow lamps. Women clad in ornate doeskin shifts were on their knees, surrounding the altar, chanting in low tones. As one moved aside to admit the half-king, Duncan froze. The platform held the body of an old man draped in a ceremonial robe of feathers.

"Conawago!" Duncan gasped, springing forward.

As he reached out to touch his friend's face, two warriors leapt from the shadows to seize him but were stopped by the half-king's upraised hand.

"Your friend is not one of us anymore," the half-king stated. "The oracle roams on the other side but is bound to my people."

Duncan stared in torment at Conawago's limp body.

A thin smile rose on the half-king's tattooed face. As he gestured Duncan forward, he began shaking a turtle shell rattle.

Though the Nipmuc's cheek was warm, he did not respond to Duncan's touch. Without thinking he pushed the robe aside to take a wrist. One of the women hissed in warning, but another, the oldest of the attendants, pulled her away. His friend's pulse was weak and slow, but discernible. Conawago was alive, barely.

"What have you done?" he demanded. The women began chanting a prayer he did not recognize.

"Done?" the half-king shot back. "Kept him alive when he was on his last breath! Enabled him to fulfill his glorious destiny!"

Duncan looked at the sentinels and the attendants then at the elegant garment he had pushed away. He had heard of such robes of multicolored feathers, used for special ceremonies. Knots of cedar smoldered in small bowls, scenting the chamber. As he pushed the robe down, he saw his friend's other hand lay on his belly, clutching the hilt of a knife. Not any knife, he knew immediately. It was the ornate knife Madame Pritchard had seen, the weapon that looked like it belonged on an altar. The hilt was carved with elaborate images and inlaid with bright stones. The blade was of flint. It had a look of great antiquity.

As he rearranged the robe over Conawago, the old Nipmuc slightly stirred, and a hoarse, whispered chant rose from his throat. The women instantly stopped and leaned toward him.

"You see now he is my bridge," the Revelator declared when Conawago fell silent. "He was discovered by my men in a cloud of smoke after we took the Lightning Lodge from those foolish Iroquois. They knew he had just returned from the other side." The half-king's eyes narrowed, as if he was daring Duncan to challenge him. "Our first oracle declared him our sacred messenger, one of the walkers among the dead. A validation of our holy quest."

Duncan could see nothing but a frail old man. His friend seemed to have greatly aged since he had last seen him. "Your bridge?" he asked in a faint voice.

It was the nearest of the old women who replied. "To the other side! The oracles, the two who travel between worlds, the ones who speak the pain of the gods."

Duncan's heart was in his throat. Conawago was wasting away in some kind of coma. "He needs help. Medicine."

"We watch over him night and day," the woman said, lowering her voice now. "I drip honey and water onto his lips, but it is not enough. It is unavoidable that he is weak. Part of him is gone over, wandering on the other side, and it has no interest in human nourishment. It is their way."

"Two oracles, you say?"

"Her life wind is almost gone," the woman said, and she gestured toward the back of the lodge. Through the thinning smoke Duncan saw now another platform against the wall. "We were wrong to cast her out. The gods have sent her back to help us. The god voice inside her told us this Conawago was a sacred one, told us he would have answers to the questions we will learn to ask. The gods painted their track on her."

Duncan understood even before he rose and saw the limp form lying on a bed of moss in the shadows. He had seen the track of her gods, under her shirt in Albany. Hetty had been known by the Mingoes, feared but also respected for her ties to the spirits. She had told them Conawago was a sacred one. She had saved him.

"She won't let go of the small one, says he is her only anchor left on earth." As the woman spoke, another attendant, wrapped in a blanket, turned. Ishmael looked up at Duncan with fearful eyes. His hand was tightly gripped by Hetty.

Duncan took a step toward the boy but was held back by one of the attending women. A low growl came from the shadows, and the woman quickly relented. Hetty had two attendants. The hell dog was there, and he did not object when Duncan put a hand on Ishmael's shoulder. The boy nodded stiffly. He was terrified, but Duncan could do nothing to help him.

Suddenly Conawago began speaking in a rough, hoarse voice, now in the tongue of his boyhood, the Nipmuc tongue Duncan had not learned. Others crowded into the longhouse, speaking in excited whispers. As Duncan was pulled out of the building, the words changed, and they were loud enough for him to hear outside.

"*Arma virumque cano, Troiae qui primus ab oris,*" Conawago called out.

Through Duncan's fog of pain and fear, the words seemed to reach something inside.

"*Italiam, fato profugus, Laviniaque venit!*"

A hollow grin rose on Duncan's face as he was shoved down the hill. The oracle, the near dead old Nipmuc, the pawn of the half-king, was reciting Virgil's *Aeneid* in Latin.

The half-king waited for him outside his tent.

"I told my people the British would break their word when they agreed not to cross the Allegheny mountains." The Revelator seemed to want to explain himself to Duncan. "The British broke their word. I told them the strong liquor of the Europeans would steal the souls of our warriors. Now drunken Indians litter the settlements. I told them join me, and the settlements along the Ohio would disappear. Now the line of burnt cabins runs for two hundred miles. When I passed through the villages of the Seneca last spring, the women asked me on what day the gods wanted them to plant their squash and maize."

"There is a long history of prophets arising in times of calamity."

"Exactly. I prophesize your future, Duncan McCallum. You are going to be taken to Fort Stanwick by some of my men. They will ask for a reward for their capture of a fugitive from British justice, to make it convincing. When you are taken back to the general you will let him learn of the French secrets."

"The French lies."

"The British will have to retreat from Canada. They will be denied their victory. The French will see our strength and ally with me. The Iroquois Council will beg to join me. We will seal the frontier with a wall of thorns."

Duncan returned his steady gaze. The half-king was worried about the Grand Council. He had promised his followers that the Council would embrace their cause. "You mean the Iroquois have refused to treat with you," Duncan asserted.

The Revelator ignored him. "You will agree tonight, or by this time tomorrow, Conawago will be sent to live entirely on the other side and you will begin dying just like that Delaware. He took five days to die. I have peeled away the flesh of a living man's face, turned it into a living, screaming skull. My men laughed to see it. Five days is an eternity in such pain. We will take your fingers and nose the first day, then your feet before we take your face, McCallum." He spoke the words like a vow, then with a click of his tongue a guard appeared and pulled Duncan back toward the torture post.

The half-king followed, and when Duncan was on the ground, tied to the post, he abruptly kicked him in the ribs. "Messages came from the North. Their teacher has taught them well, don't you think?" he spat at Duncan. One by one he dropped five slips of paper onto the ground beside him before kicking the lifeless Delaware and marching away.

A guard lingered with a torch, waiting for him to examine the papers. They were all done in the hands of children. Not just any children, and not, he suspected, of their own free will. The first was a skeleton, over the name Jacob, then a grave with a cross over the name Noah. Next was a skull over Abraham and a coffin over Abigail. The last was an angel over Hannah, who had also penned *Pray for Mr. Bedford, tortured for our lives.*

IT WOULD BE spring on the other side when he searched for Conawago. He would find the old Nipmuc on a mountain trail, watching the warblers that always filled his heart with joy. At the summit they would sit with old bears in the night and watch shooting stars.

Duncan lingered at the edge of sleep, drifting again and again into visions of how he might meet Conawago on the other side. Sometimes they were alone in lush forests, encountering strange animals that no longer existed on earth. Sometimes they sat at a fire with Duncan's father and grandfather, exchanging tales of mortal lives. Sometimes Duncan was walking endlessly in a dense fog, hearing Conawago's voice but never finding him.

He sensed movement beside him and turned to see Sagatchie rubbing the rope that bound him against a rock at the base of his pole. No guard was to be seen.

"I am not leaving," Duncan warned the Mohawk.

Sagatchie looked at him, confused. "I seek not to escape, Duncan. I seek to free you, to go with you to the oracles." Duncan had explained to his companions about Hetty and Conawago. "It is a job for a Nipmuc warrior, but you will have to do it." He kept sawing at his ropes as he spoke. "When you have the flint knife in your hand, you will become a Nipmuc warrior." A stone flew out of the shadows, grazing Sagatchie's temple, and he stopped.

"I don't understand," Duncan said.

"It's why he clutches the knife to his chest. A Nipmuc would never be a slave to a man like this half-king. But he would never take his own life. The warrior's duty falls to you."

"We could never fight our way free."

"I will fight whomever blocks your way to the lodge. Once you are inside it should be but the work of a moment. Just position the flint blade over his heart and pound the hilt."

For a long moment Duncan could not speak. "I could never kill him, not Conawago."

Sagatchie sighed. "Then I will do it, though it is best that he be released by a friend."

Sagatchie was wrong, Duncan kept telling himself, but the Mohawk's words kept echoing in his mind, mixed with visions of his father calling him to death. He had no choices left, except one. He could let Conawago be slowly killed by the half-king as he himself died at the torture post. Or he could die performing the warrior's duty.

He drifted into a fog of despair and fatigue. He would do better in the next life, he mused. This life had been one misadventure after another, just a series of fits and starts with no real purpose, no anchors except for Conawago and the gentle Sarah Ramsey. He had wanted nothing more than to be a doctor among his beloved clansmen, but the Highland life had been systematically destroyed, leaving him a transported criminal, an indentured servant, a fugitive who found his way into prison every few months. Now, here, it ended, in the camp of a bloodthirsty prophet.

A new vision seized him. Conawago was escorting him into a council fire where Scottish and Indian chieftains spanning many centuries silently passed around a pipe. From somewhere in the shadows behind them came a melancholy song. *I am coming home, mother,* the hoarse, faltering voice chanted. *On the wings of my eagle I fly.*

"May the old ones embrace you. May the old ones sing your name in the dawn." These were the words of a tribal ritual, a refrain in response to a death song. Suddenly Duncan realized they had been spoken near his ear. He was abruptly awake. Beside him Sagatchie gazed into the shadows ahead of them, reciting the mourning words. A bright moon had risen, making his features clearly visible, and the stoic warrior's face was full of emotion.

"I am coming, Mother," came the song again, "with a fat deer on my back," the voice croaked from in front of Duncan.

His heart rose into his throat. The dead Delaware was singing.

Chapter Nine

"He knows he is about to cross over," Sagatchie whispered, his voice full of admiration. "I have known many Lenape," he declared, more loudly. "Your tribe may be broken, but its warriors are not."

The song faded away. Words came in faltering gasps. "There was a time . . . when the Lenape . . . were the masters of the forest. All along the great rivers tribes trembled at our name."

"With a thousand such as you my friend, you would be masters again," Sagatchie replied.

"How are you called?" came the weak voice.

"Sagatchie of the Wolf clan of the Mohawk."

"I am Osotku of the Beaver clan, though few of my clan yet survive."

"Where is your hearth, Osotku?"

"In Pennsylvania along the Forks of the Delaware . . ." The phrases came piecemeal, punctuated by groans of pain. "Near Nazareth. My wife waits in our cabin with our four children. Some damned European said the land was given to him by his government. He said I had to pay him eight pounds or he would drive my family out. I went for furs so my family would not be slaves. I had enough to pay for the land, but these dogs who follow that Mingo butcher said the furs were theirs. I said they do not own the animals, that the furs belong to the one who does the work for them." Another agonized groan cut off the words, and Osotku's head slumped onto his chest. "I am coming home," he moaned.

"They do not own what the spirits have provided," Sagatchie agreed.

The voice from the shadows came ever more slowly, in struggling breaths. "It took fifty of these damned Huron and Mingo dogs to kill me."

A warrior's glint suddenly lit Sagatchie's eyes. "Hurons? Do you know the clan of these Hurons?"

"Porcupine clan, and Fox clan."

"You have not seen the Wolverine?"

Duncan glanced in surprise at his friend. In the solemn moment of the Delaware's death he wanted to speak of tribal clans.

Osotku seemed to welcome the question. Sagatchie and he were speaking as two fellow warriors. "They were the dogs who took me on the lake, but when the oracle with the great hound arrived, they went north. The one with the iron head took my furs and my ears with him. His name is Paxto. You know his clan?"

Sagatchie spat the name like a curse. "Paxto! He was the one who attacked our council fire and destroyed it many years ago," Sagatchie explained. "Our blood feud with the Wolverines goes back to my father's father's time."

Osotku seemed to fade in and out of consciousness, in and out of reality, for he raved now, speaking names none of them knew, of stalking animals in the forest and of other events of his too-short life. "Black angel came last night," he murmured, "fluttering about with a laceback. Come to see the handiwork. A fine son," he groaned after a moment, then, "this cabin will be ours forever." Later came, "I knew the crossed boys in the Ohio years ago. They liked games of chance. They always cheated."

His words died away. He coughed, and a dark smear of blood oozed out of his lips. Duncan clenched his jaw at the thought of the agony the man was suffering. Slices from his flesh. Amputations. Spikes of wood driven into his torso. Yet there was no hint of self-pity or fear from the warrior. Duncan would not serve as the half-king's pawn, but he doubted he would ever be able to show such courage or endure such prolonged pain. His medical training told him there would be ways for him to end such torment early.

"They say there's murder on the other side now," Osotku said suddenly. "Europeans have found their way in and are killing the first men. I don't know what to believe. I will find out soon. Don't tell my family . . . about that story. I don't want . . . them to be frightened when they cross over." The man fell silent, then after another minute the song started anew. "I am coming home, Mother. Make the sky clear. I am coming home on wings." The words grew fainter and fainter until at last Duncan did not know if he was only hearing the song in his own mind.

Duncan was going to die just as the Lenape died. A great emptiness grew inside him. He felt shame at knowing he could never die so nobly.

"May the old ones embrace you. May the old ones sing your name in the dawn." The whispered chant was taken up again not just by Sagatchie but also by Kassawaya now. Duncan gazed at the moon for a long time, eventually realizing he too was whispering the mourning chant.

The moon was high overhead when Duncan was awakened by a shower of dirt. Sagatchie had twisted about so his legs faced Duncan, and he was kicking towards him. "The guard ran away," the Mohawk reported. "You said Conawago lies in that lodge at the top of the village. There is a disturbance up there." As he spoke, frantic voices were raised. Torches were being lit. He turned to the sound of running feet, and to his horror he saw three warriors speeding toward them, one with a torch and two with scalping knives drawn. He began pushing himself upright against his post, intending at least a few well-placed kicks before he succumbed. But they were on him too quickly. Before he could make sense of their intentions, they had cut his bindings and were urgently pulling him toward the lodge on the hill.

At least a hundred figures stood outside the small structure, watching it in nervous silence. Duncan was led past them and escorted inside, to the low platform where Conawago still lay.

Only the oldest of the native women who had tended him earlier was still there. She took Duncan's hand. "He called out from the other side. He said, get the Scot with the yellow hair. Give him his pack so he can rally the spirits, he said. You must call the gods, he said, because they are confused and fleeing!" She gestured to one of the guards, who dropped Duncan's tattered pack at his side.

Duncan took several long breaths, studying Conawago, trying to understand. Then he slowly nodded. "Everyone must leave," he said. "Heap more cedar on the corner fires, then make a circle around the lodge and chant the mourning song until you hear my call."

He stood silently over his friend when the chamber was emptied, pulling down the robe and gazing at the flint knife. Sagatchie would say the gods had given him the opportunity to perform the warrior's duty. Instead he pulled up the robe and took the old man's hand. "I will do this my friend, but I do it to call you back. You are still needed in this world. The children need you. Your nephew needs you." Duncan's eyes misted. "I need you," he whispered after a moment, and to his joy the leathery hand squeezed his.

A hundred voices began chanting outside.

He leapt up, unloading his pack to reach the bundle wrapped in old muslin at the bottom, the only thing of his old life that had come with him across the sea. He thrust the thin reeds in his mouth to moisten them as he reverently laid out the intricately carved drones and chanter. It was minutes before the drones were tuned and the bladder filled with air, but at last he clamped the blowstick in his teeth and fingered the chanter.

The first notes of the pipes always wrenched his heart. A door opened somewhere inside his mind and images flooded out, of his grandfather in his fishing dory, his mother laughing as lambs frolicked around her, his youngest brother riding on their father's broad shoulder. He paced slowly around the platform as he played, choosing the old solemn tunes, the music of Highland ritual. Before leaving the chamber, he extracted the snakeskin he had taken from the ashes of Hetty's hut and tied it around his head.

When he finally stepped into the entry, every torchlit face locked on him, wearing expressions of awe and, on some, fear.

As he began to circle the small lodge, walking through the scented smoke of the cedar boughs, the members of the Revelator's army dropped to their knees. Several Scots scattered among them raised their bonnets in salute. Macaulay, near the front, stood with half a dozen other Highlanders, his eyes clouding, his bonnet held tightly to his chest. On his second circuit the ranks parted to make way for the half-king and his guards.

"Enough!" he shouted. He had obviously been elsewhere, or asleep, not aware of the summons that had come through Conawago. "Enough!" he repeated as Duncan continued, staring defiantly at him. The half-king's eyes were wild with anger. Scar, at his side, lifted his war ax. Duncan played even more loudly. He would rather die like this, with his clan's pipes in hand, than tied to a post.

The Revelator grabbed the ax from his deputy and was advancing on Duncan when a high-pitched scream rose from inside the lodge. His pipes sputtered to silence.

The scream continued for longer than Duncan would have considered possible, a high ululation that uncannily seemed to match the sound of the pipes, as if it were some response from the other side. Those gathered nearest the entry suddenly shrank back as an otherworldly figure materialized out of the shadows inside. The half-king gasped and stepped behind his warriors.

The creature's hair was matted with thick red pigment, which ran down her bare shoulders. She was naked except for a cloth looped around her waist, her skin covered with dried moss and feathers of many colors and shapes. Where patches of skin showed there was only a slippery, slimy substance. Several of those nearest him looked back in alarm at Duncan as though they were convinced he had summoned the creature from the other world.

Not until she spoke did recognition dawn in Duncan.

"They are angry!" the woman cried out in a scratchy birdlike voice.

"The gods say you ignore the ways of the people!" Her pale eyes were wild. "The gods say treat with the Grand Council or be damned!"

"It's just the damned Welsh woman!" the Revelator growled, but no one seemed to hear him. It was indeed not Hetty Eldridge before them but Hetty the seer, Hetty the witch who had once frightened the tribes so much they had sent her back to the Europeans. The half-king could not eject her, for his disciples had embraced her as an oracle.

She did a strange dance now, a stuttering step of two paces forward and one back, bobbing her head like a bird all the while as she murmured words Duncan could not understand, waving long skeleton arms at the assembly. Not exactly arms, just femur bones extending beyond her hands that she gripped so tightly they seemed part of her body. She shouted the haunting words in a harsh, screeching voice, her head now raised to the moon, then every few paces she halted, lowered her head, and aimed her bones at the ranks of frightened onlookers. Nearly every Indian gripped his or her protective amulet. Then finally she swept her bone-arm around the assembly and stopped when it pointed to the Revelator. She spoke now in the tongue of the Haudenosaunee. "The gods say the Council must be respected!" she screeched, then she switched back to her alien tongue before taking up her jarring dance again. The Revelator tried to reach her, but she kept moving in and out of the crowd, which closed about her as she passed. The words were long mouthfuls of consonants, sounds that began to sound oddly familiar to Duncan.

"The old ones say the piper and the Nipmucs speak for them! They must bring the truth of the Revelator to the Council!" she cried when she stopped again, then relapsed to the strange language.

Suddenly Duncan recognized the tongue, if not the words. Hetty was speaking Welsh.

"With the piper and the Nipmucs, we will reach across and bring them the truth of the Revelator!" she screeched, then she collapsed in a cloud of feathers.

THE CANOES SANG the waters, the Haudenosaunee were fond of saying in describing swift water passages. For two days their narrow bark vessels did indeed sing. They had help from the half-king's men over the ancient carrying place to the shore of the lake called Oneida, and their two canoes had then raced over the smooth waters and into the river that would take them to the central hearth of the Haudenosaunee at Onondaga Castle. Duncan and Macaulay, whom the Revelator had insisted would escort them, paddled the first canoe with Conawago lying on blankets, tended by Ishmael. Sagatchie and Kass, themselves representatives of the Haudenosaunee whom the oracle had said the half-king must respect, propelled the second with Hetty between them, nearly as weak as the old Nipmuc. She too had an attendant, who lay beside her, sometimes licking her like a docile puppy. The hell dog had leapt into the canoe when they had laid her inside, and no one had been inclined to resist him.

After nearly sinking when an old patch on the canoe had sheared away, Duncan insisted they make camp in the early evening to allow Conawago a hot meal and a comfortable night's rest. They had pulled their vessels onto an island where a grove of pines provided a soft carpet of needles near a sandy beach. Duncan's old friend had been rapidly improving, confirming his suspicion that his condition had been caused by something ingested, not physical injuries. When he had awakened in the canoe and realized who the youth at his side was, Conawago's joyful cries had echoed over the lake.

Duncan and Ishmael settled Conawago against a tree. Then, as Ishmael sat at the old man's side, Duncan followed a path down which Hetty, also much stronger, had disappeared. He found her kneeling beside the river's edge, rubbing wet sand through her matted, tangled hair. Farther down the beach, Sagatchie and Kass were repairing the damaged canoe with fresh bark and pine pitch. The leak had started so abruptly Duncan had thought they had collided with a log. Had Duncan not quickly stuffed a blanket into the hole they surely would have sunk in the deep water.

"What you did at the half-king's camp," he said to her back, finding it oddly awkward to speak to the woman. "I'd be tied to a post missing parts of my body by now if you hadn't . . ."

"I warned you, son," she said without turning. "You didn't know how to speak to the Revelator."

"Meaning I should have poured honey over my body and rolled in feathers and moss?"

The Welsh woman made a grunting sound that may have been a laugh as she rubbed sand on her skin. "That old Seneca woman who tended us knew me from years ago. She told me the half-king was feeding your friend mushrooms that kept him on his back and brought his visions. Everyone was talking about how he had just appeared in the Lightning Lodge, speaking in a tongue no one could recognize. If the half-king had been alone I'm sure he would have killed him, but his men were scared and insisted Conawago had come across for a reason. They would not touch the sacred knife he clutched, for they said it was a weapon of the old gods."

Duncan cocked his head in surprise, not at the word of Conawago but at Hetty. She was speaking to him like some elderly aunt.

"I made her stop those mushrooms." Hetty kept clearing the dried honey from her hair as she spoke. "He is one of the old ones who must be preserved. The knowledge of all the forest people resides in his heart."

"I had a grandfather who kept our old ways alive," Duncan said. "I would have given my life to preserve him. But the English army hanged him."

Hetty glanced over her shoulder. "You weren't going to preserve Conawago by taunting the Revelator. You were a fool to seek him out."

"I wasn't necessarily seeking out the half-king, Mrs. Eldridge. I was following you and Ishmael."

"So you would throw your life away in pursuit of an old woman and an orphaned boy?"

"And five lost children captured with their schoolmaster. You are the one who sought the half-king," he reminded her. "You expected the half-king to have your son. Did you see signs of him, or the children?"

The Welsh woman sluiced water through her long greying hair before finally turning to Duncan. "I have never had need of money, but I went to the settlements because those damned lawyers only respect money. All these years I stayed in that cramped town sewing lace so English prigs would look pretty at their dancing balls. I hate towns. I only did it for my son." She grabbed a handful of hair and began wringing the water from it. There was no longer anything sinister about her. She was just a tired old woman.

Duncan hesitated, confused by the remorse in her voice. He realized he had missed the most important point. "The half-king also sought you. Why? How did he know you?"

She ignored his questions.

"Then why do this, why change your path? You should be going north, to the Saint Lawrence, that has to be where the raiders went, where your son and the children are. Runners came from the North with drawings from the children. They are alive. Henry Bedford is the strength of those children. He's been keeping them safe, at God knows what cost."

She did not reply. Something at the camp had changed her mind about where to search for her son or how to obtain his release. Her performance as the screeching oracle had been calculated to free them to go south.

"You must be very proud of him," he ventured. "He's very brave." He could not bring himself to share what he had read on Hannah's note. The schoolmaster was being tortured to save the children.

She found a piece of moss knotted in her hair and bent to untangle it.

He realized she would talk no more of her son. "When you spoke to me in Albany," he tried instead, "you said White George stumbles. I did not understand then. You meant King George. You knew about the Revelator when no one else in Albany did."

"I am a witch, boy."

"When I was young a band of mummers came to the market town near my home. My father took me. They had an African witch who danced and shook rattles and terrified me. Later I looked under her tent and saw her preparing for a performance. It was just an old hag who was blacking her skin with burnt cork."

"You are a fool if you believe only what your eyes see." She straightened, and her eyes narrowed. "Shall I tell you how you will die, Duncan McCallum?"

"I want to know how five children will not die."

The words brought a hard, intense stare from the woman. "There's an island in the North," she replied. "The children will enter, but no children will leave."

A shiver ran down Duncan's spine. He could not tell if it was the old aunt or the witch who spoke now. "Then tell me this: Why did you go west toward the Mingoes when Mingoes tried to kill you in Albany?"

Hetty's uneven grin revealed a missing tooth. "You don't think I know how to make a Mingo arrow, boy? I burnt my own cabin down."

He stared at her in disbelief. A dozen questions leapt into his mind, but then he saw Hetty looking over his shoulder. He turned to see Ishmael standing on the bank above them, looking at them with a pleading expression. "I don't know what to do," the boy said.

Conawago was bent over Macaulay. The big Scot had lain down for a quick rest but wasn't getting up. He seemed to be in a restless sleep. Duncan checked his pulse. "He probably hasn't slept in two or three days," he said. "Just exhaustion. Leave him be."

When Macaulay awoke in the evening, he accepted a mug of one of Conawago's teas then leaned against a tree to listen with the others as Sagatchie and Conawago told tales of heroes who were now constellations in the sky. Even Hetty offered a legend, of dragons that fought in the skies of a long lost land called Wales, flying so high they became creatures of the stars as well. Ishmael, lying on his blanket and pointing out shapes in the sky, took delight in learning that while he had always known the cluster of stars overhead as the Dancers, the Welsh called them the Pack of Dogs, the Scots called them the Sisters, and the English called them the Pleiades.

The moon was high when Duncan awoke in a sweat. He had been dreaming of dead Scots again, but this time his father had not pointed at him from the gibbet but toward a dull glow beyond a hill. When he reached the top he discovered Conawago tied to a post, singing his death chant as flames consumed him. Huge warriors encircled the fire, joining in his chant, facing outward to assure no one disturbed his dying.

He sat in the moonlight, trying again to link the pieces of the puzzle before him. Dead Mohawks at Bethel Church. Captive children being taken north to be killed. A missing treasure of the British king. A witch who sought out the half-king. He threw wood on the fire and by the flickering light examined once more the slips of paper he had brought from Henry Bedford's school. The raiders had only killed the children whose names matched those of the families at the settlement. What was different about these children? Why did the raiders trouble over them? He turned the papers over and not for the first time puzzled over the lines and arcs drawn on the original side of the paper. The strokes were bold and deliberate. They could have been part of a design, a drawing for a mechanical device. He extracted the musket ball he had cut from Conawago's shoulder and rolled it between his fingers, gazing up at the moon.

With a sudden start he found the hell dog at his side, but the creature simply settled down with his head on Duncan's leg. A nighthawk trilled from a nearby tree. A woman laughed. A duck called out from the river.

A woman laughed. The hell dog was suddenly up and alert, circling the fire. It glanced at Duncan then looked toward the river. Duncan grabbed his rifle and together they stole down the path. They halted in the shadows as two figures rose up out of the water, thirty feet apart. Instinctively he raised his gun, then he slowly lowered it.

The water glistened on their naked bodies as Sagatchie and Kass approached each other on the sandy beach. The dog cocked its head in curiosity. Kassawaya spoke softly, Sagatchie laughed, and the Oneida woman pulled him down with her onto the sand. The moon would not be refused.

Duncan touched the dog's head, and they retreated back to camp.

The corporal was not inclined to stir in the morning, and Conawago insisted he was strong enough to paddle, so they laid Macaulay in the canoe. By early afternoon he had a raging fever and was thrashing about so much they had no choice but to pull onto the riverbank. Duncan clenched his jaw as he studied the soldier. He was hot to the touch, and pustules were erupting on his face.

"I'll be fine," the corporal said in a hoarse voice. "Just a bit of tea, lad."

They stayed on the shore, making an early camp. The tea Conawago brewed from several different leaves quieted Macaulay's ragged breathing, but Duncan knew it would bring only temporary comfort.

"A little rest," the burly corporal kept repeating. But Duncan had seen the misery in his eyes, and he conferred with Hetty then urgently ordered Sagatchie and Kass to stay away, to make their own camp down the river.

As the setting sun washed the camp in a coppery light, Macaulay asked to be propped up against a tree. "I was only in that damned death cave less than an hour," he groaned. "It's like that cursed darkness followed me out of the ground."

"People can get smallpox by brushing someone on the street or standing in a tavern crowd," Duncan said in a tight voice.

"Standing in a tavern," Macaulay repeated. "Let's say it was from kissing a bonny lass," he added, forcing a smile. Duncan saw fear in his eyes now. Hetty, who had confirmed that she had survived several smallpox epidemics in the past, had stayed in camp and now appeared with a small birch bark pail of water. She tore off a patch at the bottom of her skirt and began wiping Macaulay's brow.

"I survived Ticonderoga," the corporal said, as if in protest. "Every man in my squad died, but I swore I wouldn't let that damned fool English general get me killed. I fought the French up and down the lakes."

"Is he dying?" Ishmael asked as they gathered more firewood.

"He began dying the moment he followed us into the lower depths of the iron hole."

"But he's built like a bull."

"The army loses more men to disease than it does to battle."

Ishmael jerked around as a sudden roar burst from the camp. Duncan ran back, expecting a bear. It was the Scottish bull, raging at the hand fate had dealt him. Macaulay, impossibly, had hauled himself up and was stumbling toward the river, bellowing his anger. He faltered as Duncan arrived, staggering toward the river, struggling to lift one leg, then the other. As Duncan reached him he collapsed with his arm in the water.

"The damned fever . . . If I can but cool the flames in my head," Macaulay moaned as Duncan hauled him upright. He had used up his strength. They had to half-drag the big man back to his pallet of pine needles, where he dropped into unconsciousness.

When Macaulay woke it was hours later. He stared up at the gibbous moon. They both knew he would not see the sun again.

"I remember sailing into Stornaway harbor with a boat full of halibut," Duncan said, raising a weak smile on the big Scot's face. "My grandfather would trade the fish for tweed from the islands. There would always be women in the square working the cloth, singing the waulking songs," he said, referring to the ancient rhythmic chants used by groups of island women as they kneaded the hard fibers on planks. "It was magical. He had to drag me away when they were singing."

"Aye, my mother used to make me sing them with her as we chopped peat out of the moor," Macaulay remembered. As Hetty wiped his brow, Macaulay tried to sing in a faltering voice, but the effort ended in a spell of ragged coughing.

"I'm sorry, lad," the deserter said after a long silence. He fixed Duncan with a weak but steady gaze.

"Not your fault," Hetty replied, stroking his head as though he were her little child. Ishmael held the corporal's hand.

"That's not what he means," Duncan said.

The corporal gazed toward the moon. "'T'is a grand notion, is it not? Raising the colors of the clans on this side of the sea. Think of the gatherings we'll have. The flash of the plaid as we dance the swords, the singing of the lasses." His weakened hand opened and revealed a worn knot of white ribbon that had been pressed tight in his palm. It was the white cockade of the Jacobite rebels. "Take it, lad."

Duncan stared at the ribbon but made no move to lift it from Macaulay's palm. "I had an old uncle who was a riever," Duncan said, referring to the highwaymen of Scotland. "He said there was no dishonor in taking a man's cows if he were fool enough to let you, but you never killed a man for them."

"We're not talking cows, Clan McCallum." Macaulay pointedly used the form of address for clan chiefs. "We're talking about taking back what was taken from us, setting the scales in balance. I seem to recall a lot of cannons and nooses used against us."

"Innocent men and women were slaughtered at Bethel Church. They had no stake in that cause."

"It's war, lad."

"When were you going to perform your act of war, Corporal?" Duncan asked. "While we slept? A quick blade to the throat?"

Hetty's hand, about to wipe the man's brow again, stopped in midair. "Duncan, do not speak such nonsense," she said in a tight voice.

"Sagatchie said the patch on the canoe that pulled away had been pried at with a blade to loosen it. It would have been the easiest way, to have all three witnesses from Bethel Church drown."

Macaulay gazed up at the sky without responding. He was past lying.

"When we were in the iron hole, you asked about the settlement where MacLeod died. It was only much later when I realized I hadn't said anything about a settlement. You were not guilty of insubordination. You were sent in there to watch the boy."

The hell dog paced around the dying man, sniffing at his limbs, then pushing Hetty away with its muzzle.

"The half-king spoke of a letter taken to the general," Duncan continued, "a supposed message from me to the French. The conspirators didn't even know I existed until the day I was shoved into the prison hole in

Albany. You disappeared after we escaped. You told them about me, and they saw that I could be their perfect pawn. That's when they laid their plans for the forged letter. The deserters who attacked Sagatchie were looking for us, following us, just as Hawley was, but Macaulay's dirk in his back stopped that."

Duncan spoke to Hetty now. "When Macaulay went ahead with you, it was to let the half-king know I was coming. But you interfered with his plans, Hetty, when you made sure we would be going to the Iroquois Council. The half-king was furious but he could not stop it. There could be only one reason Corporal Macaulay came with us. The Revelator gave him a mission, a special task."

The brawny Scot turned his head toward Duncan, his eyes full of melancholy. "I protested, lad, said you were harmless." His words were labored.

"But the half-king insisted," Duncan said. "He is at war. He received word from the North, word about the children that somehow made him confident that he would win over the Council even without us. He had to let us go because the oracle demanded it in front of his followers. But we could do more damage than good to his cause, so he told you to kill us. It had to be you, since you were the only one in his camp who could get close to us."

Macaulay did not disagree.

"How many Scots take orders from him?"

When Macaulay did not reply, Duncan tried another tack. "Tell me this, then, Corporal. Did you come with us out of the iron hole to escape or because I showed an interest in Ishmael?"

"You have it wrong, lad. I was not following the half-king's orders when I went into the hole."

Duncan hesitated. His gaze drifted back to the white cockade still in Macaulay's hand. He had thought the big man's talk about the clans rising was his fever talking, but now he was not so sure. "You're saying it was a Scottish officer who sent you? Who, Macaulay, who ordered you into the iron hole? They killed you by doing so."

Macaulay looked away, throwing his arm over his fevered brow. Duncan sat, waiting for him to speak, but soon realized he had lost consciousness again.

It was after midnight when Conawago found Duncan where he kept watch by the river. "He asks for you. I think he has little time left."

When Macaulay reached out for Duncan's hand, his grip was as weak as a bairn's. "It's all in secret, lad. There's white cockades all over the regiments now. I ne'er heard a word about killing women and children. I don't know where it starts. Someone near the top. If I knew I'd tell ye so ye can trade for yer life when the general takes ye. I did wrong by ye. I kept hoping ye would give me reason to dislike ye." A fit of rattling coughs seized the big Scot. His lungs were filling with fluid. When he spoke again his breathing was labored. "Back home in Stornaway, a priest would come at the end and listen to the dying man's confession."

"I am here, Corporal."

A bitter grin twisted Macaulay's face. "I'm sorry for the sixteen men I've killed in battle," he said after a few struggling breaths. "I could have just wounded most of them, but I chose not to. I'm sorry for the two men I've killed in anger. I'm sorry I have not written me precious mother these four years past. I'm sorry for the wenches I've abandoned and the profane words I have spoken. I'm sorry I did not believe me mother when she said me grandmother was a selkie, kin to the seals." He turned away in another fit of coughing, then reached out and pulled Duncan closer. "Look past the savages to the good the cause can do. Ye can make a good life in the North, with yer own people."

The effort of speaking seemed to have sapped the little strength the Scot had left. Macaulay reached out for Duncan's hand, and when Duncan looked down, the white cockade was in his palm.

It was a long time before he opened his eyes again. "It's time to call them in," he whispered in Gaelic, and for a moment Duncan thought it was just a fevered rant. "Can you reach them from so far away, lad? I worry that being so deep in the woods I'll just drop into the heaven of the tribes."

"I can reach them," Duncan promised, and when he turned Conawago was extending his pack to him.

An owl returned the call when he piped his first few notes. He started with one of the odes to Bonnie Prince Charlie, then tunes the island clans used when sending boats out to sea. Conawago sat at Macaulay's side and gripped one of his hands, while Macaulay's other hand clutched his dirk. Sometime during a haunting ballad for selkies or a call to battle, the tormented Highlander crossed over to the other side.

Chapter Ten

"*N ai raxhottahyh!*" the old man intoned over the fire of the Grand Council of the Iroquois. "Hail my grandfathers, hearken while your grandchildren cry to you, for the Great League grows old!"

Duncan sat in the shadows behind Conawago, watching, trying to catch the Haudenosaunee words as they were spoken. Conawago had warned him that nothing in the town that was the heart of the Iroquois world would be as it seemed. It would be simpler and more complex than Duncan expected, uglier and more beautiful, the old Nimpuc had declared. Any notion of a grand woodland palace had quickly disappeared when they reached the Onondaga village. Onondaga Castle on its face appeared to be just another worn palisaded town, not much larger than others he had seen. In fact it was not as well protected as many since its population was scattered outside the walls in small lodges and cabins along the riverbank. Only now as Duncan began to relax, grateful for the simple pleasure of warm tea and a safe, soft place to sit, did he begin to notice the subtle differences, the hints that something greater lay hidden beneath the surface.

Cedar smoke wafted from several large, shallow bowls along the perimeter of the central plaza, the scented air calling in the spirits. There were poles arranged around the clearing, many of them intricately carved with turtles, beaver, bears, and other signs of the Haudenosaunee clans. The plaza itself was in fact a shallow bowl of packed earth, with flat tiers rising like concentric rings broken by an aisle that led directly into the largest of the longhouses. It was the simplest of amphitheaters, perfectly designed for public speaking. Duncan had met an old Dutch trader months before who spent an evening speaking with him of his years with the woodland tribes. The Iroquois leaders were not feared warriors, the Dutchman had declared, but feared orators, known for breaking entire woodland nations with the force of their words.

There was a rigid liturgy in all Council meetings, Conawago had explained to him. There would be no business conducted until the members had expressed respect to the spirits and gratitude for what was known as the Iroquois Peace. Deceased chiefs, some gone for centuries, would then be praised, and the ancient laws of the League invoked, the most sacred of which was that war may never be fought among tribes of the League. It was on this last point that the speakers now lingered, Conawago explained in a whisper. The Mingoes were, in the view of the Council, a subordinate tribe of the federation, yet under the self-proclaimed half-king they were acting apart, without the blessing or authority of the Council. As the old chiefs began the second hour of oration, a wiry, leather-faced elder dominated the discussion, an Oneida named Custaloga. He was one of the few on the Council who had served as a war chief, decades earlier, then become a peace chief, now second ranking on the Council. The old man, easily as old as Conawago, had a noble, refined air about him, and those on the Council and those who sat behind them listened in rapt silence as he spoke of past glories of the League.

"Hearken while your grandchildren cry." Duncan did not understand all the words the wise old sachem spoke, but he knew those and recognized them again and again in Custaloga's speech. The sachems who made up the council, and the old matrons sitting behind them, with whom the sachems frequently conferred, were clearly distraught. The federation, so powerful for hundreds of years, was starting to show age and decay.

There was a strange fierceness in the old man's voice, and Duncan saw now that whenever he paused he glanced at an aged woman sitting close by. In the last century, the League had been hit hard by enemies from the North. Entire Iroquois settlements had been annihilated, and the French and northern tribes had laid ambushes that had killed scores of Iroquois warriors. The town where they sat now was not the original Onondaga Castle. Another one, another capital town, had been destroyed, most of its inhabitants massacred, in a surprise attack by the Hurons. Custaloga and the senior chief, Atotarho, had been there, had witnessed the near toppling of the federation. Over half of the Haudenosaunee population had been lost, entire towns obliterated, many loved ones captured and taken into slavery by Huron and other enemy tribes.

Nearly every member of the Council spoke, and as they entered into the third hour, with the sun sinking low, Duncan found his gaze wandering, seeing now Ishmael walking with Kass along the palisade wall, where sentries armed with muskets walked. The big braziers that burned cedar, lit whenever the Council was convened, were being supplemented with more fires and pinepitch torches. Young braves carried firewood inside the adjacent lodge, where the main Council fire, the perpetual hearth of the League, was kept burning. Their day's labor finished, Iroquois families were filing in through the gate, settling in the growing shadows around the Council ring. The faces of young and old alike seemed fixed with the same expression of solemn anxiety.

Conawago touched Duncan's arm. A group of newcomers, one of them wearing European clothes and a wide-brimmed black hat, had appeared in the shadows and were urgently speaking among themselves. As he watched, all but two retreated toward the river landing. The remaining two approached the Council ring. One of them, wearing a doeskin shirt with ornate quillwork, was being urged into the ring by his companion, a tribesman who wore the cut-down blue jacket of a British navy officer.

Custaloga rose and paced around the ring, pointing to the newcomer. "It is the nephew of Custaloga," Conawago whispered. "He has been living among the Senecas, in the West. He is called Black Fish, once a mighty warrior." The man being brought into the ring no longer had the appearance of a great warrior. His belly bulged out, his face was aged beyond his years. Yet as Custaloga related Black Fish's history and his blood ties with those present, then draped a strand of white wampum over his nephew's hand, he was greeted with sober deference.

The man spoke too fast for Duncan to follow, but he saw Conawago's face tighten as he listened. "Black Fish has visited all the major settlements of the League to explain that he has the same dream every night," Conawago explained. "Such a dream will be taken as an important sign by the tribes, one that can never be ignored." As Duncan leaned closer the old Nipmuc began translating the man's exact words.

"Now is the time of night that the graves gape wide and let forth the ghosts!" Black Fish exclaimed in a louder orator's voice, raising his face toward the rising moon.

Conawago's translation ended as Black Fish's speech grew more animated, and even louder. The Nipmuc stared in mute surprise, worry etching his face. The middle-aged warrior was shouting now, leaping about and swinging his arms, jerking his body and crying out in pain from invisible wounds. He was acting out a terrible struggle. As he finished he dropped to his knees and raised his hands toward the heavens and began repeating the same phrases over and over. Duncan needed no translation. "The Revelator is sent by the gods! The Revelator is our father!" he cried out. "The Revelator is sent by the gods! The League will die without the Revelator!" He shouted louder and louder, flailing his arms against his chest as if possessed until finally collapsing onto the ground.

The man in the blue jacket rushed forward to help Black Fish to his feet and escort him away. His speech had sapped all his strength. Conawago studied him intensely as he disappeared among the onlookers. Duncan saw that the other elders watched as well, most with deep alarm on their faces.

"His story spreads around to every Iroquois hearth, exciting all those who hear it," Conawago explained. "Black Fish has been there, to the other side, Duncan! Sometimes he is abruptly summoned and falls down and is instantly transported there, always to the same place. At first he wanders in a thick fog but then spirits of the long dead find him and take him to a huge bark lodge." Conawago paused, gazing into the fire. He was clearly troubled by Black Fish's message. "In it sits Dekanawidah and the other great chiefs who were the founders of the Iroquois League, and his heart fills with joy. But then the ghost of a huge Englishman approaches the founders from behind, raising a sword, intending to stab the ancient one, to kill the first god. Black Fish then sees behind the intruder the shapes of the other original spirits, lying dead with knives in their hearts. Spirits. The spirits have been killed! Suddenly a man runs past Black Fish and wrestles the Englishman. It is the half-king, and he beats down the Englishman and shouts out that he will save the founders from the other English demons, shaped like humans but with horses' heads, who approach through the mist. Then the spirits declare that the half-king is their revelator, who shall speak for them on earth. Dekanawidah declares that if the League does not listen then the places they hold sacred, the places that connect the Iroquois to the other side, will be destroyed. That which cannot fall will fall. That which cannot burn will burn. And when all the original spirits die, the gates to the other side will be closed forever. "

Conawago took a long, heavy breath. The Nipmuc was clearly shaken by the words. "He says after his first vision he found the Revelator lying in the forest with bears sitting all around him as if to protect him, and though the Revelator was dead, the biggest of the bears bent over him and breathed into his mouth and the dead man sprang back to life. Ever since, the Mingoes bend their knee to him, and now the Haudenosaunee must as well if they wish to survive."

The Council had no response to the terrible pronouncements of Black Fish. Most of the Council members silently stared into the fire. Suddenly the old sachem Atotarho rose, followed by the other members of the Council. The leader spoke a quick syllable, and the silence was broken, the Council dismissed.

As Duncan turned toward Conawago, the oldest of the matriarchs, who had sat behind Atotarho, appeared at their side. "We wish you to come with us," she said in a near whisper, as if wanting to avoid being overheard, then introduced herself as Adanahoe.

As they passed through the palisade wall, Custaloga joined them, holding a torch. He greeted Conawago as an old friend and guided them to the top of the ridge overlooking the town.

"Onondaga Castle has been built half a dozen times, in different places but always near a sacred ground to keep the Council anchored to the spirits," Custaloga said when he halted. "We do not speak openly of such places. Many in the tribes would not know exactly how to find them. The Council members know and sometimes take their families there, or young ones who show promise of becoming a chieftain." The old sachem studied the town below, lit by the moon and torches, then led them up a steep ridge behind the first, along a path that was a channel between high boulders. Soon they reached a flat near the top, an expanse of ledge rock where stones were strangely twisted and misshapen. "The Mouth of Dekanawidah we call this place," Custaloga explained. "For many generations we have come here to listen. The voice from the other side was low, like a whisper. Often we could not understand it, but it was always reassuring because we knew it came from the other side."

He halted at a gnarled piece of rock in the center of a shallow bowl of solid stone. Surrounding the bowl were boulders as high as a man's waist, painted with tribal symbols. The center rock was shaped roughly like a human head, and a strong cool current of air blew from the crack that was its mouth.

"I came to sit with it last night. I stayed all night, speaking old words in the hope it might heal itself. But it will speak no more to us," Custaloga said in a melancholy tone, and he lowered the torch.

Duncan saw now how the rock around what had been a narrow mouth was chipped and broken and the surface of the rock itself strangely blistered.

"I would always come here on the night of the full moon. Last month when I arrived it was on fire. The rock was on fire!" The old man explained in an anguished voice. "I never would have believed it had I not seen it with my own eyes. And now the mouth will speak no more." The sachem looked up at them. "Then tonight Black Fish spoke, who has not been here for years. That which cannot fall will fall, he said. The side of the mountain fell over a sacred cave near the Oneida towns. The Oneida had honored the spirits there for as far back as memory reaches. Now that which cannot burn has burned, and the gods stop speaking with us." The old chief wiped his hand along the rock and raised it, spilling out grey powder. "It is dust."

Duncan bent low to the stone and rubbed his finger along the surface. A dark greasy residue came away on his finger. He sniffed it. It was not gunpowder, nor any substance he knew. It would have been easy enough to smash the mouth with a hammer, but rock could not burn.

"It is dust," Custaloga repeated in a mournful tone. "Without the spirits we become dust."

No one replied.

By the time their silent, troubled procession returned to the palisade, the Iroquois families had dispersed, but there was new activity outside the Council lodge. The sachems had held their meeting before the inhabitants of the Castle and now continued their business more privately, within the lodge. Custaloga motioned Conawago and Duncan inside, following the other elders. Duncan paused outside the entrance and quickly scanned the shadows, finding Kass with her arm around Ishmael's shoulder. The Oneida woman nodded at Duncan. She would stay with the boy as the sacred work of the Council proceeded.

The longhouse was like no other Duncan had ever seen. The beams that supported the large structure were carefully worked, bound with joints and pins, the supporting posts all carved with images of forest life. To the left of the entry was one of the chambers typically used as a family's apartment, separated by walls of sewn skins. But this chamber held two older women. One, an elegant looking woman whose braids had red yarn woven through them, was solemnly stringing beads while at her side the second chanted a low song. They were assembling a wampum belt, one of the official messages sent from the Grand Council, said to be empowered by the spirits. Above them, arrayed on plank shelves, were cylinders of birch bark bound with sinew. A similar container lay before the women. The containers all held wampum belts, he realized, some probably going back generations. He was looking at the archive of the League of the Haudenosaunee.

Beyond the chamber was a great open space extending the full width of the building and twice as deep. The Council members were sitting in a circle, some on low split log benches, some on fur cushions around a large fire ring where fragrant wood burned. As Conawago began leading Duncan toward one of the empty benches near the back, Custaloga motioned them in the opposite direction. They hesitated, glancing uncertainly at each other. The chief was directing them to an open place beside himself and Atotarho, a place of great honor beside the perpetual hearth.

As Duncan and Conawago completed the circle of the Council, Atotarho began an invocation of the spirits, extending a smoldering shank of tobacco to each of the four directions. One of the old women behind the sachems began a singsong chant, pausing at intervals for others to respond. "*Ak wah*," the sachems repeated in unison at each pause. Yea truly.

Duncan found himself studying the chamber from which the great League was governed. Garlands of feathers hung along the wall behind the speakers, some composed entirely of hawk and eagle feathers, others entirely of the red and yellow feathers of small songbirds. Battered war axes hung between two such garlands, cornhusk dolls between two others. Along the adjacent walls hung robes of fur and feather and stretched doeskins adorned with figures of animals, trees, and many symbols Duncan did not recognize. Some of the skins seemed to be of great age, and he realized they told stories of events from prior centuries. He saw Conawago's eyes straying as well, and he knew the old Nipmuc yearned to study the robes and chronicle skins.

Custaloga, now wearing a fox fur on his shoulder, was speaking. His rich voice was slow enough that Duncan could understand many of his words. He was describing the Haudenosaunee nation, sometimes gesticulating to the doeskin pictograms on the walls.

The League of the Haudenosaunee was without rival. Every tribe from the great salt water to the Ohio country feared the Iroquois and also loved them, for they knew the Iroquois brought harmony. Because no tribe would dare bring war to defy the Grand Council, the peoples of all the woodlands lived in peace, at one with the spirits. Custaloga's speech was interrupted by long pauses in which he pointed at the old chronicles on the wall, as if to invoke their stories. Duncan saw now the bloodstains on some of the old skins, the charred edges of others. A sadness entered the sachem's voice.

This was in the past, Custaloga admitted. The seventeenth century had been the pinnacle of Iroquois empire. Then the French had armed the northern tribes, and the League had been battered in battle after battle. He pointed to a skin on which scores of humans lay sprawling on the ground while others were being led away in captive straps.

When Custaloga finally sat back in the circle, another chieftain rose to receive a long birch bark container from one of the female elders. He paced around the circle with the container before stopping before Atotarho and ceremoniously opening the container. The old sachem lifted out a long pipe and held it aloft, calling for the gods to open their hearts and come join the circle of elders.

The pipe was filled with tobacco, lit with a burning cedar stick, then slowly carried around the ring, each chieftain solemnly taking it to his lips. When the sachems were finished, the pipe was extended to Conawago, then to Duncan, who found his hand trembling as he accepted the ancient instrument. He felt like a small boy before ancient sages.

"Have you come to speak of the final fate of the Haudenosaunee?" The words were spoken by Atotarho the moment Duncan handed back the pipe, so abruptly and in such well-formed English that Duncan stared at the Council leader in mute confusion before realizing they were directed toward Conawago and himself.

"I have come," Conawago replied, "to discuss the fate of our gods."

The words seemed to offend several of the sachems, who murmured words of alarm until a strong voice rang clear from the shadows. Sagatchie stepped forward, pointing out that no one had properly introduced the great Conawago, eldest of the Nipmuc tribe, who had once been the spiritual caretakers of all the forest people. He reminded them of how Conawago and Duncan had helped the Onondaga chief Skanawati restore honor to his people the year before, and how they both wore the mark of the dawnchasers.

The words brought a sober repose to the circle, and when Conawago spoke again all eyes were on him. He explained that the Revelator had sent them to ask the Council to join the cause of the half-king.

"Ask or demand?" asked Atotarho.

"It is not for me to impose another's will on the Council."

"What does the Revelator offer our people?"

"He would stop the rum that poisons many of the tribes. He would unite all the tribes to retake their lands. He would bring back old ways."

"The Revelator's path is full of blood," the old chieftain observed.

"The path without the Revelator is full of blood," Conawago replied.

The sachem's nod was solemn. "If the gods are asking, how can we refuse?" He directed the ancient pipe to be rekindled and passed around the circle.

Conawago puffed on the sacred pipe before answering. "But first," he finally replied, "we must be certain of who is asking. Is this Mingo called the Revelator a war chief or a peace chief?"

The chamber was suddenly very still. Duncan realized his friend had asked the essential question. The anchor of the great federation, the reason it had endured for so long, was the separation of warriors from the wise old sachems. War chiefs were not permitted to sit on the Council or to determine the course of a tribe's action, only those called peace chiefs were able to do so. Otherwise, the woodlands would have been in a constant state of war. It was only the peace chiefs, and the matriarchs who always advised them, who could send their people to war, and only then did the war chiefs play a role. For the Council to yield to the vengeful renegade leader would be to turn its back on its sacred law.

Atotarho nodded very slowly and raised his hands into the air over his head as if beseeching the heavens. He turned to Adanahoe, sitting behind him, who whispered in his ear, then the first chieftain gestured toward a small figure sitting beside the female elders. In her simple doeskin dress, Hetty Eldridge looked more relaxed than Duncan had ever seen her. Some of the lines in her face had vanished. Her hair had a twist of red wool in it, after the Mohawk fashion. Beside her the hell dog watched attentively. The sachem waited until Hetty stood, stepped toward Duncan and Conawago, and sat behind them. They had their matriarch as well. Atotarho motioned for Duncan to take the pipe again, then waited for Duncan to exhale a long plume of smoke before speaking. "Why have you chosen this journey, McCallum?"

"A wise old Nipmuc was tortured and killed. Children were taken."

"Are you the protector of Nipmucs, then?" the elder sachem asked.

Duncan glanced at Conawago, who kept his gaze on the head of the council. "I do not sleep well when innocent people are slain."

Melancholy entered the elder's eyes. "Then you may never sleep well again."

"So just as in our tribe, the old one is the peace chief," Custaloga inserted, motioning toward Conawago, "and the young one is the war chief." He pointed to Duncan.

"Just as with the Haudenosaunee," Duncan essayed, "the challenge for both is knowing what is worth fighting for." He paused, but when he received no response, he continued. "Once my people fought for lords and flags and princes. They were a brave and joyful people who only wanted to be left alone. But they were destroyed by bullets, cannons, and swords. The rest of us were scattered like autumn leaves."

"So now you fight for innocent men and lost children," replied Atotarho. "I fear, Duncan McCallum, that old men and children are taken from this world every day. The world shrugs it off."

"There is more owed to the innocent men and children of Bethel Church."

The last two words took the breath away from the old chieftains. Duncan realized they had not heard the place of the massacre until that moment. No one spoke. Several of the council members abruptly reached for their amulets. Adanahoe broke into a wail.

DUNCAN'S MOTHER WAS crying, frantically reaching for him as he edged over the cliff. His fall toward the rock surf far below was strangely slow, but they both knew he was dropping to his death. No matter how far she extended her arms, they were always just out of grasp. She called out desperate words, but he could not understand them. She had an urgent message for him before he died, and he could not even understand it. Then, impossibly, she was speaking in the Haudenosaunee tongue.

"You are needed, Duncan." The words came in a different voice now, and someone was shaking his shoulder. He opened his eyes, and a gentle finger on his lips stifled his protest.

Kass pulled away his blanket and pointed to a figure who waited behind her. "The mother of the Grand Council asks for you." Through the dim light Duncan saw Adanahoe, holding a tallow lamp. "Bringer of first light," he said to the old woman. "It is what your name means?" Adanahoe silently nodded, and Kass put a hand on his arm. "One of the lost children is her grandson," she said.

The Council had been slow to explain its connection to the children, but Duncan's mention of Bethel Church had clearly seized the hearts of the Iroquois leaders. Chieftains and matriarchs alike had leaned forward as he had risen at the bidding of Atotarho to describe what had happened at the Mohawk settlement. When he finished, he had extracted the bits of paper taken from the schoolhouse wall and read the names on each.

When he had recited Jacob Pine's name, Adanahoe had reacted with an anguished moan. When he read the name of Noah Moss, a tear had rolled down the leathery cheek of old Custaloga. For each name an old chieftain or matriarch had extended a hand for the paper. They studied the papers in tormented silence before returning them with trembling hands. Few of the tribes could read, and most just referred to writing as word pictures and tried to relate the symbols to the pictograms they used in their own records. But the slips of paper Duncan had shown them had seemed precious to them, and before returning them to him, each had pressed the paper to his or her heart.

The two women now led Duncan out of the longhouse where he slept into the starlit night. Only a few torches remained burning. A solitary guard stood in front of the log structure into which Duncan was led.

"Why do we steal about in . . ." The question died with a shiver of fear. The walls were alive with monsters. Hideous faces stared out at him though a haze of cedar smoke. A grotesquely long face with bulbous eyes and a huge twisted smile sneered at him. A beastly countenance with huge red eyes and a crooked nose glared down at the intruders. Five, ten, a dozen of the terrible faces glared from the walls. As Kass pulled Duncan through the torchlit chamber, he saw that she too was uncomfortable under the gazes. The spirit masks used in Haudenosaunee ritual were among the most sacred of objects. The tribes believed that once the masks were consecrated they were alive and had to be reverently cared for, even nourished with offerings of food. They were closely guarded when not in use by the secret False Face societies. To have so many together was, Duncan suspected, extraordinary, and this house was probably the only place in all the League where it was done.

A soft rhythmic drumming rose from the shadows, like the pulse of the spirits inhabiting the chamber. He found himself resisting as Kass tried to lead him on. The masks had a strange hold on him. The room was like a dream chamber, a place where men and spirits mixed. Kass pulled more insistently, leading him down a short, dark corridor to a chamber at the rear of the structure. She pushed aside a heavy skin that covered the entry and gestured him inside.

The room was lit with flickering bear fat lamps. More deerskin chronicles hung on the walls, some bearing images of the False Face masks, others outlines of bison, elk, and giant bears, animals not seen in the eastern forests for many years. Custaloga and the elegant woman Duncan had seen weaving wampum belts sat with Conawago on the floor before a bowl of smoldering tobacco.

Custaloga's face was lined with melancholy and confusion. When he looked up he seemed unable to speak. Adanahoe appeared out of the shadows and motioned Duncan to a blanket on the floor then sat beside him, gesturing for Kass to complete the circle around the smoldering bowl. "Bethel Church was our greatest secret. We sent the most promising ones," the first mother of the Council explained, "the ones who would best learn the European ways. They were to become our bridges to our future, the council decided. Each was the grandson or granddaughter of one of the great peace chiefs. They took new names, English names. Hickory John persuaded us it was for the best, for the good of our people, and he promised to look after them. They were the precious seeds of our new people, who would know how to live alongside Europeans, not underneath them. They would teach those ways to the rest of our people. Tushcona," she gestured to the belt weaver, "made a chronicle so those in the future would know of our plans."

The slow pulsing in the shadows grew closer. Tushcona the belt weaver began to softly shake a turtle shell rattle in time to the beat as Adanahoe continued. "There are those who say this stealing of our children is an act of the spirits, that they are telling us something. There are those who say we cannot interfere or the spirits will punish us. There are those who say it proves we must join the half-king. There are those who say we must go to war over such a grievous act, but we know not on whom to wage such war. Some of the Council have gone out in the moonlight to pray under the old trees."

The gentle rattling and the quiet pulse of the drum filled the silence that followed. Conawago gazed at the rising thread of fragrant smoke. Custaloga closed his eyes and bowed his head. Tushcona, still working her rattle, began a whispered prayer. Adanahoe began rubbing a rough wooden slab with a smooth stick, making a sound like the rustle of grass in the wind.

At last Custaloga lifted his head and looked at Duncan. "Would the spirits lie in order to us to protect us?" he asked.

Duncan had difficulty speaking. He felt so inadequate, so small, in such company. "The twisted path of my life shows I understand little of what the spirits want."

The old man studied Duncan, then Conawago, before replying. "I think the twisted path of your life shows the spirits have often sought to use you. What is needed now are those of both the forest world and the European world, who belong to neither." The aged sachem leaned forward. When he spoke, his words had the sound of a solemn vow. "When the killer of gods is pushed out of the spirit world, we will need you to bind him down, to keep him from returning."

Duncan's mouth went bone dry. He knew he should protest, should laugh, should run away, but he could not move.

A new rattling sound disrupted the ethereal music of the chamber. Duncan forced himself to turn, and his heart leapt into his throat. A god was kneeling beside him, staring him in the face.

A long bloodred mask with a twisted mouth fringed with black hair was inches from his face. Wrapped around the arm of the man behind the mask was a messenger of the gods. The diamondback snake was huge, its head held firmly in the god's hand, its tail shaking in a strange harmony with the reverent drumming and the murmured prayer.

Duncan was not sure he had not already entered the spirit world.

"It is said you can read the dead," the old woman said. "What we need is for you to read the dead god."

IT WAS NEARLY dawn when they finally emerged from the spirit house. Several elders sat outside the door, waiting. One of them rose and gestured their small group to follow him. They made a silent procession out of the gate, to a circle of frightened men and women at the river landing.

Hetty stood at the edge of the circle, clutching Ishmael to her breast. Their guide pressed forward through the throng then stopped abruptly. The chieftain turned and gestured for Duncan. His gut tightened as he sensed the elder's intent. For now a reader of the human dead was needed.

Black Fish would witness no more miracles. Duncan knelt at the body. The man who had energetically recounted the killing of gods and the resurrection of the half-king had been set in his death against a stump. The empty sockets where his eyes had been were fixed on the setting moon.

Chapter Eleven

"Never before has there been such a belt," Conawago said. There was wonder in his voice, mixed with confusion. They had made camp at the water's edge after their first day of travel from Onondaga Castle, and as Kass, Sagatchie, and Ishmael readied their camp for the night, the old Nipmuc sat at the fire gazing at a dark belt of beads in his hands.

They had been summoned into the Council lodge after Duncan had finished examining the body of Black Fish. "This is not a time for great war between the forest tribes," Atotarho had declared. "But it *is* a time for little war between certain men," he concluded, and he gripped both Duncan and Conawago on the shoulder while murmuring a prayer. He took the wampum belt from Tushcona and extended it in both hands to them. "We know you will show no fear when the time comes," he declared as Conawago accepted the belt, then he retreated into the shadows.

Adanahoe then appeared. "It had already been decided before the killing," the matriarch announced. The belt would have indeed taken hours to weave. "The Council cannot act as the Council in this matter. But these children are the Council's great hope. A secret war is being waged against us, and we cannot stand idly by," she had said as Conawago gazed at the belt with wide, disbelieving eyes. "This killing leaves us no time.

The half-king will think it was the work of the Council, an act of hostility against him. If things are not made right, there will be open war between the tribes. Keeping the League alive is the most sacred of our responsibilities, and we will have failed. The forest will run with blood."

As they paddled northward, Duncan had spent much of the day trying to understand those words and the strange symbols on the belt. The killing had indeed changed everything. To have a prominent disciple of the Revelator murdered virtually in the shadow of the Council lodge would outrage the half-king and be seen as a sign of weakness on the part of the Council by the Iroquois people. The League could not declare war on the rebellious tribesmen, nor would it join the Revelator. The belt meant they would fight in their own secret way, using Duncan and Conawago as their surrogates.

Duncan had been given almost no time to ask about Black Fish, learning only that the dead man had arrived with four others in a large cargo canoe with red eyes painted on its bow, and the man in the naval jacket who had accompanied Black Fish to the Council ring was a ne'er-do-well Seneca named Rabbit Jack. Duncan kept revisiting the scene of Black Fish's arrival in his mind's eye. There had been other men accompanying Black Fish and Rabbit Jack, including one whose face had been obscured with a wide-brimmed European hat, but they had stopped abruptly and turned back. Something or someone at the Council ring had caused them to retreat. But the only thing that could have been unexpected was the presence of Duncan, Conawago, and Hetty.

Now at their campfire, Conawago kept staring at the belt, turning it over, holding the beads close to his eye as if they might hold some tiny secret. There was a hollow amusement in his voice when he finally spoke. "That's me," he said with a low chuckle, pointing to the larger of the stick figures in the center of the belt, the one who held a spear. The three-inch-wide belt consisted almost entirely of purple beads, making it a black belt in the parlance of the Haudenosaunee, a war belt. The two figures in white beads, one larger than the other, did not signify a big man and a small one, but a young one and an old one. Conawago pointed to the smaller figure, "And that's you. Tushcona said the image had come to her in a vision." Over the heads of the figures was a small half-circle with rays coming out of it. The Council had decided to send the dawnchasers to war.

Two other patterns were woven at either side of the stick figures. The first was a set of wavy lines: three vertical waves then at the top right two similar but much smaller horizontal waves. On the opposite side were two white rings, one inside the other.

"Water," Duncan suggested, pointing to the wavy lines.

Conawago nodded and gestured to the vertical lines. "The big lake, the inland sea called the shining water. Ontario. And at the northeast corner—"

"A river," Duncan put in, grasping the simple eloquence of the lines. "My God, it's a map to a river at the northeast corner of the lake. The Saint Lawrence." They exchanged a worried glance. The Saint Lawrence was the boiling point of the war. The long river valley was swarming with enemy troops and enemy tribes, with the British army and navy about to descend on them.

"Some of the tribes call it the River that Never Ends," Conawago said, foreboding in his voice as he traced the concentric circles with his finger, "for it seems to have no headwaters and two great mouths, one in the inland sea and one in the salt sea."

Duncan looked up to see Sagatchie, back from collecting firewood, staring at them. Being given a war belt was always a solemn and auspicious event, and though Sagatchie and Kass seemed confused as to its intent, they knew its source could only have been the Council.

As his companions laid out their blankets and dropped wood on the fire, Conawago kept staring at the belt, as if he could see things in it that were invisible to Duncan.

Suddenly Sagatchie grabbed his gun and sprang into the shadows. Duncan instinctively pushed Ishmael down and checked the powder in his rifle's firing pan as Conawago and Hetty stepped behind trees. A low growl rose from the hell dog at Hetty's side.

Duncan's heart clenched as he heard the determined chant that came from the river, but then he realized it was no war chant but one of the harvest songs used in Iroquois fields.

Conawago broke from cover, running to the bank with waving arms, then stepping in knee-deep to pull the canoe ashore.

"Custaloga!" Sagtachie said in surprise as the chieftain stepped onto the bank. The Mohawk ranger gave a respectful nod to the elder and watched in mute amazement as Adanahoe and Tushcona the belt weaver climbed out behind him.

Adanahoe set a bulging pack down, clicking her tongue in disapproval as she saw the carelessly laid fire. She knelt and began rearranging the logs, then she crisscrossed several more from the nearby pile. "There are huckleberries on the bank downstream," she declared, pointing to Duncan and Sagatchie.

"Grandmother," Duncan said, "why have you left the castle?"

The old woman stood tall, straightening her doeskin dress. "Jacob Pine," she said, tapping her breast with her hand, then pointed to Custaloga then to Tushcona, reciting the names of Noah Moss and Hannah Redfern. "They are our children's children. Their parents are dead or away in the fighting. The other grandparents are too weak to travel."

"You don't understand," Duncan protested. "Where we go will be a place of great danger, a place of death."

The old woman's face burned bright with determination. "Those who wage a little war still need a little army. Long before he was a peace chief, Custaloga was a great war chief." As she spoke Custaloga stepped to her side, touching the war ax on his belt with a fierce glint in his eye.

Duncan looked at Conawago, then Sagatchie, in exasperation, hoping they would know the way to ask the elders to return to their town. "We cannot," he said. "I mean, you are too valuable to the Haudenosaunee people. We can't risk—" Kassawaya stepped beside Adanahoe, as though in warning, her face as stern as those of the elders. Duncan turned to Conawago with a plaintive expression. "Tell me what to do," he pleaded.

"I think what you need to do," the old Nipmuc said with a grin, "is go pick huckleberries."

A STRONG NORTHERN wind stirred the surface of the great inland sea called Lake Ontario, covering it with short choppy whitecaps. Duncan studied the small fleet of warships trapped by the wind in the harbor below Fort Oswego. Three sloops of war with a dozen guns each lay anchored close to shore, and strung between them like beads on a necklace were two dozen of the long boats used for transporting troops on the inland waters. The fort was being used as the launching point for the troops that would invade French Canada up the Saint Lawrence from the West.

If the solid, symmetrical stone fortress overlooking the harbor was the perfect symbol of England's military order, the town below was the symbol of the chaos of the frontier. A handful of small inns and taverns, some little more than large huts, rose up along the rutted roads. Ramshackle lean-tos, log houses, even small bark lodges sprawled along muddy paths that led toward piers built along the wide river. Only half a dozen stone houses at the mouth of the river offered any sense of permanence. Scores of tents lined the long flat field on the east side of the fort, with soldiers erecting more as they watched. Militia and regular troops were arriving, assembling for the northern campaign. Duncan looked uneasily back toward their own camp, a quarter mile upstream. They could never maneuver their canoes on the lake in such a wind. They would have to wait in hiding, Duncan told himself, but then Sagatchie touched his arm and pointed to the log piers jutting into the river. The wide cargo canoe with red eyes painted on its bow was beached by the nearest pier. Rabbit Jack and the other traders who had fled from Onondaga Castle were in the town.

"I don't know if I would recognize him," Duncan said.

"He loves that jacket." Sagatchie surveyed the riverfront as he spoke, then his gaze settled on a rundown log structure built into the bank. "And he will bear the mark," he added, and set off at a trot back toward their camp.

By the time Duncan reached him, the Mohawk ranger was already speaking with their companions. Duncan was about to explain that they could not travel on the lake that day when he saw Adanahoe unrolling their blankets, and he realized Sagatchie had broken the news. Conawago straightened and motioned Duncan in the direction of the settlement. "If someone killed Black Fish for telling the story of the half-king and the spirits, we must know why. Those from that canoe will know."

"Perhaps he didn't die for telling the story," Duncan suggested. "He had a heavy scent of rum about him. Maybe it had more to do with him getting drunk after telling it."

Conawago stared at the river as he weighed Duncan's words. "You mean he may have divulged something his killer did not want others to know."

"A drunk man can boast. A man who played a trick on the Council might be very proud of himself."

"No!" Conawago shot back. "You saw him. He held the beads, Duncan!" In the old Nipmuc's world it was not possible to lie to the Council.

"A man with a dark heart may not speak with honor," Duncan pointed out. "Words can become snares for the unknowing."

"Stop this!" Tushcona cried out. "I thought you understood our ways. Do not pretend a member of the League could speak other than the truth to the Council. It is the sacred duty of all. It is not possible to hold the beads and lie."

"He spoke and then he died," Duncan replied.

Conawago frowned at him, unhappy that Duncan would press the elders.

"Whatever the reason he died," Duncan continued, "word will get back quickly to the half-king that on the very the night the Council was asked to support him his disciple was murdered. No matter what words we use now, that will be the message the half-king will hear. Vengeance is in his blood. We have seen what he does to those who anger him."

Sagatchie slowly led Conawago and Duncan back toward the docks, pausing to step into shadows whenever boats carrying soldiers and militia passed by, then stopping at the wide canoe. Two wooden chests of cargo covered with blankets were still in the vessel, though no guard watched them. The Mohawk stepped into the canoe, threw off the blanket on the first chest, and opened it. There was nothing inside but four small bags of cornmeal and half a dozen of the cheap axes used in trade. The second held nothing but a smaller chest packed in straw. Wooden panels divided the inner chest into half a dozen compartments, holding nothing but sawdust. Sagatchie ran his fingers through the sawdust, lifting some in his palm and watching with a confused expression as it blew away. "Those who belong to this canoe were supposed to be traders, who called at the Iroquois castles to spread the promise of the half-king. They received nothing in trade. Their cargo was a ruse," he said with a pointed glance at Duncan. "Onondaga Castle was their last stop. They are traveling back to the half-king."

A cool anger grew on the Mohawk's face. He covered the chests again and pointed toward the hut built into the side of the bank. Sagatchie and Duncan stepped through its flimsy leather-hinged door into a smoky, foul-smelling chamber where several Indians and rough looking trappers were tossing white and black pebbles in a circle marked with flour on the dirt floor.

"They have to bet to play, but first they pay the owner," Sagatchie said. As he spoke a stout man in a leather apron took a coin from a tribesman, who then extended his forearm. The proprietor reached out with a stick of chalk and left a broad white mark on his skin then dropped the coin into a bowl on the table beside him. "With that mark he can play all day," the Mohawk explained and gestured Duncan toward the plump man's side.

"Five men from that red-eyed canoe woke me up this morning to buy a jar of rum," the proprietor explained, "and to begin their games." Duncan saw that his bowl held not just coins but silver links from jewelry, brass pins, and even a piece of crystal rock. "My customers usually play for hours. Those five left around noon, the only ones to leave so far today."

"Meaning the only ones with the mark will be those from that canoe," Conawago observed when Duncan reported the news, and he gestured Duncan onto the muddy street.

The settlement was alive with activity. They found themselves weaving around women carrying huge piles of firewood on their backs or dragging branches on the ground. An old tribal woman sold fish strung on vines, another small pumpkins stacked at her side. A boy carrying a bundle of sassafras roots on his shoulder passed by, leaving a scented trail. Conawago and Duncan had reached the end of the outermost street and were about to continue their search closer to the fort when Sagatchie stepped out of the shadows. "Two of them are in the stable below the fort, sharing a jar of ale."

"You found them so soon?" Duncan asked. "How did you . . ." As he glanced further into the shade of the trees, he realized he did not need to finish his question. Patrick Woolford sat against a big oak. "You were already looking for them," he concluded.

Woolford nodded. "I saw the canoe this morning. Red eyes on the bow. It's been calling on every Iroquois settlement this side of Lake Cayuga. Even here they have been recruiting men for the half-king, offering a new ax and a pint of ale to each man who agrees to go north."

Duncan quickly explained the murder at Onondaga Castle.

"If we had any sense we'd throw the lot of them behind bars," Woolford groused. He rose and made a quick gesture toward the trees, and four more men wearing ranger green emerged from the deeper shadows, two Iroquois and two sturdy bearded men. Woolford offered a few quiet words, and the men left at a brisk walk toward the fort.

"There's an old stable behind these trees where we made our camp. We will bring them all back for a chat. We want none to flee to the renegade camp. Wait there, Duncan. Need I remind you you are still a fugitive from the army's justice?"

Woolford took off down the street with Sagatchie. Duncan and Conawago waited until the ranger was out of sight and resumed their own search. They had wandered down nearly half the town's paths and streets, studying every man they passed, when Conawago grabbed his arm in alarm. Provosts were walking down the street toward them. As they watched, however, two of the old women carrying a bundle of wood between them stumbled before the provosts, scattering the wood, then falling to the ground to block their path. Duncan did not understand Conawago's chuckle until the women raised their faces toward them. It was Hetty and Tushcona the weaver. They had interfered with the provosts to give them time to hide.

As they watched from the shadows, Conawago silently gestured to an old man dragging several long branches along the road. Custaloga glanced up but pretended not to know them. As he watched, the old Oneida seemed to stumble, turning the branches sideways as he did so, blocking the path of two tribesmen walking up the track. Duncan did not notice the white marks on their forearms until two of Woolford's rangers suddenly appeared behind them and grabbed their elbows. Their army of Iroquois elders was at work.

A moment later a sharp whistle rose from further down the street. Woolford and Sagatchie were pulling Rabbit Jack between them.

"Hold there, Captain!" The sharp, angry command came from the prim and powdered officer who had sent Duncan to the iron hole. Duncan lowered his head and fought the impulse to run.

Woolford stiffly acknowledged the older man. "Colonel Cameron."

Cameron wore the scarlet, gold, and lace of a senior British officer, but beside him were two stern grenadiers in Highland plaid. "Have you no grasp of our sensitive relations with the tribes?" Cameron snapped.

"I have some experience in that regard, sir. I mean to question these men."

"Nonsense!" Cameron thundered. "Do not play the magistrate, Woolford. I will not abide insults to our brave companions in arms!" He gestured to his escort, who pulled the prisoners from the rangers. "You are too bold, sir, entirely too bold!" the colonel snapped.

The ranger officer was clearly struggling to keep his temper under control. He glanced at Duncan, whose face was known to Cameron, then brought a knuckle to his temple like an obsequious recruit. "Too bold," he repeated. He was about to turn when a figure leapt out from an alley and launched itself onto Rabbit Jack's back. The Mingo seemed more amazed then hurt as Hetty screeched Indian epithets and pummeled him with her small bony fists. Rabbit Jack laughed as the grenadiers began prying her off. She did not want to give up, and she clutched his blue jacket as she was dragged away. As she dropped into the dirt the hell dog leapt beside her, baring his teeth at the Mingo as he retreated, still laughing.

"There was another man in that canoe," Woolford reported to Duncan. "Before that fool Cameron interrupted, I told Rabbit Jack he was going to hang for murder. He laughed and said we had the wrong man, that we should speak with the poet. He said it is the poet of death who teaches the flock how to leave bodies behind."

The poet of death. He sounded like a European. Duncan looked to Sagatchie and Kass. "We were all at the Council," Sagatchie said. "No one watched the landing where those from the red-eyed canoe made their camp."

"Several men arrived together at the council fire," Duncan said. "But only two came forward, Rabbit Jack and Black Fish. The others backed quickly away. One of them was a tall man in European clothes, wearing a wide-brimmed hat."

"The fox will back away when it sees a wolf at a kill," Sagatchie observed.

Duncan broke the silence that followed. "If this poet is here, then Rabbit Jack will probably be running to him now."

"I think that particular hare will hop to a tavern," Woolford said. "And poets are known to be partial to ale."

They resumed their search, more wary than ever of the scarlet coats, tracing reports of Rabbit Jack calling at two taverns, asking after a tall man in a black hat. At last an old Oneida hawking baskets pointed to a two-story stone structure overlooking the river, the most substantial of the town's taverns. With a glint of victory in his eye, Woolford directed Duncan to enter the rear door while he and Sagatchie stood outside the front. They would snare Jack as he fled.

Duncan entered the back of the building and stepped to the cage-like alcove built into the corner from which the tavernkeeper dispensed his beverages. Beside the cage a plump woman with rouged cheeks sat, rolling three silver beads back and forth on the table. Duncan hesitated a moment, realizing they matched the beads he had seen in the bowl at the gaming hut. When he asked for a warrior in a naval jacket, the old Dutchman pointed toward the entry. "Left not five minutes ago."

Duncan darted out the door so quickly he did not see the halberd that tripped him until he was sprawled on the ground.

"Not so fast, laddie. You could crack your brainpan." An ox of a man wearing the bearskin hat of the grenadiers bent and pulled Duncan to his feet. Duncan looked through the ring of provosts that surrounded him to see the red-eyed canoe gliding past the tavern. Rabbit Jack made an obscene gesture at him then with a laugh slapped the back of a lean, black-clothed man who sat on one of the wooden chests. The brim of his black hat was too wide for Duncan to see the face of the poet of death.

The big grenadier pushed Duncan back inside, to a table where Conawago now sat. The old Nipmuc absently lifted the deck of worn playing cards on the table and began shuffling from hand to hand. Duncan kept his eyes down, painfully aware of whispered commands and grumbling, of chairs scraping the floor.

Suddenly the tavern was quiet. There were no more soldiers, no more patrons, not even the tavernkeeper. Duncan rose uneasily and was eyeing the rear door when Woolford stepped out of a doorway along the opposite side of the room. With a look of apology he opened the door wider to reveal a private dining chamber. The ranger captain gestured them toward the candlelit table where a solitary man sat waiting.

Duncan at first did not recognize the figure since he had never seen him in civilian clothes. "General Calder!" he said with a shudder, and he spun toward the rear door before realizing provosts were undoubtedly standing outside.

"The proprietor serves an excellent applejack," Calder said, gesturing to a clay bottle beside several pewter mugs, another deck of cards and a set of draughts. "Sit down, McCallum," he said when Duncan hesitated. "There is no point to arresting you since you make such light work of my prisons. And last I heard, your dead body had already been dragged out of the hole. I'm not sure even I have authority to hang a dead man."

Conawago gave a restraining tug on Duncan's arm as he stepped to the table. The old Nipmuc seemed more curious than afraid of the general. Duncan followed and sat beside his friend.

General Calder silently filled four mugs, motioning Woolford to join them, then pushed two across the table before raising his lined countenance toward them. "A dispatch rider off his route, tied to a solitary wheel of an army wagon, deep in a lake. It would sound like one of those ridiculous conundrums posed for the entertainment of philosophers. Except that I was conducting an inspection at William Henry and decided to see for myself. Nothing ridiculous about the bloated corpse of a loyal soldier. Normally a missing dispatch rider means missing dispatches. But his dispatch case was still sealed when the horse you borrowed found its way to its stable."

Duncan looked from Woolford to the general before replying. "You haven't found the payroll," he stated. Neither man returned his gaze. He pushed his chair back to leave.

"We haven't found the payroll," the general reluctantly confirmed. "And one puff of wind in the wrong direction, and the house of cards built of our recent military successes will collapse." When he finally looked up at Duncan, his face was dark with worry. "People think we win our wars because we have more troops, more cannon, more bullets. But that is seldom the case. Our secret weapon is discipline. I have the best disciplined troops in America. And that discipline has gone to hell. Three thousand men are en route here, and I don't know how many I can rely on when I take them north. I have no money to pay them, have had none for months. Many of the best-loved members of their regiments have been imprisoned for insubordination. I have several thousand savages who may turn against us at any moment. When they do, all that will be left of his majesty's army will be scalps hanging on tribal lodgepoles." A bitter smile rose on Calder's face, and he drained his mug. "Where is the king's money, McCallum?"

"I did not take it."

The general filled his mug again. "That verdict has yet to be rendered. But your friends say I could benefit from your intellect, that you have something of an instinct for the mysterious ways of men in the wilderness."

"You cast your net too wide," Duncan said. "Look to your own."

Anger flared in the general's eyes. Duncan extracted the pieces of paper he had taken from the Bethel Church school. He laid them with the writing of the students facing down.

"Paper is scarce in the frontier settlements," he explained. "Everyone uses both sides." He began arranging the papers to line up the disjointed arcs and lines on them, fitting them together like pieces of a puzzle. "I took these to try to understand the captured children, but they tell me more about the captured coins."

Calder pushed the candle closer. "A drawing of a cabinet?"

"A door?" Woolford suggested.

"The detail of a chest. Or rather an elaborate coach seat that opened like a chest."

The general sighed. "I am weary, McCallum. I have no appetite for your games."

"The payroll wagon was built in Bethel Church."

Calder frowned. "That information was secret. But yes, the quartermaster chose to contract with the Mohawk builders. A gesture of respect to our woodland brethren. But the drawings for it would have been surrendered on delivery of the vehicle."

"As I would expect. But someone made a second set and it was kept even more secretly. When they were no longer of use, the schoolmaster must have found them and salvaged the paper for his students."

Calder made a gesture of dismissal toward the papers. "What purpose would a second set of plans serve?" he asked. "The pay chest was impregnable. It could only be opened with two different keys, which had been sent north with different dispatch riders the week before."

"Keys that did not work," Duncan stated.

Calder offered no disagreement.

"A second wagon was built with the same secrecy as the first," Duncan continued. "An identical wagon. The Mohawk builders did not suspect anything because it was arranged for, and paid for, by officers in uniform, perhaps even the same officers. They were building another for his majesty as far as they knew."

The general went very still.

"It would have taken them at least three months to build," Duncan continued. "Add a month for the second set of drawings to be made and sent to them, say a month of planning. Meaning the scheme was hatched just after the defeat of the French at Quebec. What was it the French needed most then?"

"A few thousand regular soldiers and a few tons of munitions."

"All of which are expected soon, with the arrival of their next fleet any day now. Which means all they really needed was time. They're getting it. What they did was to assure you lost confidence in your troops, in your ability to act swiftly in delivering the killing stroke. The theft of the payroll was meant to change the tide of war."

The general looked like he had bitten something very sour. He lifted the bottle as if to fill his mug once more then lowered it. "You have an active imagination, sir." There was no confidence in his voice.

Duncan balanced a structure out of the cards on the table, two walls and a roof. "Those involved knew the routine, knew the wagon's schedule and that it would stop for a meal at the settlement." He took a draught piece and pushed it inside the card structure. "The second wagon waited in the barn. Some of the escorts were part of the conspiracy, including the driver. The others went inside for the meal." He pushed a second draught piece into the back of the house of cards. "The paywagon was driven into the far end of the barn, the horse team switched to the new wagon and driven out." He extended a finger and pulled out the wooden disc. "It would not have been difficult to make the new wagon look road worn—just throw some dirt on it, maybe add a scratch or two. The only one who would likely notice a difference would have been the driver."

Woolford muttered a curse. "He was one of those reported as a deserter."

The general frowned again. "You suggest I should act based on such wild speculation?"

Duncan reached into his waistcoat pocket and dropped a musket ball on the table. "I cut this out of Conawago's shoulder two hours before we arrived at Bethel Church. A bateau fired on us. We thought it an honest mistake by a British vessel, carrying military cargo north. But this is not the seventy-seven caliber of a British Brown Bess."

Woolford scooped up the ball, weighing it in his palm before lifting it to his eye, then nodding. "Seventy-two," the ranger declared. "A French bullet."

"The stolen wagon was on the bateau," Duncan continued, "without its wheels. One of the wheels was used to drown the dispatch rider. The others will be on the bottom too, in a line going north from that dock. They tricked the inhabitants of Bethel Church with a false contract. They tricked the army into thinking the original wagon was in the North. They tricked anyone looking at the bateau into thinking it was on army business. It is the imagination of your enemies you should worry about. They have been playing you exceedingly well."

Calder bristled. "What are you saying?" he demanded.

The reply came from the shadows. "What he is saying, General, is that you think you have this beast by the throat when in fact all you have is the tail." William Johnson emerged from a second, darkened chamber.

"I am going north," Calder snapped to Duncan, as if he had to explain himself. "Johnson and I will crush the French beast if I have to lead every battle myself."

Duncan and Woolford exchanged worried glances. Johnson poured himself some applejack.

"Then the beast has already won."

The general looked up in surprise. Conawago had at last spoken. Duncan would not long forget the stare the old Nipmuc fixed on Calder. Along with cool anger was an unexpected pity.

Calder's face flushed with color. He had swallowed enough pride. Being baldly rebuked was too much. Duncan saw him glance at the door, where his provost brutes waited.

Duncan's own words came out with more acid than he intended. He would not let Calder harm Conawago. "You listen like a British general. What is needed is an American general."

Venom rose in Calder's eyes.

"The French did not steal your payroll," Duncan said. "They simply cooperated with the thieves."

"You said it was raiders!" Calder spat.

"If the French had the money," Woolford inserted, "they would be spreading bounties so fast every settler in Canada would be racing to join them at Montreal. Our reports say instead they have trouble keeping their existing militia from deserting."

Calder stared into his mug for several long breaths then turned to Duncan. "Tell me what you mean to do, McCallum."

"Five Iroquois children were kidnapped by the thieves. I thought at first it was just an afterthought, that some warriors saw an opportunity to win a few pelts in the slave market. But now I understand. Taking those children was as important to the raiders as taking the king's silver."

"What do you mean to do?" Calder repeated.

"The coins were meant to reach the French, but it was never a French conspiracy. The half-king is at the center of this. To him the French are only a stepping-stone. What he needs, what he must have, is the Iroquois Council. Silver means nothing to the Council. The children are the descendants of the Council, future members of the Council. They are the real treasure of the Iroquois. I am going north with my Haudenosaunee friends to save five innocent children."

"Five innocent children," the general repeated in a mocking tone.

"I admire your charitable instincts," Johnson offered as he lifted the candle to light his pipe. "But the lives of every European and half the Haudenosaunee will be forfeit if we don't stop this damned half-king. We have been so obsessed with the French that we have let this monster rise up right under our noses. He has slipped past and is closing in on the Saint Lawrence. Once he truly combines with the French, our path to Montreal is blocked. They will close the choke points on the river, and our campaign will be finished. Once he combines," Johnson added, "the French will have King's George's treasure."

"Without the children," Conawago inserted, "the half-king does not have the Iroquois. Without the Iroquois his plans fail."

Calder had had too much. "Ridiculous! Do not presume to teach me about diplomacy! You will not go another mile north!" the general barked. "I have sent trained emissaries to treat with the renegade. My nephew Marston is a lieutenant on my personal staff and is seasoned as a diplomat in the Low Countries. This damned mischief maker will be bought off like every other savage, and I will rally my troops to finish this war."

"Have you heard nothing I've said?" Duncan demanded. "The Revelator is not acting alone. He has powerful allies. He is convinced that he has a destiny of greatness. He will not treat with you. There is only one authority that troubles him, only one that will cause him to hesitate."

The general's sneer was aimed first at Duncan, then Conawago. "A dead Scottish clan? An extinct woodland tribe?"

Johnson blew a plume of smoke into the general's face. Calder's hand closed into a fist and then relaxed, as if he accepted the rebuke.

In the brittle silence, Conawago produced the belt of purple beads and solemnly unrolled it on the table.

The general began to wave his hand as if in dismissal, but Johnson pushed the hand aside as he leaned forward. "God's breath!" the Irishman gasped. "What have you done?"

Duncan had no reply. Woolford bent over the belt, tentatively pushing its edges, turning over one end to study the knots. He and Johnson exchanged somber glances. "It is indeed the work of the Council weaver," the ranger whispered.

"A bunch of cheap beads," Calder said. "A child's plaything."

"I assure you," Johnson said, "this is anything but child's play. If you understood, General, you would be shaken to the bone. Such a belt carries the full power of the Iroquois League, the word of the Council, and the touch of the gods. It has to be satisfied, as the elders would say. And this kind of belt is only satisfied with blood."

"You are speaking like some drunken mummer."

Johnson looked at Conawago, as if for help, but the Nipmuc would not speak. The Irishman paced around the table, feverishly working his pipe. "These gentlemen," he finally said, indicating Duncan and Conawago, "are on a mission of blood for the Grand Council of the Iroquois League. A secret mission."

"Nonsense," Calder snapped. "We are all on a glorious mission for our blessed King George, to assure British victory over the damnable French. To establish British freedom over this continent." The general's words were dismissive, yet he could not take his eyes off the belt. The longer he stared at it, the angrier he seemed.

"And what, General Calder," Conawago asked quietly, "does this continent look like when it has become entirely British?"

"Sir?"

"Where in your British freedom are the Iroquois, where are all the men chained to labor by British indentures, where are the Lenni Lenape, the Huron, the Shawnee, and the African slaves?"

Duncan shifted to the edge of his chair, ready to stop the blow that surely would come.

But the general only clenched his jaw. "When the French are defeated, you will see that the hand of the king is merciful." He saw Conawago's disapproving frown, and his anger ignited once more. "And if you are not prepared to make sacrifice in that cause, then you are my enemy!"

Conawago replied in a quiet voice. "Then you do not understand who your enemies are, sir." He sipped from his mug before continuing. "For generations," Conawago explained, "the Iroquois tribes have been the bridge, the buffer between the French and the English. The English have supplied guns and goods and signed treaties with them because they kept the French at bay. After so many of their people were lost to war and disease in the last century, their connection with the British became the real source of Iroquois power, assuring they would be respected by all. They have fought as surrogates for British soldiers, died instead of those soldiers. Do you need reminding it was they who died for Colonel Johnson's victory at Lake George, not British troops?

"Remove the French threat, and the leverage of the Six Nations is gone," Conawago continued. "They become just another impediment to British expansion."

"Nonsense," the general snapped back. "The king has always remembered his friends. They have nothing to fear." The general looked to Woolford, as if for confirmation, but the ranger captain just stared impassively at the belt.

"You do not know who your enemies are," Duncan repeated. "Let us go north. The half-king has no tolerance for diplomats. He has warned that any outsiders who came before him would become his men or hollow men. Your nephew is in grave danger."

"This half-king is little more than a child who speaks in the riddles of children. And you, sir, are so naive in the ways of the world that you are frightened by him." The general abruptly rose. "Damn you, McCallum! If you had not connived to obtain the protection of the Iroquois Council,

I would have you in irons! You will not go north! You will not meddle in affairs of the state! You will not interfere with the progress of my northern campaign! Venture another mile to the north, and I will forget my generosity. You will be dragged back to Albany and chained to the wall of the iron hole until you rot!" Calder marched to the door and turned. "This tavern is closed! You will sleep here tonight while I decide what to do with you!"

Duncan watched the door, half expecting provosts to bring manacles. When he turned he found Johnson and Woolford still staring at the wampum beads. Conawago had taken his mug to the water barrel on the far side of the tavern.

"Do you have any notion of the gravity of this belt?" Johnson asked Duncan. The Irishman kept his hands away from it now, as if he were frightened of it.

"I have seen war belts before."

"Not like this you haven't. These aren't just two men on the belt. They are you and Conawago. It's a very old thing, something I have only heard about at council fires but never seen."

"They knew Conawago and I had a chance of getting through where a large war party would not."

"When I was a wee lad, my grandfather would speak of the heroes of old," Johnson explained, "who would leave on holy missions to slay dragons and other preternatural beasts. The names of the heroes were inscribed on stones out on the moors where they had fallen. The Haudenosaunee have similar legends of heroes sent on impossible missions to save the tribes from grave harm. Solitary warriors sent to turn back huge war parties or force fierce beasts back to whence they came. There are still shrines at special trees deep in the forest kept to honor them, though more and more of the trees are being forgotten. Those heroes are said to have carried belts like yours, for their missions of little war."

"I don't understand."

Johnson looked to Woolford as if for help. The ranger's face took on a melancholy expression. "Accepting this belt is like a vow. The images aren't just a map, Duncan." He pointed to the rays over the stick men. "Do you understand what this is?"

"We both ran the dawn runner course. They sent their dawnchasers."

Woolford grimaced. "Would that it were true. No. It is a gate, a threshold. He pointed to the waving lines, then the concentric circles. Two men must go up the Saint Lawrence, to a place the Iroquois call the hole in the world. Then the two men must go into the hole, across to the other side. It is not just a prophesy. It is a truth in the eyes of the tribes, a promise, a duty now."

Duncan looked at Conawago, who lingered at the water barrel, staring pointedly into the water as if waiting for Woolford to speak the words to Duncan he had been unable to. "Across?"

Woolford folded the belt very carefully, not looking up. "Conawago and the elders know. They are certain these mysteries must be resolved on the other side."

"Speak plainly, damn it."

When Woolford did speak, it was in a whisper. He looked up with anguish in his eyes. "You promised to die, Duncan."

IT WAS LATE in the evening when Woolford returned to the tavern, admitted by a provost who warned the ranger he would have only a quarter hour with the prisoners. Woolford dropped a linen-wrapped bundle on a table and uncovered a loaf of bread and a cold leg of mutton. Conawago rose from the hearth. He had chosen to sleep since they had been locked in the tavern, as if to avoid Duncan.

"There was news," he announced as Duncan began to eat, "a letter from Albany."

Duncan paused, sensing the hesitation in his friend's voice.

"Duncan," the ranger continued uneasily, "there was no time to send to that lawyer in New York town. I discovered the name of the magistrate in Albany who passed sentence on Eldridge, but the crusty old fool wouldn't see me." Duncan took another bite as Woolford stepped to the water barrel for a drink. "So I wrote to Sarah Ramsey," he said into his mug.

Duncan's head snapped up.

"The Ramsey name is still well respected in the colony," Woolford quickly continued, as if fearing Duncan would interrupt. "She wrote to him, saying Lord Ramsey desired that the particulars of the Eldridge prosecution be sent to me here."

"I do not want Sarah to be burdened by . . ." Duncan said stiffly, searching for words, "by all this."

Woolford ignored him. "The magistrate reports it was a most peculiar case. The victim had been tied to a tree and had his fingers cut off. The arrest warrant was issued because Eldridge was heard to threaten the man. At the hearing he said it must have been a savage who tortured the Dutchman. He said it must have been a Huron. A week later, Eldridge escaped the jail. It was taken as a sign of his guilt."

"A Huron?" Conawago asked. "Why would he say that?"

"Don't presume on my relationship with Sarah," Duncan warned.

"She has great affection for you, Duncan," Woolford countered. "One of the comeliest lasses in the colonies. And one of the richest. Don't tell me you never think of her."

Duncan tore away a piece of bread and stared at the table as he ate it. "Not a day goes by without me wondering whether she is safe, whether she is working the fields, whether she is continuing to learn to read."

"But?" Woolford asked.

It was Conawago who answered after an uncomfortable silence. "But Duncan doesn't think he deserves her." The tavern was apparently a place where hard truths had to be spoken.

"She would leave Edentown tomorrow if you offered to build a cabin with her in the wilderness," the ranger declared.

Duncan's reply was a whisper. "All I have to my name is a rifle and a set of tattered bagpipes. I am the prisoner of a general and have apparently promised to go north to die for the Iroquois Council," he said, exchanging a sober gaze with the old Nipmuc. "Which I will be honored to do if Conawago wishes it." He turned back to the ranger. "I beg you not to discuss her further."

Woolford solemnly dipped his mug at Duncan and nodded.

They ate for several minutes without speaking, until Conawago finally broke the silence. "A Huron," he said again. "Why would the schoolmaster say that?"

THE SOUND OF the horn roused Duncan from his troubled sleep on the hearth of the tavern. Through the window he could see soldiers running from the fort to the landing dock. A young officer bolted into the big stone house where the general slept. A ship was approaching from the North.

Duncan found the door unguarded. By the time he reached the dock, the general was there with Woolford, studying the little brig through a spyglass. The sailing ship pulled a smaller boat behind it. Calder lowered the telescope and fixed Duncan with a gloating smile. "The triumphant return."

"Being towed home?"

"As I explained, McCallum, my nephew Marston had things well in hand. We shall hear his report of how this half-king is standing down, deferring to us as we complete our invasion force. We will—"

"Sir," Woolford interrupted. His face was pale. He had been using his own telescope. "You must return to your quarters. Please. I beg you."

Duncan and the general turned, confused by the tightness in the ranger's voice. Duncan looked back at the brig. There was none of the cheering he would have expected upon the return of a victorious mission, no celebratory cannon shot. The men in the boat under tow were strangely sober and still.

"We found them drifting five miles offshore, sir," an officer on the brig reported in an uneasy voice as it slipped alongside the long dock. As the crew hauled in the towline, none of the men in the smaller craft moved to acknowledge Calder. The general, clearly off put by the snub, reached the end of the dock in several long, eager strides. "Marston! Pray, what news! Marston lad, when do we . . ." His question faded away with an anguished groan. Woolford rushed forward to grab his arm as the general swayed, about to collapse.

There were five soldiers in the boat, all sitting stiffly upright, not moving. Duncan approached slowly, puzzling over the strange T-shaped frames of saplings behind each man that were lashed to the benches on which they sat. He saw now how each was also lashed to the neck of the man it supported. Then as the boat was turned, he saw the empty faces and understood the terrible truth.

The general's nephew and every other man wore only his uniform coat, unbuttoned. The shirts that would have covered their bellies were gone. Their bellies were gone.

"Mother of God!" Woolford cried.

Two of the junior officers who had joined them dashed to the side of the dock and retched into the water.

The men had been eviscerated, dressed like butchered deer, before being propped up like mannequins. The Revelator had promised only hollow men would return.

When the general looked back to Duncan his face was ashen, his voice a dry croak. "Go," he moaned, "take your pitiful band north and stop this demon."

Chapter Twelve

A man who takes a peaceful passage at sea for granted soon finds the gods spitting in his eye. Duncan heard the words of his grandfather, mariner of the western isles, so vividly he could smell the peat smoke on the old man's clothes. He braced himself as another swell crashed over the bow of their little brig.

Duncan had underestimated the inland sea. When they had begun their sail north, he had described it as a pond to the ship's commanding officer. It had no tide, had no currents, none of the rocky shoals that plagued the vessels of the Hebrides in Duncan's youth. The bearded naval lieutenant who served as captain had smiled patiently and pointed to a bank of clouds on the northern horizon.

They had had difficulty convincing their Iroquois companions to board the vessel, trying to explain that it would provide the quickest passage into the Saint Lawrence, where the Revelator's bands were converging. Custaloga had wanted, but not received, assurance they would hug the shoreline, for the natives almost never strayed more than half a mile offshore. Even Sagatchie, intrepid warrior and ranger, had to be coaxed by Woolford to set foot on the ship. Conawago, veteran of several transatlantic crossings, had finally cajoled the elders by telling them the vessel was nothing more than a big lodge on the water.

Now Duncan looked back with guilt toward the small aft cabin where the Iroquois huddled, holding their bellies, clutching their protective amulets, some bent over buckets. He gripped a shroud line as the sturdy vessel heaved over another swell, raising his face into the wind-driven spray. Like his grandfather, he had always preferred to take his storms in the open. As much as he regretted his companions' discomfort, he could not deny the thrill that welled up inside when the storm had hit. More than once as a boy his mother had angrily fetched him from his grandfather's side as they stood on seacliffs in the teeth of a gale. The blood of the Furies ran in their veins, she had fumed on such nights, and more often than not his grandfather would escort Duncan to bed before going back into the storm with his pipes. Duncan would steal to the window in the loft where he slept and wait for the lightning flashes that would illuminate the old man playing the pipes at the cliff edge. He had been convinced that his grandfather was a living part of the storms, stirring the winds to greater force with his pipes. Every few weeks Duncan still woke to the image, the sound of the howling pipes and the answering winds echoing in his head.

Duncan let the cold water soak him and the spray slash his face as the little ship heaved and rolled. He had been so blind, so scared, so confused the past weeks. Answers to the terrible mysteries plaguing them always seemed to be lurking close, but always just out of his grasp. His vision was obscured. He loathed his growing sense of being one more victim, of being beaten down by unseen hands. If he was meant to die on this quest, he wanted to understand why. His despair battered him worse than the storm. He wanted to be, he needed to be, scoured by the elements. His grandfather had told him that sailors who survived storms at sea came out new men, with brighter souls and stronger hearts.

As the ship lurched again, he glanced behind to confirm that the captain still firmly held the wheel, then he saw a new shape clinging to a line. With a gasp he released his hold and sprang across the slippery deck.

"Ishmael!" he cried above the din. "This is no place—" Another wave crashed over the deck, choking away his words. He dove for a line to keep from washing overboard and grabbed the boy with his free arm.

"The elders say the gods are angry at us!" the boy cried. The wind slammed a gull against the mast, and its lifeless body dropped to the deck. The boy looked at the dead creature, then at Duncan, as if it proved his point.

"No, Ishmael!" Duncan shouted into the boy's ear. "This storm is driving us to where we need to be. The gods aren't trying to kill us, they are just seeing if we are up to the task they gave us."

Ishmael gazed uncertainly at Duncan, then a determined grin grew on the boy's troubled face. They remained motionless, not speaking, as the wind and water lashed at them.

"You can hear her," Duncan said when the wind ebbed for a moment. "Every ship has her song in a storm."

Ishmael cocked his head, then slowly nodded, telling Duncan he understood. The wind had reached such a velocity that the taut lines and fittings of the masts were resonating with a low hum.

"This is one of the real things, isn't it?" the boy declared.

Duncan nodded. A wild and unexpected joy pulsed through his heart. They were, together, hearing a voice of nature, the voice of gods, as some natives would say. For a moment he was his grandfather, standing with a young boy witnessing the rawness of the earth, humbled by the power of what the natives would call the real world.

"What she does is real too," Ishmael said, and Duncan glanced at the boy uncertainly before making out a sound of higher pitch. He missed the woman when first scanning the deck behind them, finding her in the wind-driven spray only when her chant grew louder.

Hetty Eldridge had wedged herself between the low cabin wall and a post of the port rail. The repetitive Haudenosaunee words she spoke were fast and slurred, but he could make out enough to understand. They had been the first Iroquois words he had ever heard, invoked in a raging storm of the north Atlantic. She was speaking to the black snake wind, the spirit who brought storms.

His heart wrenched. Surely she was too weak to hold on much longer, but he didn't dare release the boy. It seemed as though the strength of her spirit alone was keeping her in place. Her face was a terrible mixture of defiance and fear. He watched with increasing desperation as her hand lost its grip on the railing. He had seen a man washed off a deck. One moment the sailor had been darting for a loose stay, the next a wave had reached out and he was gone. The black snake wind could be a prankster, Conawago had once told him. It delighted in bursting the arrogance of humans. Duncan cursed it now for making him choose between the old woman and the young boy. He unwound his arm from the rope that held him and showed Ishmael how to twine his own arm around it.

Before he could move, another wave, bigger than those before, crashed over the bow. He doubled over, holding Ishmael close. The captain was having trouble keeping the rudder straight. The ship shifted dangerously into a wallow between waves, and as the officer struggled to regain control, another wave hit the ship broadside.

"Hetty!" Duncan cried out as the woman lost her grip and slid across the shifting deck. With an anguished groan Duncan began to release himself, then a figure darted out of the cabin hatch, scooped up the woman with one arm, and seized the mainmast with the other, pressing her tight against it as another wave hit.

Woolford offered a grim nod to Duncan, then pulled a length of rope from his waist and quickly bound the woman to the mast. Hetty, looking dazed, did not protest her restraints, even silently accepted the gag that Woolford tied around her mouth before retreating into the cabin. The words of the Welsh witch, Duncan realized, had been disturbing the elders.

A quarter hour later the sun broke out of the dark clouds, and the angry water subsided to low rolling swells. Woolford reappeared to take a dazed, sodden Ishmael from Duncan. Two sailors sped to the stern, where they relieved the exhausted captain.

"Our friends took poorly to the weather," the ranger observed, nodding to the hatch, where the Iroquois were filing out. Sagatchie looked as if he had fought a battle. Kassawaya's hands were shaking. The Iroquois elders gathered around Hetty, who seemed not to notice them. Her eyes, aimed toward the distant shoreline, were empty and unfocused. Two dead seagulls lay at her feet.

The captain, so fatigued he seemed to have trouble climbing down to the main deck, nodded his gratitude as Duncan offered a hand to steady him. "That blow was as good as two days' sailing. We'll be entering the Saint Lawrence by tomorrow afternoon," the bearded officer declared in a hopeful tone, then he turned to call on his men to raise more sail.

Hetty groaned like an injured cat. "No, no, no!" she screeched, and they turned to find her gazing in anguish at them. She seemed not to notice Sagatchie, who was untying her, but she had clearly heard the captain's report.

"I would have thought you joined the others in wishing for dry land," Duncan said, but then he saw the snakeskin entwined around the woman's hand and suddenly understood why she had come on deck. She had not been trying to banish the storm, she had been encouraging it. "Where would you have us go, Hetty?"

The Welsh woman produced a small wooden cylinder from the folds of her dress and clutched it tightly in her hand. "Away," she murmured forlornly. "Away from all that must be. Away from the hole in the world, where death awaits." Suddenly she looked up at Duncan as though just seeing him, and she thrust her hand behind her. As he reached out, she moved with surprising speed, ducking down and twisting past Duncan and Woolford, darting to the ship's rail.

Duncan leapt as she raised her hand, but too late. She threw the object in a long arc over the water.

He reacted without conscious thought, dropping his waistcoat and slipping off his shoes as he climbed the rail. Ignoring Hetty's wail of protest, Ishmael's fearful cry, and Woolford's angry curse, he launched himself over the side.

Even before he reached the water he heard the captain shouting frantic orders. He did not look back to make sense of the hurried activity on deck, just kept focused on the little speck of brown on the surface forty feet away. A few powerful strokes brought the wooden object into his grasp. He treaded water, staring in confusion at its ornate carved symbols. By the time he looked up the ship was over a hundred yards away and picking up speed. He would soon be alone on the wide inland sea.

"I seem to recall," came a voice from behind him, "this is not the first time you have thrown yourself off a ship. At least you waited for the storm to pass this time." Duncan turned to see Woolford standing with a bemused expression in the bow of the ship's dinghy.

Ishmael stared at him wide-eyed as he climbed over the ship's rail. "How could you do . . ." The boy seemed to have trouble finding words. There was more fear than wonder in his voice. "All that water. A man should be lost in it. You must be fish."

Duncan hesitated over his strange wording then saw that the boy was clutching his amulet. He glanced back at Conawago on the raised aft deck. The old Nipmuc was listening. Duncan had begun to realize that it was unsettling to the Indians, especially Conawago, that he had grown so close to them, in many ways become one of them, but had not embraced a spirit protector. "No Ishmael, there is no spirit of trout or pike inside me."

"A mighty sturgeon perhaps," the boy ventured.

Duncan offered an uncertain grin. "Nor sturgeon."

The boy studied Duncan with the eyes of a wise old man, then spoke with disappointment in his voice. "But anyone can see it, the thrill of a spirit touching you, pushing you, as you parted the water. Another man would have been pulled into the depths."

Duncan looked back to Conawago, half suspecting that the old Nipmuc had put the words in the boy's mouth. He did not know why he was so reluctant to admit the truth of Ishmael's words, for he indeed felt something thrill inside him when in the water.

"At the old hearths an uncle or shaman would present you your amulet when you came of age." Ishmael spoke like a patient kinsman. "Those close to your heart would know your spirit animal, though none would say its name for fear of frightening it away." There was an odd melancholy in the boy's words now, though Duncan did not know if it was for him or for the loss of the old hearths.

"No," Duncan said, though the word pained him. "It was not the way at the hearths of my clan." He looked down at the strange talisman in his hand, the object Hetty so desperately wanted no one to see. The images carved around the cylinder were intricately crafted. A leaping deer, a beaver with a branch in its mouth, a songbird, a horse, a cow, a bow, a hayfork. Tribal images and farming images. He scanned the deck. Hetty was nowhere to be seen.

"She took that off Rabbit Jack," Woolford stated as he looked over Duncan's shoulder. "You saw the way she pounced on him, like she was possessed. She tore at his waistcoat and belt pouches and pulled away a small wooden thing. We were so busy dealing with the provosts I forgot about it until now."

Duncan shook the cylinder and heard a rattle inside, then twisted it. One end moved along a nearly invisible seam. He pried it loose and upended the tube. Four small silver links tumbled onto his palm, pieces of a finely worked necklace or bracelet. He held one up to the sunlight and realized he had seen identical links, in the bowl at the gaming shed in Oswego and with the painted woman at the tavern.

"Grandfather's." Duncan looked up to see Ishmael at his side. The boy stared at the cylinder with haunted eyes. "My grandfather carved that."

"That can't be," Duncan said in confusion. "Hetty just took it at Oswego."

"Look at the bottom," the boy said.

Duncan turned it over. On the bottom was an elegant mark carved into the wood, the letters H and J between a spreading tree.

He looked back at the hatch where Hetty had fled. Which had she so desperately wanted him not to see, the silver links or the carving from Bethel Church?

FOLLOWING THE STORM the night sky was like crystal. A thousand stars beckoned. The wind had slackened, the clouds had vanished, and the reflection of the moon stretched for miles over the still black water. Duncan stood at the rail with Conawago, who fingered the wooden tube carved by his kinsman. He had no words to ease the old Nipmuc's troubles. The bodies lined up in the smithy of Bethel Church would haunt their sleep as long as they lived. But just as real to Conawago were the killings on the other side reported by the half-king's followers. Spirits were not supposed to die, and if they did they would face nothing but interminable blackness until the end of time. But that was not the unspeakable horror that kept the old Nipmuc's face clouded and his tongue uncharacteristically silent. The words of Black Fish had stabbed at Conawago's heart. When all the original spirits died the gates of the other side would close forever, Black Fish had testified to the Council, holding the truth beads in his hand as he repeated the words of the dead. Then the people of the forest would become no more than dust. They would be no more forever. The looming end of the tribal world had weighed heavily on Conawago for years, but he seldom spoke of it, and when he did it was of events in a possible future, a future that might yet be avoided. But suddenly messages about that ending were coming from the other side. It had become real, happening before them.

"I never meant for you to die, Duncan," Conawago said suddenly, still facing the water.

"Two lives to stop the Revelator and save the gods seems a fair price." Conawago offered no reply.

"I told you," Duncan said, struggling to keep emotion out of his voice. "My family has been calling me. I never expected to my life to be finished."

Conwago turned. "Finished?"

"Polished over decades like the gemstone that is your life."

The Nipmuc slowly shook his head. "Not a life to be envied. A slow torture, watching first your family then your entire world be destroyed over decades."

"But I have bested you, my friend. I managed to accomplish all that in a few short years."

Conawago's eyes narrowed. "In all of the time I have known you, I have never before heard words of self-pity from your lips. They dishonor the clan leader who lives within you."

It was Duncan's turn to stare out over the water. "You are right. I am sorry," he replied after a moment. "In all the time I have known you, I have never feared for you so much. Do not let me believe you would give up life so easily."

"Our gods are tired. I am tired. I begin to feel as though the bones of my soul are broken."

"The gods," Duncan said, "have much to answer for."

The words brought another brooding silence.

Duncan tried to make small talk with Conawago, pointing out the shimmer on the horizon he took to be the northern lights, even offering to borrow Woolford's lens so they could look at the mountains on the moon.

"We will find a way," Duncan said at last. "We have to find a way to survive, for Ishmael's sake."

The desolate expression with which Conwago answered his words chilled Duncan to his heart. His friend felt honor-bound to die, despite the terrible cost to Ishmael. After several more minutes of painful silence, he wandered toward the stern, where Woolford, doing his best to help the elders forget the torment of the storm, had persuaded the Iroquois to sit and listen to him recite his favorite bard.

The ranger captain had just completed a soliloquy from one of Shakespeare's comedies, to the obvious enjoyment of the elders, and he began a dialogue from *Romeo and Juliet*, engaging the grinning captain as the officer stood with one hand on the wheel. It warmed Duncan to hear Custaloga, Tushcona, and Adanahoe laugh.

As the cook brought mugs of hot tea to the Iroquois, Woolford enthusiastically began his favorite soliloquy from *Hamlet*. "To be or not to be, that is the question." Well into the famous passage he slowed his tempo for dramatic effect. "To sleep, perchance to dream, ay there's the rub, for in the sleep of death what dreams may come."

"This Hamlet," Custaloga interrupted, suddenly very sober, "he had trouble on the other side too? So after he died, what dreams did come? What were the visions in the death he spoke of? What did his people do about them?"

Woolford reacted at first with the impatience of the actor interrupted. "It was just Shakespeare's way of expression."

"But this Shakespeare is from the place of your birth. Have you not asked him?"

"He crossed over more than a century and a half ago."

Custaloga nodded, as if it somehow proved his point. "Then he must have powerful dreams from the other side, to make you speak his words today."

Woolford looked to Duncan as if for help. Neither was inclined to argue.

"Speak more of his dreams tomorrow," Adanahoe said as she rose and stretched, ready for slumber. "Tell us what the spirits told him. Tell us of the time of night when the graves gape wide."

The woman's words seemed to surprise Woolford. He stared at the woman as she stepped toward the ladder that led to the cabin hatch. Conawago stepped out of the shadows, looking at the ranger with intense curiosity.

Tushcona yawned and followed Adanahoe. "Did he speak of the beasts with wings?" she asked as she passed them.

Woolford seemed to grow uneasy. "Why would you ask that?"

The woman seemed not to hear as she disappeared down the ladder. "They are creatures of the spirit world," Custaloga explained. As he stepped across the moonlit deck, he looked into the sky as if he might glimpse the creatures, then spoke in afterthought before descending the ladder himself. "The four beasts had each of them six wings, and they were full of eyes and did not rest night and day."

Woolford grabbed Conawago's arm, as it to keep the Nipmuc from leaving. "Where did they get those words?" he asked in an urgent tone. Sagatchie, who had been watching the water, turned in confusion toward them.

Conawago shrugged. "The elders are famed for their memories of speeches. It is how the culture of the Iroquois is passed down. They are Black Fish's words, from his dream, from his visit to other side . . ." The old Nipmuc hesitated as he felt Duncan's intense stare.

"You never told me," Duncan said.

"I did not translate every word. I told you there were beasts guarding the original spirits."

"And the four beasts had each of them six wings about him and they were full of eyes within, and they rest not night and day," Woolford recited.

Conawago cocked his head. "You were at one of the other villages where Black Fish told his dream?"

"It is from the Bible, Conawago. A passage about the end of the world."

Conawago began to shake his head as if in disagreement, then paused as he saw the way his companions gazed at him. "What book?" he asked the ranger in an uneasy voice.

"Revelation."

"Revelation," Conawago repeated in a whisper. His face clouded as he looked at Duncan. "I am sorry. I am an Old Testament man." He seemed to grow weaker, and he lowered himself onto the stern bench. "The graves gape and let forth ghosts," he said.

"Now is the time of night that the graves gape wide and let forth the ghosts," Woolford recited. "*A Midsummer Night's Dream.* Why would you and Adanahoe both—"

"Something else Black Fish said that night. Words he repeated all over the League."

"Surely not," Woolford said. "Why would he . . ." His words drifted away as he looked from Duncan to Conawago's ashen face. "What else?"

"When he started to relate his dreams it was like theater," Conawago recalled. "But speeches before the Council often have a theatrical flair. At some of the smaller castles it was said there was a burst of yellow and red smoke in the fire which he leapt through. There is a certain expectation of drama. The words are supposed to be long remembered." The old Nipmuc shrugged. "He started by saying it is time to be frightened because now the lion roars and the wolf howls at the moon."

Woolford shook his head as if in disbelief. "Now the hungry lion roars and the wolf behowls the moon. Shakespeare again. *A Midsummer Night's Dream* again. Next you'll tell me he saw men with the heads of asses."

Conawago's voice grew small. "Men with the heads of horses were among those attacking the gods." He looked up sheepishly. "Not many in the tribes have seen an ass."

Water lapped at the side of the ship in the silence that followed. In the distance came the mocking cry of a loon.

"My God, the Delaware," Duncan said, looking at Sagatchie now. "He was telling us before he died. He knew the boys in the Ohio, he said, and they liked to cheat. We thought it was just more raving. He was talking about the half-king. He was warning us!" He saw the confusion on Conawago's face. "They gave you mushrooms to bring hallucinations," he said to his friend. "The words spoken by Black Fish weren't his words. Someone prepared a script for a disciple of the half-king to use with the League."

"Someone at the Council saw through it, and killed him," Woolford suggested.

"No. Black Fish was no great orator, or traveler to the spirit world. He had a good memory, as his uncle does, but also a taste for liquor. He was watched over by his companions in the red-eyed canoe. He was killed by one of them. He had found some rum and couldn't be trusted to keep his secret. He was likely to boast that he was part of a ruse against the Iroquois League."

"If men cannot be trusted before the Council," Conawago murmured toward the water, "then the world indeed collapses around us."

"It was meant to be his final performance," Woolford said in a near whisper. "Spread the tale among the other castles, sow the seeds of fear, then finally present to the Council."

"But shrines were destroyed," Conawago pointed out. "More than the hand of man was involved. A sacred cave was buried when the mountainside above it shifted. I heard a sacred tree burst from the inside."

"Either could have been done with gunpowder," Woolford observed.

"Gunpowder doesn't burn rocks," Duncan said. "We saw it, at the mouth of the gods near Onondaga Castle. It was as if lava had risen out of the earth and melted the stone."

"Certain gunners can burn rocks," came a voice from the dark, "burn the earth, like the devil himself."

Duncan looked about in the darkness for the speaker before realizing it came from the captain, still standing at the wheel.

"Beg pardon," the officer said. "None of my concern."

"How?" Duncan pressed. "How do you burn rocks?"

"Why with water, what else?" came the bitter reply. When the captain saw the insistent look on Duncan's face, he called for the first mate to take the wheel and gestured them below.

A minute later they stood before the heavy door that marked the ship's magazine. "Not just gunpowder in here," the captain explained as he unlocked the hatch. "There's always signal rockets and flares. But lately the navy board is experimenting with old recipes for Greek fire, the fluid that ignites with water and burns like the fire of Hades. Made of quicklime, saltpeter, sulphur, and bitumen, though the exact recipe is a secret kept by London. They heard rumors the French are equipping their fighting ships with it."

"We need to see how you burn a rock," Woolford said.

The officer seemed reluctant to go further. He sent for the gunner's mate, who knelt at a wooden chest lined with straw. Inside was a smaller chest that was divided into a dozen smaller compartments, each of which was lined with sawdust. He carefully extracted a small glass jar. Duncan exchanged a pointed glance with Sagatchie. They had seen such a chest, in the red-eyed canoe.

Back on the main deck the gunner's mate produced an old cracked ceramic bowl, a bucket, and a long grappling hook. He upturned the bowl in the bottom of the bucket and poured the jar's acrid-smelling contents over it. "Ye paint yer rock like this," the mate explained, "then toss on some water." He quickly hung the bucket at the end of the pole and extended it from the ship's side, over the lake. "Greek fire be like a viper. If y'er gonna release it git away fast." As he spoke the captain used the ladle from the water butt to toss a few drops into the bucket. Instantly the bowl burst into white flame, and the mate lowered the pole to set the bucket adrift. "It has to burn itself out. Water just makes it angrier." The bucket began to tilt, its molten contents spilling into their wake. They stared in uneasy silence as a narrow line of burning water traced their passage over the blackened lake.

IT SEEMED DUNCAN had barely lain down when the pounding of feet overhead awoke him. He rolled off his hammock and was far enough up the ladder to hear the frightened shout that came from the lookout.

"Boat ahead, port bow!" came the call from the mizzentop. The sailor quickly corrected himself. "Vessels on the starboard and port bow!" he called to the deck. "Blessed Mary!" he moaned a moment later. "The buggers are everywhere!" he shouted in desperate confusion.

Moments later Duncan had joined the captain on the lower shrouds, studying the shore they were now hugging. At first he saw nothing but a long point of land, then he thought he was glimpsing scores of logs in the water beyond the point. As he focused his glass the captain uttered a fearful gasp and cast a worried glance at his limp sails, then extended the telescope to Duncan.

It was not logs coming toward them. Duncan looked down into the anxious faces of Woolford and Sagatchie.

"Canoes," he reported, "Fifty or more, full of warriors. The half-king's men."

The captain's voice cracked as he called out orders to his meager crew. "Battle stations!"

"No," Duncan said.

"My cannons may be small, sir, but those vessels are fragile."

"They are fast and able to come at us from all sides," Woolford rejoined from the rail below them. "If just twenty of those warriors make it on board, we are finished."

"What do you suggest?" the captain asked, looking in despair at his pennant. The wind was quickly dying. They were as unlikely to outrun the canoes as outfight them.

Duncan and Sagatchie stepped to the rail and studied the advancing warriors. The sailors on deck seemed frozen in fear. They had all seen the gutted men sent back by the half-king.

"I always wanted to play the admiral," Conawago suggested with a sly grin.

Duncan gazed at his friend in confusion, but Woolford's eyes lit with understanding, and the ranger turned to the captain. "You're going to surrender the ship to the tribes."

"Never! You saw what they did to the last British who fell into their hands!"

Woolford held up his hand. "Not those tribes."

Duncan slowly grasped Conawago's intentions. "You and your men must go below and stay out of sight," he instructed the captain, then he quickly conferred with Woolford and Conawago.

The old Iroquois reacted energetically. By the time the canoes reached the sluggish brig, they were ready. Conawago, with a light in his eyes Duncan had not seen for weeks, stood at the wheel wearing the uniform jacket of the captain, looking every bit the mariner. Ishmael, attired like a cabin boy, stood at his side holding a compass box. All of the old Iroquois were on the deck, each of them wearing an article of clothing borrowed from the crew, who were concealed below, some holding slow match to fire the cannons if desperate measures were called for. Hetty was stretched along the bowsprit, her flinty face aimed outward, looking for all the world like a ship's figurehead.

Sagatchie stood in the mizzentop with his rifle, Kass in the foretop with her bow and quiver. Duncan, alone of the Europeans, stood on deck.

The half-king's men slowed as they reached the ship, spreading out to encircle the brig at the radius of a bowshot. Only one canoe glided forward, its passenger standing, holding a long ceremonial spear. With a chill Duncan recognized Scar, who had directed the torture of the Delaware Osotku and taunted them with his necklace of the man's fingers.

"These are the waters of the Revelator's nation!" the half-king's Huron captain shouted. "You will surrender the king's ship to us!"

Conawago made a show of working the captain's sextant, seeming not to notice the intruders at first. He handed the sextant to Ishmael then made a dismissive gesture toward the Huron. "As you can see, this king's boat has already been surrendered to the tribes in a greater cause."

"To you?" the Huron scoffed. "An old man and a boy?"

The reply came from old Custaloga, who appeared at the rail holding a boarding pike at his side like a staff. "To the Grand Council of the Haudenosaunee."

"Then you obey the Revelator's summons?"

"Revelator?" the old Oneida chieftain asked, keeping his voice loud enough for those in all the canoes to hear. "I know not of such a man. We obey the summons of the spirits." The hell dog appeared at his side, baring its teeth toward Scar.

The Huron hesitated a moment, looking at the dog. "To join the Revelator's cause," he asserted.

Duncan watched uneasily, glancing at the cabin door where the crew waited with weapons at the ready. One misplay and the deck would be running with blood. Custaloga lifted his pike and shook it as if to make sure the onlookers saw the strips of white fur hanging from it over streaks of fresh red paint that looked like dripping blood.

"To patch the hole in the world," Custaloga declared matter-of-factly. He was revered as a great orator, and he spoke with slow eloquence, gesturing now to the warriors hovering in the canoes. "We are pleased you have come to join us on this quest. You can be at our side when we all cross over. The navigator sent by the spirits says we have only a few hours remaining. Time enough for you to prepare your death songs."

The Huron leader opened and shut his mouth several times, but he had no reply. He had seen the faces of his men. Many seemed to sag. Those with weapons in their hands lowered them. Some began backpaddling. The Revelator's warriors had lost their lust for blood.

"Please!" Custaloga continued, "stay with us. You are wise to surround us this way. We need you as our noble vanguard, the first to cross over! The Speaker of the Dead shall tell you which of you shall have the honor to cross over first! She has walked that path many times! Your people will speak of your sacrifice for many seasons to come!" He aimed his pike toward the bow. Tushcona, sitting out of sight below the bowsprit, took her cue to uncover a brazier of smoldering tobacco. Hetty pushed herself up from the bowsprit on which she had been lying, rising up out of the smoke.

When Conawago had told the old Iroquois that Hetty had to look more the role of a spirit chaser, Tushcona had quickly taken charge, demanding the red jacket of one of the brig's marines and ordering Kass to gather up the dead gulls before sending Ishmael for the big cartouche bag she had brought with her.

Even Duncan, aware of the ruse, was unsettled. There was nothing artificial about the creature who hovered over the bow now. Hetty was indeed a spirit chaser. The red coat had been sliced so that not one but two pairs of long gull wings extended from her shoulders and back. Feathers had been sewn with quick stitches along the sleeves. From the red band that covered much of her head dangled long red shreds of cloth looking like bloodstained hair. Along the front, on either temple, had been sewn the head of a seagull. Her hands, inside the feathered sleeves, clutched the legs of a gull, so that instead of fingers appearing at the end of the sleeves, the scaled and clawed feet of the great bird extended.

"Beaver! Bear! Turtle!" she screeched, pointing with one of the horrid appendages to one canoe, then another, and another. She recognized the markings among the Huron and Mingoes and was calling out the names of their clans toward the sky. "The black snake wind has shown us the way," she called out. "The honor to be first to leave this world will be yours!" She pointed to another group of canoes. "Wolverine!"

Duncan did not miss the gasp from above and saw Sagatchie instantly raise his rifle. He halted before aiming, controlling his instinct. Custaloga had heard too, and he reflexively pointed his pike at the same group of canoes. The reviled destroyers of the Council hearth so many years before, the clan who had massacred the inhabitants of Onondaga Castle, were within striking distance.

The Huron leader tried to try to speak again, but then the canoe beside him turned and began furiously paddling away. He lowered his spear in confusion, then barked a rebuke to his own paddlers as they began to turn his canoe.

"We will have proof the Council is not against us!" the Huron shouted furiously. He still had a dozen canoes with him, and their warriors stared hungrily toward their traditional enemies. A man in one of the closest stood and waved his war ax. He wore an old bowl-shaped iron helmet on his head, a pot helm that was a vestige of another century. The iron head, Osotku had said of the Huron who had captured him and begun his torture by slicing away his ears. A sound like a growl escaped Sagatchie's throat. It was the Wolverine clan and their chief Paxto who had stayed. Kass lifted her bow. The man in the helmet shouted in the Huron tongue, and those around him answered with furious war cries. He was not about to let Hetty deprive him of the chance to spill Iroquois blood.

"The first mother of the Council is its proof," came a steady voice. Adanahoe was walking along the rail, pulling on a ceremonial robe. Both Conawago and Custaloga stepped quickly forward to pull her back, but she stopped them with a raised hand then bent to lift the hinged section of rail that opened to the ladder that ran down the hull.

"The Revelator will be pleased to have the first mother at his fire," Scar declared with a victorious sneer.

"Do not do this," Conawago begged the old woman. "We have seen what the half-king does to his captives."

Adanahoe tightened her robe about her with a determined glint. "They will not be turned back by mere words," the matriarch replied in a low voice. "Look at them, like hungry animals. Their blood is on the boil," she said to her companions. "I do not know about this god or that god, I just know you must live and go for the children."

"And for you," Tushcona added in an anguished voice.

Adanahoe squeezed her friend's hand. "My fate has not yet been woven," she said to the belt weaver, then she defiantly turned and climbed down into the canoe that sped forward to receive her. Duncan watched her canoe glide toward the shore, humbled by her bravery. The half-king's camp was in a fever pitch, had eviscerated the last outsiders who had come to interfere with their plans. The gentle old matriarch would gladly let herself be hollowed out if it meant saving the children.

"IT'S NOT WHAT I expected the hole between the worlds to look like," the captain declared as he carried the last of their party's baggage ashore.

Duncan looked up uneasily at the ruined buildings on the heights of the island, then took the officer's proffered hand without reply. The captain had kept a nervous watch as they had threaded their way up the maze of islands in the river, as if expecting the flotilla of canoes to reappear at any moment.

"I suspect no enemy warrior will dare venture near your ship again," Duncan offered.

"You may be right, sir, but I will not breathe easy until I have twenty miles of open water between me and this damned river. This archipelago is like a series of traps for any vessel bigger than a dinghy." The captain offered a hollow smile then ordered his men into the ship's launch. He had readily accepted Duncan's terms, agreeing to leave his passengers at the island chosen by Custaloga provided he leave them with the larger skiff and food supplies. Tushcona had also requested axes, as if she meant to do battle.

When Custaloga had pointed to the cliff that jutted like a ship's bow in the middle of the river, a seaman had called out to ask if the old Iroquois had found his hole between worlds. The elder had offered a patient smile. "To the river this ship is a hole between worlds, neither sky nor water. The water resists holes, and in the end water always prevails."

The words had not only wiped away the grin on the sailor's face, they had shaken him so badly he had backed away, tripping over a bucket. Not a sailor had spoken another word.

At first Duncan had thought Custaloga had simply chosen the island with the best vantage over the unfolding river, for the height would surely give a view for miles in every direction. But as they reached the switchback trail that led up the steep walls, Ishmael cried out and ran to Conawago, who put a steadying hand on his shoulder and pulled him up the trail away from the water's edge. Duncan lingered, watching as the Iroquois elders paused at the same spot, touching the amulets of their protective spirits and murmuring soft words toward the weathered white stones of the shore before beginning the climb.

Only when Duncan and Woolford, last in line, shouldered their packs and stepped to the trailhead did they see that among the sun-bleached stones, obscured by their shape and color, were dozens of human skulls.

THE RUINS THEY had seen from below were the burned-out shells of a large barn and two sheds. Hidden behind them was an abandoned three-story structure of stone, perched over an overgrown field that stretched to the low but steep ridge that bisected the island. Despite being overtaken by vines, the stone building was sturdy and well crafted. Once there had been crops in the field, and here and there stalks of maize poked up among the weeds. Behind the ruined barn a small vineyard had been planted many years before, and to Ishmael's delight the rangy, weed-choked vines still yielded bunches of fat red grapes.

Duncan scouted the site with Woolford and Sagatchie, discovering scraps of polished leather and long rows of stones that appeared to have been recently stacked into defensive walls. In the shadow at one end of the house were trestles recently nailed together from wood salvaged from the barn.

Sagatchie bent to pick up a small brass disc. *"Français,"* he said, holding it up to show Duncan the little *fleur-de-lis* embossed on the button.

Woolford checked the priming of his rifle and studied the landscape with new worry as the hell dog began sniffing the ground like a predator sensing a trail. "The French army was here, no more than a month ago."

"I know this place," came a low, worried voice behind them. Kass had a blanket draped over her shoulders, as if she had grown cold. "It is called the Island of the Ghosts. War parties have stopped here for many generations, and trading parties. One of the old skins on the Council House wall tells the story of how a small group of Iroquois stole into a war camp of Huron on the island with the ruined stone castle. They rescued captives and gave them all their canoes to flee in, then they stayed to attack. Ten of our warriors against forty of theirs. We still sing of their deaths at our campfires."

A shiver ran down Duncan's spine. Tushcona's belt predicted that he and Conawago would become dead heroes. "Why are we here?" he asked. "Why did Custaloga bring us to a place of dead heroes?"

"I wish I knew," Woolford said as he reached for his pocket telescope. "I don't like it. The French know Johnson and the general will be bringing troops up the river toward Montreal," he added as he scanned the horizon. "If I were them I'd set an artillery battery here. We've seen the signs of a scouting party. I wager they will be coming, very soon and in force. If we linger we are lost."

But lingering was exactly what the Iroquois elders intended. When Duncan and his companions returned to the house, a large cooking fire had been lit. Tushcona was directing the others with the air of a matriarch arranging a family meal. A cask of cornmeal had been found among the supplies left by the navy, and she was directing Conawago as he shaped little loaves and set them under upturned clay pots beside the fire. Grapes harvested by

Ishmael lay spread along the makeshift table of planks and trestles. Bacon and beans left by the captain were cooking over the open flames.

Duncan and Woolford retreated into the house, passing through a large kitchen with a walk-in hearth then into rooms stripped of furnishings. Shards of plaster with hints of bright paint clung to the plank walls. They could make no sense of the stately, incongruous structure until they reached the largest of the chambers, where the walls remained largely intact. Their plaster was covered with scenes of the Bible, painted with amateur but devout hands.

"A church," Woolford said.

"No," Duncan replied, pointing to faded names that had been ornately painted along the back wall, over a long table that had been partially dismantled for firewood. *Frère Jean, Frère Samuel, Frère Pierre, Frère Stephen.* "Not exactly."

"A monastery," came a voice behind them. "Or at least the beginnings of one." Conawago stepped into a pool of light cast by one of the windows. "I was brought here by my Jesuit teachers to visit for a few weeks as a boy. I heard the news that Queen Mary had died, making William of Orange a widower, while seated in that very kitchen, drinking hot cider on a stool by the fireplace."

"Surely not," Woolford argued. "That was in the last century."

Conawago ran his fingers along the names in the wall with a sad smile. "Sixteen and ninety-three to be exact." The Nipmuc's energy and enthusiasm for life often made it easy to forget that he had lived more then four score years. "The abbey of Saint Ignatius," he continued. "It was a grand scheme funded by the king in Paris for a few years. He sent soldiers to help construct these first buildings. I remember a parchment on the wall of the kitchen showing plans to build several buildings such as this one, in a square with a central courtyard. A monastery and school were to be established at a point between the warring tribes of north and south, to act as a buffer. It was intended that novices be taken in from all the tribes. They would become a tribal army of missionaries. I remember when I was here there were half a dozen native monks. The abbot was very proud of his native children's choir. They all lined up and sang for us, liturgical chants in Latin. I was deeply moved. He meant to take them all to Paris to perform for the king. After the singing we played lacrosse, the monks against the children."

"What happened?" Woolford asked.

"Years later a Huron chief came to visit his son, who was a novice here. He became furious when he saw his son's garment and his gentle demeanor, said the black robes had turned him into a woman. He returned with his warriors to put an end to things. When they came the Jesuits just prayed. The Hurons threw them over the cliff then fired the big barn. They were about to burn the abbey house when a terrific storm blew up and extinguished the fires. A very bad omen. They fled, and half were lost when their canoes were upset by the wind. It is said that no Hurons have ever returned to this end of the island, that it is taboo to do so."

"A sanctuary then," Woolford concluded. "Is that why we are here? We didn't come all this way to hide."

Conawago did not reply, and Duncan and Woolford followed as the old Nipmuc pushed on, up the wide, winding stairs to a corridor of small identical rooms, the cells of the monks. "Samuel, Jean, Pierre, Stephen, Victor, Frederick, Louis," he read the names painted on the first doors as he walked down the long hall. "I met these black robes. I wasn't certain about their vengeful God, but there could be no doubt about their courage and reverence. They stood alone in the wilderness, made an oasis here for a few years with naught but their crosses, Bibles, and virtue for protection. They died unmourned, without confession." He paused to read a Latin inscription on the wall like an old scholar. "Some say they were therefore not permitted into heaven," he added with a sigh, "that at night they can be seen wandering with the others over the island."

Woolford removed his cap. "The island of ghosts."

"War is closing in on all sides, and Custaloga brought us to a long-dead monastery?" Duncan asked after a moment's silence.

"This island has always been known for something else, long before the abbey. This was the island's side of light. The monks meant to help ease the misery, to break the dark side." Conawago made a cryptic gesture toward the low ridge that divided the island.

The others. How many monks could there have been, Duncan asked himself. A dozen? Certainly no more than twenty. There had been many more skulls on the beach.

Duncan was about to press for more of an explanation when Tushcona called them for her feast. She would not let anyone eat until they offered a long murmured prayer, spoken too low and too fast for Duncan to understand. He made out a plea for the safety of Adanahoe and *saderesera*, the grandchildren.

Their company was hungry but also weary. After their makeshift banquet, the Council's weaver, assisted by Hetty, took charge, assigning rooms as if she were a tavern keeper, assuring everyone they could sleep soundly without a sentinel since the building was protected by the old black robes. Tushcona paused in a small chapel at the end of the second-floor corridor. Duncan, still bewildered by her behavior, followed and saw emotion flood her countenance as she studied the simple wood-paneled chamber. Centered on the plaster wall above a low shelf was a pale spot where a crucifix had hung. Tushcona smiled as she saw it now lying on the windowsill, broken into several pieces but salvaged. Someone had bound the shards together against a piece of wood with strips of sinew. The old Iroquois woman lifted the broken cross and reverently leaned it upright on the shelf. She turned back to the window, hesitating a moment before running her fingers along the front lip of the sill. She made a tentative pulling motion then uttered a syllable of surprised pleasure as the front board of the sill fell outward on hinges to reveal a narrow compartment. Inside was a rosary and several beeswax candles.

"How could—" Duncan began to ask, but Conawago was suddenly at his side, squeezing his arm to cut him off. They stepped aside to let the old woman set the candles in the dusty sconces along the corridor of sleeping cells. Ishmael followed, lighting each one with a taper.

No one needed to stand guard, the old woman reminded them again, and she ushered Duncan and Conawago into the last of the chambers where their blankets and packs awaited, putting a finger to her lips as though it was now time for silent meditation in the cells.

Duncan slept fitfully, then woke abruptly, his mind boiling with images of Adanahoe as a ghost and warriors hacking at monks with their war axes. The floor planks creaked as he made his way down the corridor, checking on the sleeping figures as he passed each cell. Ishmael had chosen to sleep curled on the floor nestled against the big dog.

He pushed open a narrow door and found a twisting stairway that led to the third floor. Lifting a candle from a sconce, he ventured upward, into another corridor. Half the space was finished into cells. He passed into another chamber, still in rough timber, used for storage. Crumbling wicker hampers were lined against one wall, filled with rotting clothing. On a shelf behind them were small wooden boxes, each with the name of a monk and two dates. He opened the hinged top of the first, marked *Brother Luc, 1652-1687.* Inside was a small bible, a writing quill, a ring, and a lock of blond hair tied with a red ribbon. On the bottom was a piece of parchment with a narrative in French.

Brother Luc, dove of Christ, was martyred on the northern shore of Lake Huron, it began, going on to explain that he was the son of a lowly shoemaker in Burgundy who as a teenager had answered God's call to live among the tribes of North America. Luc had opened half a dozen missions and christened over two hundred aborigines before being burned alive for administering European medicine to Ojibways dying of fever.

Duncan closed the box reverently, realizing now that it, like the others, held the personal effects of monks killed by the tribes they had sought to convert.

He ventured toward the pool of moonlight cast through the window to find a makeshift chapel. A rough bench bore a cross made of white birch sticks set on a piece of white ermine fur. Other benches faced the altar. On the adjacent wall, charcoal pictograms had been drawn in the fashion of those he had seen on the chronicle skins of the Iroquois Council. But as he raised the candle he saw that these did not depict hunts or raids. A stick figure with a beard carried a cross on his back up a hill. In another scene the bearded man sat with others at a long table, in another he distributed fish to a crowd of smaller figures.

The Mohawks of Quebec, Conawago had told him, were all Christians. There was something strangely poignant about the little chapel built by Christian natives in the crumbling Jesuit outpost. In the lands of Duncan's youth, the violent Reformers of Calvin had torn down chapels, even entire cathedrals, but on some nights his grandmother had taken him to a tiny chapel in a cavern overlooking the sea where an aged defrocked priest had presided.

He stared through the window at the black sky over the blacker river. The apocalyptic destruction of the Highlands had broken the faith of many Highlanders. It had been years since he had been in a church. He looked out at a bright star rising over the water. *"Ave Maris Stella."* The words left his tongue unbidden. The old priest had been a fisherman and often opened his nighttime rites at the mouth of the cavern with an invocation toward the ocean. Hail, Star of the Sea.

Despair crept into his heart. He could not remember ever feeling so broken, so adrift, so filled with foreboding. Murderers who lied about gods and thieves who stole treasure and children roamed the wilderness, and try as he might he could not pierce the mysteries that connected them. Armies waited ahead, lusting to soak the land in blood for the sake of distant kings. His companions expected him to lead them to the truth, to an end to the violence and a restoration of the old ways, but he could not shake the feeling that he was only leading them to their deaths.

As the moon rose over the black rim of the horizon, he extinguished his candle and faced the little birch cross, glowing silver in the moonlight. He was head of a dying clan, companion to a dying tribe. The monks of Saint Ignatius had vowed to bridge the peoples from different sides of the sea, and when they failed they had calmly prayed as they were thrown over the cliff.

"*Ave Maria*," he whispered, then continued more loudly. "*Gratia plena, Dominus tecum.*"

He did not know how long he prayed, but the moon had climbed well clear of the horizon when he looked back out the window. The overgrown field was bathed in soft light. Suddenly he saw movement along the low ridge, two slow figures who stopped and bent at intervals along the crest. He shot up and silently slipped down the stairs.

The rocks at the northern end of the ridge provided cover as he ascended, rifle in hand. The two figures were less than fifty paces away when he reached the top. The amorphous shapes glided over the silver landscape. This was the Island of the Ghosts, and this was their hour.

He gasped as he stepped around a boulder to find another phantom. Kassawaya sat as still as a statue, her bow in her lap, an arrow nocked and ready. She showed no surprise at Duncan's appearance, and he realized she had probably been watching him since he left the abbey.

"I have heard of this place all my life," she whispered. "Be good or you'll be sent to the Isle of the Ghosts, my aunts would say. No one ever comes back from the Isle of the Ghosts, my mother said once when I broke a favorite pot of hers. I had to go away to a hut for five days when my first moonblood came on me. At night I had visions of a place where lost, weeping souls wandered aimlessly. I thought it must be this island."

Duncan gazed uncertainly at the Oneida woman. Her words seem to come from someone vulnerable, even frightened. But the countenance he saw was of someone else. Her playful strength, her strong will, her energetic nature were so dominant they often eclipsed her comeliness. In the moonlight, as unmoving as the rock she sat on, bow in hand, she could have been a statute of wild Artemis, goddess of the hunt.

Her gaze shifted, from the ghosts on the crest of the ridge to its far side, to a small, dark valley that the rising moon had not yet lit. Her expression grew hard, and sad, and when Duncan asked what was there, she offered no reply.

He moved on, warily approaching the two phantoms, grateful for the rifle in his hand. They were moving toward him, stopping every few feet at large rocks along the crest and bending over the rocks before continuing their strange passage. Duncan dropped to one knee and waited for the ghosts. The nearest was ten feet away when it raised an arm to throw back the cowl that covered it.

"Tushcona, is it you?" Duncan asked, confused to see the old woman.

She put a finger to her lips then gestured to her companion, who reached into a sack and extended a small object to the Iroquois elder. A small loaf of cornbread. Duncan looked at the line of rocks behind them and saw now that each held one of the small loaves. He had thought they had baked the loaves for their journey, but instead they were giving them to the Isle of the Ghosts.

The two grey figures remained silent when they reached the last rock, only a few feet from the unmoving Kassawaya, then turned to walk back along the crest. They passed Duncan without a word and continued, Duncan a step behind, until they reached a large flat boulder that marked a trail leading down into the shadowed valley.

"I don't know who I am," the old woman suddenly replied. Her companion sat on a rock on the opposite side of the path and removed the cowl of her monk's robe. It was Hetty Eldridge. Duncan, feeling like an intruder, took a tentative step backward, but Tushcona gestured for him to sit on the ground between the two women.

"I was born to a Shawnee clan," the weaver of the Council belts confessed. "But my parents were killed in a Huron raid when I was in my eighth summer. They captured over twenty of us, children, young women, and several of our warriors. They brought us here for the trading. Other war parties came in with European prisoners."

As she spoke moonlight began to filter into the valley beyond. Duncan's heart leapt, and he grabbed his gun as he saw the rows of upright figures.

Tushcona showed no alarm. "I thought we would stay a day or two when they tied us to those terrible posts. But we had to wait for the market. More parties came in, from the North and the West, to buy new slaves.

Every post was used, many with two prisoners tied back-to-back. I was there," she pointed to a tall grey shape midway down the nearest row.

Posts. Duncan was looking at *gaondote* posts, prisoner posts sunk in the ground in two long rows separated by a wide avenue. There were a least two dozen in each row.

"It became like a festival for the war parties and slavers. They were on the way home, with prizes of war. There was rum. I was tied with an English boy, a good boy who sang songs and began teaching me my first English words. His father and mother were there too and would sometimes call out to him, though they always paid for it with a blow from a club. On the tenth night they tied his father to a long pole and hoisted him over a fire while they danced. They roasted him alive to celebrate their victory. He screamed and screamed, and when the boy screamed back they knocked him unconscious.

"The next day some Abenaki came, friends of the Huron. They paid in pelts for all the surviving English children, over a dozen, but they never untied them. One by one they slit their throats, in revenge for some raid English soldiers made on their camps. Only after the bodies began to smell did those Hurons untie them and throw them over the cliff.

"For generations war parties have come here with captives. So many children died. Scores of children, hundreds even. We could have done more to stop it. We should have done more."

Duncan stood and looked out over the flat with its ranks of posts. It was a torture ground where unimaginable suffering had been inflicted, the blood of so many lives spilled. And it had become a worm eating into the souls of the old Iroquois, who could have stopped it and hadn't. He walked along the nearest posts, touching each one with only his fingertips, thinking of the belt, the elders, and the night in front of the Council. This dark place of torture was the hole in the world. But he had not understood the connection until that moment.

"The children will be brought here," he said to Tushcona.

"If they survive, yes. They are in the hands of the Huron, who adhere to the old ways. There are those among them who would pay much to see my granddaughter's life spilled out on the ground here."

"But that is not why the half-king took them."

"He took them to force us to his cause. If he is not successful he will give them to the Huron." Tushcona walked with him now, though she seemed reluctant to step too close to the posts.

"How?" Duncan asked. "How could the half-king have known the children were from the elders? The secret must have been known by so few." Secrecy had been their protection, their shield.

Tushcona seemed not to hear. "Sometimes those who came from the North liked to buy a slave and leave it tied to a post to starve." The old woman pointed a finger toward the second line of posts. "There were two such men dying, an Oneida and a Nipmuc, when I arrived. No food, no water. They would make songs for rain because then they could open their mouths and live another day. At night when it rains I still hear their songs."

Duncan began to understand the island. "It's why they built the abbey here," he said. "The monks wanted the cruelty stopped."

Tuschcona nodded. "They tried. They would sometimes walk among the prisoners, saying their prayers, offering food and water when it was permitted. When no one bought me, the Hurons decided to starve me too. They kept the monks away and nearly killed one when he secretly brought me a crust to eat in the night. But a French trader came, and the monks got him to trade a cask of rum for me."

"How long did you stay with the monks?"

"A few months. Some of those Christian Mohawks of the French decided to take me to Onondaga Castle. The old castle. A warrior there took me for a wife. We had a fine son. But they both died when the Wolverines came."

Hetty stepped to their side, as if she did not wish to be alone. Duncan noticed now the haunted way the Welsh woman stared at the little valley. "You knew the posts too?"

She put a hand up on a post as if she needed support. "The abbey was destroyed by then," she said. "The western tribes would bring furs to trade. I was eighteen years old. I was so scared. The ghosts were here then too. The ones who had died of starvation were the worst. They would howl for food in the night, but I was the only one who could hear them. I wanted to help them but never knew how."

A chill ran down Duncan's spine.

She touched the scars that circled her wrists. "I struggled so much I wore away the skin and flesh, almost to the bone."

Duncan stared at the Welsh woman, not understanding but somehow believing her. He turned to look up at the rocks with the loaves. "So tonight you finally feed them."

As she spoke, new shapes emerged from the shadows. The other elders, with Ishmael and Conawago, appeared over the crest, carrying the axes brought from the brig.

Tushcona stepped before Conawago. "The posts still bind those who died at them. I watched a Nipmuc warrior die at the second post on the north side."

Conawago hesitated. "Surely those of the Council should—"

"No. You are the chosen ones." She handed an ax to Duncan. "You two shall release the first ghosts to the other side. They will let the old ones there know you have arrived to make good on your word, tell them you are coming to stop the killing of the gods."

The posts were thick, but the old wood was brittle and their blades sank deep. As Conawago and Duncan alternated their swings, the old Nipmuc chanted, with a phrase on each stroke. "We are coming," he said with the first swing, then, "do not die," with the second. "Do not forget us," he said with the third, then he repeated the words, over and over, his determination growing fiercer with each bite of the ax. Whether he was speaking to the lost children or the fading spirits Duncan was not certain. He joined in the chant.

They had the first post down in minutes. When they had leveled four posts, the elders lit a fire at the center of the slaveyard and rolled the posts into it. After each of the elders had helped cut down a post, they took up positions at the fire, throwing tobacco in it and singing the songs that called for the spirits to take notice. They had taken down nearly half the posts when Woolford appeared, taking an ax from a weary Conawago.

Duncan had the sense that his ax was growing lighter as they leveled the posts. Ishmael exclaimed with joy as a meteor shot overhead. He became aware that all of them, including Woolford as he swung the heavy blade, were singing a new chant, a spirit chant used by warriors. Not for the first time on their strange journey Duncan felt as if he were caught inside some ancient myth of the tribes. He paused and looked at Hetty and Tushcona at the fire, sparks flying around their heads, then Conawago, who swung his ax again, looking more like a fighter than the gentle philosopher Duncan knew him to be. This was how the old tribesmen fought their wars.

They were only done, Tushcona insisted, when every post was cut and burned. It was arduous work, and by the time they were finished Duncan felt as if he had felled an entire forest. He collapsed beside Conawago by the fire. The soaring flames and singsong chant were hypnotic.

He was not certain if he dozed off, but Conawago's touch on his knee brought him back to full consciousness. The sky had lightened to a dull grey, enough to illuminate the crest of the low ridge. As he followed Conawago's gaze, his heart leapt into his throat. For a moment he was certain he was looking at a line of ghosts staring down at them from the ridge. But then the figures began to descend the slope in a line of attack, shoving a frightened Kassawaya before them. They were vengeful warriors and were ready for battle.

Chapter Thirteen

Woolford grabbed his rifle. "Stay with Conawago!" he desperately whispered before darting into the shadows. Duncan reached for his own rifle.

"No!" came Conawago's quick command. "Caughnawags."

The warning did little to dispel Duncan's fear. The Caughnawags were the northern Mohawks, who had been converted by French Jesuits in the prior century then exiled to Canada when the Iroquois fell into the British sphere of influence. They prayed to one God but gave homage to their war axes as well. They were the most numerous of France's allies on the northern frontier and second only to the Hurons in their reputation for ferocity. They did not consider themselves part of the Iroquois League, for they were French Indians, and those of the League were British Indians. For decades they had led raids deep into British territory, including the infamous massacre at Deerfield, in the Massachusetts colony.

Duncan struggled against his impulse to grab his weapon as the enemy closed around them. Each warrior carried a musket, though they kept the barrels down as they surrounded those at the fire.

"They spoke to me in Mohawk," Kass groused, glancing at Sagatchie. She was obviously shamed by her capture.

"Because they *are* Mohawk," said Custaloga, his eyes on a stern middle-aged warrior wearing a sash of skunk pelts. "Because the same blood flows in their veins and ours."

The warrior with the fur sash stepped forward. "You have made good use of the wood here," he declared in a deep slow voice.

Duncan realized the man was offering support for their night's work, although his sober expression gave no hint of friendship.

Custaloga offered a tentative smile. "Our northern relatives sometimes recover captives and bring them back to us," he said to Duncan, though loudly enough for all to hear.

The chieftain in the black-and-white fur shrugged. "The Hurons and Abenaki will be furious."

Custaloga shrugged back. "Chief Tatamy, you and I know that Mohawks do not wage war on women and children."

The stranger called Tatamy stared at Custaloga with a stony expression, as if to rebuke him. His gaze shifted to Ishmael as the boy stepped in front of Conawago, holding a stick like a club, and a weary smile flickered on his weathered face. "Mohawks do not wage war on women and children," he agreed.

"Then you will help us recover the five lost children of the Council," Duncan interjected. The moment the words left his tongue, he knew they had been too hasty. The Iroquois had not even begun the rituals of hospitality.

Tatamy frowned his disapproval.

"This person is Duncan McCallum," Conawago apologized as he gestured to Duncan. "A wretched Scot who is still learning the ways of true humans."

The chieftain shook his head, expressing his own regret, then sighed and gestured to several warriors standing behind him. "If you would share your fire," he said to the elders, "then we would share our fish." The warriors stepped forward, extending vines strung with huge trout.

As the fish were cleaned and spitted for roasting, Custaloga and Tatamy spoke of the difficulties of their respective journeys and offered each other water to wash away the grime of the trail. It was a version of the Edge of the Woods ceremony, a cornerstone of Iroquois diplomacy, in which those who met at the end of a journey offered to clear the soil of travel and extract the thorns of difficult trails. The two chieftains then offered gourds of fresh water for each of the other's party to drink.

When he finished, Custaloga stood with his gourd before Tatamy. "You would refuse me the honor of treating with all your warriors?" he asked pointedly.

Tatamy worked his jaw, clearly struggling for a moment, then turned toward the ridge and gave the call of a meadowlark. Two men rose up from the shadows and began descending the ridge. They had not covered half the distance to the fire before a third figure darted down from the field of boulders and disappeared over the ridge. The two chieftains were letting Woolford flee. The presence of the ranger captain, who fought bitterly with Caughnawags in the field, would have been an awkward distraction to the business of their makeshift council.

The sharing of the fish and the remaining grapes retrieved from the abbey erased all tension. The Caughnawags and those who lived in Onondaga Castle might be enemies, but they were also family. Soon several were speaking of common relatives. In times of peace, Duncan learned, Mohawks on one side of the Saint Lawrence would often take spouses from among the other. The northern warriors, many of whom wore crosses around their necks beside their spirit amulets, treated the Iroquois elders with wary deference.

At last Tatamy rose and conferred with several of his men. "We will now go to the stone castle," he announced, gesturing Custaloga toward the abbey, as his men dispersed toward either side of the island to keep watch. Conawago waited until the two chieftains were nearly at the crest of the ridge before motioning for Duncan to follow with him. The two chieftains were already in the main chapel when Duncan and the old Nipmuc reached them. Tatamy was kneeling before the battered altar. When he rose, his face held more worry than anger.

He looked to Duncan with challenge in his eyes. "Say the words," he said.

"I have come to find five children."

Tatamy looked at him without expression. "Say the words," he repeated.

Uncertain, Duncan looked over the chieftain's shoulder to the writing on the wall. "*Gloria Patri et Filio et Spiritui Sancto.*" He read the first line of the prayer, then continued with the unwritten remainder, still in Latin. The northern chieftain closed his eyes to listen better, as if the words transported him to another, more harmonious time.

"English," Tatamy said when he finished.

"Glory be to the Father, the Son, and the Holy Spirit," Duncan recited.

"*Français,*" the chieftain pressed.

When Duncan spoke the French words, then offered them in Gaelic, there was more curiosity in Tatamy's eyes than challenge. "My mother," the chief observed in a distant tone, "always said there must be a different god for each language." He stepped forward and abruptly pulled down the shoulder of Duncan's jerkin, exposing the top of the dawnchaser tattoo on his shoulder. "You collect gods like beads, McCallum."

"My mother taught me that each man must take his own god into his heart. A strong man knows it does no harm to his god to respect that of another."

Tatamy stared impassively. "Do you think you will patch things on the other side by tricking the gods?"

"Those who seek to play tricks with gods do not deserve their protection."

Tatamy cocked his head at Duncan but offered no reply.

"But sometimes I wonder," Duncan added, "if it may be the gods who play tricks on us. Making good men kill each other because of the color of the flag they stand under."

Tatamy frowned and walked along the religious murals on the wall before turning back to Duncan. "The men I will take you to will probably kill you. They kill a spy almost once a week," he explained in a matter-of-fact tone. "Hang him. Shoot him by a wall. In the winter they like to tie a rock to him and drop him through a hole in the ice over the river. It has become something of a sport to the French officers and the Huron chiefs."

"I will not go the French army."

Tatamy grinned. "But our officers are much prettier than yours. Even their monks wear lace. And despite the fall of Quebec, they are still convinced they will be the victors."

The meaning of the warrior's words slowly sank in. "You're saying the half-king is already with them or soon will be. I will not expose my companions to the wrath of the French or the half-king," Duncan said.

"It is your choice," Tatamy said, and with nods to Custaloga and Conawago he took his leave. As he reached the door he turned and tossed something shiny to Duncan.

Duncan stared, struck dumb, at the coin he caught. In his hand was a Spanish dollar stamped with the broad arrow symbol of the British army.

MONTREAL'S LONG OUTER wall stretched for nearly a mile along the river, punctuated at regular intervals by cannon barrels. A surprising number of steeples reached above the wall, reminding Duncan of towns he had seen in the low countries of Europe.

Any lingering hostility had gone from Tatamy after he had spent hours speaking with the Iroquois elders. Now he conducted them into the enemy city with the air of a stealthy warrior.

"Hospital, outpost barracks, fur depot," Tatamy explained with quick gestures as they glided past a group of stout buildings situated near the water, outside the western end of the fortress. The water gates along the riverbank were scenes of intense activity as boats of stores were unloaded, watched over by stern sentinels in the bleached wool frocks of French infantry or militia in woodland dress. Artillerymen were firing cannons in long-ranging shots to calibrate their balls and powder. Duncan's gut clenched with every shot.

"Any language but English," Conawago warned as they beached their canoes and Duncan donned the soft wool foraging cap tossed to him by Tatamy. Most of the chieftain's men had parted company before the portage around the falls miles above Montreal, but the half-dozen who remained flanked their small party as Tatamy led them through one of the gates guarded by militia, who wore caps matching that of Duncan.

The town was a thriving mercantile center. Rich convoys of fur-laden canoes from the West and North had been arriving for decades. The streets hummed with activity of merchants and craftsmen. A cobbler worked at his bench before the open door of his shop. Shelves of pewter lined the window of a shop with a huge wooden candlestick for its sign. The size and affluence of the buildings he saw matched many he had seen in New York and Philadelphia, though the great stone structure near the town center was larger than any he had seen in the British colonies. Dogs played with scraps of fur. Aged women, both of the tribes and of the French, hawked baskets, apples, fish, and crocks of syrup, crying out their wares. Along a stone wall, half a dozen old, frail-looking Indian men and women dressed in little more than rags held out bark containers, or just leathery palms, in search of alms. As they rounded the corner Kass hesitated, then retreated to pull Sagatchie away as he stared at the beggars. Duncan paused as he realized Hetty and the hell dog were settling along the wall at the end of the line of beggars. She shook her head adamantly when Duncan gestured her on.

"We'll be here when you are ready to leave," she said in French, turning to the haggard woman beside her, who was admiring the dog, and beginning a conversation.

They worked their way down another block of merchants then Tatamy signaled for them to wait in the shadows of an alley as two officers in uniformed finery passed by, speaking with excited gestures, toward the ramparts.

"Pretty lacebacks," Ishmael whispered at Duncan's side.

As the boy stepped away, he grabbed his shoulder. "Lacebacks. Why did you say that?"

Ishmael shrugged. "Lacebacks," he said again, pointing to the officers' uniforms whose lace collars were visible below blue tricorns. "Lacebacks flutter around. Like Osotku said. I told you they took me to see him, to scare me. He said to me 'black angels and lacebacks flutter around.'"

Duncan had heard the words too but had dismissed them as the ravings of a dying man.

"You knew what he meant?"

"Not until later. That night they came to look at Conawago and Hetty, the half-king's oracles. A French officer and a priest. I guess he was what you call a priest. Fancier than a monk. He wore a robe but also a gold necklace and a black cloak with red lining. A laceback and a black angel."

Fancier than a monk. A French officer and someone high in the Roman church had come to observe the half-king's progress. He waited until the rest of his companions had followed Tatamy then warily stepped behind them as the Mohawk led them to the stone tower. They were being taken to the center of the Roman church in Canada.

In his youth Duncan had seen cathedrals the size of the one Tatamy led them to, but they had all been in ruins, laid waste by Calvin's reformers. Despite his foreboding, he longed to linger to study the stained glass and the gothic carvings along the pews and altars, but Tatamy hurried them through, to a small arched door behind a row of confessional booths. The northern chieftain paused to be sure they were not followed before opening the door. He lifted a lit lantern hanging on the inside wall and led them down a flight of stone stairs, cupped from long use. Tatamy had identified a long two-story stone building across the courtyard from the cathedral as the seminary, and as they entered a long passageway, Duncan realized they were being led toward it, underground. He assumed the second door that Tatamy led them through would open to another staircase. Instead they reached a small antechamber leading to a low door, heavy with iron studs and an iron cross nailed to its center. The Mohawk gave four slow knocks, and after several moments they heard the sound of a deadbolt being released.

A small man in a monk's robe greeted Tatamy in the tribal tongue, then hurriedly introduced himself as Brother Xavier before turning toward a large candlelit table in front of a smoldering hearth. The chamber looked as though it had been built for storage of foodstuffs, but there was no longer any evidence of supplies. One wall of the vaulted chamber was nearly covered by a fading tapestry with the crucifixion scene, at the top of which hung rich pelts and ornate tribal spears. Draped over the shelves of books and manuscripts that lined the other walls were more than a dozen beaded wampum belts. Brother Xavier settled into a chair before a large manuscript volume, pushed his unkempt greying hair back on his nape, and took up his quill as if they had interrupted him in some urgent task of scholarship.

Even after Tatamy had gathered the group in front of the broad table, the man kept writing. Finally he looked up, with a smile on his long, thin face. "One of my favorite entries in this chronicle is from 1689," Brother Xavier declared in a refined voice, "when our blessed cathedral was still being built. A young Huron arrived with the tale of a white stag that had appeared along the banks of the inland sea, the great lake that takes the name of his tribe. He said the stag had come to them through a gate to the spirit world, to heaven. One of the young monks named Pierre who was being prepared to go live among the Hurons insisted on going back with the warrior. He was never heard from again. Years later that same Huron returned with one of the fur convoys and told a peculiar tale. He and the monk had found that stag. It let them follow it until they came to a valley thick with fog, though all the surrounding land was under a clear blue sky. The stag waited as if expecting them to continue into the fog with it, and Brother Pierre said it must be the way across, that they must have need of a monk on the other side. The Huron was too frightened, but Brother Pierre went on. Neither he nor the stag were ever seen again. No trace was found of him except his Bible, lying on a perfectly circular rock in a perfectly circular clearing."

Tatamy glanced at Conawago. The Mohawk chief seemed disturbed by the tale, but Conawago wore a calm smile. The monk at the table seemed to see only the old Nipmuc. "What will you say, Conawago of the Nipmuc, when you meet Brother Pierre on the other side?"

"I will ask him if the moon was full on the night he left this world."

"The moon?"

"My mother told me of a white stag that was able to fly through the sky whenever the moon was full. She called it the spirit stag."

The monk's face filled with wonder. He lifted his quill and quickly wrote on a scrap of paper, then rose and spread out his arms. "*Bienvenue!*" he offered, his greeting warmer this time. "We are honored to have the companions from the Council with us." Xavier gestured to the volume on his desk. "I am keeper of the archives." Duncan glanced around the room again. The chambers where monks worked at manuscripts were usually well lit by windows and mirrors. Xavier preferred to work in shadows.

Conawago inched in front of Ishmael, as if the boy needed protection. Brother Xavier smiled again. He seemed to know much about his visitors. "There are entries about a Nipmuc boy in the last century," he said to Ishamel, stepping to the side to be able to see the boy more clearly. "He would have been about your age, a lad of great promise, a student in the Ville de Quebec who was sent to our seminary as a novice, one of the first of the tribes to wear our robes. He was even taken to France and introduced to the king, who was enchanted with him. They spoke long into the night about the beasts of the New World. Louis XIV was fond of the notion that the natives of our woodlands were the lost tribes of Israel. The king nearly choked with delight when the boy said he had always assumed the Israelites were a lost tribe of the Americas." Brother Xavier's smile took on an air of melancholy. "But we have no Israelites to show us the way today. Just a band of . . ." the sweep of his arm took in Duncan, Conawago, Sagatchie, Kass, and the elders, "brave voyageurs."

"Whom you have invited into the belly of the monster," Duncan added. He was uneasy being at the mercy of a French monk, trapped underground. The church was known for working closely with the French army. Black angels were working with lacebacks. Their lives hung on the thin thread of their trust in Tatamy. A squad of soldiers outside the solitary door would mean the end of them all.

"You dishonor me, McCallum," the monk replied in a cool tone. "I gave my oath to the Lord above, not to an earthly king." He opened a heavy tome at the side of his table. "Our prelate opposed this when my old teacher started it. It is still considered wrong by some, even a sacrilege. But I persevere, continuing the work of translation."

First Duncan, then Conawago, stepped forward to leaf through the book. It was a Bible written in the language of the Mohawks. As he pushed the book toward Conawago, Duncan exposed correspondence underneath.

"I do not want more blood spilled," Xavier declared as he dropped another book over the letters, though not before Duncan cast a surreptitious glance at them. Several were written in Italian. Two more were addressed to Logtown, the largest settlement of the Mingoes, and Fort Detroit, largest of the French forts in the West. "The tribes must settle tribal differences among themselves. They must stop being used by European generals." He gestured to the chronicle of the missionaries. "When our brothers first landed here, they were certain they had found the lambs of God. They were naive. They were in thrall to the arrogant rulers in Rome who were themselves blinded by the gold and jewels of Vatican robes. They thought they had but to shepherd the lambs. They paid for it dearly. Nearly every missionary we sent among them in the early years died, and never easily. The deaths are recorded here in hideous detail. I was among those missions. I ventured with five other brothers into the West. The tribes tortured my comrades in front of me and sent me back to bear witness. But I went back, again and again. Most of me survived." He held up his left hand, and for the first time Duncan saw that it was missing two fingers.

The blast of a cannon, another solitary ranging shot, shook the walls. Tushcona, clearly unsettled, began low whispered prayers, clutching her amulet. The sound of the cannon seemed to prod the monk, to make his words more urgent. "They died true martyrs, do not mistake me, but their deaths were wasted. Rome kept viewing our mission as a conquest and kept dispatching their Christian soldiers to subjugate the wayward flock of the New World. For decades they refused to allow arms to be given to the tribes of the North since that was inconsistent with their vision of the natives as lambs. When the Dutch and English armed their traditional enemies, many in the northern tribes died needlessly. Rome's version of the truth has pushed the tribes into slow death."

The thunder of another gun interrupted the Jesuit, shaking the walls. He glanced resentfully in the direction of the blast.

"The history of the Jesuits is filled with contradiction," Conawago observed.

"Because they think the tribes are their children!" Xavier shot back, fire suddenly in his voice. "That is the error of their ways! The tribes are not the lambs of God! They are the lions of God!" His voice dropped to a near whisper. "They are the means by which we save our corrupted souls!"

Tushcona's whispers stopped, as did Duncan's breathing.

It was Conawago who broke the silence. "The claws of these particular lions are not the tools of the Vatican."

"Are you deaf!" Xavier snapped. "Do you hear nothing I say? That is the error of our ways! Rome has its holy saints and disciples just as the tribes have their holy spirits of the trees and water, but there is only one god, not one God from Rome and one who sits on the great turtle's back directing the ways of copper men. There is one, and he watches over our grand chess game to see which side is worthy to survive."

Duncan eyed the fierce, enigmatic Jesuit, wondering how many sides there were in the game Xavier played.

"Tell me something, Brother Xavier," Duncan asked, "are you familiar with the chieftains in the western lands?"

Xavier held up his maimed hand again. "The chieftains long ago accepted that I had paid my passage. I have spent many years in the Ohio country, have even seen the mighty Mississippi. I am a familiar face to all those tribes, and to those who trade with them."

Duncan realized that he had misunderstood Xavier, just as Woolford had not appreciated the contradictions of the Jesuits when he chose not to probe the Jesuit message route. He looked back up at the skins and spears hanging over the tapestry of martyrdom, then at the beaded belts hanging casually from the shelves. The belts, meaningless to almost every European, were the perfect medium for secret messages. A message on one could be hidden in plain sight. Xavier was no monkish scholar. Here was the secret communications center Woolford had been seeking, the nexus of the messages between the French and the half-king. The messages had been carried by the Jesuits, who regularly traveled between east and west. Xavier was a deputy of the half-king. And he had summoned them for a purpose.

Xavier fixed him with the smile of a conspirator. "There is little time left and much to do. The pieces fall together like the gears of a clock. But old feuds are difficult to extinguish. I need you to understand that only one thing stands in the way of the tribes' true destiny, preventing them from coming together at last in all their glory."

"The Iroquois Council," Duncan inserted. "But the Council will never join the cause if their children are killed or enslaved."

Xavier gave an approving nod. "Exactly. Regis overreacts. He must learn that chess is won with subtle moves."

"Regis?" Conawago asked.

Xavier made a dismissive gesture. "Before he became a leader of the western tribes, the Revelator had another name."

Duncan recalled how the half-king had fluently spoken English and French. Regis. It had the sound of a trader's son, of a half-breed. The crossed boy, Osotku had said as he died.

"He is too bold by half in dealing with the Iroquois League," the monk continued, "and he corrupts his cause by stealing their children. He was taught better. Now he talks of riches and bounties and bribes. But he has been taught that gold and silver corrupts the soul as much as the rum he loathes. It does not build on the strength of the tribes he wishes to lead. He spent so long in war parties that he forgets how to negotiate."

"So we have been brought to his peace chief?" Duncan said.

The suggestion brought a thin smile to Xavier's face. "He deludes himself and must be shown he can win his crown without stooping to the greedy ways of European kings. Our lust for gold is a disease of the soul! We must show ourselves immune!"

Duncan glanced back at Tatamy. Xavier knew much of the half-king's ways, but not all of them.

Xavier made another dismissive gesture. "I have someone who is waiting for you," he declared, changing the subject. He picked up one of his candles and led them toward the end of the tapestry. As he reached it, Tatamy lifted one corner, revealing a small arched door.

Two of the walls of the larger room they entered held barrels of wine stacked lengthwise on heavy racks, and the third shelved the heavy crocks used for storing pickled vegetables and grains. Along the far wall a wooden stair reached up into the vaulted ceiling, no doubt into the seminary's kitchens. Under the stair was a cot on which a tribal girl of perhaps ten years lay. The girl's arm was in a sling and a long jagged cut ran down one of her cheeks, expertly closed with sutures.

Xavier said nothing, just stepped aside.

Tushcona gasped and rushed forward. "Hannah!" the weaver exclaimed as she embraced the girl. One of the lost children was found.

Tears began streaming down the cheeks of both the old woman and her granddaughter.

Duncan looked back at Xavier, then at the stairway. Was the Jesuit offering them a token of good faith or baiting a trap?

The woman and child spoke with hushed, rapid Iroquois words as Tushcona kissed Hannah's forehead then examined her injuries. Finally the girl looked up and spoke in English.

"Jacob Pine saved my life!" she declared through her tears.

"I grew so tired, so hungry," she continued after a moment, clutching her grandmother's hand. "Those Hurons made us carry heavy loads, and we had to fight their dogs for the bones they tossed aside. But if we showed any weakness they would raise their axes and have our brains on the rocks. I saw it happen, to a boy from the Connecticut country, one day after we joined with another raiding party. When we paused to rest he started crying, hugging his knees and calling for his mother. When it was time to go, he wouldn't stand up. This Huron yelled and yelled, and then he hit him with his war club. His head popped like a melon. The next day I fell and twisted my ankle and had trouble getting up even with Jacob helping me. That Huron was so angry with me, he lifted his club to strike me."

Ishmael came forward and knelt by the girl. "Jacob Pine is my particular friend," the boy explained to his companions.

"He charged that Huron," Hannah said, "hit him hard enough to push the club away from my head. It just broke my arm, then cut my face when he slashed backward at me. That Huron hit Jacob too then, and cut him bad on the shoulder, but the Caughnawags ran up and pulled the Huron away."

Brother Xavier stepped closer to the girl and turned toward Duncan, as if to cut her off. "When I saw them I demanded they give up the girl, for I know the fate of captives who cannot perform work. Dead Iroquois maidens help no one. She had the care of the seminary physician." He shifted toward the Iroquois elders. "I told them I know who those five children were, that I would write it in my great book if they injured more of them."

"Your book?" Duncan asked.

"The chronicle is a living record. Once it is written, the world remembers. They all know that." Xavier hesitated and flushed at the suggestion that he used the book to shame his native flock. He was, Duncan could see, well aware of the ways the tribes had been abused and cheated with the written words of Europeans. "I mean only that I reminded them that the children must be properly respected. Honorable men do not fight with children as their pawns."

"Honorable men do not fight with children as their pawns," Custaloga repeated, directing his words to Tatamy, who remained expressionless.

The monk grew uneasy. "We should not tire our patient," he said, gesturing them back toward his library vault.

"Mr. Bedford. Is he safe?" Ishmael asked as he rose.

"They took him away, Ishmael," Hannah said with a forlorn shake of her head. "They said he was to be tortured because he tried to hide us at Bethel Church. They do terrible things to the prisoners they tie to those posts. I pray for him every night. Brother Xavier says he lights candles for him."

Hetty must have learned her son's fate, Duncan realized as he followed Xavier back to the vault. She had changed her plans, had helped them go the Council because she had decided her son was lost.

When they returned to Xavier's chamber, he produced a hand-drawn map and laid it on his table, pointing out the outposts and batteries around Montreal. A large box marked with a B indicated the British base on the southern bank five miles away. Underneath was written the name of the units in the advance positions: Fraser. Montgomery. Black Watch. All Highland units.

"The Caughnawags and Quebec militia wait for their orders," the Frenchman declared. "As thick as flies in the summer woods." He indicated smaller boxes, each within two or three miles of a British unit. "When the Scots are eliminated, the other troops brought by General Calder and Xavier Johnson will be useless. The campaign will be lost, the British initiative lost for the year. And that will make all the difference."

"When?" Duncan asked. "When has a Scottish regiment ever been defeated in this war?"

Xavier's expression was that of the cunning fox who has made a kill. "The Saint Lawrence will become a gauntlet of death for the English troops. For the glory of Rome."

"You mean the glory of the Revelator," Duncan snapped impatiently. Xavier's silent smile sent a shiver down his spine, and he looked back at Tatamy. Xavier thought they had come to listen to his terms, but Tatamy had brought them to reveal the crimes he could not speak of.

Xavier gestured toward the entryway. "We have laid pallets in the adjoining vault. You can—"

The army coin rang like a bell when Duncan dropped it on the table. Xavier's gloating expression disappeared. "You mean for the glory of the sainted renegade who had his men hammer the skulls of Christian Mohawks to steal British treasure."

The color drained from the Jesuit's face and he dropped into his chair. He had known nothing of the payroll theft.

A LOW RUMBLE of wheels on stone cobbles woke Duncan from his restless sleep in the empty chamber where he and the others slept. He lay awake in the dim light of the solitary lantern, then finally sat up, stretching, and suddenly saw that Ishmael's pallet was empty. He slipped out into the dimly lit corridor then up the passage to the cathedral. At the end of the nave, near the altar, a priest was on his knees with an old native woman, both absorbed in prayer. They took no notice of him as he stole out of the cathedral.

He circled the big stone structure and its seminary, thinking the boy may have sought a perch to watch as the ox-drawn cannons crept through the town, then he retraced their path from the river. The stone wall where the beggars sat was lit by street lanterns, and Duncan dropped back into the shadows as he spotted the boy. Ishmael was on his knees before the aged woman beside Hetty, extending a blanket to her. The woman held her palms up to decline the gift, but the boy remonstrated until at last she let Ishmael drape the blanket over her shoulders. Ishmael quickly stepped backward, as if worried she might change her mind, then bent to give Hetty an awkward embrace before hurrying toward the shadows where Duncan stood.

The boy halted as he reached the darkness and turned to watch the old women. They seemed to a mystery to him, and with a tightening in his chest Duncan realized the boy had never had women in his life. Duncan had lost his own mother and sisters, but he had been blessed with memories of good years with them. Ishmael's only family had been his grandfather, and Hickory John had been hardening him for a life alone in the world.

After several minutes Duncan stepped closer to Ishmael, who acknowledged him with a silent nod.

"That one with Hetty," the boy said, "she is a Conoy, one of the lost tribes of the Pennsylvania lands. Hetty met her many years ago, wandering in the Ohio country. She had been a revered matriarch, a leader and teacher, daughter of a great chief. She says when the great snows come, the other beggars put on crosses and are allowed to sleep in the back of the cathedral. But she won't do so because she says it affronts the old gods, that it is not the way of her people. The others laugh at her and say she has no people."

"She has a blanket now," Duncan observed.

"Is that the way of it when you are the last of your kind?" There was a catch in Ishmael's throat as he spoke. "Being laughed at? Sitting in a blanket alone in the raging snow?"

"She is not alone," Duncan said after a long moment. "All of her gods and all of her people live inside her."

As they returned to the cathedral Duncan did not object when Ishmael gestured him to a pew. They sat in silence for a quarter hour, gazing at the image of Christ on the cross over the altar and the priest who still spoke with the native woman, who was now weeping. Ishmael finally rose and without a word disappeared back down the stairway.

Duncan lingered a few more minutes then stepped to another arched doorway on the opposite side. The bell tower stairs were so narrow his elbows brushed both walls as he climbed. He emerged onto an open belfry, the highest vantage point in the city. A cool wind blew through the starlit sky. The muscles of small gargoyles jutting off the ledge below the belfry rippled in the silver light, as if the creatures were about to leap into the sky.

Below him the city lay in repose except for wagons with provisions arriving at a single gate. The city was preparing for a long siege. In the far distance, down the wide eastern stretch of the river, the rising moon silhouetted the topmasts of British warships. The clip-clop of a solitary rider echoed off the cobblestones below. A lantern moved along the top of the outer wall, an officer checking his sentries. He gazed over the open expanse of river beyond. If the British ships could advance and hold in the right position against the river's powerful currents they would pound the walls to dust. But the French artillerymen, famed for their cool, efficient fire, meant to sink the ships before they could secure their anchors. Hundreds of men were soon to die.

From his perch he could see far beyond the city, the fortifications, and the ships of war. The rolling shadow of the wild country extended to the far horizon. The European hold on the vast continent sometimes seemed so tenuous, but he knew the power of the Europeans. Gunpowder, Greek fire, and the mighty steel ax were weapons for which the natural world had no defenses. He had begun to sense something else, an awareness deep inside that had not been there before. Conawago would say it was because he had been woven into a Haudenosaunee belt. For all his effort to help the tribesmen be treated as equals by the Europeans, he was beginning to understand Johnson's claim that the humans of towns and settled lands were fundamentally different from those of the forest. The soil of the woodlands was mixed in the blood of the tribes. They were inextricable from the land, part of the wildness, part of something ancient and vital that the world badly needed. Looking out over the dim lights toward the vastness beyond, he felt the pain deep in the hearts of the elders, the essence of their anguish over the disturbances on the other side. The bond to the natural world that defined the tribes was weakening. The settlements, the armies, the endless flow of farmers were like rot in the root of their world.

He moved to the other side of the tower to gaze on familiar stars, leaning out to see the belt of Orion the hunter emerging over the horizon. The constellation had been a favorite of his grandfather's and they had often . . . Duncan froze. One of the gargoyles below was indeed alive.

"I keep thinking of what they say about the hell dog," Sagatchie suddenly said, as if they had been carrying on a conversation, "about how a great warrior is in its body." The Mohawk ranger was seated on the narrow ledge beside a stone gargoyle, one hand resting casually on its head.

"The creature has a more noble air than many men I know," Duncan replied, fighting the impulse to reach out to pull his friend to safety. There was nothing but air between Sagatchie and the cobblestones over a hundred feet below.

"I knew of that warrior married to Hetty. There were legends told of him when I was a boy. He knew how to die. He understood that a man must die at the right age, which may not mean an old age."

"Sagatchie," Duncan asked, "would it be possible to sit more like a man and less like a sparrow?"

The Mohawk's teeth gleamed as he grinned. He rose and vaulted upward to sit on the wall beside Duncan. "I try to understand the cut world, but it never gives me quiet," he said after a moment.

"The cut world?"

The Mohawk gestured toward the buildings below. "Living in cut stone and cut trees. The only time I feel alone is when I am surrounded by so many Europeans and their buildings.

"That night at the Council," he continued after a few breaths, "the elders spoke of our nation growing old. It was painful to hear but I know they spoke the truth. Worlds change. It is the way of all things. I have always known in my heart that there would be nothing better than to die for my grandfathers and for my gods. But when I grow old what will be left? What will there be to die for? Will anyone remember the names of our gods a hundred years from now? My greatest fear is that I die an old man in the cut world. I had a vision of that on the last full moon, and it kept me awake all night. I have never been frightened in battle, but that night I felt like a small boy surrounded by hungry beasts. I saw those beggars on the streets today. I cannot stop thinking of them. I fight for the British king, but when he wins the British will take our land. The land is our birthright, the essence of our people. When we have land, we have everything. When we have no land, we can only live by working for others, which means we all become slaves and beggars."

A great weight settled over Duncan's shoulders. He wanted to argue. "The wilderness is like a living thing," he offered, gesturing toward the surrounding countryside. "It will endure, like its children."

"Wilderness?" Sagatchie said. "I see British ships on the horizon. I see camps of soldiers in every direction and a river that has become a European highway."

"But beyond that the deer runs free and the eagle flies high," Duncan said. "To the West no man even knows how many hundreds of miles the wildness extends."

Sagatchie seemed lost in his own thoughts. "A warrior's life is nothing unless it ends with honor," he said, and he would speak no more.

As Duncan descended, the words echoed in his mind. A sacred belt said he was supposed to die for the tribal spirits, which at least would be a death with honor. But it was more likely he would die crushed in the European war machine.

When he stole into the darkened library vault, he thought a grey-haired monk had come to study the books. He was about to retreat, wary that the man bent by the candle might sound an alarm, but the monk straightened, yawning and stretching his arms. Duncan grinned and stepped into the light.

"It was the life they tried to push you to," he said to Conawago, who had donned one of the monks' robes against the chill. "In a robe, in a cathedral."

"If they had just left me alone with the books, I probably never would have left," his friend said. "Look at these!" Conawago exclaimed. "The treatise of Linnaeus on plant classification! The poetry of Thomas Grey! I was just reading the one on the death of his favorite cat. Drowned in a tub of fish!" When Duncan did not react he shrugged, then closed the book before him. "They had other plans for me, Duncan."

Duncan paced along the rows of books, and an unexpected thrill ran down his spine as he touched them. There were many religious tracts, but also Rabelais, Cervantes, Swift, Defoe, and Voltaire, books that would not be allowed in a formal church library. "It was you," he said, turning with sudden realization, "you who jibed with the king of France."

As the old Nipmuc folded his hands over the book, a faraway smile lit his features. "I liked that king," Conawago said, gazing at the candle flame, "though not his courtesans. He was shorter than I expected. He asked about the skills of the forest, so I took him to his royal garden and showed him how to lay a snare. His sister wanted me beheaded when we caught one of her lap dogs, but he was laughing about it for days. He wanted me to stay with him, grow up with him at Versailles." Conawago's smile grew melancholy. "I told him I had to return to America, because my mother was waiting for me."

Duncan pulled a stool close and leaned toward his friend. "I want to hear it all. I want to know what a young Nipmuc thought of the grand palace, what you ate, and the color of the king's robes."

Conawago's face lit with delight. He spoke with an energy Duncan had seldom heard in his voice, of the huge square-rigged ships in the convoy to France, of being terrified at seeing the endless ocean that first time as the convoy cleared the islands, of riding to Paris in a carriage with golden adornments. It was, Duncan realized, the salve they both needed, a carefree, intimate sharing like they knew at their mountain campfires. For brief moments the years seem to disappear, and Duncan could see the young adventurer in the old man's face. Duncan found a bottle of the monk's port, and they shared a cup as Conawago described the ridiculous fashions of the French women. At last, spent yet somehow refreshed, they drank another cup.

"Why are we here?" Duncan finally asked.

Conawago rose and dropped another log on the fire before answering. "They say if a Jesuit had been at the crucifixion he would have negotiated secret exile to some Roman isle for the son of God." He turned and poked the fire with the iron rod by the chimney. "They've been out of favor with the Pope's court for years, but that suits them best. Lingering in the shadows is more their way, manipulating events to their interests, quietly informing those in power."

"Those they chose to inform," Duncan added.

"They have always been the church's scholars."

"Back in Rome sometimes they grow too zealous about their un-orthodox ideas and their compulsion to alter the affairs of men. Some revert to quiet intrigue. Those who agitate too loudly are sometimes sent to the New World."

"You're suggesting Brother Xavier is in exile?" Conawago asked.

"He spoke about an early life at missions, but he is writing letters in Italian. I wager he has also lived in Rome. I think he is a man who would turn exile into opportunity. Some men pull puppet strings just for the delight of it."

"Or because it serves a cause they fervently believe in. Jesuits have been helping the Christian Mohawks for generations now." Conawago stirred the embers. "But I am not certain bringing the allies of your enemy into your last fortress falls into that category. And for a hundred years our sanctimonious friends have not tried to stop the butchery of the raids into English territory."

"So it is a trap? If the French were to take the elders of the Iroquois Council, they could keep the Iroquois from fighting. We are surrounded by French troops. Why are we here?" Duncan asked again.

"What was it that Delaware said to you of the crossed boy?"

"He always cheated."

Conawago nodded. "They needed you to bear witness that their beloved renegade has cheated." After Duncan had shocked him with the coin, Xavier had sat with his head in his hands listening to the details of the murders and theft.

"Before I came in here," Conawago explained, "Xavier and Tatamy were arguing about something, raising their voices. When I eased the door open after a long silence, Xavier was on his knees at that table," Conawago said, indicating a small, low table along the tapestry wall bearing a brass cross and a small image in a simple wooden frame. "'Forgive me father,' he kept saying, like the sinner in a confessional."

"Monks pray for forgiveness like everyone else."

"For a monk like Xavier, sins are more complicated." Conawago reached into his shirt and extended a slip of paper bearing two words.

"Fortress Island," Duncan read.

"He gave it to me. He's telling us where the half-king is, his camp on the river."

"Why should we believe him?"

In reply Conawago pushed the candle toward Duncan. He lifted it and stepped to the little table. He assumed the framed image would be one of Christ, but it was instead an ink drawing of an older man with long curly hair, much like that of Xavier. *Father Francis*, read the caption on the bottom.

"His sins are as complicated as his schemes," Duncan said as he returned to Conawago. "There is something more. Something he is not telling us." He shook his head in frustration. "I don't want to die in a French prison."

"Since we accepted our mission from the Council we have had one foot on the other side, Duncan. The French will let the half-king play out his hand. And we know what he intends. If we don't give him the alliance he wants then he will demand you, me, and the elders. Five of us for the children. It saves the children and gives him an even stronger hold on the Council."

"I could not bear to see the elders tied to the half-king's posts."

"Do you possibly think we would let the half-king use us against the League?"

Duncan studied Conawago uneasily.

"Don't lie to yourself, my friend. You and I are on that belt. When you hold a belt you must speak the truth. When you are woven into a belt you must live the truth." Conawago stood and fixed Duncan with an intense stare. "That first night when the elders arrived at our camp, Custaloga asked if I had a good sharp knife, and he showed me his. He said they would never be pawns to the French or the Hurons, that to do so would disgrace the League. He said they had all agreed."

Duncan did not speak for several heartbeats. "I don't understand." He did understand, but he could not admit the terrible truth.

"The warrior's duty, Duncan. If the French or the half-king try to take us prisoner, Custaloga will cut Tushcona's throat, and then I am to kill him. He made me promise. Then, he said, when you and I come across our army would be waiting."

HIS LAST BIT of hope seemed to die with the embers Duncan stared at. If they fled toward the British, or simply fled into the wilderness, they would have failed the Iroquois and would carry the dishonor for as long as they lived. If they stayed with the Jesuits and the Caughnawags, they would become two more puppets of the half-king. The elders might choose a quick death at the hand of a friend, but the half-king had promised Duncan a death of five days.

He looked to see that Conawago had retired, then rose and walked along the books again. He had at least expected Xavier to parlay to keep the tribes from destroying each other. Instead he had just brought them to see an injured Mohawk girl. Duncan looked toward the chamber where Hannah lay. Xavier had left the girl in their care for the night, and the Jesuits did nothing by chance. Had he wanted them to have an opportunity to speak with her in the quiet hours?

He paused at the end of the tapestry then pushed open the door. Ishmael sat on the stool beside the cot, speaking in hushed tones with the Iroquois girl. Duncan advanced slowly, making sure they heard his footsteps.

"I wanted to check your wound," he said to Hannah, glancing at Ishmael, who looked into the shadows as if to avoid Duncan's gaze. He bent to feel the girl's pulse before lightly touching the flesh around the wound on her cheek then turning to the bucket to freshen the cloth on her forehead. When he turned back to her, she was staring at him.

"My mother used to say I was the prettiest girl in the village." The girl's voice was surprisingly strong. "No more."

Duncan put the moist cloth on her head. "One side of your face will captivate all those who see you, the other will humble. The tribes of the forest wear their battle scars with great pride."

The girl's smile was hollow. "The rose loses its flower but never its thorn." She cast an expectant glance toward Ishmael, who nodded his encouragement. "Ishmael says I should tell you something because you understand the secret ways of Europeans." The girl lifted her blanket and produced a slip of paper on which an image had been drawn, a series of curves and lines running together.

"The kilted men who went north with us, wherever they went they made this symbol. Carved it on trees. Used charred sticks to mark rocks with it."

Duncan turned the paper this way and that, trying to make sense of it, then went still as recognition finally reached him. He asked for her writing lead and drew it again, very carefully, first a letter J and a letter R with a space between, then he joined the letters by nestling a figure 8 between them.

"Yes!" the girl said, nodding, "that is it."

Duncan had not seen the sign for years. Jacobus Rex, the cipher meant, or more particularly King James the Eighth, the last Scottish King. Although forgotten by many, it had always been a secret sign of Jacobites, a sign that got men arrested, and worse, during the last uprising.

Duncan saw now how both Hannah and Ishmael looked uneasily into the shadows past the big wine barrels. He lifted one of the candles and ventured toward them. In a small alcove beyond them he discovered another cot, on which an aged man lay propped against the stone wall. He appeared to be asleep but roused as Duncan approached with the light. A smile lit his craggy face.

"*Ciamar a tha sibh?*"

The face, and the Gaelic greeting, stopped Duncan. For a moment he was transported to another place, another time. He did not know the man, but he certainly knew his features and his accent. He had known a hundred such men in his boyhood, the old ones who bridged the generations, who piped and danced and led joyful gatherings on misty isles.

The man's voice was hoarse, as if he had not used it in a long time. "I am Clan Graham," he explained, "and you are Clan McCallum. An age ago I danced with McCallum lasses. I was no weakling but it was difficult to keep up with them," he said with a wheezing laugh.

Duncan lowered himself onto a stool and set the candle on the upturned crate by the man's bed. On the crate were several bleeding cups beside small bottles with familiar labels. Laudanum, the tincture of opium used for severe pain. Powder of Algaroth, used as an emetic. Peruvian bark, for fevers.

"Strong children those two," the stranger said, nodding toward Ishmael and Hannah. "Bodes well for America, wouldn't you say?" With visible effort he swung his legs out of the bed and sat up, bringing his face out of the shadows.

The man's hands trembled. His deep, intelligent eyes looked out from a worn, wrinkled face.

"May I?" Duncan asked Graham, reaching for his withered wrist. "I studied for some years at the medical college in Edinburgh."

The old Scot did not resist when Duncan gently took his arm. His pulse was weak and irregular. "The great college! I entertained many of its professors at my Edinburgh home. Buchanan, Oglesby, even McPhee, before he had that bother over the corpses in his classroom."

Duncan could not hide his pleasure at hearing the names of learned men he too had known and admired. They spoke for several minutes of mutual acquaintances before Graham reached behind his pillow and produced a heavy bottle. He uncorked it with a conspiratorial grin. "The best medicine of all," he said, pouring some of its golden liquid into two of the bleeding cups and handing one to Duncan. Graham lifted his cup and closed his eyes as he sniffed. "The water of life, lad."

It had been too long since Duncan had tasted good Highland whiskey, and as he let the first sip linger on his tongue, memories of other old Scots and their whiskey washed over him.

"McPhee would love to have me on his table when I breathe my last," Graham said in a surprisingly congenial tone. "He would debate with his class for hours over whether it was my lungs, my liver, or the growth in my belly that killed me. I prefer to think of it as just the harvest of a long life well lived." Graham said nothing when Duncan pressed his fingertips through the thin linen of his shirt, just stood up like a compliant patient. The tight lump beside the man's stomach was prominent. He had a tumor.

"Alice McCallum," Graham recalled with a whimsical glint as Duncan probed. "The lass had the deepest blue eyes I ever saw. A man could wander for days in those eyes. I was in love with her one summer," he confessed, holding up his arms as if embracing a dance partner. Suddenly he noticed Hannah and Ishmael standing by the barrels. With surprising grace he glided to the maiden and bowed before her. Hannah laughed, tucked her splinted arm against her body, and took Graham's proffered hand as he began humming a waltz.

As Duncan watched the aged Scot and the Iroquois maiden dance, he recalled how Graham had introduced himself. Clan Graham. It was the address for a clan chief. The Grahams had been one of the most powerful clans in the northern Highlands, and before the uprising their clan chief would have been a great laird, ruling like a king. After the uprising there were huge bounties placed on the heads of the rebel lords.

Ishmael took up the humming, and soon Graham and the young Mohawk girl began laughing so hard they had to stop. The glee on the old man's countenance twisted into a grimace of pain. As he clutched his belly, Duncan helped him back to his cot and poured him another inch of whiskey.

"I remember meeting a company of McCallum men," Graham said when he recovered. The more he drank, the more pronounced was the Scottish burr in his voice. "At the *kyle* along Skye it was, and the fools were swimming shaggy cows across the channel from the island to the drovers' camp near Lochlash. Long before you were born, lad."

Duncan grinned again. "Those were my people, Lord Graham. My uncles used to boast of the days when they swam so many cows they could walk across the channel on their backs."

Graham's laugh ended in a violent shiver, and he pointed to the monk's robe draped over the nearest barrel. As Duncan helped him into it, the good-natured old man lowered his head and made the sign of the cross, murmuring the prayer in French. "Call me Father Andre, lad. My days as Laird Andrew Graham are long ago memories."

"I understand why the girl is here, Father," Duncan said. "But you are not hiding in the vault because you escaped from the half-king." He was beginning to suspect he was looking at the real reason he had been brought to Montreal.

Graham studied him silently. There was wisdom in his eyes, but also cunning. "The Highland way of life was just that, a way of life. Are we so shallow as to think it had to be lost because our lands were lost?" The old laird grew very sober. "I've seen mountains to the west, by the inland seas, that are covered with heather and pines just like home. There are four thousand brave Highland men converging on this very city. That fool Amherst doesn't realize he has assembled the biggest gathering of Scottish fighters since the uprising in '46."

He leaned closer to Duncan. When he spoke again there was new strength in his voice. "With the western tribes, the French Indians, and the Iroquois at their side, they will be unstoppable. Neither king will have the stomach to stop them when they choose to establish a new Scottish nation around the inland seas."

Duncan stared at the man, stunned. His heart raced as he lowered his whiskey. He had been so blind. They had all been so blind. Somehow the half-king had connected to the secret Jacobite network. Regis had found an old Highland laird whom he would present at the final hour to rally the Scots. The Revelator didn't simply mean for the Highlanders to refuse to fight for the British, he intended that they would take up their own flag and fight against the British alongside the half-king. The French would be assured of their long-sought victory. He looked back at the cot under the stairs, where Hannah had drawn the Jacobite symbol. For the glory of Rome, all those in Rome, Brother Xavier had said. But Duncan did not ask the question that leapt to his tongue. "I had understood those to be tribal lands," he said instead.

"And the half-king will treat all tribes as equals. We will be their protectors, their way to counter the threat of other Europeans. Surely you want Highlanders to find their true place. You are one of us."

"Of course," Duncan quickly replied, then he weighed Graham's words. "But it is dangerous to make assumptions about the tribes."

"I make no assumptions. I have smoked the pipe with every major chief in the West."

Duncan studied the old Scot, considering his words. The half-king was not acting out of vengeance against colonists. Vengeance was a cover. He was acting out a carefully planned strategy, a grand and historic vision.

"The McCallum clan can start anew," Graham said. Though his eyes were sunken, they were sparkling now. "Build a croft by the water. Perhaps tame some bison to be your shaggy cows."

"The half-king roasts men alive."

Graham winced, as if the remark jabbed him personally. "He can be impetuous, yes," he said, and then continued to describe his vision. "We will organize companies of men to build barns and cabins. We will want a shipyard. The McCallums once built boats, I recall. Or a school, if that's what you want. That's it, lad! You'll have the first medical school for the tribes! We will build you a—" Graham's words choked away as he doubled up with pain. With a shuddering groan he clutched his belly, then suddenly Brother Xavier and Tatamy stepped out of the shadows. Xavier motioned Duncan away, as Tatamy placed a slat of wood between Graham's clenched teeth. Through his agony the old Scot nodded his thanks to the Christian Mohawk, and Duncan realized they must be old friends. He backed away, staring in confusion. With his last words the old Scot had sounded as though the rebellion was his, not the half-king's.

Xavier murmured prayers. Tatamy wiped his brow and spoke low comforting words in his native tongue. Duncan retreated to the cot under the stairs, where Hannah sat, looking uneasily in the direction of Graham. Duncan helped her settle for sleep as Ishmael curled up in a blanket by the foot of the cot. Tatamy appeared and bent over the girl to look at the stitches in her cheek.

"A Huron did that to the child," the chieftain declared.

"Have the northern Mohawks grown particular about whom they maim?" Duncan shot back. A cruel, poorly timed jab, but he was tired of being a pawn and not understanding, weary of the casual cruelty that injured so many.

Tatamy sat beside him on the second stool. "It was a French colonel who spoke first to us about the half-king who called himself the Revelator. We have been allied with the French for nearly two hundred years, and Andrew explained that alliances between France and Scotland go back even further." He shrugged. "We fight wars to win them."

Duncan was confused by the regret in the man's voice. "Those were your men at Bethel Church," he said.

Tatamy nodded grimly. "Four of them were. My best warriors, who had made raids in the South before and knew the land along the lakes. We were told it was to be a daring raid on supply lines, deep into enemy territory, that much glory would come of it. They said the Indians who lived in the town had raided our own villages. But one of my men came to me when they returned. He had been having bad dreams. He said those who died had not fought, but had sung. They were not warriors, they were peacemakers. He showed me a cross he had taken from one of the dead."

Tatamy looked up to Duncan with apology in his eyes. "The Revelator's men made sure my men gave no trouble. Our Caughnawags held their tongues until they returned home and could speak to my face. All are having bad dreams. They know now there was no honor in what they did, that the dreams are telling them they must put things back in harmony, they must rectify things somehow. It is wrong to build a new world on the suffering of good people."

Suddenly Duncan felt a glimmer of understanding. Xavier was a key lieutenant in the conspiracy, but only a lieutenant. "Father Xavier didn't know it was also being built with stolen silver," he suggested.

"The tale of the Revelator has built great hope among our people. He promises great things." The chief stared at Duncan pointedly. "We do things for him others cannot."

Duncan considered the words as he gazed at the sleeping girl. "The people of Bethel Church died, and the children were betrayed because of that treasure. Just some shiny metal."

"The Revelator thinks he must have it for his cause to succeed." The chieftain frowned. "Just some shiny metal, yes. He means to turn the world upside down with it. If something happened to it, the half-king would give much to get it back."

Duncan hesitated, first wondering if he heard invitation in Tatamy's voice then grasping the full weight of the chieftain's words. "You mean he does not have the payroll in his hands yet." He spoke slowly, responding to the mischievous gleam in the chieftain's eyes. "You mean he would trade the children to someone who did have it. But the French surely must have the coins by now. They would not tolerate him interfering with their plans."

"*Their* plans?" Tatamy asked. "Have you not listened today? The French have helped him, the French embraced the opportunity to wreak havoc in the British lines. But the plans were laid in that very chamber," he said, gesturing toward Xavier's vault, "not in some war room."

Duncan's mind raced as he gazed into the shadows where Graham laid. There had never been French generals behind the half-king's scheme. It had been a broken Scottish laird and a Jesuit monk who had unleashed the Revelator and his poet of death. But like most wild animals, they had proven difficult to control. He looked back at the Mohawk chieftain. "You suggest someone else might obtain the treasure and buy back the children."

"It is the greatest of his secrets. My men were with the raiders on the lake, were there when their bateau met another loaded with gunpowder kegs. Now the half-king calls for twenty of my men to be ready before dawn the day after tomorrow, at a cove on the far side of the river, to go to a field with rows of earthen mounds. We are to remove our crosses, be ready for a hard day's march. He wants us to look like Mohawks from the South, arrived to carry loads for the army."

"But if you don't have the coins and he doesn't have the coins . . ." Duncan said slowly, and then a grin lit his face as he finally understood. The Revelator had indeed made a fool of King George. He had made the British army transport its own stolen payroll.

Chapter Fourteen

Tatamy's men escorted them to the canoes an hour before dawn, stealing through a thick fog past work parties who hauled cannonballs onto the ramparts. Graham's words echoed in Duncan's mind. The greatest gathering of Highland military might since the uprising was approaching Montreal, and Highlanders had a long memory. There would be a new Scotland. Duncan would have a croft, a boat, a medical practice among his own people, Highland and tribal. He drifted into visions of that new world, of raising his own family, of Conawago at last finding fulfillment as he taught gleeful red-haired and black-haired children. Four thousand Highland soldiers would be liberated.

Duncan cocked his head at Conawago as the others boarded the canoes. The old Nipmuc had the wampum belt out and was staring at it. He felt Duncan's gaze and looked at him, then turned the belt toward Duncan, as if he needed reminding. They had seen the price being extracted by the half-king for that world. The elders had understood when they had woven the belt. Tatamy had glimpsed it and decided he no longer wanted to be part of the bargain.

By daybreak the mist was breaking up and they were on the opposite bank of the wide river. At Tatamy's direction the three canoes containing

Duncan, Conawago, and the Iroquois were in the front, and as they passed a small fog-shrouded cove, Duncan realized they were alone. The northern Mohawks had disappeared into the mist.

Duncan guided them warily along the wooded shore until the coughing cry of a merganser broke the silence, and two canoes shot out from a bed of reeds. The first, holding Woolford and one of his tribal rangers, circled them, offering quiet greetings. The second, holding three more rangers, took up position at the rear of the procession as Woolford directed them toward a point of land half a mile away.

Custaloga gasped as they entered the bay beyond the point. It was overflowing with British soldiers. Longboats were ferrying troops off transport ships. Mortars and cannons were being lowered from yardarm cranes onto squat gunboats. On what had been the broad pasture of a farm, troops were parading in time to loud drumbeats. A band played a jaunty tune as longboats disgorged ranks of redcoats. Scores of white tents were arranged in orderly rows on the slope above the field.

To Duncan's relief, Woolford turned toward the shore and directed their party into a grove of maples where half a dozen more rangers waited to guide them to a campfire for a hot breakfast. Woolford lingered by the canoes with Duncan, explaining the regimental flags arrayed along the waterfront.

The screech of a whistle, the double tones of a boatswain's pipe, interrupted them. As Woolford spun about, the color drained from his face. Two long boats rowed by sailors, one filled with a squad of marines and the other with officers in brocaded finery, were rapidly approaching.

"The grand bastard himself," Woolford declared in a worried voice, and he whistled sharply toward his camp. The rangers began herding their guests deeper into the forest.

"Amherst?" Duncan asked.

No reply came, but none was necessary. Oars were shipped, letting the boats coast into the shallow water. Sailors from the officers boat leapt into the water to take a heavy chair held out by the marines, followed closely by two junior officers who assisted an older, bewigged officer into the chair. As he was carried to shore, he had the air of a raja on his palanquin. His round, puffy cheeks showed signs of rouge, the brass gorget on his chest shined mirror bright. Duncan took a step backward, longing to be in the shadows.

"It is always reassuring to see our rugged frontline emerge safely from the forest," the officer announced after he had straightened his uniform.

For a moment Duncan thought Woolford was going to bow. Instead he dipped his head and touched his temple with a knuckle. "General Amherst. We are honored."

The general looked down his long thin nose at Woolford. "Do you bring word from General Calder, Captain?"

"He hopes you will not sweep away the enemy before he has a chance to join the field."

Amherst offered a thin smile, then extended a hand to one of his staff officers, who quickly opened a silver snuff box. "We will draw the frogs out," the supreme commander declared with a gesture toward his massed troops. "Then Calder will be the hammer that drives them onto our anvil." With a delicate motion he lifted snuff with his finger and thumb then pressed it up his nostrils. For a moment his eyes narrowed and he studied the camp behind Woolford, then he withdrew a handkerchief and sneezed.

"I am going downriver for consultations with the navy," he announced. "I look forward to news of Calder's arrival above Montreal." He made a vague gesture toward the forest. "Carry on," he said with a lightless smile.

"What in God's name was that about?" Duncan asked as the boats rowed away. "The king's anointed one came to show off his glittering snuff box?"

Woolford shook his head. "I wish I knew. He despises our Indian allies and anyone else who does not march to his strict beat. If I reported to him instead of General Calder, my company would be disbanded in a heartbeat."

"But you are far removed from General Calder."

"I am his eyes and ears."

"Which Amherst knows."

"Calder does not like to proceed onto unknown ground."

"The payroll was going north to Amherst," Duncan observed as he watched the retreating boats. "He must not take it kindly that Calder lost it."

Woolford nodded. "Except that Amherst ordered the payroll investigation closed. I am commanded to gather battlefield intelligence. There are not just French and their militia to watch, but Huron and Abenaki and Caughnawag camps."

"Meaning Calder is worried about them."

"He is perhaps four days away, slowly making his way up the lake to the river. It is a laborious affair, moving thousands of men. And he has little appetite for moving into the chain of islands since he knows the half-king is waiting for him somewhere along the river, with a few hundred men at last report, and more no doubt pouring into his secret camp every day."

Duncan extended the paper from Xavier. "Not so secret."

Woolford's eyes went round with surprise. "I know this place, a few miles above Montreal. The island has a high ridge on the south and east that shields it from this side. He could mass an army there and not be seen."

"But surely with Calder's strength—" Duncan began.

"His strength is hollow. One in three of his men are just recalled from the West Indies, meaning they are still weak from fever. Half the others may not be reliable."

"You mean Highlanders."

Woolford frowned, then nodded. "Several hundred are already here, with the troops that came from Quebec City. Amherst has his own watchers. He doesn't trust them."

"And what will the generals do when they find they haven't simply lost the use of the Highlanders but have to face them on the battlefield?"

Woolford's head snapped toward Duncan. "Even speaking such nonsense would be considered treason by Amherst!" His expression soured as Duncan reported what the half-king intended to do with the Scottish troops.

"What will the English troops do when several regiments of Highlanders charge their line?" Duncan asked as he concluded.

Woolford stared intensely at Duncan. He grabbed a handful of pebbles, which he angrily hurled one at a time into the water. "The grenadiers will stand and die, and all the others will break and run, as any sane man would do. When the Highlanders have their blood up, they are a machine of death." He looked at Duncan. "But if they were going to turn, surely they would have done so."

"The moment of battle has not yet arrived."

"Duncan, I cannot believe the Scots will betray their colors for a few pieces of silver. They are made of sterner stuff."

"Exactly. The money is a token, an enticement, an excuse to get them to listen. What they will hear is that they finally have the opportunity to make a strike for the clans, to pay back the king for the way he has abused the Highlands. It won't be about the money in the end."

"Surely they won't all desert just for some hollow vengeance."

Duncan showed the ranger the paper with the Jacobite symbol on it. "Thousands gave their lives in the '46 uprising to support the Stewart prince. Families gave everything for their prince. He was like some mythic hero rising up to slay the monsters that plagued them."

"You're talking history."

"That same prince still lives. At the Vatican, with the Jesuits."

"But the hold of the Jesuits here, and in Rome, has been slipping away."

"Tell me this, Patrick: Who are the lasting enemies of England, enemies for centuries? It's not just the French."

"Again, you're speaking of history."

"Then you are as blind as Calder and Amherst. The Roman Church, the Jacobites, the French. The trinity that prays for the destruction of England. I spent last night with a Jesuit monk who exclaimed with great confidence about the new world that is coming. I met an old Scottish laird who was a leader of the Jacobites. He knows Rome. He is an intimate of the Stewart prince. The Jacobites and the Jesuits mean to carve out a new kingdom, supported by the tribes and the Highland troops. The theft of the payroll, the kidnapping of the Council's children, and the rising of the half-king are all moves on the same chessboard."

The remaining pebbles fell from Woolford's fingers. He lowered himself onto a log. "My God. The vengeful shouts of a western chieftain will fade. The half-king alone is a nuisance who may put off our victory for another year, nothing more. But a plot hatched in the Vatican . . ."

"Which has been looking for retribution ever since England split from the Holy Church. Thousands of innocents died then because of the words in prayer books. If the Vatican wishes to change the hearts of thousands, it sends out an army of monks. If it wishes to change an entire country, it sends out a handful of Jesuits. The Jacobite prince is desperate and embittered, but he is a devout Catholic living in Rome. By himself he has been powerless. But a few words spoken in the right ears in the Vatican brought an epiphany, that the Roman Church and the Jacobites might have common interests with the French in the New World. When their conspiracy succeeds, every river between here and the Atlantic will run with blood."

Woolford lifted a stick and twisted it in his hands until it broke. "It's all too fantastic, Duncan. There is no proof. Every question is answered by a riddle."

"That's the point. It isn't about the riddles, it's about the riddler."

"You mean the half-king."

"No. The half-king's is someone's soldier. There is a hidden chain that reaches through the old Jacobites to the exiled prince in Rome. I know the links to Rome now. But at the other end, there has to be someone close to army secrets, someone who understands the movement of Highland troops and paywagons. This is a clockwork maze of gears, but every clock has its mainspring. Something's been bothering me ever since Oswego. Why was Colonel Cameron so protective of Rabbit Jack and the poet of death?"

Woolford shook his head. "Ridiculous. Cameron is more English than I am. Amherst trusts him implicitly. They say he was assigned to Calder's staff to keep Calder in line. Amherst values him so highly he brought him back to help plan the battle."

"Brought him back?"

"A fast escort of provosts riding with extra mounts brought him from Calder's column yesterday. He's the ranking officer of the Highland regiments."

"What exactly did he do for Calder?"

"His adjutant, responsible for administration. Same as for Amherst, at least for the rest of the campaign. Overseeing the quartermaster, the infirmaries, deployment schedules."

"Including the paymaster?"

Woolford hesitated before nodding. "And the paymaster."

"Who would have been responsible for the report on the payroll robbery?"

"He would have been."

"Get it."

"Impossible."

"You run an intelligence network for Calder. You have ways."

"I don't spy within the army, Duncan. Stealing such a report would be a hanging offense."

"You can only hang once."

"You are the one who accumulates capital offenses, not me."

"I am thinking more of how you are going to help me ransom the Council's children."

AN ARMY WON battles on the strength of musket and sword. It won wars on the strength of oxen and wagons. General Amherst was famed not for his ability in a battle line but for his prowess at moving huge amounts of men and supplies to where they would do the enemy the most damage. Duncan could not help but admire the temporary city that Amherst was building. Hundreds of men worked at erecting tents, digging latrines, cutting and hauling wood for scores of fires, even raising high poles for regimental colors.

Woolford nervously watched Duncan as they paced along the neat rows of freshly excavated earthen bunkers where kegs of gunpowder were being stored.

Duncan paused to watch one of the blue-coated artillery officers step into a pit and begin marking kegs with a piece of chalk. "Why does he do that?"

"An artillery officer's world revolves around chalk marks. Marks to show when a batch of powder was tested last, marks to distinguish the coarse powder for the big guns from the fine, which is saved for small arms. Marks to show the age of the powder. Marks to show whether the powder came from the Birmingham works or the Durham works, since each has its own characteristics. In the field, kegs have to be marked for delivery to specific batteries. They all have their own codes. And that is just the powder. There is also the shot. The munitions will go to half a dozen batteries being built along the southern bank. Those expecting to face troops will receive grape shot, those planning to face ships will get chain shot."

"There's almost no roads on this side. So they must be carried by porters. The kind of menial job Amherst would expect the tribes to do."

Woolford nodded. "He has lots of Mohawks already here."

"Under whose supervision?"

"The quartermaster."

"Who would be accountable to the adjutant. Colonel Cameron."

Woolford turned to study Duncan. "One moment you are the most zealous of Highlanders. The next you speak of them in tones of suspicion. Who are you?"

Duncan had no answer. He walked as close to the bunkers as he could, inconspicuously trying to see the markings. A pair of artillerymen in Fraser plaid passed by, then two more wearing the Montgomery tartan. It would take experienced hands to pack so many coins in the powder kegs, hands that knew the normal weight of a full keg, knew how to repack a keg without signs of tampering, hands with enough authority to control where the kegs went and with a way to guard them without raising too much suspicion. He tried to calculate how many kegs it would take. Ten or fifteen at least, more like twenty. "The westernmost battery," he said, "the one closest to the half-king. What is its mark? Who is manning it?"

Woolford frowned again then silently surveyed the magazines. His gaze came to rest on a cluster of officers around a field desk. "Wait here," he instructed.

Five minutes later the ranger led Duncan to the last row of earthen bunkers. The last pit in the last of the row had been dug at the edge of an encampment of Fraser Highlanders. The soldiers had dug one of their cook fire pits not thirty yards away and surrounded it with logs for seating. It was a place where men could linger, night and day, without being conspicuous.

He did not tarry as he walked by the bunker, but he quickly studied the kegs in sight. He could see at least four with the mark of the Jacobites.

He waited to speak until he was on a knoll overlooking the magazines. "Do you have paper and lead?" he asked.

Woolford reached into the light day pack he carried, and a moment later Duncan was on one knee, drawing a map. He marked each pit with a circle, then the one by the Frasers with an X inside the circle. "Tatamy said he would camp in a grove of birches a mile north of Montreal. One of your Mohawks must get this to him," he told Woolford. "Today."

"Why today?"

"Because tomorrow we are going to rescue the children and stop the half-king with a piece of chalk."

IT WAS NEARLY sundown when Woolford returned to the camp. The ranger captain motioned Duncan to the half-tent he had raised by tying a sailcloth between two trees. He had found some driftwood planks and arranged them on logs for a makeshift table, and he now tossed a leather dispatch case onto it.

"I copied the clerk's copy, word for word, saying it was needed for General Calder." He shook his head as he gazed at the case. "I don't know how to react," he said in a forlorn tone. "I admire the Highlanders and regret their suffering. I despise traitors."

Duncan pulled out the single sheet of paper rolled inside. It was a report sent by Colonel Cameron to the Ministry in London the week before. Cameron had conducted a thorough investigation of the robbery, he reported. The raiders had bribed the Iroquois carpenters at Bethel Church, who had secret knowledge of the locking mechanisms in the pay-wagon, then had offloaded the payroll while the escort had taken a meal in one of the houses. They had waited for the wagon to leave, then killed all the Iroquois to eradicate all witnesses. Using canoes on Lake Champlain, they had expected a fast transport back to the French lines. Witnesses confirmed seeing a half dozen canoes speeding north the afternoon of the theft, all riding low in the water, indicating heavy loads. Unfortunately, that night there had been a strong storm over the central part of the lake. Reliable witnesses reported seeing the canoes floundering half a mile offshore. The overladen canoes had been lost. The raiders had been punished by the hand of God, though unfortunately the king's treasure now lay in the depths of the lake.

"No names for the sources of his information," Duncan observed. "Only reliable witnesses. No way to verify their words."

"A friend of mine helped me get this," Woolford explained. "He and his rangers do what I do, but for Amherst. After the general read Cameron's report, he sent some of his own rangers to Lake Champlain, to Crown Point and Ticonderoga."

"And?"

Woolford seemed reluctant to continue. He rolled the paper up, but instead of returning it to the case he stepped to the smoldering fire and lit it. He held it in his hand, watching it burn as Duncan stepped to his side.

"And?" Duncan pressed.

"There was another report, one that Amherst burned after reading. The rangers found their own reliable witnesses, officers of the garrison guard, supported by the daily logs of the guard. There were no storms that day or the next, and sightings of unexplained canoes would have been recorded. There were no such reports."

Duncan paced around the fire. "Amherst knows Cameron was lying."

Woolford did not disagree. "The day after he received the report, Amherst sent for Cameron to come take over the Highland units. Then he left to confer with the navy."

"It makes no sense."

"Intrigue between officers is not uncommon. Cameron provided the army with a convenient way to explain away the loss of the treasure. Amherst proved it was a lie, but such knowledge can be more powerful when kept secret. Favors can be asked by those who have such secrets. Cameron will be bound to Amherst forever."

"Where is Cameron now?"

"Making final preparations for the advance of ground troops tomorrow. You saw Amherst leave to meet the second wave of transports coming up the river. And four outposts stretched along the southern bank of the river upstream of Montreal have been attacked and destroyed. A patrol from the half-king intercepted some of my Mohawks. The Revelator demands to see the Iroquois elders tomorrow. He will leave them a sign at a fishing camp on the southern shoreline above Montreal. He expects them to deliver the Iroquois League."

"So by this time tomorrow," Duncan said, "we will have the children or we will be tied to his torture posts."

AS THEIR MODEST flotilla of canoes approached the fishing camp just after dawn, they saw three canoes speeding away toward the walled island.

A single man awaited them.

"The poet!" Conawago exclaimed as their canoe ran up on the sand. The man sitting against a boulder did indeed wear the black clothes and wide-brimmed hat of the half-king's ambassador of death. Woolford quickly deployed his rangers to flank the campsite before joining Conawago and Duncan as they advanced on the man.

At first it seemed he was praying, with his head bowed and hands folded in his lap. When he ignored Woolford's challenge, Duncan used his rifle barrel to push up the man's hat.

Rabbit Jack had been hit so hard the white of his skull was exposed. Just to be certain, his killer had slit his belly. Blood still ebbed out of his gut. The stream of blood down each cheek told Duncan that he had not been dead when his eyes had been carved out.

A piece of paper had been placed between his two hands. *Death to Murderers*, it stated in well-formed letters. A smaller legend at the bottom said, *Fortress Island*.

"The half-king is making it clear that he does not blame the Council for the death of Black Fish," Conawago observed as he signaled the elders to approach. "He gives the killer of his nephew to Custaloga."

"He pays respect in the currency of a butcher, nothing more," Duncan said. "This man didn't kill Black Fish. He was killed by the man who killed Black Fish." He heard a splash behind him, and the hell dog rushed past him. The dog bent over the body with a strangely intense curiosity, sniffing the wounds, sniffing the clothes, sniffing the hat, before turning to look at Hetty. She was staring, transfixed at the morbid sight, and though she had been approaching, the dog's actions stopped her.

"The poet killed Black Fish, and now Rabbit Jack," Duncan observed. "He gives up his costume."

"It is an ending of sorts," Conawago added. "He considers his work to be done."

"Death to murderers," Woolford repeated. "I take no consolation from it." He whistled for his rangers.

The elders gathered in a half-circle around the dead man. Tushcona murmured a short prayer, though whether it was for the benefit of the dead man or the elders, Duncan could not tell. Custaloga placed the hat back on the man's head to cover his hideous face, then with a surprised gasp, he pulled the paper from the man's hands, turned it, and raised it for the others to see.

Tushcona rushed forward to study the writing on the reverse of the paper. The four remaining captive children had all written their names on it. Above them were two more names: Adanahoe and Henry Bedford.

"It is good news," Duncan said uncertainly as Hetty stepped to his side. "It must mean your son yet lives. His captors have at least reunited him with his students. That will be some comfort to them."

The Welsh woman's countenance betrayed no emotion. Her only response was to drop to her knees and embrace the hell dog as it burrowed its head in her shoulder.

THE BEAUTY OF the cobalt sky and the scarlet foliage reflected in the River That Never Ends gave little hint of the violence that would soon erupt. The British troops were nearly all in place. In another day the artillery would begin their savage duels.

It had been surprisingly easy for Woolford to spirit away one of the smaller work boats to meet Tatamy's men, and the loading of the kegs onto the boat after Duncan had marked them had been done in sober silence. The Christian Mohawks, like the elders, knew their actions thrust them into the crosshairs of both opposing armies. The game they played now was absolute. They would win or they would die.

All morning they had watched from the shore as canoes of warriors and long boats of Highlanders arrived at Fortress Island. By the time Tatamy's men had arrived and they had made their final arrangements, their party was inconspicuous. No one seemed to notice the boat they moored to a pine on a tiny island a quarter mile from the beach. As their own canoes finally coasted onto the pebbles of Fortress Island, Duncan looked back at the point of land where Woolford waited with his men and the hell dog, wondering if he or any of his companions would make good on their promise to return to the ranger camp by nightfall. He cast a worried glance at Ishmael, who had leapt into a canoe at the last moment, defying Duncan's instructions to stay with the rangers. "It is his war too," Conawago had sighed with a restraining hand on Duncan's shoulder.

But it wasn't a war camp that Duncan and his friends walked into, it was a Highland celebration. At least two hundred men in the plaids of the Highland regiments milled about the island campsite, and though the tribal warriors far outnumbered them, the atmosphere was unquestionably Gaelic.

A man wearing the sash of a Fraser piper played a lively tune, and Duncan could not suppress a grin as he watched a handful of Scots lead several confused but laughing northern Mohawks in an impromptu jig. A man in Montgomery plaid had crossed two swords on the ground and was performing a sword dance for a delighted group of Scottish and woodland warriors. Amused exclamations filled the air, in both Gaelic and tribal tongues, and Duncan and Conawago joined in, doing their best to keep attention away from the Iroquois elders behind them, who were furtively searching for the children.

Since reaching the New World, Duncan could not recall such a joyful collection of Highlanders. No, it had been much longer—not since the clan gatherings of the days of his youth. They wandered through the knots of men and women, pausing to help pull a long pole to raise one more army tent. Duncan found himself walking slower and slower. Something deep inside him was struggling, calling out to him. Here before him, it was saying, was the best chance he would ever have of finding a contented life. Here was the chance to live among his own kind, the proof that the Highland ways could be resurrected.

On a flat below the camp, a handful of Highlanders laughed and slapped tribesman on their backs as the Indians tried to teach the Scots how to play lacrosse. Several tribal matrons watched in amusement as a stout trooper in a leather apron sliced pumpkins with a short sword.

It wasn't contentment, but at least a faint echo of it that he felt at seeing the bighearted Highlanders mix with the tribes. A wayward ball of sewn deerhide landed at his feet. As he tossed it back to the lacrosse players, Conawago pulled on his arm as if to change their course.

A familiar tent lay ahead of them, the ornate stone-painted tent with scalloped flaps. Somber Hurons stood guard as the chieftain in the pot helm, Paxto of the Wolverine clan, and Scar, the vengeful deputy of the half-king, conferred with someone inside the tent. Too late Duncan stepped back. A sentinel spoke, the men at the tent turned, and a moment later the half-king emerged into the sunlight.

Duncan sensed movement on either side. Hurons led by Scar closed in around them. He heard running feet, and suddenly Custaloga was at Conawago's side, and Sagatchie and Kass flanked Duncan.

The half-king was adorned for a grand celebration. Over his tattooed chest was the open scarlet jacket, fringed with gold lace, of a British officer, and along the snake tattoo on his face were waving lines of war paint. A brass gorget hung around his throat. The long braids of his hair had colorful feathers woven into them. Over his doeskin leggings he wore the red, green, and brown kilt of the Montgomerys. Instead of a sporran pouch at the front, he had stuffed the full pelt of a lynx in his belt, with the wild cat's dead eyes gazing out from his belly.

He eyed Duncan and Conawago with undisguised malice. "I thought the oracle would have surely crossed over by now," he said to Conawago. "So many opportunities. It seems almost miserly for you not to oblige."

The old Nipmuc stared at him defiantly. "I will be more than ready to face the gods once you return the children and the first mother of the Iroquois."

The half-king studied Custaloga and Tushcona, then turned back to Conawago. "I am prepared to accept the Council's petition for an alliance. The first mother has been . . ." he searched for a word, "ambiguous in her representations of Iroquois support."

"We bring the grandparents of the children."

"We tremble at your mighty warriors!" he mocked. His men laughed. Scar spat at Conawago, then raised a knife and made a pantomime of slitting his throat. Conawago did not react. Paxto drew his war ax and tapped its handle against his hand as if making ready to swing it.

"You would be wise to tremble," Duncan said.

"They will be responsible for the death of their gods," the half-king snapped.

"No," Duncan shot back, "what kills gods is lying and murdering in their name."

Venom filled the half-king's eyes. "I will kill you, McCallum," he vowed. "I will kill you for five days. I will peel the skin from your face as you beg for death."

"Not today," Duncan shot back. "Not here. You won't kill a Highlander in front of all these clans," he said gesturing toward the Scots, several of whom had paused, showing interest in their exchange.

"You thought to just steal the children from us?"

"We thought we would buy them," Duncan answered, and tossed a coin at the leader of the rebels.

The half-king's eyes narrowed as he stared at the coin at his feet. "A pretty piece of silver means nothing."

"Seven thousand five hundred thirty-two of them means a lot. We could have given them back to the British so they could calm their impatient troops. We will instead exchange them for your captives."

The half-king's eyes flared. He turned and fired angry questions at the men beside him, who clearly had no answers.

"Impossible!" he snarled as he turned back. "Do not presume to know our secrets, McCallum."

"What secrets? How you built a second paywagon, how you switched it for the real one then transported it up the lake? Or perhaps how you transferred its coins into powder kegs?"

"I do not believe you!"

Duncan dropped to a knee and in the soil drew the Jacobite symbol from the kegs.

Worry flickered on the half-king's face, but it was quickly replaced by fury. "Where?" he demanded.

"One keg is in the canoe at the far end of the beach," Duncan said. The half-king barked a quick order, and two men sprinted away. "A token. You will get the remainder when we have the captives."

The rebel leader spoke another word, and they were quickly surrounded by warriors. He said nothing until the keg was set at his feet and smashed open. As the half-king kicked the keg onto its side, scores of coins tumbled out amid the black powder.

His anger burned like a fire. "Where?" he shouted.

"Where are the children?" Duncan replied in a level voice. "Where is the first mother?"

The half-king fingered his own ornate war ax as if resisting the impulse to smash Duncan's skull. Suddenly Scar leaned to whisper in his ear, and he turned his gaze to Tushcona. "We did not realize we had the Council's own belt weaver!" he exclaimed. "You will have the captives for the coins and a simple belt." He stepped up to the old woman, leaning close to her face. "You will weave a belt that declares the Iroquois alliance with us. We will parade it through all the villages. The tribes will shout for joy. The English will squirm in terror as they wait for our scalping knives."

Tushcona replied with the impatience of a peeved mother. "You do not understand the making of a Council belt, child," she chided. "My hands weave only the truth."

"Your hands," the half-king growled, "will feed my dogs."

"Then I will learn to weave with my feet."

Duncan took a step toward the woman, ready to take the blow.

"When the truth finally finds you, it will be your death," Tushcona coolly declared.

Duncan saw the amused cruelty in the half-king's eyes as he surveyed the scene. He was assessing the witnesses, thinking of killing the matriarch. Just as frightening was the certainty that Tushcona was willing to die.

"Kill the Council's weaver, and you kill all hope of an alliance," Duncan said.

The half-king gave an exaggerated grimace. "But you so make me feel the need to kill someone. You have not learned to take me seriously. Just a small death for now. One child." He muttered a low command, and one of his guards handed him a pouch from his belt. The half-king upended the pouch, and black-and-white pebbles, gaming pieces, spilled onto the ground. With deliberate slowness he selected three white pebbles and one black, then pointed to a deep shadow under the rocky ridge that might have been a cave. Two warriors stood on either side of the shadow. The half-king dropped the four stones back into the empty pouch. "The one who draws the black dies. If my belt has not been started in an hour, we will play the game again. You—" he pointed to Tushcona, "will hold the pouch as they draw, so they will know it is you who kills them." The half-king's frigid grin faded as his gaze moved over Duncan's shoulder.

"The colonel desires to honor our guests," reported a stern voice. Duncan turned to see a grenadier sergeant, flanked by half a dozen fully armed men. "There is tea," the solder said with a bow to the Iroquois.

THE ARISTOCRATIC OFFICER stood ramrod straight at the entrance to a large tent beyond the Highland campfires. Beside him stood a field table on which an orderly was arranging a surprisingly elegant tea service. The colonel greeted each member of their party with a courteous nod and gestured them to the steaming tea.

The arrogance Duncan had seen before on Colonel Cameron's face was gone, replaced with lines of worry. He offered no greeting to Duncan, only studied him with an uncertain expression until his shoulder was tapped by a grenadier. The colonel stepped several feet away and followed the man's pointing arm to a newly arrived long boat from which casks of rum were being unloaded.

"Whose are they?" Cameron snapped. "I do not recognize them."

"From Montgomerys," the grenadier reported. "And they all wear the white cockade."

Cameron gave a slow, reluctant nod. "But I said no spirits!" he snapped, then he cursed as a swarm of Highlanders and warriors alike descended on the casks.

"There'll be no stopping it now, sir," the grenadier declared.

Cameron grimaced, then dismissed the soldier and turned back to Duncan. "After our first encounter in the general's quarters in Albany," he declared, "he said you were a damned difficult person to understand. He said you spoke like a foe but acted like a friend."

"In contrast to one who but talks like a friend.'

Color rose into Cameron's face. "When I have committed to a mission, I do not shy from its consequences, however uncomfortable they may be. I have stood with my troops in many a battle, beside the British colors."

"When I lived in Edinburgh, Colonel, I made a point of reading everything I could about the uprising of '46. Camerons held huge estates in the Highlands. At Culloden, there were Camerons on the western flank, not far from the McCallums. Scores lay dead of English lead and steel at the end of the day. But soon you offered to raise more troops for the king that had killed them."

The words clearly stung the man. He motioned Duncan inside his tent and stepped to another field table, then poured a glass of sherry and downed it before answering. "It was a time for hard choices. I had friends in Edinburgh who had already taken the king's colors, who begged me to help my people. Estates that had been held by our clan for centuries were about to be seized, every male about to be put to the butcher's blade or rope, their women and children subject to unthinkable horrors. Scores of men, hundreds of women and children. If it was in your power to stop that horror, what would you have done, McCallum? Hard bargains had to be struck. It took more than mere begging for mercy to win the reprieve." Cameron stared at the little glass as he rolled the stem in his fingers. "I drank myself to sleep every night for a year. By then the army had reduced the Highlands to rubble. There was nothing to go back to even if I wanted. But my people were allowed to leave, marched past bonfires into which the army threw their pipes and every article of clothing made of plaid." He stepped to a narrow, tattered banner that hung from a tent rope and lifted it. "You can read Latin, McCallum?"

The cloth took Duncan's breath away. He stared at it without speaking, stepping closer to read the words over the image of a pelican feeding its young. "*Virescit vulnere virtus,*" he recited. "Courage grows strong at a wound." The pelican was sometimes called the Jesus Bird, for it was thought to prick its own breast to feed its blood to its young. It was a powerful and sacred image, well known in the Highlands.

"When this was first brought to me in secret, I thought it had to be a craven joke. A banner from Rome, the crest of the royal Stewart himself. Impossible, I thought. It was beyond my wildest dreams that the cause of the white cockade could be resurrected. But the banner was real, bearing bloodstains from Culloden. From the moment that spark of hope presented itself, I was duty bound to keep it alive," he said, a hint of challenge in his voice.

Duncan stared at the solemn Scot. "Who? Who brought the banner?"

"It wasn't only the banner. There was a letter from Rome, the affirmation that the one true prince is willing to take to sea, vouchsafed by the prince's own royal ring." Cameron spoke the words with the religious fervor of the old Jacobites, and as he spoke he touched the white cockade pinned to his lapel, much as one of the elders would touch his amulet. He leaned closer to Duncan. "Did you bring the Iroquois Council?"

"I brought enough of the Council to make a difference," Duncan stated.

Cameron nodded, as if taking Duncan's word as an affirmation, then pointed to the large chart on his table. It showed a section of the broad river with recent pencil marks depicting the new British batteries.

"Amherst has no appreciation of our coppery friends," Cameron said in a conspiratorial tone, "and his plans overly depend on artillery. He is quite right that these batteries will prevent French access to miles of river on either side of Montreal. What he does not expect, what he has not protected against, is two hundred savages rushing each battery from the rear. We will take them so fast they will never be able to spike the guns, without even time for messengers to raise the alarm to Amherst. We will let the transport ships stretch out in front of us before opening fire. With no room to maneuver, they will have no chance."

The colonel's words sank in with slow, sickening realization. "That's five thousand men at least, sir." Duncan's voice was almost a whisper.

Cameron's voice was as cold as ice. "Five for each Highlander slaughtered by British guns at Culloden. The wound we inflict will make them cower in London. They will know they have wakened the Jacobite beast, and they will not venture down this river again, not for many years."

From behind the curtain panel came a rough, dry coughing. Cameron pulled Duncan's arm to stop him from investigating. "Here, lad," he said, rolling up the chart to reveal another underneath. "We'll not forget your part."

"My part?"

Cameron quickly stepped to a trunk then extended a small dirk to Duncan. "You should have this," he said as Duncan accepted the knife. It was the finely worked Highland dirk he had taken from the dead dispatch rider. "You kept the general confused over the theft. You slowed his western advance. You bought us time with the Iroquois League. The half-king reached the Saint Lawrence without any attempt to stop him. We need good men, educated men. Five hundred acres at least."

"Sir?"

"You'll always be an outcast among the English." Cameron gestured to the chart. "Take a look."

The chart contained a larger view of the entire river valley, stretching for dozens of miles on either side of Montreal. Cameron pointed to large plot penciled in along the vast lake beyond the river. "I will have twenty thousand acres and will build the biggest castle in the New World. You can take five hundred alongside, or one of the large islands if you prefer. Find a maiden. Start your clan anew." Cameron turned to Duncan, expecting gratitude.

Duncan stared in disbelief. This new life kept presenting itself, as if it was his destiny. It was not a dream in the night, but here and now. He could point to the map, and an estate would be his. "You are betting with hundreds of lives," he said. "Who brought you the prince's banner?" he asked again.

The coughing started again. Cameron made no effort this time to stop Duncan as he lifted the hanging canvas that walled off the back of the large tent.

The chamber was bigger than he expected. The tattered carpet that covered its earthen floor showed faded hints of hunting scenes. On a field table sat a bright oil lamp. The robed monk looked up in surprise.

"Brother Xavier." Duncan nodded to the Jesuit, who rose and solemnly returned his nod. "He was too weak to come by himself," Xavier explained. "I wanted to be with him when . . ." his voice drifted away, and he shrugged, then left the chamber.

The man on the cot was noticeably weaker than when Duncan had left him in Montreal. His eyes had sunken even deeper. His hands seemed but skin and bone.

"Lord Graham," Duncan offered in greeting, then he quickly stepped to the cot. He realized his question about the source of the banner was answered.

It seemed to cause Graham great effort to raise his hand and move it back and forth as though to correct Duncan. He was about to speak when another spasm of coughing seized him. Duncan sat by the bed and lifted the man's wrist. His pulse was light as a feather. Every breath was a wheezing struggle. The smell of death was settling around him.

"Cameron's a good lad, son," Graham finally said. "He has been battered by his times."

"Like the rest of us."

Graham offered a weak smile. "Tribes and clans alike."

Duncan pulled the blanket back and loosened the black robe over the man's chest, pausing as his effort exposed a fine linen shirt underneath. Hanging over it was an elegant golden chain, at the end of which was a heavy golden ring set with a seal. A ring had been sent from the prince.

"And royal families in Rome," Duncan added. "There was never a conspiracy of the western tribes," he said after a moment.

"Not at first. I decided—" Graham's words were cut off by a paroxysm of coughing. The linen cloth he held to his mouth came away bloody. "I decided the world was big enough to allow battered peoples a place of their own."

"A noble idea," Duncan agreed.

"If only I had lived to see the dream fulfilled. I'd give my right arm for a few more weeks. But in his infinite wisdom, God has decided to take me to the threshold and no further. You would have been one of the strong backs I would have leaned on. Cameron always wants to speak of castles. I am more interested in churches and schools and infirmaries. A factory to allow the tribes to process their own furs—now that would be something!"

Before Duncan could reply, Lord Graham reached with bony fingers to extract a piece of rich brown fur that had been entwined in the links of his gold chain. "It wasn't going to keep me alive forever," he whispered. His breath came in short raspy gasps now. As he rubbed the fur, a small white patch appeared on it.

"King otter skin." The words came from Duncan's tongue unbidden, as if a door had creaked open in the back of his mind.

Graham dropped the fur into Duncan's palm.

The old Highlanders from Duncan's youth had always insisted the king otter, the largest of the species, was impervious to death except by a wound to the tiny patch of white on his chest. Even a small scrap of its fur was said to protect the one who carried it from any danger. "I had an uncle who kept a piece close to his heart," Duncan said. "It protected him for eighty years, but not from the English rope that took him in the end."

"It saved me from English bullets at Culloden, from vengeful arrows on the Ohio," Graham explained. "Harpoons on the shore of Hudson's Bay, a rapier in Paris, even a stiletto in Rome. But it ne'er promised immortality."

Graham coughed and pointed to the solitary bottle by his bed. There was only one medicine left for him. Duncan uncorked it and poured out a dram of whiskey.

"There had to be an emissary from the Vatican," Duncan said as the laird drank. "There had to be a go-between with the Stewart prince. There was a Scottish trader who filled the boy named Regis with such bold ideas he became the Revelator. I just never thought they could be the same man." Duncan had found the missing link in the chain, the man who tied everything together.

"Lord Andrew Graham. Father Andre," the old man said in a whimsical tone. "And many years ago, the western tribes called me the Red Bear, for the red beard I wore as a trader. I have been rich in names and adventures, in wives and friends."

"And ambitions."

Graham motioned for more whiskey. "What I have done is for my people, all my people."

"There was a man named Regis who became rich in names and ambitions," Duncan said as he filled the glass again. Here before him, he knew, was the man who had laid the seeds of rebellion within the Revelator, who had cajoled the Jacobite prince into considering the possibility of starting fresh in the New World. Here too was the man who meant to beat down the English at last by using Indians as cannon fodder, who set wheels in motion that had caused untold deaths already, including those at Bethel Church. Duncan should hate him, should wish him dead. Andrew Graham had been larger than life, a war hero, an explorer, a spy, a diplomat, a man who would make kings. In another age he would have carved out his own kingdom. But the creature before him was a shrunken caricature of that man, another broken laird, the dying old Highlander who had made everything possible, given an honored place in the half-king's camp.

Another piece suddenly slid into place. "The half-king is your son," Duncan declared.

Graham drank deeply of his whiskey. When he spoke his voice was thin as a leaf. "I've had several sons," he said, "but only Regis survives. His mother was a beautiful Mingo maid who lived among the French, and she had him baptized by them. Regis Thistle, so he would not forget his Scottish blood. When he was eight I left a bundle of furs with a Jesuit monk on the Ohio and told him to educate the boy."

"You should have made it two or three bundles."

Graham gave a bitter grin, and when he spoke his voice was steadier. "I find that one's education adapts to one's world," he said. "This world needed to be shaken. He has become my flaming spear." He began a raspy, whispered song, the Highland lament that had become the Jacobite anthem.

Duncan waited until he quieted to speak again. "For years I could not hear the name of the British king without hate boiling up inside me. It was in his name that my mother and sisters and young brother were tormented and killed."

Graham cocked his head, not fully understanding.

"Children of the Iroquois Council were taken," Duncan said. "The Revelator threatens to enslave them, or worse."

Graham drank again. The whiskey strengthened his voice. "The ways of the savage are ever hard, lad. Tooth and claw have ruled the forest since before time."

"I was thinking more of your ways, the ways of the holy Jacobite cause and a virtuous prince who waits in the Vatican. Yet nine gentle souls were slaughtered at Bethel Church in the name of the half-king."

Graham's face clouded. "I know of no such thing. There was no need for bloodshed at the settlement. The robbery was to be by subterfuge, never violence."

"It was there the children of the Iroquois Council were captured. If the half-king has his way, those children will die, all in the name of his vision. But a father's last request cannot be ignored," Duncan added. "It could be a gift, a tribute to the prince who waits in Rome. We just want to leave with the children."

A crooked smile grew on the dying Scot's face. "Colonel Cameron!" he called in the voice of the laird he once had been. "Bring me Regis!"

THE FOUR KILTED grenadiers escorting them marched in silent formation, their military discipline as tight as on any parade ground. They passed the last of the military tents and kept marching, toward the cave beyond the camp where two sullen warriors stood guard. The soldiers flanked the guards, and the lead grenadier pointed into the cave.

A short figure appeared, huddled under a blanket. As Duncan approached, the blanket dropped to reveal an Indian boy of perhaps ten. His arm was wrapped in a bloody bandage.

"Jacob," Duncan said in a soft voice as Conawago reached his side, "it is time to go home."

The boy looked at Duncan uncertainly, then turned to a larger figure who hobbled into the light, supported by a young girl. Adanahoe's face was bruised, with one eye swollen shut.

"I knew people who looked like you," the old matriarch grinned, "but they would have to be dead by now."

There was no time for response, for the children broke into joyful cries as they saw the elders and Ishmael emerging from behind the soldiers.

Embraces and tears quickly followed, but Duncan would not allow the reunion to be lengthy. He desperately wanted to be out of the half-king's reach. He spoke urgently to the elders, who quickly quieted the children. They must circle the camp, he explained, staying on the fringe all the way to the canoes.

They were less than a minute from the landing when a dozen warriors ran to block them.

"Not so fast, McCallum!" the half-king shouted. He had not disputed

Lord Graham's command, though Duncan suspected it had not been so much due to the respect of a son as the judgment that he could not argue with the venerated old clan chief in front of so many Highlanders. But there were only tribal warriors around them now.

"You heard Lord Graham give us permission," Duncan declared. "We are leaving." He glanced toward the main camp. Most of its occupants were gathered around a table where the casks of rum were being served out.

"Of course you are. Once the price has been paid."

"The other kegs are in a boat tied to the little island past the landing."

The half-king spoke an urgent command, and half a dozen warriors broke away. "One more minor payment," he said to Duncan.

"Payment?"

The half-king's smile was cold as ice. "A quick walk down the aisle, then you may go. Our generous Lord Graham would not refuse us a little entertainment."

The warriors surrounding the Revelator stepped back to reveal two score Hurons, each brandishing a weapon, facing each other to form a narrow alley. It was a gauntlet, the line of torment down which prisoners were sometimes thrust. The warriors would not step out of line, but the blows they aimed at the miserable creature who ran between them could be, and often were, fatal.

Paxto, chief of the Wolverine clan, stood at the head of one line, the bones woven into his hair rattling as he swung his war ax. Scar stood at the other, holding a heavy club. "Wolverines!" Custaloga hissed. The warriors in the lines were all of the hated clan. They would be certain to draw as much blood as possible.

The half-king seemed to take great pleasure in the frightened silence of the Iroquois. "One of you must reach the end. If the first falls, another must try, and another, until the end is reached. You can decide who runs." He lifted the long braid of Abigail, oldest of the children. "The quiet maiden?" He stepped to Tushcona and made a sewing motion with his hand. "The weaver of Iroquois fate?" He stopped before Custaloga and stooped, bending his shoulders to mock the old man. "Custaloga, the warrior who became a woman?" The Hurons began to hoot and call in derision at the Iroquois. Duncan inched toward Scar. "Perhaps Sagatchie, who shamed his people by putting on the king's uniform?"

He was still speaking when a figure shot out of the shadows toward the gauntlet, a lean man in tattered clothing whose hands were tied behind his back. The half-king casually extended a leg and the stranger tripped, sprawling on the ground. "A noble gesture, Bedford," the halfking said with another thin laugh as Jacob darted forward to defiantly stand over the man. They had at last met the valiant schoolteacher of Bethel Church. The half-king pushed the boy aside, lifting Bedford by the collar and shoving him toward Hetty.

"Perhaps you would step into our line," he said to the Welsh woman. "Nothing to fear for you, mother of so many names. One who can make snakes fly. You can turn all their axes to feathers." When Hetty only glared in response, he turned back to the Iroquois. "Ah," he said, as he reached the tallest of the women, "the beautiful Kassawaya. Just a graceful waltz with the Wolverines and you'll—"

Duncan leapt in a blur of motion. He had seen the act performed in medical school, and he knew he had but one chance to repeat it now. With all his strength he slammed the edge of his hand into Scar's neck, abruptly pressing his artery against his windpipe. As the warrior began to collapse, Duncan ducked and caught him on his shoulders, one arm over a leg, the other over an arm, draping the stunned body over his shoulders. With a war screech, he darted into the mouth of the beast.

The blows fell hard on the Huron's back. Duncan twisted, slamming the man's feet into the jaw of one warrior, twisting violently to hit another on the opposite side. A club bounced against Duncan's ear. He knocked down the ball of a war ax with the limp arm. A stick bounced against Scar's skull and onto his own, and for moment he was sure he would fall. More sticks sought to trip him, more clubs slammed onto the Huron as he twisted the unconscious man to block the blows, though several glanced off his own head. Blood was in his eyes. He staggered, off balance, then recovered, shouting out a Gaelic curse, and spun in a full circle, using Scar's appendages to strike his assailants. His arm jerked as a club drew blood from his forearm, his ankle screamed in pain as another pounded its bones.

Then suddenly there were no more tormentors. He let the unconscious body fall from his shoulders and collapsed onto his knees, gasping, blood running down his arm and jaw.

He became aware of a pair of well-polished black shoes near his face, and he looked up into the stern face of Colonel Cameron.

"Well played, McCallum," the colonel said with a cool smile. His grenadier guards rushed to stand over Duncan.

It seemed to take all his strength to turn and sit on the ground, facing the line of Wolverines. Some of the warriors stared at him in disbelief, others in fury. Several swung their clubs as if about to attack him. Savage cries broke out.

It took a moment for Duncan to realize they were coming from others in the camp, dozens of Scots and Indians who had been watching. They were cries of amusement, of laughter. A brawny Scot doused him with a bucket of water and helped him to his feet as others rushed forward. He ignored the pain of the congratulatory slaps on his shoulders as he watched Conawago and Sagatchie herd the Iroquois around the edge of the camp, joined now by the schoolmaster. To buy them time, he began to murmur acknowledgment to those who swarmed around him and accepted swigs of ale from several offered flasks. It was a quarter hour before the crowd began to break up, the Wolverines still glaring at him as he tried to inconspicuously make his way to the beach.

The elders and the children were already halfway to shore when he climbed into a canoe. He froze, paddle in his hand, as he saw the tall warriors of the Revelator's guard gathering with several Scots at the far end of the beach to land the boat with the powder kegs. The Revelator had used the gauntlet to gain time to reach the kegs. Duncan watched in horror as a keg was handed down a chain of men and a hand ax slammed into its top. His paddle cut into the water as the first confused curse echoed across the river. Furious orders followed, and more kegs were opened, all revealing nothing but gunpowder. Duncan put all his strength into his paddle, and his canoe shot forward.

"McCallum!" came the half-king's furious roar. A musket barked, and another. Balls plucked at the water around him, and then he was out of range.

He started shouting to his companions on the shoreline when he was still a hundred yards away. They stared in confusion, not understanding his desperate calls for them to run. On the far side of the high tongue of land, half a mile away, Woolford waited with his rangers.

"They opened the kegs!" he shouted as he leapt out. "They know why we are fleeing!" He pointed behind him. A dozen canoes were rapidly following them, filled with enraged warriors.

Chapter Fifteen

Despite Duncan's desperate urgings, the escape of their weary band was agonizingly slow. They stumbled through an abandoned pasture then encountered thickets of brush covering the steep slope up the open ridge they had to cross to reach Woolford's camp. The elders and the children were weak from their long ordeal. Tushcona and Bedford carried the youngest on their backs but were nearly spent before they were halfway up.

By the time they reached a vantage point at the top of the ridge, their pursuers milled along the riverbank, searching for their trail. Duncan and Conawago exchanged worried glances, knowing that as soon as they began to run across the open-faced ridge, they would be spotted.

Sagatchie helped the last of their party climb over the ledge marking the top of the slope then joined them to gaze down on the open field below. Duncan did not at first understand the sigh of satisfaction that came from the big Mohawk, then he followed his gaze to the solitary figure that stood on a boulder, staring up at them. His metal helmet was unmistakable.

"Wolverines," Duncan heard himself say. A chill ran down his spine. The blood feud between the Iroquois and the Wolverine clan was like a festering wound, and Duncan had rubbed salt into it by shaming the Hurons at the gauntlet. The half-king had sent those he knew would be most likely to bring back all the scalps of those who had deceived him.

"Run!" Kass shouted at the children and the elders, urging them desperately across the top of the ridge toward the safety of the rangers. Bedford scooped up one of the children, and Kass threw another onto her back as she ran.

Sagatchie eyed the ledge rock that jutted upward a few feet away, making something of a parapet overlooking the pasture below. A great calm seemed to settle over him. He laid his rifle on the ledge, along with his powder horn and cartridge box.

Duncan now saw Conawago staring at the Mohawk. A melancholy pride burned in the Nipmuc's eyes as he lowered his own rifle onto the rock parapet and helped Sagatchie remove his pack then extracted the little wooden container that warriors always carefully guarded on their travels. Tushcona, carrying their only other rifle, rushed to their side as Kass, Bedford, and the children ran headlong across the open ridge. Without a word she began checking the priming in the pans of the guns.

A serene smile lit Sagatchie's face. "This is what the spirits always intended," he declared in a level voice. "I know now they have not forgotten me."

Duncan followed his gaze toward the Wolverine Hurons, and his heart wrenched. He had trouble making his tongue work. "No . . ." he protested. "God no, Sagatchie. Please don't. I beg you . . ."

Sagatchie seemed not to hear him. He turned one cheek, then another as Conawago dipped a finger into the little wooden cylinder and painted the red stripes of war on his face. When the warrior looked up to the sky, he had his war ax in one hand and his knife in the other. "Hear my call! My name is Sagatchie, of the Wolf clan of the Mohawks!" he shouted toward the clouds, pressing his protector amulet tightly against his heart. "The strength of the wolf is in my arm! The speed of the wolf is in my legs!"

When he finished he turned to Duncan, who found no words as the Mohawk lay his forearm along Duncan's own in the warrior's grip.

He nodded at Duncan, still smiling, then launched himself down the slope with a joyful whoop.

They had four rifles, and Tushcona stood by to reload as Conawago and Duncan fired. When they dropped the first two Hurons who had begun to run across the pasture, the others at the edge of the field answered with screams of war. Their enemy had shown themselves, and the battle was joined. The Hurons fired their own rifles, the bullets ricocheting off the rocks around Conawago and Duncan, then tossed them aside and drew out their war axes.

Two more Hurons fell to their rifles, but Duncan's shot at the helmeted chieftain missed. The advancing warriors stopped abruptly as Sagatchie appeared out of the thicket, shouting at them, waving his war ax in challenge. Suddenly a second figure, grey and bent, scrambled out of the undergrowth to join him, swinging his own ax.

Duncan spun about to see Adanahoe, tears streaming down her face. She was holding Custaloga's pack and shirt. The eighty-year-old chief, survivor of the razing of Ononadagoa Castle by the Wolverines decades earlier, was a warrior once more and was finally facing his enemy.

Duncan and Conawago fired again, and there were only a dozen Huron left, facing the two Iroquois across thirty yards of grass. It was the old sachem who moved first, shouting out his war cry and charging directly at the Huron chief, Sagatchie a step behind.

An anguished cry broke the eerie stillness as Duncan and Conawago lowered their rifles. Kass was running at them, flinging off her pack and jacket, lifting her bow. She broke away when Duncan grabbed her arm, then leapt past them into the undergrowth of the slope.

They watched helplessly as the two chiefs danced with their axes, slashing and backing, chopping with vicious strokes. It was Custaloga who landed the killing stroke, but as Paxto fell, the aged Iroquois was covered with Huron assailants. Sagatchie leveled two of the attackers and was pulling his ax from the leg of a third when four more leapt on top of him. A mournful moan escaped Duncan's lips as his Mohawk friend fell.

Kass appeared in time to put an arrow in the Huron who raised a knife to scalp the fallen Mohawk.

Suddenly a warrior at the edge of the field shouted frantically, and the war party froze, following his raised arm toward the river. With cries of alarm they backed away, carrying the body of the pot helm chief with them.

A call from behind broke the brittle silence. Duncan turned to see Woolford and several rangers running from the far side of the point. He did not wait for them but started down the slope with Conawago at his side.

Bodies lay strewn about the field, six downed by rifle shots, seven by blade and ax. Singing a low, melancholy chant, Kass dragged away the Huron dead heaped by Sagatchie's body, then stood over the dead Mohawk. He had been sliced in a dozen places, but the blow that had taken him had been from the ax in the back of his skull. Kass said nothing as Duncan bent to remove the weapon, but as the blade came free, dripping Sagatchie's lifeblood, she seemed to lose all strength. She sagged, collapsing into Duncan's arms, then slowly, leaning on Duncan, lowered herself to her knees by the body.

Duncan turned and walked toward the rangers that emerged onto the field.

"We came as soon as we heard the shots!" Woolford gasped.

"A few minutes more and we could have made it to you," Duncan said in a hollow voice.

"The Hurons paid the butcher's bill," Woolford muttered as he surveyed the dead. "Where's . . ." his question died away. The mournful death song started by Kass was all he needed to know.

"Dear Jesus, no!" he moaned and rushed past Duncan to where Kass knelt. He dropped to the ground and buried his head in his hands.

More death songs rose as the elders arrived. Duncan and Conawago laid out the body of Custaloga beside that of Sagatchie.

"The bastards fled," Woolford said in a tight voice. "Why?"

Duncan looked about the field, realizing he had no answer. The two men quickly made their way to the river and mounted a high, flat boulder.

"That is why!" Duncan said, pointing to a long line of objects floating downstream. Woolford extracted his telescope. "Canoes and long boats," he reported in an uncertain tone.

Duncan took the glass and quickly saw the reason for the ranger's confusion. There were at least fifty canoes on the river, and they were all empty, adrift in the fast current. Ahead of them were long boats strung in a line, being towed by a lead boat in which half a dozen men feverishly worked the oars.

IT WAS EARLY evening before they began to climb over the ridge that jutted into the river. The Iroquois rangers quickly disposed of the enemy dead, but they would not move the bodies of Sagatchie and Custaloga, would not leave them alone, until long songs had been sung and long chants spoken to console their spirits.

Woolford was shaken badly by his friend's death. He had fought at Sagatchie's side for years. "He was the best," the captain said in a breaking voice when he returned to the Mohawk's body again. "The best of all of us."

Duncan studied his friend and realized that Woolford had long known what the rest of them had learned, that Sagatchie had been unbowed, that he had fervently kept the old ways alive even while bridging the worlds of the tribes and Europeans. He had been pure, never touching rum or whiskey, steadfast in the ancient ways of his people, his long rifle the only compromise he made to European technology.

When Adanahoe announced where their burial scaffolds would have to be erected, her companions were surprised but they did not argue. Woolford just nodded and sent one of his men for blankets to wrap the bodies.

Kass seemed to find new strength in reciting the death chants, yet she seemed inconsolable. The tears did not stop flowing down her cheeks as she cleaned Sagatchie's body and murmured the sacred words. As Duncan approached her, Conawago touched his arm. "The song she sings now," the old Nipmuc said. "It is not one of mourning."

Duncan backed away. "I don't understand."

"It is not a death song, it is a love song, one of courtship."

It was another half-hour before Duncan knelt beside her and explained that they would have to leave for the rangers' camp.

She seemed not to hear. "He will be strong." The tracks of her tears were plain on her face. "He is going to run like a stag in the forest and hear his father's voice in the wind."

"He was very strong," Duncan said as if to correct her.

A sad smile broke across her countenance. "You do not understand, McCallum." She flattened her palm over her abdomen. "I carry Sagatchie's son in my belly."

For a moment Duncan wanted to say it was impossible, that they had been together less than a month, and they were antagonists for the first days. But he saw the radiance that shined through her despair and the certainty of her voice. The people of the forest had their own instincts, and they knew to trust them. He knew better than to doubt her words.

It was early evening before their long, slow procession emerged upon the ridge and made for the rangers' camp. Bedford had scavenged a pistol and knife from the dead Hurons and had nervously patrolled all afternoon. Although he was obviously impatient to leave his captors behind, the Iroquois would not be hurried in their rites, nor in the slow cleansing and wrapping of the bodies. The sun was touching the western treetops when the cry of a killdeer broke through the silence of their grim column.

The ranger captain spun about, rifle at the ready, and Duncan realized it was a warning cry from one of his men. When the call repeated, Woolford ordered the company to continue, then set off in the direction of the call, toward the rising bluff that hovered over the river. Duncan followed a few steps behind.

The ranger captain was above Duncan at the top of the bluff when he froze. Duncan watched in confusion as Woolford seemed to sag, leaning on his rifle as if he were about to fall.

"The bastard," Woolford spat as Duncan reached his side. "The contemptible scheming priggish bastard."

Duncan tried to piece together the puzzle on the river. Two frigates had materialized half a mile away as well as four of the squat barge-like vessels the British called gunboats. In the fading light they were securing their moorings in a wide arc parallel to the island on which the rebel Scots and the half-king's warriors were camped.

Woolford extended the tube of his telescope and studied the vessels. "It must have been his plan all along." He turned to Duncan with a grim expression. "He brought his long boat into shore to make certain he knew where we were, and that we knew he was leaving. One of his own rangers sought us today while I was up here watching the island."

"You make no sense."

"They've been using us. Before I could stop them, my men revealed that you had gone to the island to meet with the half-king. Amherst has been away with the navy. He knows about Cameron's falsified report on the payroll theft. He didn't fail to act against Cameron. He is acting against him now." Woolford extended the telescope to Duncan. "But this," he shook his head forlornly. "Look at the gunboats! Every gun is a mortar!

"It was no coincidence that the canoes were set adrift. Those men towing away the long boats had been at the camp, brought in casks of rum despite the colonel's edict against spirits. They were Amherst's men, sent to make sure the camp was drunk tonight."

"And to make sure those on the island are trapped with no way off." Woolford gestured toward the ships. "Those are siege guns on the gunboats, fortress breakers, deployed against mere tents and huts. Amherst barely tolerates the Scots in the best of times, and he despises the Indians. This is what he wanted all along. Now his most troublesome foe and the Highland traitors are stranded in one small place. The island will be a killing ground. There won't be a man alive by dawn."

Duncan discovered he had dropped to his knees as the horror of

Woolford's words sank in. Amherst had deceived them all. He had openly rejected all suggestions of a supposed conspiracy between Scots and the rebel Indians, allied to the French. But secretly he had followed events, had bided his time so he could trap the reviled Scots and Indians together and unleash his killing machines. He intended total annihilation. Most of those on the island would be drunk, and Cameron would no doubt be distracted by his dying laird. The ships would be obstructed from view of the camps by the bluff that swept up at the eastern end.

"We have to go!" Duncan cried. "We have to take them off the island!"

"We'll be dead as soon as we are in rifle range. You killed half the Wolverine warriors. You stole the half-king's treasure."

Duncan grimaced, knowing the ranger spoke the truth. There were scores of Highlanders on the island, good men who, like so many before, had linked their fates to a losing cause. The nightmare image of his dead father flashed in his mind's eye, pointing at Duncan. His father had been telling him that he was supposed to die with the Scots on the island, the last of the Highland rebels.

Conawago appeared at Duncan's side and took the telescope from Duncan's hand. "The guns are all pointed upward," the Nipmuc said as he studied the boats.

"The mortars on the gunboats will throw explosive balls high in the air, over the bluff, and down into the camp," Woolford explained. "If there are canoes left at all, the cannons on the ships will destroy any leaving."

"The river runs fast through here," Conawago observed after a long, painful silence. "They have difficulty getting anchorage."

He offered the glass back to Duncan, who quickly saw that his friend was right. "The frigates have set their anchors at the two ends of the line," he reported, "and the gunboats are being moored to lines secured to the frigates."

The three men stared in grim silence at the vessels. Ishmael appeared at their side. "If the anchor lines were slipped, they would all be at the mercy of the river," Conawago pointed out.

"The British navy knows how to set its anchors," Duncan countered. He was gripped by a terrible, helpless paralysis. Everyone on the island would die.

Conawago bent over the boy, speaking in low tones. Ishmael broke away, running to the nearest trees.

Duncan, transfixed, lost track of how long he stared at the ships. He was vaguely aware that the boy had returned, and he cast an absent glance as Conawago and Ishmael cleared away grass and arranged a small fire.

He seemed fated for constant torment. There had been a few moments when he had glimpsed a Highland kingdom in America, but he would never give up the Iroquois children and the Iroquois League for it. Duncan had felt a glimmer of victory when he had finally freed the children. But then they had lost Sagatchie and Custaloga. Now he had helped seal the doom of dozens of Highlanders and betrayed his father. Voices rang in his head. *Take a canoe and warn them, at whatever the cost,* one shouted. *No,* another said, *you will die. They will never believe you in any event. Light a warning fire on the shore. No, even if they were warned, Amherst's intended victims still would have no way off the island.* He doubted one man in fifty would be able to swim the treacherous river.

There was more movement beside him. Hetty and Tushcona were there now, kneeling by the fire, dropping tobacco and other aromatic leaves on it. The death rites would continue into the night.

"We must take a swift canoe to Amherst," Duncan said to Woolford, "to explain why the rebels are no longer a threat, to plead for leniency."

"Even if we reached him," Woolford replied in a taut voice, "he would never agree to see us. He is probably drafting his report to London already, describing how he cleverly disposed of the Jacobite and Indian threat in one sweep. He has his eyes on a high title and estates from the king."

"We have to try!" Duncan pleaded.

"Night is falling," the ranger pointed out. "We would never make it in time. Those naval commanders love their fireworks at night. I wager they will start the bombardment within the hour."

Several items had appeared on a flat rock beside the fire. A small soft doeskin pouch. A little object rolled up in fur. The hollow wooden tube in which Sagatchie had kept his paint. On the far side of the rock the hell dog sat, looking at Duncan expectantly.

Duncan realized his hand was clutching the scrap of otter fur given him by Graham. He gazed forlornly at the English ships, then paused and turned. Conawago, Ishmael, and Tushcona stared in anticipation at him.

"You know I mourn the lost ones," he said uncertainly.

Conawago dropped more tobacco on the fire. The others retreated, leaving only the two of them in the aromatic smoke.

"This is not about Sagatchie, Duncan. This is about recognizing when the spirits are speaking to you. Could it be time for you to take your skin?"

Duncan grew very still. Conawago was talking about the most sacred of topics, more directly than Duncan would ever have expected. He was speaking of Duncan's spirit protector.

"Surely this is not the time, my friend."

"This is precisely the time. Why did it push itself to your heart? It is speaking to you. Listen."

Duncan looked down in confusion to see he was unconsciously pressing the old otter fur against his chest. For a moment the world fell away. He became aware of nothing but the gaze of the wise old Nipmuc and an unfamiliar energy quickening deep inside. Conawago turned his back to Duncan, signaling that this last mystery was between Duncan and his spirit protector. The hell dog cocked his head at Duncan then lowered it, touching the bundle of fur on the rock with his muzzle.

Duncan found himself kneeling at the flat rock. With a tentative finger he probed the lump of fur. There was an exquisitely carved animal inside. He knew it was the carving Conawago had worked on for weeks, the carving he had kept secret from Duncan. Conawago had known just as his grandfather had known that Duncan, alone of his siblings, had needed to be baptized by the gales at the edge of the Scottish cliffs. Conawago had seen the connection long before Duncan. In his mind's eye there was the sudden image of the same animal cavorting with him in the waters of his youth, of another following their canoe up the Mohawk River, even seeming to lead them. The dying laird could have given the precious token of fur to those closer to him, but something had compelled him to give it to Duncan.

With a trembling hand he touched the carving to his lips and recited a short Gaelic prayer, then an Iroquois prayer. He rolled the otter image up in the Scottish fur and inserted the bundle into the pouch. There should be a ceremony, he knew, but the benediction on Conawago's face as he turned back to Duncan was blessing enough.

When he hung the amulet around his neck he felt a surge of strength. An unexpected serenity entered his heart. He looked up with fierce determination at the English ships and instantly knew what must be done. He heard movement and saw Conawago gesturing Ishmael, Kass, and Woolford forward.

"Sagatchie kept his tomahawk razor sharp," Duncan said to Kass. "Did you find it?"

"His war ax was taken, but his tomahawk was in his hand."

"Do you think he would let me borrow it?"

With a small sad smile, Kass nodded, then turned and darted away.

"You keep a pot of beargrease in your supplies," he said to Woolford.

"To daub on wounds, yes."

"I need it."

Woolford suppressed the question that was in his eyes, stepped back, and trotted toward his camp.

Duncan lifted the container of paint and handed it to Tushcona, then peeled off his jerkin. "I want a pattern of the river on my body," he said, "and the stripes of a warrior on my face." The hell dog stepped to the cliff and sat, facing the river.

Tushcona looked at Duncan in confusion, then she followed the dog's gaze and her face lit with understanding. She thrust her fingers into the pigment.

By the time Woolford returned, the sky was a deep red and Duncan's body had been transformed. Tushcona had covered his torso with images of fish, snakes, and beavers. Sagatchie's tomahawk was strapped tightly to his waist, his amulet to his chest. His hair had been knotted at the back of his neck. He wore no clothing but his britches.

Woolford still did not understand. Then Duncan took the grease and began applying it to his skin, and the ranger gasped.

"Suicide!" he gasped. "No man could work against that current!"

"There are only two anchor lines out," Duncan calmly explained. "What do you think will happen when they are severed?"

"The boats will be swept miles downstream. But it is impossible! You mustn't!"

"Do you speak as my friend or as a captain in the king's army?"

"I lost one particular friend today, Duncan. I don't want to lose my only other."

"Most of the men on the island are nothing but pawns in a game set by others. Their only sin was false hope."

Woolford stared at him for a few heartbeats then cursed and grabbed the grease. "I will look for you at first light," he muttered, and he began applying the grease to Duncan's back.

When he finished, first Conawago, then Woolford linked their forearms to Duncan's in the warrior's grip. Duncan touched the hell dog's head, tousled Ishmael's hair, then cupped his hands to push the aromatic smoke toward his heart. Without another word he touched his amulet and sprang toward the edge of the cliff, launching himself with a long arcing dive into the silver water.

Chapter Sixteen

Duncan awoke slowly, gazing groggily up at a gull that drifted in the cool breeze, listening to the rhythmic lapping of water on the side of his boat. He sat up in sudden apprehension. The boat was empty. He was adrift on the treacherous river.

His aching muscles protested as he pulled himself onto a seat, but the pain cleared his mind. He saw now the familiar bluff above him and the trail that led up from the beach of skulls.

Tucked into a notch in the sun-warmed rocks was Conawago, puffing on the little German pipe he used in relaxed moments. Duncan had not seen him use it for weeks. "You were still asleep when we arrived," his friend declared. "I told them not to waken you, that your body is still recovering from its ordeal."

Duncan worked his tongue around his mouth, wondering about the hint of anise and mint on his tongue. "You gave me one of your potions," he recalled.

Conawago grinned. "You did not protest when I offered the tea. We had to carry you to the boat. You deserved a long sleep for your efforts. Such a spectacle."

It all seemed like a dream now. Reaching the first anchor line in the treacherous current and dying light had been far more difficult than Duncan had expected, but a grim determination had driven him, and when he had finally found the heavy anchor line, stretched tight as a fiddle string, Sagatchie's tomahawk had made short work of it. The British sailors had frantically fired their guns as they felt their vessels slip, but their shells hit only the tip of the island and the river itself. By the time he found the second line, they had the sense to send rockets into the air to illuminate the darkened river, and marines had begun to aim at him from the frigates. The muskets had only spattered the water around him, and the glow had made Duncan's work easier.

The flares came quicker and quicker, lighting Duncan's struggle to the shore of the island, his arms and legs screaming against the final effort. Fleeting, staccato images of the British calamity came with the flashes when he finally crawled onto the rocky shore beneath the island's cliff. The river grabbed the frigates much more violently than Duncan would have expected, spinning them about. In one flash the curving line of gunboats had begun to straighten. One of the boats kept firing, its shells hitting a rocky shoal near the island. Another rocket flash showed that its guns had shifted, tilting the boat. The next showed the guns sliding off, with the crew not far behind. In the next the crew was climbing onto the upturned hull. The retreating ships kept firing their rockets as they drifted downstream, desperately trying to avoid rocks and shoals. The remaining gunboat crews hacked away at the lines fixed to the drifting frigates until at last they were free of the threat of being capsized, only to drift even quicker than the frigates down the river.

Duncan had found himself laughing until, his body too spent for the return swim, he collapsed against a boulder.

When Woolford's canoe finally came into sight, the sky had lightened to a dull grey. The ranger captain spoke in utter astonishment of the night's work, then presented him with a breakfast of bread, cheese, and brandy. As Duncan ate, Woolford had produced two folded papers from his jerkin and spoke in low, urgent tones.

They had climbed up the bluff warily, half expecting to be fired upon, and the surly Highland sergeant they met on the top seemed inclined to do so. Duncan calmed him with a Gaelic greeting, and he had quickly agreed to bring Colonel Cameron.

The Scottish officer seemed to have aged twenty years overnight. He walked up the slope with difficulty, and his two grenadier escorts hovered close as if they expected him to fall. Cameron's face was desolate, but as he studied the half-naked Duncan, still adorned with paint and grease, curiosity seemed to overtake him, followed by something like awe. "One of my men said he saw a blond Indian by the light of those damned rockets, doing battle with an anchor rope. Surely . . ." Cameron lowered himself onto a nearby log. "My God, McCallum, my God." He gazed down the river, where the two surviving gunboats could be seen, grounded on distant shoals.

"Laird Graham breathed his last after you left," the colonel finally said. "We hadn't the heart to tell him we had been tricked out of our treasure. Everyone was condemning you as a traitor. But then last night you saved us from a horrid death." Cameron's gaze drifted toward the southern bank of the river. "You swam from the far shore?" he asked, as if still not believing Duncan's feat.

"I was raised in the western isles, sir," Duncan reminded him.

"If this were the western isles," Cameron said with a sad smile, "they'd be singing ballads of your exploit already, and for the next hundred years. You saved us. At least for another day," he said, gazing pointedly at Woolford, who wore the king's uniform.

The ranger captain sat beside Cameron. "You know that General Amherst thinks little of my native rangers," he began, "but I am under orders to General Calder. And Calder gave me instructions to probe the enemy defenses and gather intelligence wherever possible. I have had men inside Montreal this past week. Three days ago I wrote a report to General Calder but copied General Amherst since the news was so important. My men confirmed that the bank in the city has substantial quantities of gold and coin. Over ten thousand pounds' worth at least. I congratulated the generals since they would now be able to pay the Highland troops as soon as Montreal falls. I copied you as well, Colonel Cameron, as the ranking Scottish officer."

Cameron took the first paper offered by Woolford and read it, then read it again. He studied the ranger captain as if seeing him for the first time. "A daring stroke, Captain," he said at last with the hint of a smile. "Amherst will be unable to conceal the treasure in the bank once he takes Montreal. At least some will come out of this wretched episode with satisfaction."

Woolford extended the second paper. "Along a battlefront, communications can get confused. General Amherst was somewhere downriver, not possible to reach."

Cameron nodded uncertainly. "He said he went downstream to meet the navy and the troops coming up from Champlain. But . . ." he gestured toward the wrecked boats, "we know what he was doing."

"This is another report, dated yesterday. It recounts how I had discovered the whereabouts of the infamous rebel leader called the Revelator, the one who stands in the way of our victory. I sent secret word to you as the nearest senior officer, and you deployed to Fortress Island in force, as secretly as possible so as not to scare the enemy. You remonstrated with the Revelator. You explained to him that by your persuasion the Caughnawags were standing down. Without them, you explained, his cause is lost."

"A noble touch, Woolford, but it will not be credited when the Caughnawags begin attacking us." Cameron paused, returning Woolford's steady stare for a moment. "Surely you are not suggesting—"

"They were wavering already since so many have relatives among the southern Iroquois who came north with Johnson. Their discovery of the half-king's treachery at Bethel Church sealed their decision. But Amherst does not know it yet. You will deliver the news, Colonel. They will not attack the British forces. The half-king will soon be in retreat."

"But the navy. The attack intended for last night. It was based on intelligence about the mutiny of the Highlanders."

"You will say you had to let the rumors of mutiny circulate in order to build false confidence in the half-king, to lure him closer. You will tell General Amherst that you had no knowledge of his bold plan of bombardment, and because of his disappearance you had no way to inform him that you had been successful in your efforts. The navy will be deeply shamed by what happened to them last night. They will never let it be known that one man defeated a squadron. They can pretend that they successfully frightened the half-king away, and we can all bemoan the little tempest that apparently caused some minor havoc among their vessels."

Cameron stared at Woolford with new confidence. "It's bold, Captain." He read the report again in silence. "It's a gamble," he said with a small smile. "But why? Why would you do this?"

"Because the Scots on this island are good men. Because this war will be soon over, and I have it on good authority they will be offered the chance to remain in America as their units are reduced. I am not returning to England. McCallum is not returning to Scotland. We want such men at our sides, men who are friends with the tribes."

Cameron waved the paper toward Woolford. "Still a gamble, lad."

"We will see that the Revelator has enough canoes to begin a conspicuous retreat, proving your tale. And the ultimate prize you give Amherst will eclipse his doubts and his sentiments about the Highlanders."

"The prize?"

"The French know they have no chance without the northern tribes or the half-king at their side. Amherst has his own spies, who will confirm that the Caughnawags have withdrawn. The French will sue for peace. You will have made possible the near-bloodless fall of Montreal. Amherst's mind will be filled with coming knighthoods and banquets with the king. He will never blemish his victory with the court-martial of his adjutant."

The colonel stared for a long moment at Woolford. "If you took credit for this, Captain, you would be a major in a fortnight."

A small grin rose on the ranger's face. "Which would take me back across the sea to the next wretched war. I am staying in America."

Cameron stood and folded the papers into his pocket then looked out over the river. He spoke with a solemn, cracking voice. "Each of you has saved my life, and that of many good Highlanders." He shook each of their hands.

"It will mean no castle," Duncan said.

Cameron forced a weary smile. "It will mean my neck will not be stretched by the king's rope." He sighed and gazed on the ruined gunboats downstream. "My aspirations were born of the Old World. I see now a man has to have new dreams in this land. I will look for an early opportunity to leave the king's service for a new life here. My clan took its strength from the soil for centuries. A croft in America may be as good as a castle back home."

WHEN THEY REACHED the top of the trail, the old abbey and its grounds were empty. But Duncan spied a thread of smoke above the chimney.

Tushcona was tending a pot of stew over a small fire in the kitchen hearth. Upstairs the children were in the monks' cells, tended by the elders. Duncan paused by each cot, checking the health of the children and encouraging them to sleep.

He heard movement above and saw that the door to the narrow winding stairway to the top floor was open. Stealthily climbing the stairs, he followed the sound to the little makeshift chapel. The great brown dog was on its haunches, staring out the low window.

It took Duncan only a few minutes to find what he was looking for among the wooden boxes that lined the wall. The writing on the pasted lable was faded but still readable. *Father Francis*, it said, *1673*. Strangely, it had two dates for his demise. The inked inscription indicated he had died in 1722, but above it someone had used a lead to inscribe *1734*.

Inside the box was a worn rosary, a small carved bird, a braid of long black hair tied with a red ribbon, and two cheap copper rings, the kind bartered by traders, bound together with a strip of white fur.

No one among our missions showed more courage and faith than Father

Francis when he ventured as the first of us among the Mingoes, began the note at the bottom of the box. It went on to explain that Francis was a natural leader who soon attracted a settlement of natives around his little chapel on the banks of the Ohio and then opened the first school in the western lands. But he had gone too far in adopting the native ways, and in 1722, when his abbot discovered he had sired a son with a Mingo maid, they had taken his robe away. Francis did not stop his mission work, however, and was famous for preaching about the purity of the savage soul. He insisted on keeping European technology from his flock and fervently condemned those who tried to introduce European currency, saying gold and silver represented false wealth. It was the scourge of Europe and would corrupt the souls of his people. He had buried his beloved wife in an epidemic and a year later had been killed by drunken warriors trying to burn his chapel. His son Xavier continued the mission work and was consecrated as a monk at an early age.

Duncan closed the box and reverently replaced it, recalling how Xavier had begged his father's forgiveness when he had discovered the half-king had committed murder for an army payroll. The Jesuit's passion for the natives had made him a perfect lieutenant for Graham but in the end he too had become a pawn. Duncan gazed out over the broad river and the chain of islands that extended to the horizon. They could have been Scottish islands, and he could have built himself a croft, even a boat, and taught the old ways to a new generation. But the price had been too high.

A movement on the field below caught his eye. Conawago was walking toward two long bundles lying by the rock-strewn bluff. He had almost forgotten the last of their sacred duties.

They worked in silence, Ishmael and Duncan cutting and trimming sturdy maple saplings while Conawago and Kass erected the two scaffolds. When they unwrapped the blankets around the bodies, Duncan insisted on binding the many gaping wounds. Kass washed the bodies with water and sweetfern while he knelt with needle and thread. The elders arrived to light a small spirit fire. With cupped hands Conawago directed the fragrant smoke over the bodies, reciting a low gravelly chant that the others soon joined in. Duncan did not bother to wipe the moisture in his eyes.

Hetty joined in the chants, the hell dog watching her vigilantly from the cliff's edge, but as the others quieted, she continued with her own low, mournful song, in the Welsh tongue. When she was finished, Conawago spoke to the dead men in his Nipmuc language, and though only Ishmael understood what he said, the tone was unmistakable. There was mourning in his voice, but also apology and even guilt. With slow, painful realization, Duncan understood. His friend too needed to find a death with honor, and had expected it, had promised it, had been bound to it by the Iroquois Council. But he had failed to die.

Tushcona seemed to sense the depth of his pain. When Conawago finished, she spoke to him in a somber, worried tone. The Nipmuc hesitantly pulled out the belt she had woven at Onondaga Castle. The weaver seemed strangely unsteady as she lowered herself onto a boulder and stretched the belt across her lap. Her brow furrowed as she ran her fingers over it, as if unfamiliar with the beads she herself had woven. Then she touched the central figures and began an urgent, whispered chant. Conawago touched Duncan, and he saw that all the others had retreated several steps, leaving the weaver in the center of their circle. As Duncan stepped back, Tuchcona lifted the belt over her head and spoke toward a huge bird that had appeared overhead.

It was the first eagle Duncan had seen since the fateful day on Lake Champlain, and as she spoke the bird dropped closer. She kept speaking, sometimes pausing and cocking her head as if in conversation, then with a few powerful thrusts the bird changed course and began climbing. They all watched it until it was a speck high in the sky, then Tushcona sighed and looked apologetically at Duncan and Conawago, gesturing them toward her.

"It was fated to be two companions, one old and one young, who crossed over to save us," Tushcona explained. "The belt weaves itself. We only thought it was a Nipmuc and a Scot because you were the ones who came."

Conawago lowered his head. Disappointment showed through his sorrow. Finally he nodded his acceptance of her words. "The honor of dying was not ours this time."

Relief flooded Tushcona's face. She carried the belt to Sagatchie's scaffold and laid it across his chest, then spoke in a low voice in Custaloga's ear, as if to give him final assurance. The spirits could be at peace again. Their two protectors had made it across.

THEY HAD FINISHED the rituals, finished the farewells to the lost warriors, and were lingering in silent contemplation of the two dead Iroquois when the hell dog bared its teeth and growled toward the abbey yard. Duncan saw no sign of intruders, but Hetty suddenly hitched up her skirt and ran, Ishmael and Conawago only a few steps behind. They had not expected their visitors so soon.

Duncan lingered, watching the dozen warriors who emerged from around the ruined barns, and turned to Sagatchie's body with a new fierceness in his eyes. "We will make an end to this," he vowed to his dead friend, then he turned to find Kass and Adanahoe standing behind him with fire in their eyes. They conferred quickly, then descended in a wide circle around the abbey.

When he and Adanahoe finally stepped past the ruined outbuildings into the old barnyard, Ishmael was lying on the ground. Hetty and Tushcona knelt at his side trying to protect him from the angry Mingo warrior who hovered over him, dangling a string of scalps in his face. Duncan's hand went to his knife as two men filed out of the abbey, carrying the elders' packs. Scar glared at Duncan, who had left him unconscious and shamed at the end of the gauntlet. The man behind Scar, wearing the lynx pelt at his waist, paused, and a cruel, hungry grin rose on his face. The half-king still wore his war paint.

Chapter Seventeen

The renegade leader dropped the pack in his hand and stepped in front of his men, gesturing for them to get on with their work. They began dumping out the contents of the packs onto the ground.

"Surely, Regis, you can tell by their weight that the packs don't have what you seek," Duncan declared in a loud voice.

Hatred flared in the half-king's eyes, then he shrugged. "There will be time enough for me to become the Revelator again. Next year, perhaps the year after. The western tribes will not be quieted. We will yet soak the land in blood. Blood will have blood."

"Shakespeare?" Duncan replied. "You've learned well from your poet."

Sounds of struggle came from inside the building. Another pack flew out of an upstairs window. A child cried out in fear.

"If those children are harmed, it will be your men flying out the windows," Duncan growled.

Regis sneered and motioned to those beside Duncan. Tushcona was helping Ishmael to his feet. "We should be frightened of children and old women?" he mocked.

"You'd be surprised. This one," Duncan said, nodding towards Tushcona, "can kill by weaving you into a belt. This one," he said, gesturing to Hetty, who was helping Ishmael to his feet, "can send a snake to fly and tell the spirits how you lied to them and lied about them. And this one," he indicated Adanahoe "can kill with a finger. They are not in a forgiving mood."

"I will feed the fish with parts of your body as we travel up the river. You and I have unfinished business, McCallum."

"Aye," Duncan agreed. "The old ones said it was always going to end here. I was just an ignorant Scot who didn't know how to listen to them. But I am beginning to understand. The Island of the Ghosts. This is a place of truth, of absolutes. We are all just small people here. Wars and kingdoms are beyond us. It is why you were brought here. It is time to talk in front of the spirits, without the playacting, without the distractions of colored smoke and Greek fire."

"Time to die," Regis spat. "I have men below erecting new killing posts." He hesitated. "You did not bring us here. I am here for what is mine."

"You decided we tricked you out of your treasure. Your scouts were always going to follow us. We knew that. With your army all that silver and gold would have given you new glory. Without your army, it would make you one of the richest men on the continent. You came for what you deserve. I mean to see you get it. The generals may think in terms of regiments lost or won. We think more in terms of innocents slaughtered at Bethel Church."

"Give me the coins, and I will let the old ones and children live."

"Hiding it in the powder kegs was a masterstroke." Duncan continued. "I remember the old stories of the cunning fox. He was very clever, but he was always done in by his lies. You lied to Tatamy. You said you killed enemy soldiers at Bethel Church."

"Tatamy has a weak heart. Too much time with the Jesuits."

"You had a Jesuit teacher. Father Xavier was very disappointed that you murdered the town of Bethel Church to steal treasure. You were supposed to be his virtuous warrior. It was your virtue that made you invincible."

"He forgets what it takes to be invincible in the wilderness."

Another child's cry rose from upstairs, followed by a familiar war cry. "You have Wolverines with you," Duncan said, fighting the temptation to run to the monks' cells.

Regis's smile was like cracked flint. "Two of them decided to join me. They are very good at what they do."

"They should have gone home, should have run away from you when they had the chance. Don't they know the abbey is taboo to Hurons?"

"That long swim addled your brain, McCallum. I see we will have to work it out of you. I will take great pleasure in it," Regis said, then he muttered a name, and a tall warrior, a Huron, appeared in the doorway.

Adanahoe pointed at the man with her finger, and he jerked violently backward against the door. The dying man looked up at Regis, as if for an explanation, then with his last breath he looked down at the arrow that pinned him to the door. Blood trickled out of his wound onto his wolverine tattoo.

Adanahoe stepped forward and pulled a beaded pouch from the dead Huron's belt.

"He took that from Custaloga," Duncan explained in a cool voice. "He should have gone home," he said again.

Regis stared wide-eyed at the Iroquois matriarch as Scar and the Mingo who had taunted Ishmael retreated inside the building. She had killed with a finger. His head jerked about as he futilely looked for the source of the arrow among the ruined buildings, then he leapt forward and seized Ishmael. He wrapped his forearm around the boy, shielding himself with Ishmael's body.

"You stirred up the tribes by telling them the spirit world was out of balance," Duncan continued, "that Europeans had penetrated it and were killing the ancient ones. That world *was* out of balance, but because your words made it so. I can't imagine a greater betrayal of your people. You lied to the gods, and you lied about the gods. It was unimaginable to the Iroquois. But you were taught by Europeans."

Regis suddenly held a knife. "Two Nipmucs left," he hissed. "By the end of the day, I will see the tribe extinct! I will tie you to a post, McCallum, and throw them to you in little pieces as you watch. A Nipmuc finger, a Nipmuc ear, a Nipmuc liver and heart."

"There was no murder on the other side."

The half-king shrugged. "It came to me in a dream. Everyone knows the gods speak to us through dreams."

"You thought you could break the taboo against lying about dreams. You had no such dream."

"You don't know that!"

"It was not your dream, or Black Fish's dream. It was just pieces of Shakespeare and the Bible. You acted out a script from an old Scot and an old Jesuit, aided by your poet of death. What happened at Bethel Church was an afterthought, an unforeseen act of the play added by you and your poet."

"I am a warrior!" Regis barked. "I am the lion of the gods!"

"No. That is just more of the script, another line written by your old Jesuit teacher Brother Xavier. You are no warrior. You are an actor on a stage. Except," Duncan gestured about the nearly empty barnyard, "your audience has abandoned you."

Regis frowned as the two Iroquois matrons and Hetty closed around him. "The promise of a raid against a secret payroll wagon was what it took to guarantee French support," Regis said. The half-king looked at Hetty and hesitated. "But I was hundreds of miles away when the raid finally took place. Someone else decided the witnesses had to die."

Regis looked down, seeming to remember Ishmael, still pinned against him. The boy did not flinch as Regis pressed his blade under the boy's jaw, lancing the skin of his chin. When he saw the rivulet of blood, Duncan began bending slowly, coiling to spring. "You can buy him back, McCallum. One keg of the king's coins, and I give him to you with his heart still beating. Two kegs and he can keep his fingers. Three and he keeps his nose and ears."

Ishmael squirmed, trying to reach for the knife, and Duncan struggled to keep from leaping on the renegade. Regis tightened his grip on the boy then paused and looked at his hand. Ishmael had not tried to seize his knife, he had placed a small belt of white wampum across his fingers. The boy's eyes locked with Duncan's. They burned with the same calm determination he often saw in Conawago.

"I sat with a dying old Scot two days ago," Duncan said. "He said he had been blessed with many lives, many wives, and many sons. But only one son survived him. His flaming spear, he called his last son, destined to scour the earth clean. Regis Thistle. Your Mingo mother was fond of the French, but your father wanted you to remember your Scottish blood. He was proud of you, but his last wish was to keep you from killing more innocents."

The words reached the renegade. He lowered his knife, and for a few heartbeats he seemed lost in memories. Duncan inched closer.

"He is dead, Regis. Your father is dead. It was his dream, born to the laird who had done battle in Scotland and given you breath in the Ohio country where he traded furs and took his Mingo wife. A former laird who had once lived in Paris and Rome, and who chose exile in America after the uprising, the trader who schemed with Jesuit missionaries and traveled to the Vatican to cajole the last desperate members of the Jacobite court. Lord Graham tied it all together."

Regis stared at the beads in confusion, as if he could not understand how they had appeared there.

"There are those who say they will sear through your flesh if you lie," Duncan pointed out.

Regis did not react.

Duncan began to glimpse another man beneath the hate and scorn of the Revelator, and through him he glimpsed a chain of similar men through the years. There had not only been the Scottish laird, lost in the rising and resurrected twice as a wilderness trader and secret Jacobite ambassador. There was the Jacobite prince himself, wasting away in the Vatican. And there was Brother Xavier, who could not adjust to a new world order.

"It was always the same war, he said," Regis murmured. "The kings against the small people. Except we will finish it this time."

"Your war is over. You have a chance to make things right. Give us the killer of Bethel Church."

"Each of my men is as good as fifty soldiers," Regis snapped. "We will leave people writhing in pain all the way to the ocean."

As if on cue Scar stepped out of the building, dragging young Noah Moss under one arm.

Regis grinned.

Adanahoe pointed.

The arrow went through Scar's throat so forcefully that its point came out the back of his neck. Hetty turned and kicked the warrior as he dropped to the ground.

Adanahoe silently stepped up to the body and pulled Sagatchie's war ax from his belt.

Regis seemed to grow weary. He stared again at the beaded belt in his hand. "I did not tell them to kill at Bethel Church. He—"

"Ishmael!" Henry Bedford shouted as he leapt through the kitchen window, a pistol in his hand. The boy twisted, exposing Regis's chest, and the gun fired.

Regis's face went empty. He gave a long groan as blood blossomed over his heart. He sank to his knees, reaching a hand out as if to grapple with the schoolmaster, then collapsed to the ground.

Bedford's own face was a blank as he stared at his work. The prophet, the fierce Mingo renegade who had nearly changed the world, lay sprawled on the ground, his life's blood flowing onto the grass. There was movement at the windows above. The children were looking down at their dead tormentor.

As the elders gathered around the body, Adanahoe bent and draped the white beads over his lifeless mouth. No more would lies escape his lips.

Conawago's head snapped up at the whistle of a lark. Duncan followed his gaze toward Kass, who had emerged from the ruins with her bow and was pointing toward the burial scaffolds. The half-king's Mingoes were there, kicking at the loose dirt beneath the scaffolds.

"Tell them to stop, Simon," Hetty said.

Duncan was not certain what surprised the schoolteacher more, to hear his true name or to hear his mother give him such an order. He seemed to have trouble focusing on her for a moment, then he darted to Hetty and embraced her. "The ordeal is over!" he exclaimed.

Hetty seemed uninterested in his embrace. "Tell them to stop disturbing our friends."

Simon shrugged. "They are the Revelator's men."

"No," his mother said. "I watched them leave the back of the house before you leapt out the window. You told them to do so. You should not need a string of white beads when talking with your mother."

The schoolmaster frowned and backed away from Hetty, then turned and ran toward the Mingoes.

When Duncan reached him, Simon was reloading his pistol as the Mingoes pushed sticks into the loose soil around the scaffolds. The schoolmaster spoke with a new, plaintive tone. "Surely you understand, McCallum. I never planned to kill that man in Albany. It was a misunderstanding over a card game. He said I was cheating. I said he had no proof. He said he would get a constable. An English magistrate will condemn a Welshman or Scotsman as easily as putting an ax to a chicken's neck." Simon took a stick from one of the Indians and began probing the soil himself.

"That explains why you were hiding in Bethel Church," Duncan said, "but not what you did there. And I might understand a death in the anger of the moment. But we had the report from the magistrate who condemned you. That man, your first victim, died hours later tied to a tree in the forest. His fingers on one hand were cut off. You said it must have been a Huron. But it was just what a young Mingo half-blood learned when he ran with Huron war parties. It became a mark of the poet of death. I should have known that first day at Bethel Church. There were almost no clothes in your room there. You had already packed, because you knew the raiders were coming. I should have asked myself earlier who would have known to use Ishmael's medallion against Hickory John. I should have understood when I saw your mother's reaction to the deaths of Black Fish and Rabbit Jack, to the way their eyes were cut out. I should have understood when Black Fish spoke of his dream. You liked to use the Bible and verses of poets in your classroom. Writing a script about the other side and the resurrection of your old friend Regis was a lark for you. The two of you must have had a good laugh when you decided he would become the Revelator and you the poet of death."

The schoolmaster raised his pistol toward Duncan.

"There again I was blind. I did not understand the two of you had been raised together, had gone on war parties and learned to kill while you were still boys. From the same village, where Lord Graham used to call as a trader and kept a wife, where Xavier the Jesuit taught about the sins of the world. Osotku the Delaware warned us about Regis, said he knew him. What he actually said was that he knew the crossed boys. Two boys, two half-bloods who always cheated."

Simon looked up at the sound of more footsteps on the path. Hetty, Conawago, and Ishmael appeared. As if in warning Simon gestured to the Mingoes who had been with him, who had retreated into the field of boulders but held their axes ready, then to the plain below. Half a dozen warriors were indeed erecting new slave posts. He glanced at his mother uneasily before replying to Duncan. "What I did was teach school. All my students were from the tribes," Simon added.

"Regis handled the Mingoes and Hurons," Duncan continued. "Brother Xavier took care of the French and the traffic in secret messages, and old Lord Graham handled the Scots. But none had a connection to Bethel Church. You were the connection. You were Regis's particular friend as a boy. You learned about Shakespeare with him, and about killing. And you devised the scheme to make a duplicate wagon and steal the payroll." Duncan produced one of the pieces of paper from the wall of the schoolhouse and extended its drawing of the wagon.

Simon frowned. He wasn't shamed, he was just impatient. "You must have the coins! It's the only explanation!"

"Regis was about to say you were the one who swung the killing hammer at Bethel Church. It's why you shot him. He wasn't reaching out for help as he died, he was pointing to you. As terrible as the acts of the others might be, they were acts of war. But the deaths at Bethel Church, they were cold-blooded murder. You swung the hammer to crush the skulls of those who had befriended you, even students you taught."

The schoolmaster leveled the gun with a peevish sigh. "One keg of coins is all I ask. There is a French settlement at the mouth of the Mississippi. I can make a new life."

"You killed them all, Simon," came a tight, high voice. "They gave you a home, and you killed them."

Simon turned to look at Hetty. For an instant he was just a regretful son. "I learned to play war the European way. Come with us, Mother. I will build you a grand house in the Louisiana country."

Sadness filled Hetty's eyes. "All these years I spent sewing lace to pay for your lawyer, and you were guilty. You were just planning more murders. I sent you the last valuable keepsake I had from Wales, and you used the silver links for rum and women."

Simon seemed about to argue when a stone hit his cheek. "You killed my grandfather!" Ishmael shouted, and he threw another stone, then another.

The schoolmaster leapt to the boy, violently slapping him on the face. "Ever the disobedient cub, Ishmael!"

With a shudder Duncan saw the warriors from below ascending the ridge, the ones in the rocks slowly advancing with weapons raised. The hell dog appeared on a nearby boulder, its eyes fixed on Simon. The schoolmaster glanced at the dog and hesitated for a moment. He too would have heard how the creature was inhabited by the spirit of the noble warrior who had been his father.

He turned back to Ishmael. When he struck the boy again, knocking him to the ground, Conawago moved quickly but Hetty was faster, darting forward and covering the boy with her body. Simon grabbed the back of her shirt and heaved her aside like a sack of flour.

"You shame your father and me!" she cried from the ground, but her son was beyond hearing.

Simon grabbed Ishmael and lifted him upright. "Your grandfather's head sounded like a ripe melon when I hit it! He just kept singing like the others, the old fool."

"His was a warrior's song!" Ishmael shouted back. "I heard him! He died with more honor and bravery than you'll ever have!"

The fury with which Simon pummeled the boy was frightening to behold. He pounded the boy, knocking him to the ground. Suddenly his pistol was aimed at Ishmael.

"No!" Conawago shouted, and he charged at the schoolteacher, who shifted the gun towards the old Nipmuc.

As Duncan leapt forward, a brown shape hurdled past his shoulder.

The pistol fired, hitting the hell dog in the chest, but the great creature still clamped its jaw around Simon's throat, sending him reeling backwards. Simon dropped the pistol to beat the dog with his fists, staggering backward, struggling to get the furious animal off him. Then they were gone.

Man and dog disappeared over the high cliff. By the time Duncan reached the edge, there was nothing but a ring of ripples where they had vanished into the water.

The Mingoes roared into action, lifting war axes to strike as Duncan threw himself against Ishmael and rolled away with the boy in his arms. Conawago stood over Hetty and was raising his own club to defend her when their attackers abruptly stopped.

Impossibly, Duncan heard a bagpipe. He followed the confused gaze of the warriors toward the head of the trail from the boat landing.

William Johnson stood there, leaning on a walking stick, beside Woolford and a solitary piper of the Black Watch. Emerging at a fast trot from the trail behind them was a seemingly endless line of Iroquois and Highland warriors.

BY MIDMORNING OF the second day, Johnson and his army were gone, his flotilla of sloops, bateaux, and canoes stretching out for a mile down the river, joined by more and more Caughnawags pushing off from the bank. The Irish colonel had wisely chosen not to press Duncan for a detailed account of his travels since they last met. Indeed, the head of the tribal and militia troops had seemed to lose all interest in reports from the field of war when he discovered who lay on the scaffolds on the high point over the river. He was visibly shaken by the death of his friends. Immediately he had turned to Tushcona and Adanahoe.

"You are blinded by tears of grief. I would wipe them away with my words," he said, the opening lines of the Iroquois condolence ceremony. He had gestured to Kass to join them as they settled in a small circle to continue the ritual.

Nearly an hour had passed before one of his men interrupted to report that the half-king was among the dead at the old abbey. Johnson rose, promising to return to Onondaga Castle to conduct a weeklong mourning ceremony, then he hurried to the barnyard to look at the bodies. His eyes grew round. "I hope the Iroquois understand the miracle you have worked for them," he said to Duncan and Conawago, pumping their hands.

He had given them free rein to dispose of the bodies, and after consulting with the elders, a mass grave had been dug at the far end of the old slave-trading field. The terrifying Revelator, shaper of tribal nations, was just another renegade corpse tossed into the hole. When the grave had been filled, they had used the posts the Mingoes had raised to light a bonfire over it. The heat and ashes would bind them in the earth for many years, Adanahoe declared. The elders wanted such men kept out of the spirit world for as long as possible.

Much more care had been taken for another of the dead. After Johnson's men had recovered the bodies of the two who had fallen off the cliff, Hetty had insisted on burial in the ground for her son, but over the grave, alongside the scaffolds of the two fallen Iroquois, she had directed the building of a third scaffold. On it she had arranged the body of the courageous brown dog. If any had doubted her claims that a warrior, her husband, had lived inside the beast, none did now. Hetty had dutifully cleaned her son's body but had shed no tears and offered no words over it. Over the warrior with the four legs she had wept, then cleansed it with great care while chanting the mourning songs. Before they had raised him onto the platform, she had woven small, bright feathers into the long hair of his legs, as though to help him fly to the other side.

"He was the best of companions," Duncan offered as she worked, trying to break through her grief. He watched as she cut away a lock of the brown hair and carefully folded it into her amulet pouch. "I am sorry, Hetty," he said. "I should not have done it, but . . ."

She looked up to see the folded doeskin in his hands.

When she did not respond, he laid it flat on a rock. At the center of the chronicle of her life was the ivory ring carved with dragons. Her hand trembled as she lifted it and held it close to her eyes. "I was very young when my father died," she whispered. "My mother was sick and decided to send me to my uncle in America. On the day my ship sailed she gave it to me, saying my father had always worn it around his neck." She sighed. "In my life I had only one true love," she said and began tying the ring into the hair of the dog's neck. "He will like having dragons with him on the other side."

"I never had the honor of his name," Duncan said. "I do not know what to call the creature in my prayers." He was not sure she had heard him, and after a long silence he retreated.

"*Roghskenrakeghdekowah*," she said to his back. When Duncan turned, a tear was rolling down her cheek.

"War chief," Duncan translated, and he solemnly nodded. "I should have known." He pulled out the elegant dirk Cameron had given him. With a prayer in Gaelic, he laid the dirk against the dog's body and backed away.

Hetty had sat by the scaffold for hours, oblivious to the others, oblivious even to the brief thunderstorm that swept over the island. Although others tried, only Ishmael was finally able to speak with her and lead her back to the abbey. After a hot meal, the boy sat with her and asked her to explain the images on the doeskin.

Now the Welsh woman, looking frail and hollow, stood with the rest of them as they watched the great flotilla recede toward Montreal. It was Conawago who broke away first, followed by Ishmael. Minutes later they turned to see the two Nipmucs waiting below the knoll with shovels in their hands.

They moved in silent procession to the site of their first great fire, on the night they had burned the old torture posts. Everyone remained strangely quiet as they shifted the ashes to the side to expose the bare soil. They dug deeper, making a large square several inches deep, then they pried and loosened the packed soil until finally they exposed the first of the kegs. Following Duncan's directions, Tatamy's men had buried the kegs deep, sitting upright.

No one spoke until the kegs were lifted out, their chalk signs of the Jacobites conspicuous in the bright sunlight. Duncan, borrowing Conawago's ax, shattered the top of the nearest keg. For a fleeting moment he thought they had been terribly mistaken, for all he could see was gunpowder, but then Conawago sank his fingers into the keg and extracted a bright silver coin from the black grains.

Duncan handed the ax to Ishmael, and the Nipmuc boy, amusement growing on his face, opened the other kegs while Tushcona and Adanahoe followed, sifting up handfuls of coins from each to confirm its secret contents.

Duncan walked around the kegs. "I never thought we would get this far," he confided to his companions, and he looked up to Woolford.

The ranger captain shrugged. "I am not the director of this particular drama."

"We could take it back," Duncan suggested.

"We could," Woolford agreed. "No doubt the king would give Amherst some more initials to put behind his name."

Duncan knew his friend was as weary of kings and generals as he was.

"The troops will be paid from the booty taken in Montreal," the ranger reminded him.

Duncan paced around the kegs. It was more money than he had ever seen, more than he would likely ever see again. It could buy a vast plantation at the edge of the frontier. It could buy an entire town. A handful scooped from one keg could buy out his indenture, the deed of servitude that still hung around his neck. He and Conawago could make a stately home on a mountain, bigger than Johnson's own mansion, furnished with a grand library where Conawago could spend his last years reading to his heart's content. He could build an infirmary to care for the tribes.

He realized the elders, even Conawago, were staring at him. Wealth was an alien notion to them. Piles of coins had been used against the tribes ever since the Europeans arrived. Many had died, so many more had suffered, because of these very coins. The martyred father of Xavier had been right. Gold and silver worked against the spirit of the tribes. These coins in particular had only brought treachery and death.

Ishmael broke the spell. The boy stepped up to a keg and lifted a coin. "They are very heavy," he said to Conawago, "and you can't eat them."

For the first time in weeks, Duncan saw a smile on his friend's face. The old Nipmuc embraced the boy.

"I think," Duncan said, "we should take these to those who paid the greatest price."

They stacked the open kegs near the three scaffolds, on the bluff where the hell dog had fallen with the schoolmaster. Duncan listened reverently as Adanahoe spoke in her native tongue to explain to the dead how justice had been dealt to the Revelator and the poet of death.

When she finished, she looked at Duncan expectantly. He was not sure where the words came from, but he knew their rightness as soon as he spoke. "The Revelator lied when he spoke of murders on the other side," he explained. "But it was the dreams of the Council who told us it was a lean and hungry time on the other side. When I was young, we would bury the dead with coins so they could buy food along the long path to the spirit world. The ghosts here may have had a few corncakes, but that would never be enough to see them all the way."

Conawago, as always, instantly understood. He lifted a shilling from a keg and handed it to him.

"This," Duncan said, extending the coin for all to see, "buys our friends a kettle of pumpkin stew." He threw it in a long arc over the cliff, far out into the river. The splash stirred the others out of their spell.

"We are on the island of the starving ghosts," Kass reminded them, then she shouted out Sagatchie's name and threw another coin into the water far below.

Tushcona joined in, then Ishmael, and Hetty, and soon all the company was throwing coins, calling out names of dead they had known, including those of Bethel Church. They emptied one keg, then another. Woolford energetically lifted a full keg and dumped it over the side. Birds gathered overhead, not diving, but attentively watching. Ishmael pointed out an otter frolicking among the ripples. One keg followed another, emptied now by the Iroquois children and elders. For the first time Duncan saw laughter on the faces of the Iroquois, young and old, as they gave up the king's coins, one silver splash at a time, to the river that never ended.

Epilogue

Mrs. Margaret Eldridge was a Welsh widow whose family had been lost in the North, Duncan explained when they reached Edentown. Hetty looked every bit the part in her simple blue dress, her hair combed and pinned at the back. They had paused in Albany during their long return journey, where Mr. Forsey had readily agreed to provide several dresses for his former seamstress. His generosity, Duncan knew, in no small part reflected the relief Forsey and his neighbors had felt when the true identity of their party was revealed.

They had caused quite a stir at the outskirts of Albany. Sentinels on the wall of the fort had raced for their officers. Townspeople had taken one look at their party and shut themselves in their houses. A church bell rang in alarm. Only by Woolford running forward to explain the apparent invasion did the army call off its confrontation.

Their company had lingered a week at Onondaga Castle in condolence ceremonies for the heroes who now stood perpetual watch at the Isle of the Ghosts. On their last night at the Haudenosaunee capital, Adanahoe had called for a celebration. The old matriarch had waxed eloquent about the successful return of the children, the bravery of those who had died at Bethel Church, the reconciliation with the northern Mohawks, even

Duncan's discovery of his protector spirit. Afterwards the Council had insisted on dispatching an honor guard of two dozen warriors to escort Duncan, Conawago, Ishmael, Kass, and Hetty to the Hudson. The Iroquois, wearing amused expressions, had filed into Albany between ranks of nervous soldiers.

When they finally emerged from the forest onto the open lands of Edentown, Sarah Ramsey ran barefoot from the field where she had been harvesting maize. She paused before him, examining him from head to toe as she pushed back her auburn curls, then rushed forward for a long, silent embrace before warmly introducing herself to Hetty and Ishmael. A smile slowly grew on the boy's face as he took in the sturdy stables, the stone-walled smithy, and the simple cabins. Edentown, Duncan realized, was not unlike Bethel Church. The young Nipmuc shyly tugged at Conawago's arm and asked to go see the great oxen that worked the fields.

"Ishmael would fit well in our little school," Sarah said to Duncan as she sat with him on the porch that evening. They had enjoyed a simple but joyful supper on a table set up outside the stone great house.

"He could help the younger ones," she added. As town proprietress she had decreed that every student learn both English and a tribal tongue.

"I would like that," Duncan replied. "Conawago would like that."

"The children will be eager to hear Ishmael speak about the heroes of the spirit war."

"Spirit war?"

"Do not be so modest, Duncan McCallum," she chided. "The tale is for all to see on the kitchen table."

When Sarah saw the confusion on his face, she took his hand and led him into the kitchen. Kass sat at the table speaking in the tone of one of the Council storytellers to a spellbound gathering of settlers, both tribal and European. Before her was a broad doeskin of the kind Duncan had seen on the walls of the Council lodge, one of the chronicles of historic events in the centuries-long saga of the Haudenosaunee. Except Duncan recognized the scenes painted on this one. The figures were small, for there were a dozen separate panels—a church, a cave, a dog, a prisoner bound to a post, a circle of people listening to an orator, a fortress, a ship, an island in a river, a city, a battle between warriors, ships crashing into rocks, and three grave scaffolds with a spirit gate over them.

"The Council said it should be shown to your people first," Kass explained to Duncan. "Then I am to take it to every Haudenosaunee town so the tale lives in the hearts of all the Iroquois. By the time I am done, I will have Sagatchie's son with me."

It was their skin, their chronicle, the tale of their quest to find the truth and rescue the lost children. Duncan looked up after studying it to see Sarah and Conawago smiling at him. Your people, Kass had said.

Kass was pointing to the crashing ships now. "Then on the shore of the great river, the Scottish warrior at last discovered who he was, and his protector spirit showed him the way to save hundreds of lives."

It was deep in the night when their gathering broke up. Through his fatigue, Duncan became aware of Sarah and Hetty speaking in the tongue of the Iroquois on stools by the smoldering hearth. Hetty had been uncomfortable being thrust among so many strangers, but Sarah's easygoing nature had won her over. One ghostwalker, orphan of the tribes, had recognized another.

He found Conawago on the front porch, looking up at the moon beside a pile of blankets. Sarah knew they always had trouble adjusting to beds after weeks of sleeping under the stars. Conawago motioned him toward the stable where Ishmael already slept on a mound of straw, and they bedded down beside the boy.

Duncan woke to the sound of a hammer ringing on iron in the smithy. The day was already hours old. He sat up to find Sarah on a stool, watching him with the fragile smile he knew so well. He accepted the mug of tea she extended then looked about. She spoke before he could ask where his companions were.

"Ishmael had a dream, Duncan," Sarah announced.

His grin faded. He darted to the entry, looking anxiously up and down the settlement's only road.

Sarah appeared at his side, took his hand, and silently led him to the schoolhouse where as a fearful ghostwalker she had once been Duncan's student. The classroom was empty. A piece of heavy paper lay on the instructor's table, folded into a letter with Duncan's name inscribed in Conawago's elegant hand. With a sinking heart he settled into the chair and opened it.

> *I found Ishmael outside after midnight staring at the moon. He told me he had the same dream the past five nights. Hickory John was shivering on his scaffold. He told the boy he needed one of the old robes from the Nipmuc hearths. I explained to Ishmael that his grandfather meant a buffalo robe, but that I had not seen one for many years. Then we saw a shooting star in the western sky.*
>
> *I am taking the boy west, Duncan. I mean to show him the great spirit mounds in the Ohio country and keep going west until we find buffalo. We will make a robe and carry it to Towantha on his scaffold above Bethel Church, then find a safe place to hide the flint knife of our people. I will write in two or three months if I can.*

Duncan felt a terrible emptiness in his chest. It was a long time before he looked up. Sarah was sitting at the desk where she had been a student. "He told me," she said.

"The war," he said, his voice cracking. "The hostile tribes. The winter. The Mississippi." There were so many hardships, so many dangers. "I may never see him again."

"He had to do it, Duncan. He needs the time with the boy. The boy needs the time with him. The last two Nipmucs." She looked over his shoulder, and he turned. On the piece of slate on the wall, Ishmael had written a verse. *We know what we are,* it said, *but know not what we may be.* On the way to Albany Woolford had taught the boy Shakespeare.

"There was one more thing, Duncan," Sarah continued. "As he left, Conawago said Hetty could manage the household."

"Why?"

"I don't know. Conawago said I must give you this. He said to apologize to you for holding them back from the river." She stood and upended a pouch of heavy coins on the table. "Eight pounds exactly."

"Eight pounds," he said absently, then he hesitated and picked up a coin. A smile slowly broke through his melancholy. Conawago was still looking after Duncan. "Hetty can manage the household," he repeated.

Sarah did not understand, but she returned his smile.

"There are some Nipmuc travel songs I shall teach you," Duncan said as he rose.

Her smile grew wider.

"You and I are going to Nazareth, in Pennsylvania," he explained, and he took Sarah's hand. "There was another warrior who was a hero in the spirit war. We are going to buy a farm for his widow."

Timeline

1400s (estimated). The Iroquois League is established as confederation of Mohawk, Oneida, Onondaga, Cayuga, and Seneca tribes (later joined by Tuscarora), with an organized system of leaders adhering to principles of governance designed to control intertribal warfare. At its peak the Iroquois League exercised power over tribes from the Atlantic to the Mississippi.

1664. The Iroquois League formally recognizes the Covenant Chain that binds it in a political and economic alliance with Great Britain.

1739. Mutiny by 43rd Highland Regiment, the first of several mutinies against English officers by Highland troops.

1742. William Johnson, Irish trader based on the Mohawk River, is honored for his embrace of tribal ways by being formally adopted as a chieftain of the Mohawk tribe.

1746, April. At Culloden Moor near Inverness, the Scottish Jacobite rebels, including many Highland clans, are defeated by British forces, breaking the rebel army and forcing the Jacobite leader, Bonnie Prince Charlie, to flee into exile. In the aftermath of Culloden, the British send punitive expeditions into the Highlands, destroying many traditional Highland clan communities. These campaigns, and the concurrent Act of Proscription, which outlawed the bearing of arms and even the wearing of Highland kilts, effectively ended the traditional Highland life for many clans.

August. The Iroquois League abandons its longtime neutrality in the ongoing struggles between Britain and France and under the leadership of William Johnson begins organized resistance in French Canada.

1754, July. At Fort Necessity, an overwhelming force of French soldiers and Indian allies attacks Virginian troops under George Washington, who is forced to surrender the fort and leave the Ohio country. The defeat galvanizes the British government, which begins deploying regular army troops along the western frontier.

At Albany, colonial delegates meet in the first effort to join the American colonies. Benjamin Franklin, pleading "Join, or Die," invokes the structure of the Iroquois League in promoting his Albany Plan for union.

1755, April. William Johnson is appointed as Superintendent of Indian Affairs and also given command of colonial troops.

July. Along the Monongahela in western Pennsylvania, the British army, under General Braddock, is defeated by combined French and Indian forces. Of the front column of twelve hundred men, a thousand are casualties. This defeat, in which Braddock was killed, painfully demonstrates that rigid European military tactics will not succeed against the wilderness style of combat, resulting in new emphasis on irregular ranger forces and light infantry.

September. William Johnson leads a mixed force of colonial soldiers and Mohawks in defeating French forces at the southern end of Lake George. Iroquois chief King Hendrick (Teyonhenkwen), once feted in London, dies at the age of eighty while leading an attack against French.

1756, May. War is formally declared between England and France as hostilities expand into what becomes the first global conflict.

1757, January. New Scottish regiments (Montgomery's 77th Foot and Fraser's 78th Foot) are organized in the Highlands and arrive in America later in the year.

August. General Montcalm attacks and captures Fort William Henry at the southern end of Lake George. After the surrender of the British forces, French Indians, defying Montcalm's orders, massacre retreating British troops and civilians. This battle and the ensuing massacre were immortalized in Cooper's *The Last of the Mohicans*.

1758, May. British forces under General Forbes set out from Philadelphia to attack Fort Duquesne, constructing the first east–west road across the Pennsylvania mountains and thereby opening the region to rapid settlement.

July. A vastly superior British force under General Abercromby attacks the French under Montcalm at Fort Ticonderoga. After a series of costly mistakes, including ordering Highland troops to charge heavily manned entrenchments without artillery support, Abercromby withdraws with severe British losses.

August. After a monthlong siege, British forces capture the French port of Louisbourg on Cape Breton Island, the strongest fortress in

North America. In retaliation for the massacre at Fort William Henry, the British expel eight thousand French colonists from Cape Breton.

1759, July. General Amherst, new British commander, captures Fort Ticonderoga and Crown Point on Lake Champlain.

September. After a bloody three-month campaign, British forces capture Quebec. In final battle on the Plains of Abraham, both the French and British commanding generals, Montcalm and Wolfe, are killed.

1760, April. After enduring a winter-long siege in Quebec, British forces are attacked by the French and win a second battle on the Plains of Abraham.

July–September. British troops move up Lake Champlain and up the Saint Lawrence from Nova Scotia while thousands more move northward from Fort Oswego on Lake Ontario to converge on the last French stronghold at Montreal. After negotiations with William Johnson, the Caughnawags (or Northern Mohawks), France's most formidable native allies, withdraw from the field. The French surrender Montreal, giving Great Britain effective control of North America east of the Mississippi.

1761. In the aftermath of the British victory, General Amherst dramatically changes British relations with the tribes, cutting off the support that had sustained many natives for decades and fomenting unrest along the frontier.

1762. Tension between the tribes and settlers erupts into a tribal uprising, led by Chief Pontiac and driven by the anti-European teachings of the Delaware Neolin, known as the Prophet. General

Amherst orders distribution of smallpox-infected blankets to tribes on the Ohio.

1763. Campbell's Highland regiment mutinies over arrears in pay.

1764. William Johnson negotiates peace with the western tribes after Amherst is recalled to London.

1765. The Stamp Act is imposed on American colonies as a direct result of financial strain caused by the French and Indian War. This is the first of several related crises in American–British relations that eventually lead to the American Revolution.

Author's Note

In 1755, as the early flames of the French and Indian War ignited the American frontier, French raiders slaughtered eleven unresisting Christian members of the Delaware tribe at the Moravian settlement of Gnadenhutten in Pennsylvania. Years later at a settlement reprising the same mission name in the Ohio lands, frontier militia captured ninety-six Christian Delaware men, women, and children, lined them up, and one by one, as the victims prayed, crushed their skulls with mallets.

The tales of the Gnadenhutten massacres, upon which the Bethel Church killings are loosely based, have always wrenched my heart, not just for the obvious brutality inflicted on innocents but also for its deeper symbolism. The tribal victims had assimilated, had trusted, had suffered stigma from their own tribes for their embrace of European ways and European faith. Few episodes in our relations with Native Americans more poignantly raise the question of who were the savages and who the enlightened humans. The incidents just as vividly reflect the deep capacity for spirituality of the woodland tribes, an aspect seldom reflected in our history books but one that had profound effects on many Europeans who befriended them.

While that spirituality animates my leading characters, the plot of *Original Death* is built around the final stages of the bloody mid-century war between Britain and France. Although I have applied a novelist's license to certain details, the broad elements of the conflict reflected herein are faithful to the historic record. The late summer of 1760 brought the final act of that war as combatants closed on Montreal. General Amherst, infamous for his contempt for Native Americans and colonials, deployed troops with Colonel William Johnson from Fort Oswego up the St. Lawrence to rendezvous with regiments arriving from Lake Champlain and a naval fleet sailing upriver. It is remarkable that Amherst dared to assemble several thousand Highland troops for the campaign, not simply because he was creating the largest gathering of Highlanders since their bloody uprising fifteen years earlier, but also because many of those troops were restless, having not been paid for months. King George's army was chronically short of cash, and silver was in such short supply that the military resorted to using Spanish dollars stamped with the army's broad arrow mark. Senior officers were uncomfortably aware that Highland units had mutinied in the past. During the not-too-distant war between Britain and its colonies, no fewer than six Highland regiments would mutiny in America.

Montreal did indeed fall without serious bloodshed, in large part because the powerful Caughnawag Mohawks abruptly withdrew from their alliance with the French as a result of appeals from the Iroquois League and William Johnson. That larger-than-life Irish baronet, who entered battle dressed like an Iroquois warrior, shaped relations with the tribes for two generations. These pages cannot do justice to this complex, colorful adventurer and adopted chieftain; readers who wish to explore his life more deeply would be well rewarded by Fintan O'Toole's biography *White Savage*.

Our popular history texts tend to dismiss mid–eighteenth-century America as a turbulent waypoint on the journey to revolution, but those who take the time to pierce the smoke of battle will find an astonishingly rich tapestry. Scientific discovery, religious freedom, literary expression, technology, and public education were all blossoming, while at the same time the fabric of entire societies was being ripped apart. The Iroquois, whom Franklin was fond of calling the Romans of the New World, were glimpsing the demise of their once mighty empire. Highlanders struggled to keep their identity alive even though their livelihoods depended on the very British who had gutted their homeland. Orphans and exiles of a dozen European cultures were trying to rediscover themselves at the edge of an ominous wilderness.

The backdrop of *Original Death* draws from this fertile context. That world was indeed populated with Christian Mohawks, self-exiled Jacobites, Iroquois rangers, disillusioned missionaries, tea-sipping warriors, and the traumatized former tribal captives I have called ghostwalkers. The Forsey Brothers were actual military clothiers in eighteenth-century Albany, former iron mines were being used as prisons, and in the West, a charismatic tribal leader who called himself the Prophet was joining with Chief Pontiac to unleash a bloody rampage against Europeans. Also leaving tracks in chronicles of the day was the natural affinity between Highlanders and Native Americans that anchors this series. Major General David Stewart, renowned recorder of the Highland experience, wrote that when the first Highland troops marched to Albany, "Indians flooded from all quarters to see the strangers, who they believed were of the same extraction as themselves and therefore received them as brothers."

We have been taught to look for the roots of the United States in the war that began in 1775, but the seeds of our nation were planted in these earlier battlefields. This was when British prejudice against natives and colonials began to impinge on the lives of thousands, when these same colonists came to realize they could muster effective fighting forces without relying on British officers, and when many colonists began thinking of themselves as Americans. The polarizing measures soon to be imposed by London were directly linked to these years, including the hated revenue laws designed to pay debts incurred during this earlier war.

These years also marked the beginning of the end for the woodland tribes, and a sense of inevitable tragedy was seeping into the tribal consciousness. The Iroquois Council struggled to maintain its integrity as unfamiliar forces pushed to compromise age-old traditions. In a very real sense it was the honor of the Iroquois people and the bond of duty they felt to the British that caused the Mohawk allies of the French to lay down their arms, assuring British victory in the long and bloody war. Less than a generation later it was that same sense of duty that finally broke the back of the venerated Iroquois League, for its steadfast alignment with the British sent the Continental Army into Iroquoia on a path of destruction that rivaled Sherman's march to the sea in the next century. In the end it was not Hurons or French or western tribes but American soldiers who annihilated what historian Sidney Fisher labeled the "greatest advance in civilization" that Native Americans ever achieved.

—ELIOT PATTISON